# Elysium
## A Saga of Slavery and Deliverance

*The Plantation Series, Book IV*

## Also by Gretchen Craig

**NOVELS**
*Always & Forever*
(The Plantation Series, Book I)
*Ever My Love: A Saga of Slavery and Deliverance*
(The Plantation Series, Book II)
*Evermore: A Saga of Slavery and Deliverance*
(The Plantation Series, Book III)

*Tansy*
*Crimson Sky*
*Theena's Landing*
*The Lion's Teeth*
*Orchid Island*

**SHORT STORY COLLECTIONS**
*The Color of the Rose*
*Bayou Stories: Tales of Troubled Souls*
*Lookin' for Luv: Five Short Stories*

# Elysium

A Saga of Slavery and Deliverance

*The Plantation Series, Book IV*

## Gretchen Craig

Pendleton
Press

Published by Pendleton Press.
Copyright © 2015 by Gretchen Craig
*www.GretchenCraig.com*

*Kindle e-book edition available from Amazon.com.*

**ISBN-13: 978-0692535806**
**ISBN-10: 0692535802**

# Elysium
## A Saga of Slavery and Deliverance
### *The Plantation Series, Book IV*

# Chapter One

## *Louisiana*
## *May, 1867*

Lily Palmer stood on the top deck of the paddle steamer, her heart beating like a hummingbird's. Calm down, she told herself. Everything was going to be all right now.

Standing on tip toe, Lily's six year old daughter peered over the railing, mist from the paddles beading in her hair. "We're slowing down, Mama."

Over Maddie's head, Lily read the sign she'd been looking for all these many miles. Toulouse Landing. She'd done it. She'd saved them.

The pilot commenced his delicate maneuvers to position the ship for docking. The starboard side nudged the pillars. And they were home.

"Home" sounded like a place to draw you in and welcome you, a place of warmth and familiarity when, in truth, Lily had not seen Uncle Garvey or his small farm since she was a girl. His letter of invitation had been kind, though, and its timing fortuitous. Without it, Lily would not have known where to go when she and Maddie fled Philadelphia.

"Do you remember what to do when you meet Uncle Garvey?"

"I'm to curtsey, to say 'How do you do, Uncle Garvey?' and if he seems nice, I may kiss his cheek."

Lily smoothed the unruly wisps of hair off Maddie's face. "Perfect."

The crew rattled out the gangway and lashed it into place. "Ma'am," a boatman called up to them from the lower deck. "We're ready for you."

Lily drew a deep breath. This was it then. Their new life. There was certainly no going back.

Maddie clutched her hand so tight it hurt, but Lily wouldn't let go for the world. Maddie had every right to be anxious, torn from home, rushed to the river and aboard a boat headed west with no time to say goodbye to anyone. Maddie had mentioned her father only once. That first day, she'd said, "What about Daddy? Isn't he coming with us?"

"No, sweetheart. Daddy is staying here." And that was all either of them said about him.

It was a peaceful scene onshore. A dozen dark-skinned men lounged at their ease waiting to load their wagons with the crates and kegs the boat delivered. Not slaves, these men. Not anymore.

Beside the nearest wagon stood the only white person on the levee, a well-dressed young woman shading herself with a lacy white parasol. Next to her a dark young man in khaki-colored pants and a white shirt leaned against the same wagon, his arms crossed over his chest. He turned his head to say something to the elegant woman. She tossed back her head and laughed.

No sign of Uncle Garvey, but as soon as Lily crossed the gangway, the young black man strode forward.

"Mrs. Palmer?" he said as she stepped onto the levee.

"Yes."

"I'm Thomas. I'm to take you to your uncle."

A broad-shouldered white crewman rudely pushed past her and shoved a meaty hand into Thomas's chest.

"Get out of the way, boy!"

Thomas fisted his hands. Lily pulled Maddie close, watching the inner struggle so clearly flit across Thomas's face.

He made his choice, loosened his fists, and took a step back.

That was not enough for the greasy white man. He snarled and shoved him again. "I said move!"

His peaceful decision flew away, and Thomas shoved the man back.

The white man rammed his fist into Thomas's gut.

"Stop that this instant!" The well-dressed woman's commanding voice carried over the idling steam engine.

Thomas was on his feet again, lunging for the white man, his fist thrown with all the force of his shoulder behind it.

The woman marched into the fray, her closed parasol now a weapon. Fearless, she poked the boatman with the parasol and ordered him to back off. As huge and threatening as the man was, he stood down.

"Don't!" Thomas hissed at the young woman.

The white man wiped his hand across his busted lip and spat at Thomas's feet with a sneer on his face. He turned to stride away, but not without throwing a curse and a slur over his shoulder.

"Just don't!" Thomas said again through clenched teeth.

In the long moment while Thomas and the woman locked eyes, Lily read an entire story. Thomas was angry, that was easy enough to see. And this dark-haired young woman was anguished. Before she forced her expression into a blank mask, hurt and sorrow shone in her dark eyes.

A connection, an emotional one? Between a former slave and an expensively-dressed white woman? There was a history here.

Though her face was ashen, the lady turned to Lily as if nothing had happened.

"You must be Mrs. Palmer. I am Musette DeBlieux. We are to be neighbors." Miss DeBlieux's smile was wide, but Lily saw the strain around her eyes and mouth.

Lily shook her hand, then introduced Maddie.

"You'll be worn out from traveling. When you have settled in with Mr. Bickell, I will call on you, if I may."

"I look forward to it," Lily said. Indeed she did. She admired a woman who could turn a parasol into an instrument of power. And, she admitted, she was curious. For a young black man to speak to a white woman with such heat, and with such familiarity, was truly, well, unexpected.

That white crewman's hostile feelings, she supposed, were not surprising. With emancipation, every community down here was upside down, everyone unsettled and emotions high. But set back behind Toulouse, Uncle Garvey's farm promised to be a refuge. It was much smaller than the great plantations. Elysium, he'd named it – Uncle Garvey's own paradise. She prayed it would be as peaceful as she remembered. She needed peace.

Thomas led them to the wagon, tension radiating from his back like waves of heat off a pavement. Without a glance back at Miss DeBlieux, he stowed their bags and helped her and Maddie onto the bench.

Thomas flicked the reins and the mule clomped along to a rutted lane leading away from the river deep into the land behind Toulouse, the DeBlieux plantation. Uncle Garvey's place had no direct access to the Mississippi, a significant disadvantage when it was time to transport goods. But, his letter had explained, the DeBlieuxs were happy to share the dock where a small steamship stopped and collected his produce to take sixty miles downriver to New Orleans.

3

"*Heaven*, that's what my Lena called this place," Uncle Garvey had written. "Only she'd been reading a book about the ancient Greeks, so she called it *Elysium*. And it is a pretty place, Lily. More birds than you can ever name, green all year round, no snow and ice of a winter, no street cars clanging the live long day. Come see how you like it, Lily. If you can stomach it, I want you to have the place, such as it is. The only child I have left, your cousin Avery, he says he don't want it. You remember he hit it big out in California and he don't want to ever see Louisiana again. Ungrateful wretch. But I do miss him. Someday, I'm going to San Francisco like he's been after me to, but I like the notion that there's a future here for some of my own."

It was a pretty place. The air felt soft on Lily's skin and carried the scents of roses, black earth, and jasmine. Seemed like every inch of land was covered in green.

They passed the DeBlieux house of Toulouse plantation. It was an old Creole house, large and comfortable looking, but not so grand as the mansions with tall white columns she had seen along the banks of the Mississippi. Of course, the Yankees had burned some of them half way to the ground.

At the end of the lane, they turned into Uncle Garvey's yard. Over the porch, a small plank was burned with the letters to spell *Elysium*. Heaven. And maybe it was. The house was snug and welcoming with the porch rails painted bright white, the clapboards a soft gray like worn cypress. A bed of bright petunias bordered the porch and a vine of honeysuckle wound round the post all the way to the roof.

Uncle Garvey stepped out onto the porch. Lily would have known him anywhere. He looked much like her father might have if he hadn't died early. Her uncle had a bushy white bird, wispy white hair on his head, an expanding middle – and a smile on his face.

He stood on the porch with his hands on his hips watching them climb down from the wagon. Lily, uncertain how to greet him – it had been years since she'd seen him – hid her hands in her skirts so no one could see them trembling. So much depended on her and Maddie making a home here, but she had spent too much of the last years being afraid. She swallowed once and stepped onto the porch, her hand held out. But Uncle Garvey wasn't having any of that. He opened his arms wide and gathered her in. Lily felt she'd waited a long time for a hug like this, total, warm, and loving. Not since Papa died had she felt simple kindness in another person's touch. She leaned into his chest and closed her eyes. Everything was going to be all right.

"And who is this?" He bent to peer at Maddie. "Do you know, I believe you're the prettiest little girl I ever saw."

Maddie hid behind Lily's skirt, but she smiled.

"What do you say, Maddie?" Lily prompted.

Maddie responded to her cue with a lovely curtesy. "How do you do, Uncle Garvey?" Then she reached up for him to bend over again and gave him a kiss on the cheek.

"Oh my, what a charmer, Lily."

The rest of Lily's tension eased out of her shoulders. Uncle Garvey was glad to see them.

"Well, come on in. You haven't met everybody yet."

Lily took Maddie's hand and followed her uncle into the hallway where it was cool and dim.

"They're at the back of the house, I expect."

In the kitchen, Lily found a tall black woman and an even blacker man. These would be Uncle Garvey's former slaves who'd stayed on with him even after emancipation. His letter had made it clear that they belonged on the place. They were to remain here as long as they wanted to be here.

"You must be Rachel," Lily said.

The woman dipped at the knee.

"And you're Peep."

"Yes, ma'am."

"And hiding behind Peep is a new friend for you. Dawn, come out here and meet Maddie." Uncle Garvey held his hand out and a big-eyed child peered around her daddy. "Come here, darling."

Dawn took his hand and eyed Maddie from beneath curling eyelashes.

"Maddie, this is Dawn. Dawn, you two can push each other in the swing after while."

"Soon as Miss Lily get settled," Rachel said, "I'll put supper on the table, Mr. Garvey."

"Come on, then, Lily. I'll take you to your room."

In the shadowy hallway upstairs, Uncle Garvey turned to her. "Lily, you have come without your husband?"

She'd known she'd have to explain this. She'd run it through her head over and over, yet still it nearly choked her. "Frederick passed away, Uncle Garvey."

"My dear girl." He took her hand and patted it. "Then I am doubly glad I could offer you a home. You are not alone, my dear."

Lily blinked away the tears on her lashes. "Thank you, Uncle Garvey. You'll never know how much your kindness means to me and Maddie."

Maddie had gone ahead into the room to explore. Lily would have to tell her about her daddy, but not today. She took Maddie's bonnet off and washed her face. The room they were to share had pale blue walls that made the air feel cooler. The bed cover was lace over batting, the curtains were the same lace, and a landscape adorned the wall beside the door. A wash stand, a chest of drawers, a dresser with mirror, and a straight-back chair completed the furnishings.

Lily stood in the middle of the room and just listened. It was quiet here, like Uncle Garvey's letter had promised. She breathed in, closed her eyes, and let the peace seep into her bones.

This would be home for her and Maddie from now on. No more shouting. No more bruises. No more fear.

"Oh look, a little stool!" Maddie cried as if she had discovered a golden egg or at least a silver goblet. She dragged the stool over to the pegs on the wall, stepped onto it and hung her bonnet up.

"This is a good place, Mama?"

"Yes, sweetheart. I think this is a very good place. I smell supper, don't you?"

Uncle Garvey led them into the dining room still chatting with Lily. Then he suddenly hushed. His eyes ran over the table where there were three places set.

"What is this, Rachel?"

"We got people here now, Mr. Garvey."

Lily watched confusion flicker over her uncle's face, and then embarrassment. It came to her then. They'd all been eating together at this table until she and Maddie arrived.

Lily didn't know what to do. Should she assure Uncle Garvey that whatever he was accustomed to would be fine with her and Maddie? But she had never eaten with black people before. Surely it wasn't proper, especially here in Louisiana.

Rachel decided it. "Ya'll sit down. The biscuits coming out in a minute. Miss Maddie, you sit here where there's a pillow in the chair."

All of them were quiet while they seated themselves. Uncle Garvey had lost his smile, and Lily was sorry for it.

Peep came in with a pitcher of water and filled their glasses, and still no one spoke until Maddie, bless her, broke the tension. Her eyes on the platter of hot, golden biscuits, she said, "Can I have honey on my biscuits?"

"Biscuitsssss?" Uncle Garvey teased. "How many biscuits you planning to eat?"

"Fourteen!"

With a smile, Uncle Garvey caught Lily's eye and winked. "Let's pray," he said. He reached his hands out for Lily's and Maddie's and led the prayer Then it was a feast of new and old foods. Biscuits, of course. Shrimp steamed with peppers and rice, stewed okra, black-eyed peas, creamed corn, ham, pickles, sliced onions, pear compote.

"Tell me about the farm, Uncle Garvey," Lily said.

"Well, I don't know what I'd like to talk about more, honey. We got seventy-five acres here. Hardly bigger than a single cane field on the big plantations, but it's been enough for us. My Lena and I raised our family here years ago, and now the four of us – mostly Thomas and Peep since my bones got creaky -- we manage to grow enough for a profit at the markets and have plenty for ourselves. We got a creek runs down the back, and we got two mules, a few steers, a milk cow, chickens of course, a bunch of hogs. Maddie, Dawn can show you the piglets after supper."

*We*, Uncle Garvey kept saying. He and Rachel, Peep, Thomas and Dawn worked together, lived together, ate together. And now here she and Maddie were, intruding on the family they'd made.

"Most of the plantations around here near about ruined," Uncle Garvey went on. "It needs a lot of labor to get a crop of cane turned into sugar. These planters been depending on slaves, but aren't any slaves anymore. People want to be paid to work, and it's going to take a while for it to all get sorted out."

"And your place, Uncle Garvey?"

Her uncle smiled. "Not much has changed on our place. I gave Rachel and Peep and Thomas their papers way back, before the Louisiana legislature made it impossible to free a slave. Little Dawn had to wait for Lincoln's Emancipation. Since then, they do their work just like always."

Peep came in with a glass of frothy milk and set it down in front of Maddie. "That milk just come out of the cow, Miss Maddie. Good as anything you ever drink."

"Peep," Uncle Garvey said, "we pretty much been sharing the profit we made all along, haven't we?"

"Yes, sir. We pretty much has," Peep said as he refilled the water glasses.

"Only right. I can't work the place by myself, and it makes plenty for all of us."

When Peep left the room, Uncle Garvey leaned toward Lily and said in a low voice, "Quite a love story, Rachel and Peep."

Lily smiled. "Oh?"

"Peep's been with me since he was a sprout. When he got to be of an age, he came to me and said, 'Mr. Bickell, you ought to buy this girl from over at the Brown's. She be a big help to Miss Lena.' I said, 'Is that right?' I thought maybe the rascal would grin – I knew he was sweet on a girl somewhere in the neighborhood -- but he looked like he'd swallowed a burr. 'They say they gone sell her off. And if Mr. Brown try to do that, I think I'm gone have to take her away with me.'

"I can tell you, I did not expect to ever here Peep say he'd run off, not Peep. So Lena and I talked it over. We had some savings, sold the second wagon, and bought Rachel from Walter Brown. Never saw anybody so happy as those two, as starry eyed as any lovers ever were."

Lily put her hand over his. "What a good man you are, Uncle Garvey."

"I've seen worse. But Lily, what I mean to say is, you and Maddie can have a good life here with Rachel and Peep."

"Thank you, Uncle Garvey. Thank you."

He patted her hand. "Now, we won't be seeing much of young Thomas. He has better things to do than hoe weeds this summer." He radiated pride as he told her, "He aims to be a delegate to the state convention."

"A delegate?"

With a chuckle, Uncle Garvey said, "You'll find we don't sit down two minutes in this house without talking politics. You know every state has to pass a new state constitution, with certain requirements, before its allowed any representation in Congress?"

"Yes, I do." Lily had read the *Philadelphia Enquirer* from start to finish ever since the war started. She knew all about the terms for Reconstruction. "For the first time, the black people will vote to choose these delegates, isn't that right? It is momentous, I can see that. And Thomas means to be a delegate?"

"He does indeed. Our Thomas is going to be an important man in this state." Uncle Garvey turned his attention to Maddie. "And you, little lady. Looks to me like you ate all your squash. You want me to butter you another biscuit?"

Lily had never felt so humbled or so grateful. Because Uncle Garvey claimed her for his own, she also had Peep and Rachel, who were kind, and Dawn, and the ambitious, handsome Thomas. It was like inheriting a family as well as a home.

# Chapter Two

Musette sat in front of her mirror, but all she saw was Thomas's angry face.

She'd thought she was doing the right thing. No, she hadn't thought. She'd simply reacted to seeing Thomas being mistreated. She'd have done the same for anyone, wouldn't she? Wasn't she responsible for all these people who had once been slaves, whether they were from her own place or not? They might be emancipated, but they were not free from abuse by angry white men.

She closed her eyes. She had vowed to be honest, at least with herself. She jumped in to save Thomas because she loved him.

She leaned her face into her hands. The look on his face when he'd hissed at her. She'd humiliated him far more than that racist pig who shoved him. Should she apologize?

Musette laughed. What would her Grandmother Emmeline think if she knew her great granddaughter contemplated apologizing to a black man?

She picked up her hairbrush and went about making herself presentable. The dark circles under her eyes did not surprise her. She hadn't slept well. She hadn't slept well for weeks, in fact. She had committed an unpardonable offense, falling in love with a black man. An ex-slave, in fact.

One who did not love her back.

If he had, they could have followed her sister Simone to New York. She too had fallen in love with a black man. Gabe was a free-born, mixed-race, light-skinned doctor, to be more precise. Two white sisters in love with colored men. What was wrong with the DeBlieux daughters? It began, she supposed, with maman's own beloved half-sister Cleo who was also of mixed blood. The DeBlieux family knew very well how little skin color had to do with character.

Of course, Simone and Gabe could not live together in Louisiana or anywhere else in the South. They'd gone North where they could expect to sleep through the night without burning torches being thrown through their windows.

But Thomas did not love her. They would not be marrying and moving to New York.

He liked her. That was all. She had gathered several of the slaves from the neighborhood even before the war was over and taught them to read. Thomas had learned fast, and she had fed him books and more books. They'd talked on after the other students had left, had read poetry together and laughed together. They *knew* each other.

Musette had suitors during the seasons in New Orleans, and some of them had been amusing, but none of them had reached beyond the barriers of courtesy to find the real Musette DeBlieux. Her mother was Josephine Tassin from the Creole planter aristocracy. Musette grew up speaking French, thinking French, knowing she had blood kin among the black slaves. And her papa, Phanor DeBlieux, had been a poor Cajun boy from the back bayous. His liberal ideas had earned him the animosity of some of the planters. "This equality nonsense," they told him. "You're giving these ignorant blacks ideas."

Musette simply didn't see things the same way as other young men and women of her class.

And she was lonely. Twenty-two years old, and alone.

And not just because her mother and her younger sister were in New York visiting Simone and Gabe and the new baby. If only Papa were here. He'd been such fun. They'd been a happy family, the five of them, but Papa had moments of despair, too. He'd hated slavery. He'd explored ways to share the wealth of the plantation, to pay wages or sharecrop – every option led to threats from other planters that he would be burned out. He couldn't do that to Maman. Toulouse Plantation had been in her family for generations. Instead, he taught his three daughters that everyone, white or black, was a human being worthy of respect.

And look what that enlightened thinking had done for them. Simone could never live in Louisiana again, Gabe could not return, and Musette had a pain around her heart that might never go away.

Well, she was mistress of Toulouse for now, and so she must call on her new neighbors. She twisted her hair into a careless bun and tied her bonnet on. If Thomas happened to be around, well, she would pretend nothing had happened.

Footsteps clattered up the stairs. "Miss Musette, you better come."

"What is it, Glory?"

"Thibault wandering off toward the road again, and he ain't got a pass."

Musette hurried onto the veranda, then raised her skirts to rush down the stairs. Thibault had been born simple, and now, as he aged, he'd become even more confused.

She could still see him down the river road heading for the Chamard plantation. He only ambled wherever he went. She could catch him.

She trotted after him, calling his name. He stopped and waited for her.

"Where are you going, Uncle Thibault?"

"I going over to Cherleu to see if Josie there."

"She's visiting Simone and Gabe, remember? Besides, you need a pass to leave Toulouse."

Thibault frowned. "I thought we weren't slaves no more and don't need no more passes."

"You aren't a slave, Uncle Thibault. Not ever again. But there are still people who will give you a hard time if they find you on the road without a pass. Maman and I don't want anybody bothering you."

Thibault's face broke into a brilliant smile. "You belong to me, don't you? You Josie's girl."

"That's right, Uncle Thibault."

The Tassin family certainly was a tangle. Musette's grandfather Emile had had two children with a beloved slave woman. They were Cleo and Thibault, which made Thibault Musette's half-uncle. Cleo had run off to New Orleans as a girl to live as a free woman, but Thibault could never have made it on his own. He'd stayed on Toulouse where he could be taken care of, and there was not a soul on the place better loved.

"I do belong to you. That's why I don't want you having any trouble on the road. Come on back. I'll write you a pass and you can go visit your friends on Cherleu. Maybe Valentine is sitting on the porch wondering where you are. You can have a big glass of lemonade with him."

"I always like a lemonade, Josie."

Musette smiled. "I know you do. Come on home, then you can walk down to Cherleu."

~~~

The visit with Mrs. Palmer and Garvey Bickell went well enough. Musette was welcomed into the parlor where they were served coffee and coconut cake. Mrs. Palmer was several years older than Musette, and the mother of a child, yet the two of them found enough common interests that Musette thought they might become friends.

They both liked books. Musette had always wondered what people who didn't read filled their minds with. She thought of reading as rather like furnishing the rooms in her head. Though she realized that she did a disservice to people who didn't or couldn't read. Their minds were enriched by keen observation and imagination. Certainly Thomas's mind was already sharp and mature before she taught him to read.

One of the many adjustments she and the other slave owners had to make. This notion that because Negros couldn't read – had not been allowed to read – that they were somehow unable to think. And that former slaves were too child-like to be independent. Her face grew hot at the presumptions white people made.

Thomas was right to be angry with her. He was a man, just as much as any man with white skin. But when she interfered between him and the ugly boatman, she had treated Thomas as if he were a boy.

But what good would an apology do? It wouldn't make him love her.

They'd been close all those months when Thomas was learning to read. Or Musette had felt close to him. She had felt no barrier between them when they'd discussed John Locke or Thomas Jefferson. When they'd laughed at Voltaire's silly Candide. But she was a year older than he and maybe he saw her as nothing more than a sort of older sister. But of course their ages were irrelevant. The truly insurmountable barrier between them: Musette was white, Thomas was black.

"Sugar in your coffee, Miss DeBlieux?"

"Yes, please."

Thomas had been bent over picking beans in the north field when she drove by. His sweaty white shirt stuck to his back and her gaze had lingered. Thomas was so perfectly male. Muscled chest, narrow hips and strong thighs. She had never touched a man, not like she wanted to touch Thomas. Perhaps she never would.

Someday, maybe, she wouldn't ache so.

While she ate coconut cake and chatted with Lily Palmer, she heard Thomas come into the kitchen at the back of the house, heard his voice murmuring though the rooms. Maybe he'd wait for her at the wagon. Maybe she could have a few minutes with him.

Philadelphia being closer to New York and therefore to Paris, Lily was a few months ahead of Musette in knowing what the latest styles were. Waists were moving up a bit, and the monstrously huge skirts were slightly slimmed, often bunched up in the back to form a kind of bustle. They agreed any reduction in the circumference of their skirts was welcome.

Musette in her expensive wardrobe felt small and plain next to Lily in her modest cotton dress. Lily had soft wavy light brown hair, and slate blue eyes, and hands that had never been darkened by the sun. Musette's hair and eyes, like all her Creole and Cajun cousins', were dark, her skin what you would expect of a woman raised in the Louisiana sun. And while Lily was taller with a slender waist, Musette wouldn't even call herself dainty. Just short.

With a secret laugh at her own generosity, she decided not to hold Lily's loveliness against her. Musette liked her. She was intelligent and witty and very nice.

"You and Mr. Bickell will come to the picnic next door on Cherleu. Mr. Chamard has a big to do every spring."

"Even in these hard times, he'll have a party?"

"As long as there are peaches on the trees and crawfish in the bayou, that's what he told me."

"But Mr. Chamard doesn't know us, Musette."

"He knows your uncle, and believe me, you will be most welcome. Mr. Chamard has never met a man or woman he didn't like. Especially not a pretty woman. He'll expect you there, I assure you."

Musette said her goodbyes. At the door, the moment before she stepped out onto the porch, she closed her eyes for an instant in silent hope that Thomas would be outside waiting for her.

Her heart thumped hard when she saw him at the wagon. He'd brought a bucket of water for her mule and now leaned against the wagon in his characteristic stance, his arms over his chest, his ankles crossed. He'd put on a fresh shirt. For her?

She stopped ten feet away. "Thomas."

"Miss Musette."

Neither of them smiled.

"You're still angry with me."

He didn't deny it. Musette looked at the trees, at the mule. Finally she made herself meet his eyes.

"Do you know why?" he asked.

13

She nodded. "Yes. I realize."

"That's not the first time, Musette."

Here he was angry with her and a little piece of her heart hummed – he'd never called her simply Musette.

"I don't want you interfering like that again."

She shook her head. "No. I understand."

Maybe he'd walk home with her. They could lead the mule along behind them. They could talk.

"Mrs. Palmer says you've turned in your papers to run for the constitutional convention."

"That's right."

Musette almost said she was proud of him, but that would be condescending, just like stepping between him and a bully had been.

"You think you have a chance?"

"I don't see why not. Folks know me around here. I can read the briefs, thanks to you."

She nodded. "And thanks to the good brain you were born with."

"You'll notice pretty near every man and woman in the quarters is learning to read."

She flushed. She could not please him. She didn't know how.

It was impossible anyway. What she wanted, it could not happen. With her heart filling her throat so that she didn't know how she could speak, she said, "I guess I'll be going."

He reached around to his back and pulled a slim book out of his waistband. "I finished your Walt Whitman."

Musette flushed again. What had she been thinking, giving a man a book of poems that talked about, well, the sensuality of the body. He'd know she had read that poem. "I mind how once we lay such a transparent summer morning/ How you settled your head athwart my hips and gently turn'd over upon me/ And parted the shirt from my bosom-bone, and plunged your tongue to my bare-stript heart." And those lines about his "love-spendings." Her face felt like flames.

He moved the water bucket out of the way and took hold of the mule's reins. "I believe Whitman is a man of true democracy – those lines, 'Stranger, if you passing meet me and desire to speak to me, why should you not speak to me?/ And why should I not speak to you?'" Thomas looked at her, and if he saw her red face, he did not say so. "He could be writing about you, couldn't he? A white woman who dared to speak to black men, to even teach them to read."

She fell into step beside him and they walked down the lane. At least her bonnet would shield her flushed face from him if they were side by side.

"But what do you think about 'I Was Looking A Long While'?" He opened the book with one hand and read, "'I was looking a long while for a clue to the history of the past,' then he goes on and says he found it 'in Democracy – (the purport and aim of all the past).' That word 'purport' means 'meaning' or 'sense'?"

"Yes. Its significance."

"The purport of history is in democracy? I don't know how he can say that living in a country full of slaves."

"I don't know what he meant by 'purport' either. But the word 'aim.' If he means that history is meant to lead us to democracy, he has a very optimistic view of humankind."

They walked on, Thomas thumbing through the book.

Musette said, "There are other poems in that book I don't understand, but I remember one he wrote about going with the slaves of the earth the same as with the masters. Something about entering into both."

Thomas gently closed the book. "He's a great man."

Musette laughed. "Not everybody thinks so. Some people would have him horse-whipped. But yes, I think he is a great man."

He held the book out for her to take.

"You keep that one. Simone left a copy in her bedroom."

"Thank you. I'd like to read this to the others."

For these last ten minutes Musette had breathed happiness. Thomas talking to her, thinking with her, walking with her. She could smell the clean linen of his shirt, the lingering sweat on his back. Her heart beat so hard she feared it would make her bodice tremble. She wanted to touch the hand that held the book. To look into his eyes and have him look at her with the same wanting.

They were at the turn-in to Toulouse. "I'll go on back," he said. He held the book up. "Thank you for this. I will share it, and I will remind the others how generous you are."

He had not said her name again. "You're very welcome to it. All of you," she answered, just as if she felt nothing at all.

# Chapter Three

Lily opened her eyes and stretched. She felt ... rested. That had not happened in a long while, especially not since she'd left Philadelphia. By the time they'd made it to Toulouse Landing, she'd been a brittle shell, smiling and serene on the outside, empty and dark on the inside. After what she'd done to Frederick ... She had not intended ... God knew she had not intended.

She covered her face with her hands. Maybe she should have stayed in Philadelphia. Maybe the courts would understand she'd only meant to save herself. But no, the courts would not take her part. She'd heard too many tales of a woman beaten beyond endurance who finally appealed to the court, but because the man who hurt her was her husband, the judge sent her back home with him.

There had been Maddie to think of, too. When Frederick had turned on a six year old child, had struck his own daughter – he'd never done that before. She could not trust him to never strike her again. And so she'd prepared to leave him.

They were safe now. No one in Philadelphia knew about Uncle Garvey, no one knew she had any ties to Louisiana at all. And if they traced her to Gillian's house in Parkersburg, her sister would say Lily had gone to Minnesota. They had a great-uncle near St. Paul. She had no idea if he was still alive, but the connection was real.

She rose without waking Maddie and walked to the window to greet the early morning. The air was sweet with the scent of petunias, the shrubs and trees every shade of green from dusty olive to deepest forest. It was hot here, dear God, it was hot. But beautiful. Maddie could be happy here. Lily did not expect happiness for herself. In fact, she did not deserve it, but maybe she could find peace.

Peaceful or not, she meant to make a life here. Today, at Bertrand Chamard's picnic, she would smile and she would mean it. If there were dancing, she would dance. She pulled on her best day dress, a pale green calico with tiny yellow flowers pressed into the design. Around her neck she wore a green ribbon. Not a glamorous look, but she would do.

When they arrived at the picnic the sun was high and hot. Tables with linen cloths were laid out under the shade trees. Pitchers of lemonade and bowls of punch shared the table with a coconut cake, a pineapple cake, and tarts made with last summer's peach preserves, everything covered with fine gauze to keep the flies off. The other tables displayed all the bounties of a summer garden.

Maddie and Dawn had no interest in the food. They raced off toward the children playing Red Rover on the lane running beside the house. White children and black children, Lily was surprised to see, but the only black adults she saw were women serving drinks and plates of food and men setting out more tables and chairs.

Musette met her and Uncle Garvey with hands extended in welcome. "Isn't this the perfect day for a picnic? Come and meet everyone."

Mr. Chamard was a handsome man for all his sixty years. His hair was still thick and more dark than gray. His eyes gleamed with intelligence and good humor.

"Hello, Bickell. I see you've brought your family." He took Lily's hand and bowed over it with more gallantry than Lily had ever seen in Philadelphia. "Mrs. Palmer, I believe."

Lily dipped a curtsey. "Mr. Chamard. Thank you for including us in your lovely gala."

"I expect to see a great deal of you since we're neighbors. Bickell and I play poker now and again, but we could be persuaded to more gentlemanly pursuits if a lady were available to keep us company." This welcoming speech was accompanied by a kiss of her hand, which he had somehow not yet relinquished, and the open appreciation of very warm brown eyes.

Musette laid her hand on Lily's arm. "I'm taking Mrs. Palmer to meet Nicolette, Mr. Chamard. Perhaps you will entertain Mr. Bickell with talk of, oh, I don't know, guano?" She gave him an impish smile and drew Lily toward a cluster of people sipping punch in the shade.

"I thought if I didn't get you away from our host, he would charm you half to death."

Lily grinned. "But you like him."

"I adore him. Every female in the parish adores him. I believe my mother ... But yes, I like him. He and Maman and I are sticking together to figure out how to run a plantation with wage laborers. But now I want you to meet my cousin."

A fashionably dressed woman in white muslin and two handsome men in light linen suits turned at their approach. The woman greeted Musette with a big smile and a hug, carefully holding her glass of punch to the side. They kissed cheeks, then Musette introduced them.

"Nicolette is Bertrand Chamard's daughter. This is her husband Captain Finnian McKee, and our friend, Major Alistair Whiteaker. This is Mrs. Palmer. She is Garvey Bickell's niece come to stay, I hope."

One seldom saw a true beauty in this world, but this woman's face was a perfect oval with a generous mouth, creamy skin, and gray eyes under dark eyebrows. She looked to be about five months pregnant. She smiled as she shook Lily's hand. "I'm sure my Aunt Josephine – Musette's maman, you won't have met her yet – I'm sure she also will be very happy to have another woman in the neighborhood."

Captain McKee, Nicolette's husband, was a fine looking man with dark eyes and a black moustache. "Hello, Musette. How do you do, Mrs. Palmer."

Lily felt the tall blond man's attention on her. He was observing her intently from eyes of a startling blue. She made herself look away.

"Do I detect a Boston accent, Captain McKee?"

"You do. I fear I will never sound like a man of New Orleans, but that is what I am now. Alistair, however," he said gesturing to the blond man, "is Louisianan born and bred."

"Good morning, Miss DeBlieux. You're looking lovely as always," Major Whiteaker said. Then he offered his hand to Lily in chivalrous style, palm up for her to place her hand in his. Quite formally he bowed. "Mrs. Palmer."

Lily swallowed hard. The skin of her hand, bare in this heat, felt the slight pressure of his fingers long after he let go.

"You are here with your husband?" Major Whiteaker enquired.

"No, sir. I am a widow." It was merely the truth. Frederick was dead. She was a widow now.

Major Whiteaker executed a half bow. "My condolences."

She inclined her head. "Thank you."

"Let's sit down." Musette motioned to a servant standing nearby. "James, will you bring a tray of drinks, please?"

They arranged themselves in a circle of five, the major sitting directly across from Lily. She began to feel uncomfortable under his gaze. If she met his eyes, he did not look away. If she talked with someone else, she felt his gaze on her. He was sandy-haired and long of limb. Most men she knew had a beard or a moustache or both, but Major Whiteaker was clean shaven. He might be the most handsome man she'd ever seen. But her husband had been handsome, too.

Captain McKee perhaps was one of the many Northerners who came to the South after the war now that land was cheap. "You have a plantation, Captain McKee?" she asked.

Lily hoped the heat would explain her flushed face. Major Whiteaker's steady regard both embarrassed and animated her. If she let herself, she believed she would simply gaze back into his eyes with her mouth agape, losing herself in those deep sapphire irises.

A yellow hound sprawled at his side and Major Whiteaker's hand lazily stroked its ears.

It had been a long time since Lily had felt any joy in sensuality, but the sight of this man's long fingers stroking the dog's velvety ears roused thoughts of those fingers moving over her skin. She blinked and forced her attention back to Captain McKee, who was answering her question.

"Not I. Nicolette and I come upriver to visit her father as often as we can. We have a book store in town. Are you a reader, Mrs. Palmer?"

"Oh, yes. I have already begun borrowing books from Musette."

"What do you like to read?"

"I tend to avoid the history and philosophy tomes," she said, feeling as if she should apologize for her lack of serious intent. "I like novels and plays, both comedies and dramas."

Major Whiteaker's blue eyes lit up. "I prefer fiction myself. Have you read Molière?"

"Oh, yes. *Tartuffe!* I read it aloud to my father when he was still alive and we laughed ourselves silly."

Captain McKee grinned. "A kindred spirit then. Alistair and I, and Nicolette if she can be persuaded to sit still, entertain ourselves reading plays aloud. Nicolette of course makes each of us feel quite drab, and she is prone to giggles when one of us attempts a female part.

"When the season starts after Christmas, Musette, bring Mrs. Palmer to town," Mr. McKee said. "I'll find us a play that three women and two men can read together. We'll put all of New Orleans' finest actors to shame."

Nicolette grinned at Lily. "We three could shop together, even if all we need is ribbons." She shot a smile at Musette. "We always need ribbons, do we not?"

Musette said, "We should circulate. Lily needs to meet everyone."

The gentlemen stood. Finnian McKee smiled warmly. "Until we see you in New Orleans, then."

Lily felt she must turn to Major Whiteaker, it was only courtesy, but not until she had drawn a breath and held it.

He angled his head in a gentlemanly bow. "I shall look forward to it."

Musette took Lily's arm and walked her toward another group of people across the broad yard. "I think you've made a conquest," Musette whispered.

Lily looked at her in alarm. "Of course not."

Musette indulged in a smirk. "I see you don't ask whom I mean."

"Of course I know whom you mean. His attentions were not subtle."

"Behavior most unlike our Major Whiteaker."

"Is it?"

"Oh, he's always perfectly courteous. Friendly even. But there is always an air about him of being here only in body. Today the whole of him was present."

"A dreamy sort?"

"Exactly. And I often think he looks sad. Perhaps he's lonely." She looked sideways at Lily.

"Stop that. I have no room for a man in my life. Maddie is quite enough for me."

"I see," Musette murmured. "Here are the Johnstons. Let's go and say hello."

~~~

His hands clasped behind his back, Alistair watched her walk away with Musette. The sway of her hips set her green skirts into a gentle oscillation.

"Lovely woman. Don't you think, Alistair?"

"Hm? Yes, yes she is." He couldn't say he'd been thinking, as Nicolette implied. He'd been intent on looking at her, that's all. Not that she was the most beautiful woman he'd ever known. He supposed Nicolette held that title. Mrs. Palmer was a bit thin – a recent weight loss, he thought, since her dress seemed a little big on her. Maybe travel did not agree with her. But she was lovely, as Nicolette said. And there was a sweetness about her, and the hint of depths to explore.

He surprised himself. He had not been interested in any particular woman for a long while. Not since he'd realized Nicolette would never be his. He still loved her of course, always would. But he no longer craved her, or needed her like he needed air. He paused. Was that true, that he no longer was in love with Nicolette? He looked at her smiling face as she exchanged a glance with Finn. No, it didn't hurt anymore to see her happy with another man. He had lived through the enchantment, perhaps the bewitchment, she had never meant to impose on him in the first place.

Alistair took in a breath. He hadn't thought of it until now. Free of Nicolette's enchantment. He felt lighter at the realization. He had become accustomed to the role, at least in his own head, of disappointed bachelor. Perhaps now he was simply, a bachelor.

Nicolette took his arm. "Do you know Lily's Uncle Garvey, Alistair?"

"Of course. I thought he meant to join Avery in California."

"He does. He wants to leave the farm to his niece if she agrees to stay. She'll be Papa's neighbor, a stone's throw from Cherleu."

Alistair gave her a look. "Within calling distance, is that what you're saying, Nicolette? I believe we've had this conversation before. You are not to play matchmaker with me."

She widened her eyes in innocence. "I wouldn't think of it, Alistair." The gleam in her eye said otherwise though.

He gave her hand resting on his arm a quick squeeze. "I think I smell fried chicken. Smell it, Finn?"

"Yes, thank God. I'm afloat in punch. They're laying it out on that table under the chinaberry tree if I'm not mistaken."

The three strolled their way through friends and neighbors, some of them standing in earnest conversation, some settled on blankets with their hats over their faces. More energetic picnickers ignored the sun beating down on them and engaged in a lively game of horseshoes.

Alistair spied Mrs. Palmer talking with Albany Johnston. Johnston had several plantations up and down the Mississippi, but he was having trouble just as they all were in figuring out how to make a cane plantation work now that he had to pay wages to his workers. Alistair himself had other financial interests, railroads, for one, to tide him through these times of adjustment. He saw himself as the willow bending with the winds, not a rigid hickory to be toppled by the storm of changes sweeping the South.

Mrs. Palmer looked happy talking to the Johnstons. Happier than she'd been talking to him. He supposed that was his fault. He'd had a hard time not staring at her. As, he realized, he was doing now.

# Chapter Four

Leaving Lily in company with the Johnstons, Musette walked with Mr. Chamard to visit the party in the quarters. She hoped they weren't too late for a dish of ice cream. Mr. Chamard had ordered two huge chunks of ice from the factory in town, one for the picnic up by the big house, one for the laborers' celebration. The workers already had two ice cream churns from the days before the war, Christmas gifts from Mr. Chamard, and Musette herself had sent over sugar and cream. Nothing meant summer like vanilla ice cream.

"How's your Mr. Gale finding his work crews?" Mr. Chamard asked as they strolled through the orchard toward the old quarters. "My fellows say they won't work on the levy without an extra dollar a month. It is nasty, hard work, but – " He sighed, weary with the unaccustomed need to negotiate with his workers. "But a dollar a month." He shook his head.

"Mr. Gale hasn't mentioned that they've asked for more money, but I haven't seen him for the last couple of days. He's in Donaldsonville meeting with some of the overseers, trying to get a feel for what the next season's negotiations might involve."

"I do want them to make a living, to have a better life, Musette. I do. As does your mother. I just have to make them understand they can't get blood out of a turnip."

Musette laughed. "I imagine they have little expectation of blood from their turnips, Mr. Chamard. But I see your point."

"You heard they let Brown's crop molder in the fields last fall? He wouldn't pay them what they could get from other planters, and they walked off. I don't know if he can survive another year as ruinous as this past one."

"Mr. Brown wouldn't compromise."

"Lots of men won't compromise, Musette. There's going to be trouble, more than we've already seen."

As they approached the quarters, they could hear a smooth, impassioned voice above the noise of children playing.

Thomas, of course. He was a practiced orator by now, speaking to groups of ex-slaves like these. Explaining the laws from Washington, the issues in Louisiana. He had a firm grasp of what the whites wanted and what his people needed. He was, at twenty-one years old, already a leader of his people.

"Until we have the vote, we are not free." Thomas had a conversational style, his voice modulated to be heard but not to shout. "We have been released from bondage, but we do not yet enjoy fair play with every other man in Louisiana."

Thomas's eyes roamed over the people, catching this one's gaze and that one's, letting him know he spoke to them and for them. Every eye was focused on him.

Musette thrilled at the power in Thomas Bickell. If she couldn't have him, she could, in her private heart, claim a part of him for herself. She had taught him to read, she had led him to ideas from the greatest minds of the day.

"When the boss tells you that you must stay on the place, you may not leave to find a better wage, you may not own a gun -- he lies! Since last April, you do not have to sign a year-long contract. You do not have to have a pass to leave the plantation to go to market, to visit friends or family."

People murmured to themselves. Two years after the war, many of the old white masters tried to make the ex-slaves believe they had to live very much as they had always lived, under the white man's boot.

"The end of slavery is not just a bunch of words. We are freer today than we were even six months ago, but -- the work is not over. Until every one of us has the vote, we will have no power to protect ourselves. Until we have the vote, we will not have justice."

"I thought we had the vote!" someone called out.

"Yes. For this moment only. In September, we can vote on who we send to the state convention to rewrite the Louisiana Constitution. That's a powerful thing – we have the chance to change who gets to vote in this state for every election to come, not just for this one. But we have to all turn out on September 27th if we want to continue voting in the next election and the next and the next. This right to vote we have right now? We have to make it a permanent part of Louisiana's constitution."

Thomas's voice softened. "One more thing. If we're going to have the vote, we every one of us gone have to learn to read. If you can't read the ballot, and you can't read the papers that tell you what each candidate stands for, then you can't be sure your vote counts. We all got to help each other."

Thomas raised his head and looked right at Musette. "We got with us Miss DeBlieux." He held his open palm out to her. "How many of us can read because of her?"

Musette felt heat flash into her face. Eight men and a woman raised their hands and everyone turned to look at her. She was honored. And she was embarrassed.

Thomas looked over the crowd with a cheeky grin. "Who says Miss DeBlieux gets the first dish of ice cream?"

The crowd laughed and hollered amen.

Mr. Chamard gave Musette a one-armed hug and kissed the top of her head. "Come on. We get to be first in line for ice cream."

Once they had their ice cream, Musette sat with Mr. Chamard on the steps of one of the cabins.

"Just the way I like it," Mr. Chamard said, licking his spoon.

"Me too! Grainy and a little runny."

Two little girls in pigtails ran past, giggling and shrieking at the same time. A boy a year or so older pursued, a big grin on his face. Everyone had on their best, those who had more than the clothes they wore every day. A red head scarf here, a splash of yellow handkerchief there made the scene festive and happy.

Thomas was sauntering their way, his sleeves rolled up to his elbows, his collar unbuttoned. My Lord, what a picture of manhood he was. Musette had to look into her bowl instead of at him.

"I'm not free either," Mr. Chamard murmured in Musette's ear. "I can't roll my sleeves up or open my collar."

Musette smiled at him. "You poor thing."

"That was a fine speech, young man," Mr. Chamard said as Thomas came up to them.

"Thank you, sir. Can I get you some more ice cream?"

"I already had a piece of coconut cake and a peach tart. My valet will have something to say if I can't button my pants tomorrow."

"How about you, Miss Musette?"

Mr. Chamard stood. "I need to get back to my guests. But you stay and enjoy yourself, Musette. I think you are something of a guest of honor, am I right, Thomas?"

"Yes, sir." Thomas looked at her. "I'll see she gets back when she's ready."

Thomas took Chamard's place on the steps. "Ginny," he called to a girl in pigtails. "Miss DeBlieux and I would be grateful if you were to bring us some more ice cream."

She gave him a grin and ran off. Likely every female on the place would be happy to please Thomas, Musette thought. Ah, a little jealousy creeping in. Foolish of her.

"Did I say that the right way?" Thomas asked. "...'if you *were* to bring ice cream'?"

"Yes. Subjunctive case."

They watched the mama on the stoop across the way spooning ice cream into her toddler's mouth. "What a face!" Musette said. "You think he ever had anything that cold before? Oh, look, he wants more."

Thomas watched with her, smiling. But his mind never strayed far from the passion in his life.

"I'm glad you and Mr. Chamard came down. It helps all of us, to know everybody with white skin isn't the enemy."

"I'm proud to be here, Thomas. I do feel honored."

Thomas touched her hand. "You are. We all owe you a debt."

She swallowed and tried to pretend her heart hadn't sped up. They must have touched at times, especially at first when she was guiding his hand to write his letters. But this was deliberate. A warm, gentle touch.

It didn't mean anything. She knew that. There were dozens of people around. This was not meant to be a private moment, not meant to mean . . . what she wished it meant. It was just part of his thank you, that was all.

"You're all very welcome." She looked at him. "Truly."

He smiled at her. "I know we are."

Ginny delivered two bowls of ice cream, a heaping one for Musette, a rather stingy one for Thomas. They were probably running out.

She handed him her big helping and took his smaller one. He just smiled and dug in.

"God, that's good," he said.

"They know how to make it just right," she said.

"I didn't know there was any other way to make it. 'Cept I had it with peaches once."

Musette launched into a discussion of how to make the ice cream smoother, how much salt to put on the ice, how long to crank the churn.

"I had no idea you were a cook, Miss Musette."

She held her spoon up as if to pontificate. "It's not all about book learning, sir."

Musette startled as Ginny screamed and jumped onto the porch behind Thomas at the same time three horses tore into the quarters.

Their faces covered, the horsemen screamed out the piercing rebel yell, the same yell that had rattled Yankee soldiers and made their spines stiff with fear. They snapped their whips overhead, yelling and whirling their horses in circles.

Dust rose into the air, women screamed and grabbed for their children. Men reached for the reins or for the horsemen themselves.

Musette stood tall and shouted, "What is the meaning of this!"

Thomas took her arm and shoved her onto the porch behind him. "Stay out of this!"

Several men from the picnic came rushing into the lane – Mr. Chamard, Captain McKee, Major Whiteaker, and Mr. Johnston. "You men are on my property," Chamard shouted. "You will leave at once!"

Thomas rushed into the melee, dragged a man off his mount, and slammed his fist into the rider's face. Musette put her hands over her mouth, terrified he'd be run over by one of the horses.

A whip cracked again and Thomas fell to his knees, blood blooming on the back of his white shirt.

Whiteaker seized the reins of the man who'd whipped Thomas. The rider raised the whip to slash at Whiteaker, but he grabbed the man's arm and yanked him out of the saddle.

The third raider reached down and hauled up the man Thomas had dismounted and those two galloped off, screaming their yell, spurring their horses to pound out of the quarters -- leaving behind the man Whiteaker had taken.

With the raider on his back in the dirt, Whiteaker kicked his whip aside and wrenched the bandana off the man's face.

"Jacques Valmar, you cur," he said.

Musette rushed to Thomas, still on his knees. She was pushed aside by Rachel and Peep as they took him beneath the arms to help him up.

"I'll get the doctor," she cried, so scared her hands were trembling.

"No need, Miss Musette," Peep said. "Rachel know what to do. Ain't the first whip lash we ever seen."

Thomas was standing on his own now, his mouth grim. "Go on," he told her. He pointed his chin toward Chamard's big house. "Go on back to the picnic."

She blinked hard. He was dismissing her? As if she didn't belong here? She looked at the other faces she knew, at Rachel and Peep, at Valentine and at Smithy, her own slave – oh, Lord. What she'd just said – she was astonished at herself. Even if only in her own head, she had betrayed Thomas and all he stood for – she'd called the blacksmith for Toulouse *her own slave.* Thomas was right. She didn't belong here, she was not one of them.

Thomas's face softened and he gentled his voice. "Go on, Musette."

Chamard strode up to Valmar. "I'll have you thrown in jail for this."

Valmar spat. "On what charge? I ain't done nothing but go for a Sunday ride."

"Disturbing the peace, that's a good start. I imagine I'll think of more on the way to the jail."

Valmar nodded his head at Thomas. "Your nigger punched a white man. What you gonna do about that?"

Chamard drew his arm back and slapped Valmar so hard the man's head twisted all the way to the side.

"That's what I'm going to do about it." Chamard nodded to a man who had once been his property. "Cleavis, how about some of you locking this vermin up in the corn crib? Maybe there's a couple of corn snakes in there to amuse him."

Valmar touched his reddened cheek, then sneered as three men of the quarters surrounded him. He hadn't shaved in days. His brown hair straggled around his ears. His middle was soft, and his clothes were dirty. Perhaps thirty years old, not tall, not short. A very ordinary man except for the expression of smug superiority on his face.

"He don't look like much to me," Cleavis said as he and three other men of the quarters surrounded him. "What you think he's so het up on himself about?"

"Why, Cleavis. Don't you know? The man be white."

Cleavis snorted and shoved Valmar to get him moving.

Musette hardly noticed the exchange between Chamard and the man. She had stepped away from Thomas, but her eyes were still on him.

"Miss Musette," Major Whiteaker said. He placed her hand on his arm. "May I escort you back to your cousin?"

She allowed the major to take her back to the picnic where everyone but the servants was white. Where no one would tell her to *go on back where you belong.*

~~~

Alistair didn't like to see Nicolette rushing to meet them in this heat, in her condition.

"It was bad, Alistair?"

He nodded, the muscles in his jaw tight. "But it could have been worse. One man hurt, that's all. You know Thomas Bickell? The young firebrand?"

"Papa has mentioned him."

"He pulled one of the riders off his horse and slugged him. Another rider got Thomas with a whip."

Musette gave him a watery smile. "Our Major Whiteaker took down that scoundrel all by himself."

Nicolette put her hand on Whiteaker's arm. "You're not hurt, Alistair?"

He patted Nicolette's hand. "Not at all."

Finn strode toward them, his face taut.

"He locked up?" Whiteaker asked.

"For now. Alistair, I'd be obliged if you would keep Nicolette company while I'm gone. I'm going with Chamard to take Valmar to Donaldsonville. Sheriff Paget will at least lock him up. I'm not so sure but what the sheriff downriver wouldn't just grin and let him go soon as we're out of sight."

"What will the charge be?"

"I think we'll have to be satisfied with disturbing the peace. If we charge Valmar with assault, then the man Thomas punched could come forward and file charges against Thomas. That would not be good for Thomas."

"Musette, why don't you sit down, dear?" Nicolette said.

Alistair took one look at her face and hurried a chair behind her knees. "No wonder you feel faint, Miss Musette. You witnessed a shocking scene."

"Where is Mrs. Palmer off to in such a tearing hurry?" Finn said. "She's not going to the quarters?"

Alistair turned to see her marching through the orchard, her petticoats frothy white at her hemline. He pivoted and took off after her with long strides.

"Mrs. Palmer," he called as he approached.

She stopped and waited for him.

"Mrs. Palmer, where are you going, may I ask?"

"They said those men whipped Thomas. I'm going to look after him." Her voice trembled and her hands were clenched.

"His parents are with him, Mrs. Palmer. The quarters really is not the place for you at this time. People are worked up."

"But they whipped Thomas – "

"Thomas will be fine." Whiteaker gently wrapped his fingers around her arm. He didn't want her rushing down there, a stranger, red-faced and upset. She would not be welcome.

"The boy lives in the same house I do, Major Whiteaker."

"Yes, I realize. But his people will take care of him."

She looked at him with reddened eyes, the irises nearly lavender in this emotional state. He handed her his handkerchief. "I would like you to come back with me, Mrs. Palmer. Will you do that?"

She blotted her eyes and her nose and took in a shuddering breath. She looked through the pecan orchard toward the scene of the raid, but she relented. "Yes, very well."

He placed her hand on his arm and led her slowly back, giving her time to settle herself before they rejoined the others. She was not accustomed to racial issues being at fever pitch like they were here in the South. And it was only going to get worse. The more power the ex-slaves gained, the more some of the whites were going to punish them for it. Thomas Bickell was going to have to take care.

"Do you know who the men who got away are?"

"Maybe. But they had bandanas over their faces. No judge would honor a witness accusing a man who had his face covered."

After a moment, he said, "Mrs. Palmer."

She turned her face up to him. He gathered his courage and said, "If you would like to know more, to understand what is happening here, I could . . . we could . . ." He swallowed. It had been too long since he had asked to call on a woman. "We could talk."

He looked off in the distance. She probably wasn't ready for callers. She had only arrived a short while ago. She probably thought he was overbearing. He had looked at her too much earlier, he knew he had.

"Thank you, Major Whiteaker. That is kind of you."

He glanced at her. Was that a yes? Or simply the beginnings of a kind refusal.

"I'd like that," she added, looking up at him with a somber face.

She was much prettier when she smiled. Of course, everyone was. But he very much liked the way she looked at that moment, her eyes serious, her mouth grim.

"I want this to be Maddie's and my home. I want us to be part of everything that's here. But I ... I had hoped for a quiet life."

He nodded. Then he asked, "Who is Maddie?"

She smiled and the clouds in her eyes disappeared. "Maddie is my daughter. She's six, the light of my life."

A daughter. Of course. Why wouldn't she have children?

"I'll meet her when I come to call?"

"Oh, yes. And by then, she will know how to say, 'How do you do, Major Whiteaker?'"

Alistair thought he rather liked the idea of Mrs. Palmer having a daughter. Would three days be long enough to wait before knocking on her door?

# Chapter Five

Lily sat at the breakfast table over a second cup of coffee with Uncle Garvey when Maddie blew in like a whirlwind.

"Mama!"

Lily smiled at her excitement and was relieved to see Uncle Garvey was amused rather than annoyed at the rude interruption.

"What is it, Maddie?"

"Dawn is going to school! Right now!"

"Is she?"

"She said I can come. She's in the wagon with Thomas waiting for me. So I need my bonnet."

"Maddie, take a breath. You don't have to go to school until the fall, and even then, the school may be too far. I may decide to tutor you here at home."

"Mama, no! I want to go with Dawn. Right now! They're in the wagon."

"Maddie. Sit down and behave. This is not acceptable behavior."

Maddie slumped onto a chair, her eyes pleading.

"What is this school, Uncle Garvey?"

"It's the one Whiteaker built on his property. Set it up soon as he got back from the war. He was not yet himself, as far his health was concerned. Was a prisoner of war, you know. Anyway, first thing he did, built the school and hired a teacher."

"So it's a school for children of the freedmen."

"There are white children there, too. I would have no objection to having Maddie among them. At least until you decide what you want to do in the fall."

"Mama?" Maddie said softly. "They're waiting for me in the wagon."

Lily did not want to be a snob. She knew very well that being poor, white or black, was not an indication of character. But it was primarily a school for black children, after all.

On the other hand, Uncle Garvey gave her a little nod, encouraging her. Then he looked at Maddie and smiled.

Maddie sat up straight and beamed.

Well, then.

"I'll come too, Maddie. We'll make an outing of it and have a look at Dawn's school. But, mind, it is only an outing for today."

Maddie tore out of the dining room to get her bonnet.

"I'll get on with my chores, then, my dear. I believe you'll find the school in good order, but of course I leave the decision to you."

The mule pulled them over rutted back lanes for half an hour before they saw the whitewashed schoolhouse standing alone in a lush green meadow. A young black woman stood in the yard ringing a bell, white and black children cavorting around her. Maddie followed Dawn scrambling off the back of the wagon and made a run for it to the school house.

The young woman waited for them on the stoop, smiling warmly.

"Welcome to A. P. Whiteaker School."

Her eyes were on Thomas as she spoke, her smile just a little shy.

"Mrs. Palmer, this is Fanny Brown. Mrs. Palmer is Mr. Bickell's niece."

Miss Brown curtsied prettily. She was young and attractive, her features reflecting her ancestry. Medium dark skin – Lily had been here only two weeks and already she knew the shade of a freedman's skin was of consequence in this place, a broad nose, but rather turned up on the end to be what her husband would have called cute, and, surprisingly, hazel eyes tilted upwards on the outer corners.

"That was my daughter Maddie tearing across the lawn behind Dawn," Lily said. "Perhaps you have all the children you can handle already?"

Miss Brown's eyes twinkled. "As long as we can find a place to put them, we want them here, Mrs. Palmer."

"May we come in for a few moments? I don't want to disturb your routine, but I admit to being quite interested in your school."

"You are welcome, ma'am."

The schoolroom was well lit with five windows on the long walls, all of them open to catch the breeze, and unfortunately, to allow the flies to buzz in and out. Outside the windows, two saplings enjoyed the sun on either side of the schoolhouse, doing their best to grow into big shade trees.

The boisterous mayhem subsided as soon as Miss Brown stood in front of the class.

Lily looked around the room at the motley collection of students. Dawn and Maddie were the youngest. Then there were those children who seemed to be between eight and maybe twelve. Sitting in the back were the oldest children, some of them in the middle of their growth spurt if the too-short pants and sleeves were any indication. It must be a sacrifice for the families to send these older children to school. They were surely needed at home, working in the garden, even laboring for wages on the plantations.

Miss Brown passed a basket full of acorns around the room. "Take ten, each of you."

The older children got up and counted out ten acorns for the ones who needed help. Maddie knew her numbers and her letters, even if she didn't know what to do with them yet. She confidently counted out her own ten acorns, Lily was proud to see.

Thomas joined the older students in the back of the room, perching on the edge of a boy's desk. He spoke to them in a low voice and they all busily wrote a math problem on their slates.

The hour passed quickly. When Lily touched her hand and whispered she would be back for her later, Maddie nodded without taking her eyes from her teacher. Lily slipped down the aisle and out into the sunshine to find Thomas in conversation with Major Whiteaker.

"Mrs. Palmer." Major Whiteaker removed his hat and bowed. His yellow hound thumped its tail, happy to see her. Her heart thumped, too, traitorous thing. She had no intentions where gentlemen were concerned.

"Major Whiteaker."

"Excuse me," Thomas said. "I'll get a bucket of water for the mule."

"How do you find our school?" the major asked her. The smile on his face was proud and pleased when he looked over at the gleaming white schoolhouse.

"Where I grew up, the school had over a hundred students and three teachers, Major. This is new to me, a one room schoolhouse."

"We'll grow, or we'll have more schools. Right now we have twenty-two enrolled, though of course not everyone can come every day. Thomas says you've brought your little girl this morning?"

She didn't know how to read the intensity of his gaze. Bringing Maddie seemed to carry a significance she didn't understand.

"Maddie and Thomas's little sister are inseparable, and what could be more intriguing than school to a six year old?"

"It's good to have her here. We need the children to know one another."

"You would continue to have the two races in the same classroom, Major, once the school has grown?"

"Yes."

Lily nodded and directed her gaze at the sparse grass growing at their feet. His gaze was hard to hold as attentive and direct as it was.

"You don't approve, Mrs. Palmer?"

She looked up in surprise. "Approve? I certainly don't disapprove. I've just never . . . We never had much to do with each other, Negroes and whites, where I came from."

His deep blue eyes still bore into hers. He seemed to be waiting for something, for her to say something.

"I'm just not accustomed to, well, black and white children in school together."

His smile was gentle. "But you're leaving your child here for the day. Thank you."

The sun made his hair and skin golden. She wanted to raise her hand to his face, to relieve that hint of loneliness she saw in him.

Oh, my, Lily Palmer, she thought. Guard your heart.

Neither of them said another word until Thomas returned with the bucket of water. The major handed her up into the wagon. "May I call on you tomorrow, Mrs. Palmer?"

She should discourage him. That part of her life was over. But to say no would be discourteous. They were neighbors now.

He still had her hand in his. Lily put on a smile. "Rachel is baking tomorrow morning. I believe we can offer you lemon cake."

The smile he gave her in return was bright enough to coax seedlings right out of the ground. He stepped away as Thomas climbed into the wagon.

"Come tomorrow, Thomas. I'll have that horse ready for you."

"Thank you, sir."

Down the road, Lily said, "He's giving you a horse?"

"Loaning me one," Thomas said. "So I can get around the parish to speak to people. He's trying to help me get elected to the state convention."

"Why is that?"

"Why he supports me or why he's one of the few who cares about the rights of ex-slaves?"

"Why he's willing to buck the people like those men who raided the picnic."

Thomas shook his head. "Between him and God, I guess."

Lily thought of Frederick. She didn't need to wonder what his attitude toward Negro rights would have been. If there was no benefit in it for himself, he wouldn't care two peas whether they had rights or not. But Frederick was dead. She closed her eyes and tilted her head to feel the sun on her face. He was dead and he always would be. And she was not sorry. She had yet to work that out with God, but she could not find it in her heart to be sorry.

~~~

The next afternoon, Uncle Garvey and Lily entertained Major Whiteaker with coffee and cake. The coffee was dreadful, Lily thought. She was used to unadulterated coffee, not this brew diluted with chicory nuts, but Uncle Garvey and the major seemed to like it.

"I noticed you grimacing over our coffee the first few mornings you were here, my dear," Uncle Garvey said. "Now I see you are still not accustomed to it."

She smiled at him. "It's fine, Uncle Garvey."

"Far better than what we cooked up during the war," Uncle Garvey said. "But you soldiers had coffee beans, I believe, even when you had nothing else."

"Most of the time," Major Whiteaker agreed. "We weren't above brewing a pot of acorn mash, though."

"Oh, that sounds horrible. Wasn't it bitter?"

The conversation was easy and comfortable. Lily relaxed as her uncle and Major Whiteaker discussed the difficulties of growing cane with enough profit to pay the laborers a fair wage and to keep the plantation solvent. Nothing simple about it, it seemed.

Major Whiteaker interrupted her woolgathering. "Would you like to walk outside, Mrs. Palmer?"

Lily tensed. This was meant to be nothing more than a courtesy call, no more than neighbor calling on neighbor. But he was looking at her with those intense blue eyes, waiting for her.

Uncle Garvey stood up. "You two go ahead. I have chores to get to. Glad you came by, Alistair. Always good to see you."

So it was settled. "I'll get my bonnet."

~~~

With his yellow hound at his heels, Alistair strolled through Uncle Garvey's small peach orchard with his hands behind his back, content for the moment simply to be with her. He glanced at her. How he hated bonnets. A man couldn't see a woman's face with those huge brims. So what, he thought in some irritation, if the sun should touch a woman's face? It wasn't as if freckles were some hideous disfigurement.

Mrs. Palmer interrupted his discerning thoughts on bonnets. "You fought for the Confederacy with Mr. Chamard's son Marcel? I suppose you lost many friends."

"Yes. We all did."

"Musette said she sees a change in Mr. Chamard's son since the war. A sadness about him." Lily looked at him. "I see it in you, too. A sadness."

He could see her face now. Her eyes were penetrating. Rather bold, actually. Most women of his acquaintance did not speak of the war. Certainly not of a man's countenance.

A line appeared between her brows. "Have I offended you, Major? I beg your pardon."

"You're a curious person, Mrs. Palmer?"

She laughed. "I suppose 'curious' is the polite word for 'nosy.' Yes, I'm terribly 'curious.' Please forgive me. I do realize I have no right to speak of such things."

"And your husband was in the war?"

"No. He wasn't," she said and turned her face from him so he could see only bonnet.

Ah. No elaboration. Perhaps her husband had been infirm. A darker thought occurred to Alistair. Perhaps her husband had been one of those who paid another man to take his place in the ranks. It had been legal, but he found such side-stepping of obligation distasteful. He curved his neck to peer under her bonnet and could just see the set line of her mouth.

Well, it was none of his business, and he had no wish to distress her. After a few more moments of silence between them, he said. "We all lost friends. We all saw too much death."

Alistair drew a deeper breath. Would it ever be easy to speak of the war? "What bruises the soul, though, Mrs. Palmer, is not the dying. It's the killing. Marcel and I – we killed men. Some of them looking us in the eyes when we did it."

Alistair swallowed. He didn't wish to say more on the subject. He hoped she would drop it.

She gave him a searching look. "I'm sorry for it," she said, then continued on in silence.

Tawny curls escaped the confines of her bonnet, the perfect color for her blue eyes. When she turned them on him, he saw sadness lurking in her, too. Perhaps she knew sorrow as deep as any soldier's.

Perhaps she had loved her husband.

"How did your husband die, Mrs. Palmer? You don't wear mourning. It was some time ago?"

The turn of her head was sharp. He had overstepped himself.

"Excuse me. I seem to be suffering from the same malady as you."

"It's quite all right. He died in an accident. On the street."

She hid herself again behind her bonnet. He supposed it pained her to think of it.

He offered his arm to take her back and was relieved when she took it. Mrs. Palmer had not given him much encouragement. On the other hand, she had asked him a personal question. That did not indicate indifference. She was simply a woman who did not engage in shallow flirtation. And he liked that about her. He had had enough of silly young things whose mothers pointed them in his direction.

Two little girls came tearing around the house. When they saw him and Mrs. Palmer, they came running, their little legs kicking up their skirts with abandon. By the time they reached them, Alistair was grinning and his hound's tail wagged so hard its whole body shook.

He recognized Thomas's little sister. The white child must be Maddie. She nearly plowed into her mother before she could slow down. "Look what we found!" She dipped into her apron pocket and pulled out a bluebird feather, a glass bead, and a silver button.

"Show her what's in your pocket, Dawn."

The black child was shy, but she pulled out a cardinal's bright red feather, a bead to match the one in Maddie's palm, and a very small, dead, dried up frog.

Alistair laughed out loud. "May I see your frog?"

The little creature was perfectly preserved, right down to the toes. "What a treasure. Where will you keep him?"

He glanced at Mrs. Palmer. She was looking at him with an odd expression.

"I aim to keep him on the shelf above my bed," the child answered.

"And you must be Miss Maddie Palmer," he said to the other child.

"Make your curtsey," Mrs. Palmer said softly.

"Yes, sir. Pleased to make your acquaintance, sir."

"These dusty children are my daughter Maddie and her friend Dawn. This is Major Whiteaker."

"Pleased to make your acquaintance, Major Whiteaker," Maddie said all over again with another perfect curtsey.

The other child bent her knees in a perfect replica of Maddie's curtsey.

"Ladies," he said sweeping his hat off and bowing, "I am equally pleased to make your acquaintance." He gestured toward his hound. "As is General P.G.T. Beauregard. He will answer to P.G., however, if you care to call him."

Maddie giggled and Dawn smiled at him. He counted himself a great success if he could make one child laugh and another smile.

"Go wash up," Mrs. Palmer said. She didn't scold them for running like little heathens or for being dirty as yard dogs. She smiled as she sent them on their way.

An indulgent mother. A loving mother. He wondered if she would let him call her Lily. Too soon, perhaps.

"You like children, Major Whiteaker?"

He raised his brows. "I suppose I do. I hadn't thought much about it." He resumed their stroll. "Now that I do think about it, I am quite fond of my friend Marcel's three children."

She took his arm again. He became very aware of his lower leg where her skirts brushed against him with every step.

When she turned her face up at something he said, he saw a fine line of perspiration above her lip. He inhaled and looked away. If he kissed her, if he ran his tongue along the line of her upper lip – just thinking of it brought the taste of salt on his tongue.

At the front porch she turned to him and offered her hand. He lingered over it as he bowed. One was not meant to actually kiss a lady's hand, and so he didn't. Both of them were bare-handed, however, a bow to more informal rural life in a hot climate. Her hand was a working woman's hand, yet soft and comfortable in his.

He released it. "Good day, Mrs. Palmer."

~ ~ ~

Lily climbed the stairs to her room. She thought Major Whiteaker had genuinely enjoyed the girls and their treasures. A lovely man. A lovely, lovely man. But not for her. Next time they met, she must discourage him. Truly, she had not actually encouraged him, but neither had she made it clear she was not looking for male companionship.

She went to her mirror to take her bonnet off and was embarrassed to see beads of perspiration above her lip. She blew out a breath, resigned. Even in the heat of Louisiana, she supposed refined ladies did not perspire. But she was not a refined lady. She had always done her own cooking, her own cleaning.

She knew very well what the major meant about having a bruised soul. And Major Whiteaker was not for her anyway. Even if it made her ache to see him gazing at her mouth.

She shook her head and turned for the stairs. There were peas to be shelled in the kitchen while Rachel was busy at the wash house, laundry for two more people added to her chores, one of them a little girl who liked to play in the dirt.

# Chapter Six

Lily woke with a start, instantly alert, nostrils flared. She smelled smoke. Yellow light flickered against the lace window curtain. Then, the sound of hooves in the yard, several horses moving fast.

She leapt from the bed and crossed to the window in two strides. Twenty steps from the front porch, flames crackled around a central tower, yellow and orange and purple lighting the night, sparks swirling into the sky amid the black smoke.

Uncle Garvey burst into the room in his night shirt. He rushed for Maddie and grabbed her up. "Get away from the window, Lily! Downstairs."

Rachel and Peep were right behind them, Dawn in her daddy's arms. "I'll take the shotgun, Peep. You get the rifle. Rachel, you know where the pistol is."

Lily followed Uncle Garvey to the kitchen in the back of the house where he passed Maddie to her. He barred the door, and by the little light coming in from the moon, found a kitchen knife and handed it to Lily. "Stay away from the windows. Anyone steps on that porch, you scream! Loud!"

Maddie was awake now, quietly clinging to Lily's neck. "Don't worry, darling. You remember that prayer you learned last Sunday? You think you can recite that? Say it with me. 'You are a shield around me, O Lord.'"

Maddie repeated the psalm softly, her voice calm and sure. " . . . because the Lord sustains me, I will not fear."

"That's right, sweetheart," Lily whispered. "Keep saying it and God will take your fear away. Here we are, see how dark this corner is? You stay put, and no one will even know you're here." She kissed her forehead.

Lily collected every knife she could find and laid them out on the floor where she had an unobstructed line of sight to the door. The knives gathered around her, she sat on her knees. She'd heard a woman had no business trying to fight a man with a knife – he'd

41

take it away from her and use it on her instead. But she could throw them, one after the other. One of them might even hit him.

Lily heard Uncle Garvey loading the shotgun in the front room. Peep murmured something.

She hadn't realized it until this moment, but her hands were trembling. Fear, her old friend. She focused on breathing, in and out, in and out, slow and steady. She was a grown woman, she would not cower, not ever again. If someone stepped on that porch, she knew what to do even if her hands were trembling.

Rachel eased into the kitchen. "Come here, Maddie," she whispered.

"Where are you putting her?"

"She and Dawn be safest under the staircase. They can hide in the cupboard if those devils get in the house. And if they come in, they gone have to come through me and this pistol to get to these girls."

"Go on, Maddie."

Rachel came back and stood in the opposite corner with a pistol in her hand.

Lily heard the fire crackling out in front of the house. And nothing else. They waited.

After forever, Uncle Garvey's unhurried footsteps crossed the house. "They're gone."

He reached a hand out to help Lily rise, but then she froze.

A horse and wagon were coming into the back lane at a quick trot, the harness jangling urgently.

"It's Thomas!" Rachel ran for the back door and flung it open.

Garvey followed her, his shotgun ready.

"Thomas!"

"He's alive, Rachel. But he's hurt." That was Major Whiteaker's voice. Lily rushed out behind Uncle Garvey.

"Here, Lily, take the shotgun." Uncle Garvey let the backboard of the wagon bed down, and the major climbed into the back. They got Thomas out of the wagon, carried him into the kitchen and laid him on the table.

Lily lit the lamps and then covered her mouth at sight of Thomas's battered body. His shirt was torn and soaked with blood. His hair was caked with it.

Rachel didn't flinch. She started in cutting Thomas's shirt off him.

"Miss Lily," Rachel said. "I'm gone need a threaded needle."

"Of course." Lily rushed upstairs for her sewing basket, but first she got the girls out from under the stairs.

"It's all right. You can come out now."

Maddie and Dawn both grabbed hold of her and held on tight. She smoothed the hair off their faces. "There were bad men here, but they're gone now. You're safe, Maddie. Dawn, you're safe, honey."

She led them into the dining room. "I'll light a lamp for you and you two stay in here. Thomas has some scratches need tending in the kitchen and you don't want to be underfoot, but I'll leave the door open so you can see us."

"What's that burning in the front dooryard?" Dawn asked.

"Those men set fire to a post. They were just trying to scare us. It'll be all burned out pretty soon and you'll see it's nothing but a post."

In the kitchen, Lily held the needle up to the light to thread it from her best spool of silk, emerald green like the ribbon she had used to trim Maddie's bonnet.

"Miss Lily, please will you run that needle and thread through some of that whiskey?" Rachel said without taking her eyes from the wound she was pressing on Thomas's shoulder.

Thomas hadn't stirred since they'd brought him in. Lily got a good look at his face and saw he was unconscious. Good. He wouldn't feel the splash of whiskey in the gashes and scrapes.

When Major Whiteaker came in with two buckets of water, Uncle Garvey got a fire going in the stove and filled two pots and a kettle to heat.

Peep started wiping Thomas down with the cold water straight from the well. He dipped the rag in the basin again and again till the water was red and they could see just what was under all the blood.

"A bullet do that?" Lily asked, looking at a deep wound on Thomas's shoulder.

The major shook his head. "Bayonet."

Bruises over both of Thomas's eyes. A swollen nose. Busted lip. Scratches all up one arm. Scrapes on his cheek and hands. A fingernail torn off. Knuckles swollen and red. He'd fought back, that was clear.

Rachel poured whiskey in and around the bayonet wound. Thomas didn't stir.

"What happened?" Uncle Garvey asked.

Major Whiteaker wiped a hand across his mouth. There was a slash of crusted blood across his chin, but he seemed unaware of it. "Thomas was the first speaker, had been talking about ten minutes, when a gang of riders came galloping in, scattering people, firing their pistols in the air. Everybody ran for it, but Thomas. He'd been speaking from the back of a wagon so everybody could see him, and he didn't run, he just stood there, staring at the raiders."

"Fool thing to do," Peep said softly as he started on Thomas's head. Blood caked his hair, so there was a wound there, too, bad enough to knock him out.

"Where were the damned soldiers?" Garvey demanded. "They're supposed to prevent this kind of thing from happening."

"They should have been there, yes. As it was, they came running at the first shots, some afoot, some on horseback. If they hadn't chased the raiders off, it would have been worse."

"If the Yanks are going to impose military occupation, then they damned well ought to be there enforcing the law."

"I agree, Garvey. I'll talk to Major Bodell. He's probably spitting mad his men were not at the rally monitoring it."

Peep emptied the bloody water out the back door and filled his basin with hot water from the kettle. "Rachel, where you got that lye soap?"

"Right there – in a dish on the sideboard."

"They may have just wanted to break up a black gathering on principle, or maybe they specially wanted Thomas. I don't know. Either way, their aim is to scare the Negroes so they won't show up to vote in September."

"I'm gone need a razor to get the hair off around this gash in his head," Peep said.

"I'll get it, Peep," Lily said.

She found Uncle Garvey's razor and shaving soap on his dresser. From his window, she could clearly see the burning post. Not a post. A cross? They had used the sacred Christian cross in this desecration? Lily thought she knew all about how ugly a soul could be, but this, she had no experience with such hate.

When she got back to the kitchen, Peep had Thomas's head washed. He took the razor and soap from her. "Miss Lily, maybe you can see to Major Whiteaker's jaw," Rachel said.

The major's hair was mussed and dusty. His cream colored suit was filthy and torn at the knee. Lily thought he looked absolutely splendid.

She turned away to collect herself and gather the cloths and salves she'd need.

"It's nothing. It'll wait."

"It needs to be cleaned," Lily said. His jaw was swollen and turning a deep purple, and a bloody gash crossed his chin.

44

He dragged a chair away from the table. Lily stepped in between his open knees with her cloth. Under the sweat and the dust, she smelled that distinctive scent he wore. When she dabbed at the crust of blood, the wound began to bleed again and she pressed her cloth against it. "Were there many hurt?"

He shook his head. "Not many. Everybody got out of the way. And they were mostly interested in Thomas anyway. They tried to use the lash on him, but he grabbed the whip and yanked the guy out of his saddle."

Rachel stopped what she was doing with the bayonet wound to turn Thomas's hand over. His palm looked like it had been burned where he'd caught the lash in his hand. She went back to the wound she was stitching.

"That's when the guy with the bayonet lunged at him."

The major's breath shuddered out of him. No doubt he remembered other bayonet attacks in the war.

As Lily poured a half inch of whiskey in a coffee cup and handed it to him, Bertrand Chamard let himself in at the back door. He stood for a moment, taking in Peep and Rachel ministering to Thomas, Uncle Garvey standing near with his hands tucked under his arms.

"How is he?" he asked.

"Hurt pretty bad," Uncle Garvey said. "We'll see what God has to say, but Thomas is young and strong."

"He gone be all right," Rachel declared.

"I'm glad we were there," Chamard said.

Major Whiteaker nodded, dislodging the cloth Lily held to his chin. She patted it back firmly and he winced.

"Be still. It's still bleeding."

He gazed into her eyes, but she was not going to let that soulful look stir her. She was not. She pressed her lips together and gave him a severe look, but at a slight tug, she looked down. He had a pleat of her nightgown in his fingers. Dear Lord, she'd forgotten she was not dressed. Uncorseted, unlaced, her breasts were only inches from his face. A surge of heat ran through her.

She narrowed her eyes at him and frowned. His mouth twitched, but he let go.

"If Whiteaker and I hadn't been there – a couple of other white planters, too – I don't know what all they would have done," Chamard said, "but we – and the johnny-come-lately soldiers -- ran them off. You know Whiteaker here was a crack shot in the war. Well, he aimed at a man racing by on horseback thirty yards from him, and he winged him, too. Never knew anybody who could shoot that good with a pistol."

"Did you kill him?" Lily said softly. Oh, she hoped he had not. He had enough bruising on his soul.

He shook his head slightly. "I'm glad," she whispered.

"I imagine we know who they were, bandanas or not," Chamard said, "Some of them I see at mass of a Sunday morning."

Lily pressed the back of her hand to her nose trying to hold it all in. She'd been fine until Mr. Chamard mentioned the bandanas. Just like that, she could see it all – the dust stirred up by the horses, people running, screaming, the raiders hiding behind their red and blue handkerchiefs.

There would have been children there, and old people, everyone gathered to hear about the laws newly made and the laws yet to be made.

The major gripped her arm, whipped himself out of the chair and put her in it. "Here, drink this." He handed her the cup of whiskey she'd poured for him.

Her hands shaking, she sipped the whiskey and grimaced. She handed the cup back to him and tried to get up, but he had his hand on her shoulder. "Sit still a minute."

"I'm fine."

He raised his eyebrows. "Are you ready to put some stitches in this?" he said and pointed to his chin.

Lily blinked. She'd never stitched a wound in her life.

The major laughed. "It's all right. I thought I'd distract you, that's all."

"I could try, I suppose."

He grinned, which tugged at the gash in his chin.

"Here, let me." She got to her feet and pressed the cloth against his chin again. Both of them standing, she was even closer to him, her entire body lined up with his. All these people in the room, poor Thomas gravely wounded, and still she felt aware of every inch of her skin and his, of the heated air in the inches between them.

"I too was graced with a flaming cross," Chamard remarked.

"Good for you," Uncle Garvey said with a grin. Then he sobered. "What about our Miss DeBlieux? They leave her a cross, too?"

"No. Don't know why not, her teaching Negroes to read like she has. I left Valentine with her. I'll go back to her in a little bit."

The bleeding had stopped in the major's chin. Lily didn't know whether it needed stitches or not. Rachel would decide.

46

"I need to see to the children," Lily said. She handed the major the bloody cloth. "Keep that pressed against your chin a little longer."

"Yes, ma'am."

She found Dawn and Maddie curled up together under the table. Asleep. The night was warm and the hum of voices in the kitchen must have lulled them into comfort, into security again. She was glad, but it was going to be a task to get the two of them to bed.

"May I be of help?" The major had followed her into the dining room. Dirty and bedraggled, he looked as if he could handle a dozen raiders on his own for all his gentleness now.

"Could you carry Dawn to bed?"

"Of course."

Lily reached under the table, drew Dawn away from Maddie, and passed her to Alistair.

"Come here, sweetheart," he murmured. Dawn curled her arms around his neck without fully waking.

Lily retrieved Maddie and together she and Alistair climbed the stairs to the bedroom.

"In here," Lily said quietly. She lay Maddie in the bed they shared, and then motioned for the major to lay Dawn next to her. Grabbing a shawl, she followed him out.

Downstairs, she crossed the sitting room to watch the fiery cross burning down. Major Whiteaker came up close behind her, watching the flames.

"Mesmerizing – flames -- aren't they?" he said.

"Why a cross?" she asked without turning around. "Why do they choose to burn a sacred Christian symbol in such an un-Christian act?"

"I have not seen it done before. Perhaps it's a throwback to when the clansmen in Scotland burned crosses on hillsides. They were a combative lot – maybe the fires were to defy their enemies, or simply to call other clans to battle."

He didn't touch her, but she could feel his presence behind her. Here he was a Southerner, a Confederate soldier, a planter, a former slave-owner, yet he had taken Thomas's part. He had brought him home.

"Why were you at the rally? Why did you take sides with Thomas?"

She listened to him breathe, wondering if he were not going to answer her.

"Even men who owned slaves can believe in justice, Mrs. Palmer. We lived too long down here without it. I will have to answer to God for my part in withholding it from these people." He paused, and she gave him time.

"I want this new world to be a place of charity and trust. I want this – reconstruction, they're calling it in Washington – I want it to work. Thomas is a man who can make this a better world."

Lily turned around. He was too close, and he didn't step back. She had to tilt her head back to see his eyes.

"I believe, Major Whiteaker, you must be a very good man."

They were alone, the lantern light dim, only the murmur of quiet voices in the kitchen. She could put her hands up and place them on his chest. She thought he would welcome her touch. She thought he would kiss her, if she allowed it. She very much wanted to put her hands on his face, to feel his lips on hers.

She gazed into his eyes until he dropped his focus to her lips.

His mouth opened slightly and his head bent.

She realized she was still in her nightgown. She realized she'd invited his kiss, her yearning surely as plain as any words.

Lily dipped her face and stepped away.

"Do you think Thomas will be all right?" she said, her eyes on the floor.

"He's young. He's fit. I've seen men survive much worse."

Uncle Garvey clomped into the room, the shot gun over his arm. "I'm going to have a look around outside. You coming?" He held out Peep's rifle.

"I'll be here all night, outside," he told her. "If you need anything." Then he followed Uncle Garvey into the dark.

# Chapter Seven

Lily fell asleep about four that morning. When she heard pounding on the door, the sky was light and all she wanted was to pull the covers over her head. Surely God couldn't send any more troubles this quickly. She envisioned slaughtered chickens thrown at the door or men standing on the stoop with buckets of pine tar. Maybe she could deal with more by tomorrow, but not yet.

"Lily! Let me in!" came through over the knocking.

Was that Musette? Her heart in her throat, Lily rushed downstairs.

Musette stumbled into the house when Lily opened the door. "How is he? Where is he?"

"What?"

Mr. Chamard strode onto the porch, his face like thunder. He stepped inside and closed the door.

"Good morning, Mrs. Palmer." As he spoke to her his hand came down on Musette's shoulder and squeezed. "Forgive the intrusion. I see you are not yet dressed."

Lily put a hand to her throat. She had rushed down without even putting on a shawl. She looked from Mr. Chamard to Musette, whose face was gray.

Musette closed her eyes when Mr. Chamard said, "We are most anxious to hear how Thomas is."

Lily nodded. Musette must have been in that dress all night. Her hair was still dressed from yesterday but coming down around her ears. "He woke up about midnight, dizzy, but the doctor was here and said he will recover from his head wound. Rachel did everything right, the doctor said, and he has hopes there will be no infection."

"Infection? In his head?" Musette said.

"He has a wound, here," she said and gestured to her shoulder. Lily had guessed right. Musette was deeply attached to Thomas Bickell and she was scared to death. It looked like Mr. Chamard had been holding her back, telling her to wait for first light, and when dawn came, she cast off all his cautions.

49

"Can I see -- "

Mr. Chamard spoke over her. "I'm relieved to hear you and your daughter are well, Mrs. Palmer." He had not released Musette's shoulder.

Major Whiteaker opened the door and came in with a rifle in his hand. "I saw Miss DeBlieux rushing this way. Is everything all right?"

His gaze flickered over Lily's nightgown and at the braid hanging over her shoulder.

"We've merely come calling too early, Alistair. Excuse us. Musette and I will call later in the day. Thank you, Mrs. Palmer."

With his hand on Musette's shoulder, he turned her and firmly guided her out the door.

The major closed it behind them and turned back to Lily with a question on his face. "What's happened?"

"Miss DeBlieux has apparently been waiting for daylight to come to enquire about Thomas. If you'll give me a minute, I'll make coffee. You're probably half-starved, too."

Her bare feet were stuck to the floor for a moment, waiting for her to tell them to move. His eyes were perfectly correct, avoiding looking at her nightgown or even at her hair mussed from the pillow. But he didn't keep his eyes from looking at her bare toes.

He jerked his gaze back up to her face. "Yes. Coffee would be good. Thank you."

Lily's feet flew up the stairs then. When she came back downstairs, dressed, her hair in a neat bun, he was coming in the back door with a bucket of water from the well.

He was rumpled and in need of a shave, but he moved with the elegance of a man in white tie and tails. "I got the fire lit in the stove," he said. He had a row of five or six stitches in his chin where Rachel had sewn him up some time after Lily had gone to bed.

"Thank you. I confess to being intimidated by it, such a grand stove as this. Twice as big as the one I cooked on in Philadelphia."

Uncle Garvey came into the kitchen rubbing the sleep out of his face. "Morning, Lily. Alistair. Who was at the door?"

Lily glanced at the major, who seemed content for her to answer. "Mr. Chamard and Musette stopped by to ask about Thomas."

"How is he this morning, Garvey?"

"I thought he sounded pretty clear-headed last night considering the man has a concussion."

The major nodded. "I can send some laudanum over later, for the pain."

"Alistair, I don't know about that stuff. He's already got a head full of wool. I think I'd rather let him sip at a glass of whiskey if his shoulder pains him too much. The headache, well I expect he'll sleep through the next day or so."

All three of them stilled at the sound of a horse in the yard. Major Whiteaker strode to the door where he'd propped his rifle and picked it up before he opened the door.

"It's all right," he said over his shoulder, catching Lily's eye. "He's one of my men."

An old black man dismounted from his mule and walked up onto the back porch. "Morning, Major."

Alistair stepped onto the porch to meet him, leaving the door open behind him. "Morning, Elvin. What brings you here so early?"

Uncle Garvey stepped next to the major to see what the man had to say. Lily stood in the doorway.

"Got bad news, Major. Sorry to tell you this. Didn't come any sooner cause I don't like riding in the dark, and well, nothing you could have done about it we weren't already doing. So I waited till the sun was up before I saddled Mable here and come on. That wadn't till after we figured you might be here cause this is where that speaker lives, the one got beat so bad yesterday."

Lily saw Major Whiteaker's shoulders move to take in a breath, reaching for patience she supposed. She would like to shake the man herself for holding back the news.

"Elvin," he said calmly, "what happened?"

"Why, a bunch of men came riding through late in the night calling out that rebel yell, waving torches. Lots of people rushed out to see what the commotion was and seen them toss torches through the schoolhouse windows and set the whole place ablaze."

The major drew in a quick breath. "Fanny Brown – is she all right?"

"Oh yeah. All that whooping woke her up and she run on out of her room there in the back. Like to got run down by one of the horses, but she dodged him pretty good. She staying up at Molly's place now."

Alistair ran a hand through his hair and blew out a breath. He had been proud of that school, Lily thought. First one in the area for the freed children. Built it out of his own pocket, bought books and slates. Hired Fanny Brown to teach. It was a blow.

"You go on back and tell Mr. Hatfield I'll want to see him first thing, please, Elvin. Get Mable some water before you head back."

The major turned around. "I'll need to get on," he told Lily.

"Don't go just yet, Alistair," Garvey said. "You need your breakfast, and everything you got to do when you get home will wait for you."

"Yes," Lily added. She touched his sleeve and then pulled her hand back. "You need your coffee and some breakfast after being up all night."

He nodded. "Coffee would be good."

Later Lily would fix breakfast for everyone else when they got up, but for now it was quiet in the kitchen, just the three of them talking. They were on their second cups of coffee when Uncle Garvey said, "Well, it's started."

He nodded. "Yes, it has."

"Like you said. You and Bertrand and Johnston. Think it's going to be bad?"

"If this is how they're beginning, it can't do anything else but get worse." The major nodded at Lily. "Garvey, you've got Mrs. Palmer, Rachel, and two children in the house. I'm going to send some men to patrol the place for a few nights if you'll allow me."

Uncle Garvey scowled into his coffee cup.

"Garvey," he said again.

"Yes, all right. Thank you, Alistair." Uncle Garvey pushed his chair back and left the table without looking at either of them.

The major looked at her. "Garvey Bickell is a proud man. I'm sorry to – "

"He'll come around. We don't have enough people here to keep watch, and I don't know if our pockets are deep enough to hire guards."

"And you have two little girls in the house."

"Yes. Thank you, Major Whiteaker."

He sat back from the table and looked at the napkin he fiddled with. "I'd like it if you called me Alistair." When she didn't answer right away, he looked at her with a little half-smile on his face. "Now you've seen me in all my morning glory and fixed my breakfast."

"Alistair, then."

He focused those blue eyes on her and she twisted her napkin in her lap.

He grinned at her. "And may I call you Lily?"

"Oh. Of course."

"I've seen you in your morning glory, too," he said softly.

<p style="text-align:center">~~~</p>

Musette and Mr. Chamard returned. This time all was as decorous as a Sunday afternoon.

Lily offered coffee. They accepted. They sat in the sitting room and sipped for several minutes before Musette cleared her throat.

"How is your patient this morning?"

"Thomas has taken a little broth. He's awake."

"And clear headed?" Mr. Chamard asked. "A lot of people are depending on that young man's mind being clear."

"He's groggy and in pain. I think it's too soon to ask him to be clear-headed. That was quite a knock on the head."

"Alistair said last night it was a pistol butt got him from behind."

"A pistol butt and a bayonet," Lily said. "As if the war had never ended."

Musette had sat mute through the conversation. Now she stood up abruptly. "I'll see Thomas now."

Lily blinked. She glanced at Mr. Chamard, who was frowning.

"Musette ..." Lily began.

"I want to see him."

Mr. Chamard gave Lily a slight shake of the head. She agreed with him. Whether it was appropriate or not, however, was not an argument likely to sway Musette.

"Musette, Thomas is badly hurt, his head must ache awfully, he looks a fright. He doesn't want you to see him like this."

Musette fisted her hands.

Rachel appeared at the door to the sitting room. Had she been listening? Did she know how Musette felt about her son?

"Thomas not seeing nobody today, Miss Musette. Nor tomorrow neither."

"Rachel, I just want – "

Rachel shook her head, her tall square body blocking the door. "He's not seeing nobody today."

Musette wilted. Lily worried she might wilt all the way to the floor, but Mr. Chamard stood and grasped her arm.

"We will enquire again to see how he does." Mr. Chamard guided Musette to the front door. "Good day, Mrs. Palmer."

Rachel watched them out the window.

"You haven't slept at all, have you, Rachel? Let me feed you and then you go to bed. I'll sit with Thomas."

53

"I guess I am hungry, now you mention it," Rachel said softly, still watching the young woman who so hopelessly loved her boy.

"Come on then. I'll warm up the coffee and fix you a plate."

# Chapter Eight

Alistair stared at the still-smoking ruins of the little school. From the outside, he supposed he looked quite calm. From the outside, he probably seemed unmoved.

Underneath, however, Alistair burned. They'd set fire to the building with a young woman asleep in the back room. They'd have known that. The school teacher most always boarded at the school house.

This new group, the Knights of the White Camellia. This was the kind of thing they got up to, though perhaps a little more ambitious than most of their activities. They were determined to prevent the ex-slaves from exercising any power whatsoever. The fools somehow thought they could reverse four years of slaughter and heartache to restore the South to its delusional purity.

The Knights were likely all men he knew, some of them men whom Alistair had called friends. They were school mates, cousins, fellow soldiers. Prosperous, influential men. Perhaps untouchable men. The Knights would not welcome riff raff like Jacques Valmar, but it had been him at the ice cream raid.

When the school house was first built, the paint bright, the windows shining, Alistair had been there to welcome the children the first morning. Fanny Brown had proudly rung her bell, calling them to come learn your letters, come learn your numbers, and Alistair had felt this little white building to be a sacred place. As sacred as any church he'd ever been in. This was the way to end bondage in fact as well as in the letter of the law.

Six poor white children came here as well. The raiders would rather deny even white children an education than see a black child learn to read. He pinched the bridge of his nose. He was not blameless. He had owned slaves, as had his father and his father's father. He had been too proud to marry Nicolette when his whole being yearned for her because even though she looked white, it was known her blood was tainted. And he had waited until after the war to build this schoolhouse. He'd planned it for years, well before the war, but he had not done it.

Nicolette had been right to turn him down. She hadn't loved him, but just as important – he had slowly and painfully come to understand – he hadn't deserved her, even as his mistress.

The war had burned that ugliness out of him if it did nothing else. He wanted to do better. He wanted all of them to do better.

He stared at the smoldering ruin. All he could do was rebuild. When the embers cooled, they'd tear it down and start over, maybe make it bigger this time. Meanwhile, Fanny could keep school in the ballroom. It was big enough, and his mother was away so she would not be here to squawk about it.

First thing he needed to do was hire some guards and train them so they didn't blow each other's heads off in the dark. Enough men for his own home, for the school as it was being rebuilt, and for Bickell's place. Once again, he was thankful for all the money flowing into his bank from his railroad and steamship investments. His part-interest in the foundry in New Orleans was showing a profit too.

Chamard would take care of Toulouse. He and the DeBlieuxs were tied together six ways from Sunday, and he was sort of an honorary uncle to Musette.

The other first thing he needed to do was send a letter off to Finn and Nicolette in New Orleans. They had both taught freed people to read in their back room. And Finn had been a Yankee. Alistair shuddered at the thought of a flaming torch crashing through the book store window. All those books, dry as kindling, Nicolette perhaps upstairs, the flames spreading.

He wouldn't wait for the mail boat. He'd send a man to town to hand deliver his letter to Finn. William was still with them, too, that great brute of a man. Only one eye, but an able man nonetheless. He would give his life to protect Nicolette. As would Finn. As would he himself if it came to that. Nicolette was blessed with mother, father, step-father, brothers -- Lily Palmer's face rose in his mind. Who was there to care for Lily now her husband was dead?

Alistair strode off to recruit a cadre of guards from among the laborers on the place. He'd talk to Major Bodell tomorrow – cross burning in people's yards fell under his purview, his and the Freedmen's Bureau.

~~~

By Thursday, the swelling around Thomas's eyes had gone down and he could see again. His headache was mild enough he could ignore it most of the time. The doctor still would not allow him out of bed, however. The wound in his shoulder had not sufficiently closed for him to feel comfortable it would not open and bleed again.

Lily had to agree. Thomas had lost enough blood between the wounds and the pint the doctor had bled from him. The doctors in Philadelphia, at least the younger ones, no longer were certain that bleeding accomplished anything but to whiten the complexion of the afflicted, but Lily had certainly not argued with Doctor Huggins. Her own father had sworn he felt better after a bleeding, whatever the ailment.

Fanny Brown came to see Thomas at the end of the school day. Lily took her back to Thomas's room, stuck her head in the door, and asked him if he was decent for company.

Thomas frowned. "Who is it?" he mouthed.

Lily mouthed back, "Fanny."

Delight chased relief across Thomas's face. He set aside his book and when Fanny entered the room, he scooted up in the bed and smiled at her like the prettiest girl in the world had just walked in.

"Hello, Thomas."

"Fanny. You didn't have to come all this way."

"It's not so far." She handed him an oiled paper packet. "I brought you some peanut brittle. Unless your jaw is too sore?"

The room was small. One straight back chair, a small table, and a washstand. Still, there was a bed. Lily left them, but she also left the door open.

She settled in the sitting room with the mending. She could hear the murmur of their voices, talking, sometimes laughing. An hour later, Fanny was still in there, reading aloud it sounded like. Lily headed to the kitchen to help with supper. She was happy to be Rachel's under-cook, shelling peas or slicing carrots or shucking corn, anything but dealing with that cantankerous stove.

Before everyone sat down to eat, Rachel loaded up a tray with two over-full plates and took it in to Thomas and Fanny. Lily smiled to herself. Rachel approved of Miss Fanny Brown.

It was quite a different scene the next day when Musette returned. She chatted with Lily for a while, but Lily did not find it hard to read her. Musette was putting in the time with social niceties so that it would seem only incidental when she asked about Thomas.

"How is he?" she asked, sipping at a cup of coffee.

"Better every day," Lily said.

Musette set her cup down and stood. "I'll just pop in and say hello."

Lily suspected Musette's visit would not be welcome. Who else could Thomas have been thinking of yesterday when he had mouthed "Who is it?" with a frown on his face.

"I'll see if he's awake, shall I? He still needs a great deal of sleep."

Lily's shoes tapped through the house, loud enough to warn him she hoped when she approached his door. She tapped softly and looked in on him. He was in bed, reading by the light of the open window.

"Miss DeBlieux is here to see you," she said softly and raised her eyebrows in question.

Thomas quickly shook his head, but it was too late.

"Good morning, Thomas," Musette said over Lily's shoulder. "I'm so glad I caught you awake." She swept past Lily and took the chair next to the bed.

Well, Lily thought. Musette was bold, she'd give her that. She caught a glance from Thomas and came into the room herself. He moved his leg over and she sat on the edge of the bed. They would have a nice little talk for a few minutes, the three of them, Lily thought. And then, really, Musette must go.

"Oh, my." Musette said, getting a good look at the bruises on Thomas's face. "You're quite a lovely shade of purple, Thomas."

He dipped his head solemnly. "Thank you, Miss Musette. I am partial to purple myself."

She grinned at him. "I'm glad to see you feel up to reading." She nodded at the book spread upside down and open on his knees. "*The Negro in the American Rebellion*. William Wells Brown. I haven't read it."

"Major Whiteaker loaned it to me."

Musette pulled a slim volume out of her reticule. "I've brought you a copy of Whitman's *Drum Taps*. It's been out a couple of years but I've only just been able to get a copy. I think it's at least as good as *Leaves of Grass*."

Thomas accepted the small volume bound in green leather. "Miss Musette has a taste for racy poems, Mrs. Palmer," he teased.

Musette blushed, of course. "That's not all that's in there, Lily. He is quite political, Mr. Whitman is."

"And poetical," Thomas said on a laugh.

"You're awful. I should bring you only John Milton from now on."

Well, this wasn't so bad, Lily thought. They were friends, and had been for some time. Surely Musette hoped for nothing more. But, Lily knew she did. She fairly glowed to be teased by Thomas Bickell.

Lily stood. "Well, we mustn't keep you from your rest."

Musette understood. She rose. "I'll call again to see how you are."

Thomas gestured with the book. "Thank you for this."

"You're welcome, as always."

Lily closed Thomas's door behind them and there stood Rachel. She might have been a granite sentinel she stood so solemn and still. "Miss Musette," she said.

Musette hesitated. "Hello, Rachel."

"You could get my boy killed," she said quietly. "You know that."

"I – Rachel, I only -- "

"You stay away from here."

Musette's face paled. She glanced at Lily, then ducked her head as she strode to the hall table and grabbed her bonnet. She rushed out as if demons nipped at her heels.

Lily met Rachel's gaze. Rachel had been harsh, but that was her boy lying in there beaten and stabbed by white men. If they suspected he had anything to do with a white woman . . .

Lily nodded. Rachel took a breath and let herself into Thomas's room.

Musette did not return to the house. Fanny, however, came again on Saturday. By then, Thomas refused to lie in that bed another day and sat on the back porch with her. The two of them shelled peas, bowl after bowl, as they talked. Lily was in the kitchen cleaning up from mid-day dinner and did not try to listen, but one cannot close one's ears.

Fanny talked about the children who came to her, about teaching in Major Whiteaker's splendid ballroom, how all of them could hardly concentrate the first day for gawking at the green silk wall covering, the light glinting off the polished floors and the mirrors.

So Alistair Whiteaker was rich. She supposed she knew that, but hearing about a ballroom and silk wall coverings – Lily had never known anyone with that kind of wealth. She supposed his home was one of those grand affairs with the white columns and the wedding cake trim. She was much more comfortable in Uncle

Garvey's unpainted house with not one but two porches and a rather splendid stove which she was slowly learning to master.

Thomas was incapable of not talking about politics. He knew who the leaders were in the neighboring parishes, what their positions were, their strengths and weaknesses, and Fanny seemed well-informed herself. Thomas outlined the points he wanted to see covered in the new state constitution. Fanny promised to help him polish his next speech.

They were well-suited, these two. Lily wasn't surprised when Rachel came in from tying up cucumber vines and made a big pitcher of lemonade for them.

Lily had had one ear open for Maddie and Dawn who were in the sitting room playing cards with an old dog-eared deck Uncle Garvey had given them. But now they were far too quiet, so she left the very interesting courtship on the porch to see what they were up to.

# Chapter Nine

After breakfast, Thomas left the house with a vigorous intent, but he had to slow down to accommodate all the strains and bruises and aches and pains. Gray-faced by the time he'd crossed three fields to Cherleu, he knocked on the back door. Valentine, who always acted like he half owned the place, let him in.

"I reckon, from the looks of you, you out of that bed too soon, son."

"Valentine, I get enough fussing at home. Mr. Chamard in?"

Bertrand Chamard was at his desk. "Thomas. Sit down. How are you healing up?"

"I'm doing fine, sir."

Valentine stood at the door, his arms crossed. Chamard delivered a mock bow his way. "You might as well sit, too, Monsieur Valentine, if you're going to hover anyway."

Valentine smirked and took a chair. He and Chamard were of an age, Thomas noted, and had likely been together their whole lives. They had worked out their own dynamic of master and slave, now master and employee. They seemed to enjoy it.

"What can I do for you, Thomas?"

"You can tell me what our chances with the law are. The sheriff going to go after those men who stampeded through the rally?"

Chamard drew in a breath and blew it out. He looked at Valentine first, then he said, "Probably not."

A fly buzzed round and round. Outside, somebody whistled.

Thomas managed to keep his voice steady, but he didn't try to disguise the cold rage he'd been bottling up for days. "I wasn't the only one got hurt that day. A little girl got her leg broke when she didn't get out of the way of the horses fast enough."

"Thomas," Valentine said. "Don't go off and do something stupid."

Thomas looked at him. This man had been a quiet, steady presence among the slaves all his life. People listened to Valentine.

Thomas shifted and gazed out the window where the rose garden bloomed with reds and pinks.

"Is justice stupid then?"

"Yeah, Thomas, sometimes it's stupid."

"Think a moment, Thomas," Mr. Chamard said. "The Army will pressure the sheriff a while, Major Bodell telling him to round up the ones who broke up the rally. But what's the sheriff going to do, even with the best will in the world? They were masked and hatted, every one of them. All they got to say is, "No, Judge, that wasn't me.""

Thomas frowned, his thumb rubbing hard across his other fist.

"And," Mr. Chamard added, "say you find these men. Say you kill them, or say you just bust them up pretty bad. What do you think happens next? There'll be gangs of pissed off little white men, on horseback and armed. They won't care who's innocent and who isn't. They'll kill and likely rape until they get enough of it. That little girl will be healed up by then, and you'll be dead."

"You're saying there's nothing I can do."

"I didn't say that," Mr. Chamard said. "You're meant to do plenty, Thomas Bickell."

"You meant to be a delegate to this convention," Valentine said. "You meant to get us the vote. When every black man vote, we elect a black judge, a black sheriff. That's when things gone change. You got plenty to do."

"Meanwhile," Mr. Chamard said, "we'll ask around, see if anybody knows who did this. I'll talk to Whiteaker, too. If we by some miracle get proof, then we'll take it to the sheriff."

Thomas didn't know what he'd thought Chamard could say different. Maybe he'd thought Chamard would smile his famous smile, say a few charming words, and, *voila,* the sheriff would arrest the raiders, throw them in jail, and plant briars all around the doors and windows so they'd never get out.

Thomas nodded. He nodded again and then rose.

"Something else," Mr. Chamard said. "I want you to go to a tailor in Donaldsonville and get fitted for a suit. Soon as you can get to town, you go in and get measured. A man going to the state convention needs a suit. And a hat."

"Shoes, shirts, ties," Valentine added. "Handkerchiefs."

Mr. Chamard laughed. "You go with him, Valentine. Thomas, you are a lucky man. Valentine is the finest valet on the Mississippi. He'll have you dandified and prettified to a turn."

"When's the next time you speak?"

"This Sunday."

"Well, let's get to town and put that tailor to work."

"Mr. Chamard, I'm very grateful. You've given me advice all these months, about how to organize a rally, how to spread the word. I don't know how I'd have got started without you. I can't accept the suit, but I thank you."

"Thomas, you need that suit," Valentine said. "You want people to vote for you to be a delegate, you got to look like a delegate. I'll have you back before supper, I expect."

"This isn't just about you, Thomas. Remember that."

"No, sir, it isn't, is it? Then I thank you."

~~~

During the war, before Thomas's first visit to Donaldsonville, the sound of Union artillery had rumbled down the river all the way to Toulouse Landing. When it was over the Union had taken Donaldsonville away from the Rebels.

A few weeks later, when Thomas turned fifteen, he and his friend Cabel declared themselves men and slipped away from home to join the other slaves pouring into town. They had hidden in a nasty ditch when they heard the sounds of horses coming around a bend in the road. Texas Rangers, who had come to defend Donaldsonville from the Yanks, had not conceded defeat and continued to patrol the area, harassing the Union Army and punishing any loose slaves they encountered. Having only the brain of a fifteen year old, Thomas had thought it a great lark to elude the famous Rangers.

When he and Cabel arrived big eyed and impressed, Donaldsonville was bustling with soldiers in Union blue, some of them drilling with their rifles, some setting up artillery for the inevitable counter-assault from the Rebs. The Yanks put them to work alongside the hundreds of escaped slaves building the fort along the levee. Thomas wielded a shovel, pushed a wheelbarrow, and toted lumber as the walls went up. They'd been giddy, he and Cabel, being part of the struggle, part of history.

Before the week was over, Peep, Mr. Bickell, and Cabel's daddy had found them. Thomas had burned with shame to be taken away like he was some run-away child, but when he got home and his mother had cried all over him, he'd decided he'd have to stay home, at least for now.

That's when Musette DeBlieux had taken him and his friends on. They'd been her first students, and after Cabel learned, he must have taught a dozen others to read.

Thomas turned to Valentine sitting next to him on the buckboard. "Can you read, Valentine?"

"Sure can. Not good as you, but I can make out a piece in the newspaper if I work at it."

"One of Miss DeBlieux's students teach you?"

"Nah. I learned long afore she was born. Mr. Chamard, he taught me after the candle was supposed to be blown out of a night. Taught me most everything his tutors threw at him till we got caught. That's when I was put to work in the field."

"I thought you'd always been in the house."

"Wadn't in the field long. Half a year, maybe, then Bertie – Mr. Chamard – he brought me back up to the house after he promised his mama he wouldn't teach me no more. Too late by then, though."

Thomas pondered that. Most white people thought teaching a slave to read was next thing to armed robbery. It put ideas into their heads, made them dangerous. It wasn't done. In fact, it had been illegal. Miss DeBlieux, bravest woman he knew for getting herself involved with all of them, hadn't tried it till it was clear freedom was on its way, and then she had to be careful who amongst her neighbors found out. And here Mr. Chamard had done it years and years ago.

Thomas decided to just ask him. "You and Mr. Chamard brothers?"

"Yeah, but I'm the good looking one, ain't I?" Valentine laughed. "Yeah, we got the same daddy. Not the same mama, of course." Valentine was quiet awhile. "We was brothers for true when we was little. After he got big enough to go to school up in Opelousas, it wadn't the same no more. Couldn't be, naturally. But we got on, the two of us."

"You never thought about running off?"

It took him a minute to answer. "I thought about it when I were a young man full of juice, sure I did. But here's how it was. I was four when Bertie was born, and I been looking after him ever since. Used to wipe his snotty nose. Used to, he'd follow me around like I had bacon in my pocket. Our daddy whipped us about the same, too, till I got too old to whip and by then Mr. Chamard was sick and Bertie went off to school. He's my little brother, that's all. And it didn't take me long to have younguns of my own on the place. Wouldn't never leave them."

"And now? You can read, you could go most anywhere and get a job."

"Marcel – Bertie's boy – he was with my Val when he got killed at Port Hudson. We grieved together, the three of us. Bertie and Marcel loved him, too. We're family, Thomas. That's all. We're family."

They'd gone another quarter of a mile when Valentine said, "You ought to understand that. Your Mr. Bickell act like you all are family, too."

Thomas nodded. "Yes, he does. But if he hadn't freed us a long while back, if the war had not ended slavery, then I couldn't have stayed. I'd have run."

"Well, we different there, then. But I'm still proud to see you turning in to a leader. Our people gone need men like you to finish fixing things."

They approached Donaldsonville from the south, the levee on their right, plantations on their left, some of them blackened ruins from the Union bombardments. The road was full of wagons coming into town carrying produce or people or building materials. Some of the old buildings still stood, but lots of Donaldsonville had succumbed before the Union took it over. The streets were full of the noise of hammers and saws, the clang of blacksmiths fashioning hasps and clasps, nails and hooks.

The Army was still here, too. Charged with keeping the peace, enforcing the laws, trying to preserve the newly-granted rights of the freedmen, they kept a garrison right here in town. Most every street you'd see a soldier or two going about his business.

Valentine left the wagon and mule at a livery and walked them down the dirt street to a store so new the unpainted pine wood still smelled fresh.

The tailor was occupied with a white man when they walked in. He gave an abbreviated nod toward Valentine and continued his transaction with the man dressed in a fine black suit. Thomas knew nothing about fabrics beyond cotton and wool, but from the cut and fit and luster of the wool, even he knew he was looking at quality goods.

"When might you expect to get your superfine in, Mr. Moltrey?"

"Perhaps ten days. Maybe two weeks, depending on the weather."

"You'll send word."

"Of course, Mr. Tanner."

Once the well-dressed man left, the tailor turned to them with a smile. "Valentine. Mr. Chamard ready for a new suit?"

"Not this time, Mr. Moltrey. He wishes to outfit this young man in a suit with all the accoutrements."

Thomas gave Valentine a look. He might have been listening to a cultured, educated man. Accoutrements? And where was the accent?

Mr. Moltrey's smile disappeared. He gave Thomas a quick once-over.

"I don't believe I have time just now to make anything new. Perhaps Tafferty down on 3rd Street."

"That's too bad. No time even to run up a few waistcoats for Mr. Chamard?"

Moltrey's smile reappeared. "Waistcoats for Mr. Chamard? Did he specify fabric, color? I have his measurements – unless you believe your master –" Moltrey coughed, realizing what he'd said. "I have his measurements. You could pick them up next Tuesday, shall we say? Let me show you the jacquard silk that came in this week."

Stroking his chin, Valentine said, "No, I believe Mr. Chamard would be displeased if I burdened you when you are already overtaxed with orders. I'll see if Tafferty can handle the waistcoats as well as a suit for Mr. Chamard's *protégé*. Good day to you."

Mr. Moltrey's mouth hung open as they turned and walked out the door.

"I believe you enjoyed that," Thomas said.

Valentine grinned. "I never liked that man even if he is the best tailor in fifty miles."

"Will Mr. Chamard be annoyed that his waistcoats will come from another shop?"

Valentine snorted. "Like he knows where I get his clothes. The man wears whatever I put out for him. Now if it was his boots, he'd take more notice. The man likes his boots. Besides, he don't need no waistcoats."

They dodged horses and wagons to cross the street and head up third. *Tailor, Haberdasher, Boot Maker* the sign above the door said.

Mr. Tafferty, a light-skinned black man himself, was delighted to take Thomas's measurements and Valentine's instructions. Valentine wanted the hemline of the trousers to break just so over the top of the shoe, and the coat should be no longer than the upper thigh, four buttons. Two linen shirts, one tie, small clothes, socks. The boots, he told the cobbler at the back of the shop, should have heels no more than an inch and a half, rounded toes, not pointed.

Once they were on the road and the traffic had thinned out, they ate the packed supper the cook had sent with them. Over his second ham sandwich, Valentine said, "Have to be fair. Likely Moltrey is feared that if he made a suit for a black man, those same scoundrels who burned Major Whiteaker's school gone burn down his new shop. Probably not worth taking the chance."

Thomas shook his head. "I don't believe that excuses him. If we don't stand up to the forces of chaos and disorder, then we will live in chaos and disorder."

Valentine slapped him on the shoulder. "Spoken like a born orator."

~~~

Alistair tied his horse to the rail at the back of the Bickell house and stepped onto the porch where Thomas sat with a book in his lap. He gave Thomas a once-over. "You look pretty good considering. How's the shoulder?"

"I'm moving it a little more every day."

Alistair chose a chair and stretched his legs out, his hound P.G. curling up beside him.

"Have you found who was with Valmar?" Thomas asked.

He shook his head. "I know more about who it wasn't than who it was. The Knights of the White Camellia say they were not involved. Not in this particular assault anyway."

"They would deny it, of course."

"I'm inclined to believe them. I know a good many of them, unfortunately. They are not shy about their convictions, or about claiming credit for advancing their aims with means fair or foul."

"So we don't know who busted up my rally and scared people half to death. A lot of them won't come to a rally again, not if there's going to be violence."

"And therein lies their success, intimidating people into submission. As for who did it if it was not the Knights, there are plenty of angry men down here, men who were wealthy and aren't anymore, men drifting with nothing to do but fume they lost the war. I've heard rumors, that's all. Nothing to act on. And you?"

"The same. But if your rumors and my rumors are about the same men, that must mean -- "

"Not necessarily, Thomas. We need proof if we don't want the whole parish going up in smoke. If people thought the white men we charged were innocent . . . It would be like the Mechanics Institute all over again, and we don't want to feed that beast."

Alistair suspected he knew some of the white men who'd perpetrated the massacre at the Mechanics Institute. The Radical Republicans had convened a convention in New Orleans the previous July to address the hated Black Codes, statutes that attempted to put the freedmen back under the white man's boot. Peaceably assembled outside the Mechanics Institute, the overwhelmingly black crowd were attacked by armed police and white supremacists who indiscriminately fired into the unarmed Negroes. More than two hundred black men died that day.

Alistair watched the muscle jump in Thomas's jaw. He was young and passionate and talented. They didn't need a man like Thomas charging in the wrong direction.

"Give me your word you won't go off and do something before we can prove it. Thomas?"

Thomas blew out a breath. "All right. You have my word on it. I still want to know – who are the whispers about?"

Well, Thomas had promised – no hot-headed foolishness. "Fisher, Shipton, and Valmar."

Thomas stared at him. "Those are the same names I hear."

Alistair met his gaze. "That doesn't prove they did it. You know that."

Alistair sat a little longer, and finally brought himself to say it. "Your Mrs. Palmer accepting company this afternoon?"

Thomas gave him a look and a little smile. "Shall I ask?" He stood to go in the house and turned back. "That's silly. Come on inside with me. I imagine she's in the parlor."

Alistair looked down at his dirty boots. He hadn't changed his shirt since this morning. "I'm not really fit for the parlor. Maybe she'd like to walk out in the orchard. It's cooler under the trees."

Thomas went in and a few minutes later, Alistair heard Lily's light step coming through the house. He got to his feet and held on to his hat. He didn't know why he should be so shy. He wasn't some green boy.

"Here you are out here," she said, holding the screen door open. "Thomas said you're too dusty for the parlor, but you look fine to me." She smiled at him. "Come on in and I'll give you a glass of lemonade."

"Lily, I'm a mess. I thought maybe you'd like to get out of the house. It's not bad in the orchard this time of day. Or maybe you'd like to walk down to the levee and look at the river. Always a breeze coming off the river."

"Let me just get my bonnet."

"If ... of course."

"What? 'If' what?"

He might as well just tell her. "If you wear your bonnet, I can't see your face half the time. Makes it hard to talk to you."

She touched her hair and looked at the floor. He'd made her self-conscious. You'd think he'd never talked to a woman before.

She raised her head and smiled at him again. He felt his stomach drop back into place. She wiped her hands on her apron, untied it, and hooked it on the wall peg.

He held his arm out for her, and P.G. sauntered alongside him as they walked up the lane.

So. Now he had her, what were they going to talk about? He didn't feel a single word rising to the surface of his brain.

"How's the school coming along?"

Ah. He could talk about the school for an hour or three, not that she'd agree to walk with him that long. "They've nearly finished the roof. We're still waiting for the window glass to arrive. Somebody over in Vacherie is making the desks."

"I gather you're investigating the raid on Thomas's rally."

He nodded.

"The sheriff won't help?"

"He's doing what he can. The Army no doubt is pressuring him to make arrests, but you don't arrest somebody you know you can't successfully prosecute. Proving identities – it just isn't going to happen when the criminals were all masked."

"But when all the ex-slaves have the vote?"

"We're a long way from that. This vote in September, the legislature authorized it for this one time only. It's the convention that must write Negro suffrage into the constitution if Louisiana is to be a state again."

"And that's why they targeted Thomas."

"Exactly."

They ambled along the lane, comfortable together. He was glad she wasn't wearing those ridiculous hoops. Silliest fashion he'd ever seen, worse even than a gown being bedecked with ribbons and bows and laces and flounces till it must have weighed twice what a dress ought to weigh.

Lily's pale blue dress was modest, but very becoming. There were slanted tucks leading down from the bosom, showing what a little waist she had. And a generous . . . well, a gentleman did not speculate what was underneath a woman's clothes. He smiled to himself, as if there were any truth to that.

She was walking along, her hands behind her back, her head bent. He was so very taken with her, but he needed to know her, and she needed to know him. His own ideas were not popular, and she would have to be able to live with that. She sent Maddie to his school, but maybe that was mere convenience, a way to keep a restless six year old entertained.

"What do you think, Lily? About Negroes going to school?"

She looked at him in surprise. "Well, I'm for it, of course. They're going to need to read and write and figure to make all of this work."

He reached for her arm and placed her hand on his sleeve. A primitive sort of ownership settled over him. A sense of the last obstacle being swept away. He felt lifted by a surge of well-being, of optimism, of – did he dare think it – of happiness. He was going to marry Lily Palmer. Ridiculous, he knew, as little time as they'd known each other, but there it was. He'd just have to give her time to realize it.

Still, he wanted to be fair. Race was a complicated issue, one she may not have had the need to think about as much as he had. Even though she seemed pleased with the school, with Fanny Brown and the students, letting her own child attend in the fall was a different level of approval.

"Lily, I think I need to clarify something."

She tipped her head to look at him.

"I encouraged you to let Maddie come to our school, but you're new here, you'll be making new friends, making a place for yourself. I didn't make you aware that many people, neighbors up and down the river, are still hostile to the ex-slaves becoming literate. Having your child associate with the Negro children will not be acceptable in all circles."

In fact, there were women in Alistair's social set who had cut him to the bone when they learned he'd built a school for the Negroes. Curled and powdered, these ladies in their satin slippers and lacy shawls hissed *traitor*, and worse, behind his back.

"I'll give that some thought, Major."

If she couldn't extend her tolerance so far, to allow Maddie to be burdened with what some people would see as a taint, he could accept that. Her first obligation in life, after all, was to her child.

"People knew about your school – that's why they burned it down," she said with a line between her brows. "They'll know you're rebuilding, too."

"Not many secrets in this parish, Lily. I'd bet before dawn two or three hundred people will know we strolled down to the river together."

Lily laughed, as he hoped she would. This was so much better, no bonnet obscuring her face. When she laughed she threw her head back and he could see her mouth and the sparkle in her eyes. When they were married, he'd persuade her to throw all her bonnets out.

He helped her climb to the top of the levee where they could walk onto the Toulouse dock.

"It is cooler here," she said. "And here comes a paddle boat."

"How did you find your trip down the river on a steamship? Had you been on one before?"

"Never! Maddie was exhausted every evening just from the excitement of watching the towns and the forests and the fields go by."

"But it was not exciting for you?"

She looked away. In a moment, she said, "Alistair, forgive me if I'm presumptuous, but I must make something clear to you." She kept her gaze turned from him. "I don't intend to marry again. Ever."

What he thought of as simply a pump for blood suddenly showed him it was more than that. It felt like a lead weight in his chest.

"Why is that, Lily?"

She stared at the steam boat churning by.

"You loved your husband that much?"

She gave him a sharp look then turned her head back to the ship. But without her bonnet, he could read her face. So it wasn't that she'd loved her husband too much to marry again. Did that mean she'd hated him? Hated being married?

"You're still young, Lily."

She shook her head. "No. I won't marry again."

She turned abruptly and headed down the levee. She had said "won't," not "can't." Maybe someday she'd trust him enough to explain that to him. As it was, the lead weight turned to something less dense, like maybe copper, or even tin. Whichever, he did not think "won't" was so hopeless. Whatever "won't" meant could change.

# Chapter Ten

Thomas looked up from the length of leather he was braiding on the back porch when he heard voices coming around the house. Four men appeared. A delegation, in effect. Thomas welcomed them, inviting them to take the other cow-hide chairs.

"You all look like you got something on your mind."

"You know who Jacques Valmar is," Valentine said.

"Won't likely forget a man left a whip lash on my back."

"Paget locked him up, all right. Couldn't do anything else with Mr. Chamard and Major Whiteaker standing right there waiting for the door to clang shut behind the bastard. Course he had to let him out on bail the next morning."

Thomas nodded. He knew that much.

"Yesterday, Valmar had his day in court. The court charged him with disorderly conduct. That's all."

"Any more than that, Thomas," Valentine said, "then Valmar would have counter charged with assault."

"I understand. So what did the judge do?"

"Fined him a dollar."

The five men contemplated that for a while. Finally, Reynard, who chewed on a sliver of pine wood, said, "Could have just dismissed the case. A dollar fine is something, anyway."

Cabel stood up. "It's something, but it ain't enough. Valmar is going around the parish boasting about what he done. The major says the Knights of the White Camellia wouldn't have scum like Valmar with them, but he was one of them stampeding the rally in Donaldsonville. He had on a hat and a bandana, but I knew him."

"Can you prove it?" Valentine asked.

"No."

Cabel paced from one end of the porch to the other. "Thomas, two of our women were raped later that night you was beat up. Both of them from up in the north of the parish. Rumor is, one of the rapists was Valmar."

Thomas wiped a hand across his mouth. "I didn't know that."

"Nobody wanted to tell you, you half dead yourself."

Reynard spit over the porch rail. "Dead is what they ought to be."

Thomas shook his head. "Look, they deserve killing, I'm not denying that. But we got to be smarter than that. You understand, Cabel? Reynard? No violence. We got to obey the law if we want them to."

Cabel stopped pacing abruptly. "You want to do nothing, then? Cause the law ain't doing a damn thing."

"The law will do something when we get proof. We got to have more than witnesses who saw somebody wearing a hat and a bandana."

"I'm working on that," Valentine said. "These pigs ain't going nowhere. We got time to gather evidence. That's what they want. Evidence."

"There's things we can do short of killing a man," Cabel said.

"No beating him up either. I can tell you first hand it's punishment, being beaten, but – again – all we'd do is rile folks up and the violence would escalate." Thomas looked at each man. "No beatings."

Cabel, ever on a short fuse, blew up. "You act like you don't give a damn two of our women got raped. You act like you okay with waiting till *some day* when this magic evidence gone turn up. You don't know these women, so it's nothing to you."

Thomas stood up and stepped up nose to nose with Cabel. "You know that is not true." Cabel pushed and pushed, all their lives he had done that. He pushed until he pushed too far, and then – .

"You take it back, or you step off the porch with me. Won't be the first time I busted your stupid head."

Cabel's eyes glowed he was so riled. His hands were fisted as tight as Thomas's were. Thomas was going to have to beat him – or get beaten more likely since he wasn't healed up all the way from the last beating. Whichever, he was taking Cabel into the yard if he didn't take it back.

"Cabel," Valentine said.

Reynard talked around his sliver of pine. "Those white devils sure would be happy to see our finest tussling around in the dirt. Yes, sir, you do us proud beating the shit out of each other."

Cabel glanced from Valentine to Reynard. He opened his hands and stepped back. "All right. So you care."

Thomas was still furious with him. Damn hot head. It was because he didn't know those two women that he could think about it without turning himself into a fool as hot as Cabel.

"Sit down, son," Valentine said softly. Thomas sat, but he could still hear his heart beat thumping.

Cabel looked at Alfie. "You ain't said nothing yet. You happy to let Valmar walk around bragging about what he done?"

Alfie's hair was grizzled, his eyes pale with cataracts. "Ya'll ever seen a man tarred and feathered?"

No one had. "It's a sight, I tell you. Now, Thomas got the right of it. Ya'll all know that. But a tarring and feathering, it don't do no lasting damage to the body. What it do is make the man a laughed-at fool. A man been tarred and feathered ain't going to strut around all proud-like once he been shown a fool."

Thomas wiped his brow. His head still ached from the concussion, but it didn't make him stupid. "It's still violent," he said. "It's still assault."

"Well, then, I reckon we learned something from the white bastards. We all got hats. We can get ourselves some old rag to wear around our faces. Who they gone charge with assault?"

Thomas had to laugh. They were going to do this with or without his blessing. "What'd you come around here for if you're going to do the opposite of what I say?"

Valentine grinned at him, but only for a moment. "Guess we didn't need to. Look, ya'll. We got to get Thomas elected to the convention in September. We was foolish to come over here and involve him. Any hint he ain't respectable gone cost him votes."

"Should of thought of that fore we come over here then," Alfie said.

"Well, we gone fix that. Thomas, you telling us to bide our time, wait for the law to make things right. You are a wise young man. We going to do exactly as you say, ain't we, boys?"

"Yes, sir. That's what we gone do."

"Yeah, me too. I gone do what Thomas say."

"Cabel?" Valentine said.

Thomas knew he'd smirk. He did.

"Sure. Just what Thomas say do, that's what I'm gone do. Always have, always will, right, Thomas?"

Thomas snorted. "Right. You were always docile as a lamb."

They talked for a while about getting people ready to vote for the first time in their lives, about how the cane was growing, about who was paying what wages.

"You hear Gracie Evans found her people? The ones sold off seven, eight years back."

"Where were they?"

"Witherspoon, the agent over to the Freedmen's Bureau – he found them on a Bureau list, working at a place down below New Orleans. Gracie going down there to be with them."

"All right," Valentine said, standing and stretching. "We gone go on, Thomas. Gone heed what you say from here on in. Ain't we, boys?"

Oh yes they surely were, they all said.

Thomas went back to braiding the strips of leather, worrying as he worked. If they acted in any way against the law, it would hurt them in the long run. But he'd said his piece. He had no more authority than anybody else, when it came down to it. He guessed he ought to be flattered they'd come by at all.

~~~

Five nights later, it was Saturday and Tully's Tavern was full. By eleven o'clock, most of the patrons were far gone. Happy, some would say. Inebriated, in truth.

Three men in hats lingered in the shadows, patient and quiet. Along about midnight, men started dribbling out of the bar. Some of them were too far gone to walk straight while others walked the extremely careful gait of a drunk compensating for the undulating road.

"That ain't him," Reynard whispered. "Wait."

Eventually, Jacques Valmar tottered out of the tavern. But there were other men with him.

The three shadows followed along until the drinkers began to split off for their own homes. The tail stayed on Valmar. Donaldsonville already had some streetlights up and they watched him saunter into the pool of light on the corner. They pulled up their bandanas and melted around the light, staying in the shadows. They had maybe fifty yards before the next streetlight. Plenty of time.

"Case somebody can see in the dark, let's act like we all good friends."

The other two nodded. They increased their pace till they were only ten feet behind him. Valmar hadn't noticed a thing.

"Hello, friend," Cabel called. "You not going home yet, are you? Come on with us, we'll buy you a drink."

Valmar whirled around and nearly lost his balance. "Who the hell are you?"

"Now don't be that way, Jacques. All the drinking we done together, and you act like you don't know us?"

Cabel and Reynard wrapped their arms around his shoulders in a tight grip. "Come on with us. We got us a jug of shine. We gone have a good time."

Valentine, the tallest, reached around Valmar from behind and got a gag in his mouth, then tied it tight at the back of his head. Valmar struggled, of course, but he was drunk and they weren't. They had him off the street in under ten seconds.

In a dark alley, they tied his hands behind him and wrapped a rope around his ankles, him all the time grunting and carrying on. They hoisted him like he was a log and carried him to the wagon.

"Damn if he don't wiggle like a eel."

"Wrap that quilt around him. Two of us can sit on him while you drive."

Taking the back roads, they drove by a little moonlight and a little starlight until they'd traveled most of an hour.

"Here's the cut-off. I ain't heard nothing from our guest in a while. You ain't suffocated him, have you?"

"You cain't hear him snoring up there? He's dead asleep."

At the end of an old logging trail, they came to a clearing where an old man sat at a campfire, a big pot sitting near the flames.

"Remember," Valentine said. "No names."

"You got the pine tar warm?"

"Yeah," the old man said. "It just right. Not too hot, not too cool."

"Let's get these bags open then."

They had three bags of feathers. "That gone be enough?" Valentine himself had not collected feathers. He had been a valet and a butler all his life. He did not condescend to enter chicken yards.

"It be plenty," Alfie said.

They couldn't collect that many feathers on the quiet, chickens being excitable creatures, so there were others in the neighborhood had a pretty good idea what they were doing tonight. Couldn't be helped. Nobody whose chicken yards they'd raided would talk, anyway.

"Wake him up."

Two of them went to the wagon and rolled him out of the quilt. "Come on, get out of the wagon."

"He's too stupid with liquor to know what's going on."

"Give him a slap across the face."

That woke him up considerable. He tried yelling and he tried screaming, but the gag kept him pretty quiet.

Reynard untied his ankles and he tried to kick past his kidnappers. They simply knocked him to the ground. "Hush up, not nobody out here to hear you anyway."

"And be still." Valentine shook his head. "One of you sit on him so I can get his boots off."

"Look at them boots. They cowboy boots, ain't they? All shiny and new." Reynard held a boot up to his foot for size. "Reckon they too little, and they call attention to themselves anyway."

"Pull his pants off."

"His underbritches, too?"

"Yeah. Them too."

"Better do the pecker before we do the tar," Alfie said.

Cabel made a great show of unsheathing his big hunting knife. Held it over the flames and let the light glint on the metal.

They were all in on this. The law didn't say a thing about scaring a man half to death, and flashing a big blade would add to the quality of the experience for Valmar.

Valmar started screaming. Muted through the gag, it was tolerable.

Naked and scared, his privates right out there for all to see -- the excitement, the fear, whatever it was, gave the man an erection.

"If that don't beat all," Reynard said.

"Just makes it easier," Cabel said. He approached with the knife. "Hold him still."

Cabel sat on his knees and readied himself to shave the hair off Valmar's private parts. Cabel figured there wasn't likely to be a law against shaving a man's privates.

He held the knife up for Valmar to get a good look at it. Then he grinned. Valmar went crazy, bucking and screaming through the cotton in his mouth.

The men contemplated him in his throes. "I reckon we going to have to skip the shaving, what do you think?" Valentine said.

"Couldn't help but cut him, him flailing around like that."

"Well, hell." Cabel stood up and put his knife back in its sheath.

Reynard approached with a small tin of red paint. "You want to do it? It was your idea."

"Pretty good size pecker on you, mister. Likely lots of folks will enjoy looking at it when we get you back to town."

Valmar was shrieking, his eyes huge and rolling, like a horse half scared out its mind.

Cabel brushed bright red paint all over Valmar's privates from the base of the sack right on out to the tip of the pecker. He stood back and looked at his handiwork. "Now that's a sight."

"Where we start with the tar? Feet or head?"

"Head. He got to stand on his feet while we do the rest. Get him up and tie him to that pine tree over there."

Alfie swabbed pine tar all over Valmar's back, on up into his hair, in his crack, under his arms. They opened one of the bags and all of them patted feathers all over him.

"All right. Turn him around." They tied the rope around his neck and his knees, his arms pulled back to surround the trunk behind him.

Pine tar, then feathers.

"Leave the feathers off where there's red paint." The only other place they left unfeathered was the soles of his feet.

The four of them stood back to admire their work. Most of the feathers were white, but there were some nice reddish-brown ones too. Made a nice effect.

Cabel stepped up to him and hissed into his ear. "You ever touch another colored woman, even if it's just her elbow, I will cut your pecker off and stuff it down your throat. You'll wish you'd bleed to death, but I'm gone make sure you don't. And you can be sure everybody in the parish gone know there ain't nothing in your pants no more."

Valmar's eyes rolled at Cabel, then rolled right back into his head.

"Put him back in the quilt so the feathers don't rub off against the wagon bed."

They left Alfie to stomp out the fire and scatter the ashes. By the time they got back to town, it was maybe an hour before daylight. They tied him upright to the bell post in the square. "Reckon we better leave the gag in," Valentine said. "No need to wake folks up before dawn."

"What about them boots?"

"We ain't thieves. Leave 'em there."

They slipped out of town and were half way home by the time the first citizens of Donaldsonville discovered the monstrosity in the center of town.

# Chapter Eleven

Lily enjoyed Rachel's company, whether they were working in the garden or the kitchen or sitting on the back porch watching the fire flies of an evening. In Philadelphia, she'd never known a Negro personally, but she'd had the same preconceived notions most people did, she supposed. She hadn't expected the wisdom and humor of a Rachel Bickell. And after the years that Frederick had tried to keep her for himself, after the isolation and loneliness, Lily was so very glad to find a friend in this kind woman.

With the dawn sky still rosy, Lily tied an apron over her work dress and headed to the garden to help Rachel hoe weeds. Here in this rich earth, in this sun, it was a challenge to keep the weeds from overtaking the beans and corn and squash.

Lily now knew just how many plantings they could get in a season. Just how many bushels of beans they'd sold in New Orleans last year, and how many in Donaldsonville. The same for melons, tomatoes, okra, squash, corn, and even scuppernongs. Uncle Garvey kept meticulous records, and he set her down in the evenings for tutorials in running a farm.

She went to bed every night exhausted and actually slept straight through the night. No waking in the dark, remembering and regretting. She woke in the morning eager to be up and . . . just living. Every day presented new challenges like training her body to endure the rigors of bending and stretching and hefting bushel baskets.

Maddie's little face had lost that pinched look that had come on her so gradually the last year that Lily didn't know when it had first appeared. Probably when Frederick's drinking got so bad and he was as likely to throw things at Lily as talk to her. Now Maddie was sun-browned and having grand adventures with Dawn.

The Lily who had never been cowed, never been hit, never been screamed at re-emerged. She laughed and smiled. She welcomed every sunrise. The fear she'd lived with for years was just gone.

The guilt that had threatened to overwhelm her the first few weeks – that was not gone, but it had retreated to a background hum. Sometimes she was so overcome with gratitude she had to hide tears from the rest of the household. Sometimes she closed her eyes to pray silent thanks to God. And sometimes she just found Uncle Garvey in the barn or the shed and put her arms around him.

It wasn't wrong to just let herself live. She had not planned that awful moment, she had not meant it to happen. God would forgive her even if a jury wouldn't.

~~~

Since the day Rachel had sent her away, Musette had not returned to the house, but Lily went to Toulouse to sit on the gallery and sip lemonade when it was too hot to work. Nothing was said about Thomas, not a word. But they had plenty to talk about. Farming, books, fabrics, New Orleans society. As a Creole belle, Musette remembered how gay everyone had been before the war. At Mardi Gras, people danced all night and ate crawfish and étouffée and gumbo and oysters at dawn.

"The papers were full of talk of war, of course, but that last season, we celebrated as if nothing in our world would ever change. We ladies had extravagant gowns made of yards and yards of silk, the gentlemen smoked their cigars and bet on their favorite race horses. But we knew what was coming."

How easy it must have been, Lily thought, to forget, for a moment, that all that good living, all that good fortune, was gained from the misery of black slaves. Did Musette think of that? Lily thought she did. How could she be in love with Thomas and not think of that?

Two weeks passed before Lily saw Alistair again -- she no longer thought of him as Major Whiteaker, simply Alistair. Of course he stayed away, she told herself. She'd as much as told him to. She had no business missing him.

She had done the right thing, telling him she was unavailable. It hurt, though, at the time, and still. He was a man she could love, and she yearned to love again. But to marry him, she would have to tell him she had killed, and that she would not do. She could not bear the look on his face if he knew the worst of her, and she had to think of Maddie. No one must ever know Frederick did not die in a traffic accident.

And then there he was Sunday morning at church. She was already seated when she heard his voice behind her, greeting friends and acquaintances. He appeared at the end of her pew. She tried to look only marginally glad to see him, but his gaze was quick and penetrating. She didn't think many people kept secrets from Alistair Whiteaker.

"Miss Maddie, I see you have space for one more person in your row. May I sit with you?"

"How do you do, Major Whiteaker," Maddie said, scooting closer to Lily to make room for him. "Do you see?" she whispered. "I have my best shoes on. I polished them myself."

"Did you indeed?" he said as he settled and propped his hat on his knee. He leaned over and spoke to her ear as if they were conspirators. "They may be the shiniest shoes in the whole church. Do you think people can see them from the back pews?"

Maddie laughed. "Oh, silly."

They hushed as the sermon began. Lily had never seen him in church. Was he not Catholic like most Louisianans? But his was an English name, not French Creole. And might a Catholic not come to a Protestant church if he wished? Had he come to see her? Of course not. The parish was full of women who would welcome his attentions, and she had not. Then why was he here? She argued with herself long enough that she had no idea what Reverend Tyrone droned on about.

Maddie had grown very still sitting between her and Alistair. In fact, she was asleep, cuddled against Alistair's side, his arm around her.

He looked up and met her gaze. The small smile and the tender look in his eyes near broke her heart.

~~~

Alistair knew Garvey and his family would be at the Baptist church. Chamard had let that slip, inadvertently of course. Alistair smiled grimly. His friends had decided he needed a wife, and they'd even chosen her for him. He glanced at Lily sitting there, her damned bonnet obscuring her profile. They'd chosen right, this time.

She'd looked him full in the face for an instant before she adopted an expression of only mild friendly interest when he appeared at the end of her pew. But in that instant, the look in her eyes had fed every one of his hopes. And now little Maddie had trusted him with her sleepy self.

He was afflicted with moist eyes this morning. Dust, or pollen, probably. He cleared his throat and tried to listen to Reverend Tyrone. Ah, now he remembered why he hadn't been to church for months. And months and months. If Alistair didn't watch himself, he'd be snoring next to Maddie.

At the final "amen," Lily stroked Maddie's arm. "Wake up, sweetheart."

On a great sigh, Maddie pulled herself upright and looked around. "Did I miss it again?"

"What's that, Maddie?" Alistair said.

"The angels singing. Uncle Garvey said if I could stay awake this time I'd hear angels singing."

Alistair glanced at Garvey who raised his eyes to the ceiling in a very poor semblance of innocence. Lily's mouth was twisted in a vain attempt not to laugh.

"You can ask your Uncle Garvey all about it on the way home."

They collected Rachel and Peep and Thomas from the back of the church as they exited. Alistair was not surprised to see Fanny was with them. She had no family, and Rachel seemed to have decided that she was the one for her son. Thomas looked pretty pleased himself. Fanny's head was bent to the side, Thomas whispering in her ear. She smiled and he smiled.

Sometimes things did work out so that everybody was happy. Sometimes Cupid got it right without putting two people through torment before letting them find each other.

In the churchyard, everyone lingered to talk to their neighbors, squinting against the bright sun. P. G. got up and stretched before he wandered over to stand with his master.

Alistair stood next to Lily wondering what to say. He couldn't see anything but her chin from this angle. She was too short. Or he was too tall. Anyway, the brim of her bonnet hid her face again.

Lily spoke first, thank heavens. "We haven't seen you here before. Is this not your church?"

He gave her a rueful smile. "It is. But, you know . . . " What did she know? What was he going to say? She was looking right at him, waiting for him to finish his sentence. "Sundays are a good day for sleeping in."

She raised her eyebrows at him. "You, Alistair? I'd thought you filled every minute of every day building or planting or . . . " She waved her hand vaguely.

That made him feel better. She didn't know what to say either. Like a couple of kids.

~~~

Musette emerged from the sweltering church into the bright sun and pulled the lace mantilla from her head. She dabbed at her face with her handkerchief, her hair curling in unlady-like tendrils against her sweaty neck.

The church yard was full of her fellow Catholics, French Creoles, Cajuns, a few Irish families, and a number of German families who had been in these parts as long as her own. She visited with people she'd known all her life, nodded at others too far away to chat with, and strolled on toward the shade where Thibault had settled and snoozed during mass. She knew everyone here, yet she felt herself a stranger. Maybe it was just that she missed her mother and Ariane. She was unaccustomed to being alone so much.

It wasn't that, though. She was lonely all the way to the bone. If her mother and sister were here, she'd still feel apart, still feel adrift.

Twenty-two. A spinster. She only wanted what other women wanted. A husband, a family of her own. But she wanted it with Thomas Bickell. What a fool she was. Sometimes she indulged in the fantasy that once Thomas had achieved suffrage for black men, he would be ready to move on. They could live in New York. He could practice law. They would read books together, talk to new friends about ideas and plans, make love every night. They'd be happy.

"The flowers were lovely, Miss DeBlieux," the priest said, intercepting her. "Thank you again."

She supposed Father Antoine was not a bad looking man if you could overlook his yellow teeth. But she found his sermons condescending and trite, and worse, he was as bigoted as any man she'd ever known. "You're very welcome, Father. Have you reconsidered your thoughts on supporting Thomas Bickell as a delegate to the convention? He is going to be a strong leader in this parish."

Father Antoine's smile was as real as crocodile tears. "I've been so busy, you see. Three funerals since I spoke with you. And two weddings. And a christening."

"Yes, you do have a great many of us relying on you, Father. Which is why people listen to you. They know your leadership and they know you as a wise man of discernment."

Father Antoine wagged a finger in her face. She could have snapped her jaws and bitten it off. The man was a weasel, always was and always would be. But he was the most important priest in the parish.

"Now, now, Miss DeBlieux. You needn't try to flatter me." He gave her another of his crocodile smiles. Odious man. "I'll make up my mind in my own good time."

"Of course, Father," Musette said, trying to look chastened. She doubted it was convincing. "I know you see everyone in the parish as God's children and want what's best for everyone, white and black. We need fair-minded men like you in such tense times."

"You're doing it again, Miss DeBlieux." No crocodile smile this time. No smile at all.

With that, he sailed off, his black cassock swinging round his legs. She hoped his starched collar rubbed his neck raw, she hoped his wool robe would be so drenched with sweat that his stink would radiate for miles.

The problem was, she didn't have the gift of charm. She should have left it to Mr. Chamard to speak with Father Antoine. He could spend five minutes with a man, hand him a cigar, put an arm around his shoulders, and the man would be his. Took only two minutes with women, and that without the cigar.

She supposed she should have left it to Thomas himself. Had he spoken with Father Antoine yet? Would he think it worth his time? How likely was it a Catholic priest, whose most important congregants were white planters, would favor a black delegate?

Feeling useless and frustrated, Musette climbed into the carriage by herself.

She really should just hush. Everyone knew her sister had married a mixed race man. And that man's white half-brother had been a shepherd in the Underground Railroad, an institution her white neighbors were only just learning about, greeting the news with rage and indignation.

She had no credibility. "Of course she'd side with the Negroes," she supposed they would whisper. She had no trouble imagining a sneer on their faces when they said it.

She gently touched Thibault's shoulder. "Wake up, Uncle. Time to go home."

He startled and shook his head. "I think I must have dozed off."

"Maybe you did. You ready to go home?"

"Let's do that," he said.

Thibault flicked the reins and got the horse moving. Musette opened her parasol as the carriage made a little breeze trotting down the river road.

Wild honeysuckle grew alongside the road to sweeten the air. Musette inhaled and willed herself to lighten her mood. She was prone to feeling sorry for herself, that's all. She was a realist, wasn't she? After four years of war, how could there be any idealists left in the South? Any white ones, anyway.

She forced herself to pay attention to the fields they passed, how far along the cane was growing, was it higher than her own, thicker, greener? None of the houses on the river road shone in their former splendor. They all needed paint, some of them needed windowpanes replaced. Where raw wood showed, she knew the owners had had some capital left to repair the damage the Yankees had done.

Perhaps she'd ask the Gales to have dinner with her when she got home. Andrew Gale's father had been overseer of Toulouse before him, and Musette and Andrew had known each other all their lives. They were not social equals, but they were friends, of a sort. And Musette was sick of eating alone with nothing but a silent house to keep her company.

Ahead of her, the Baptist church had just let out and people were still standing in the yard visiting. Idly, Musette looked to see who among her neighbors were there.

With some surprise, she saw Alistair Whiteaker standing at Lily Palmer's side. She had not thought he attended church anymore. There were the Gerald Jacksons and the Harold Jacksons, Andrew Gale and his family, Eugenia Harris, Minette and Charles Holmes. Peep and Rachel.

And Thomas. With a young woman.

Fanny Brown, Alistair Whiteaker's teacher. Two of the few people of color in the parish who were literate, of course they'd be acquainted.

Musette's fingers curled into claws. That girl, she'd probably sought him out. She probably thought she was good enough for him. Could she read Walt Whitman with him? Could she make him laugh? Did she even know who Fyodor Dostoyevsky was?

"You want I should pull the wagon over? We know some of them people," Thibault said.

Over in the churchyard, Fanny Brown put her hand in the crook of Thomas's arm and Thomas looked down at her, smiling. Musette could not draw a breath.

"Mam'zelle," Thibault said again, "you want us to get down and talk with folks?"

Musette dipped her parasol so that no one in the churchyard could see her face. "No," she said, her voice hardly audible. "No," she tried again so Thibault could hear her. "Just take me home."

~~~

Out of the corner of his eye Alistair saw Rachel lean in to speak to Garvey Bickell. Garvey strode over to them, threading through the church goers, a big smile on his face.

"Rachel tells me we got a big lemon cake at home. Why don't you come on home with us for dinner?"

Alistair looked at Lily who was staring at the red scar on his chin. Well, she wasn't scowling at him to keep him away at least.

Maddie tugged at his hand. "Will you come to my house, Major Whiteaker? Dawn and I found some more buttons in the yard."

"Oh, well, that settles it. Thank you, Maddie. Garvey. I'll be happy to join you."

They drifted across the yard, stopping to say hello and exchange Sunday pleasantries with friends and neighbors. "Would you rather I excuse myself, Lily?" Alistair said quietly.

She gave him a quick look, revealing what the bonnet kept hiding from him. "Of course not. Why ever would I want that?"

He raised an eyebrow at her.

"Well, I certainly didn't mean I never wanted to see you again." She sounded angry.

As she turned, her bonnet hiding him from her as well as the reverse, Alistair smiled.

At the wagon, Maddie held her arms up to him to be lifted into the back. Lily accepted Alistair's hand getting into the wagon. With Peep and his family, Fanny Brown, Garvey -- the mule had a heavy load to pull, so Alistair mounted his horse to ride alongside. Thomas rode on the other side where he was close to Fanny Brown, Dawn sharing the saddle with him.

Before Garvey twitched the reins to start, Maddie climbed over her mother and called to him. "I could ride on the horse with you, Major Whiteaker," she offered.

Alistair grinned. "What a fine offer. Ask your mother, Maddie."

"Mama, Major Whiteaker would like me to ride with him. I don't mind."

Lily laughed. "My child is not shy, as you see. Are you sure you'll be comfortable?"

"Quite sure," he said. He reached down and lifted Maddie out of the wagon and onto the saddle in front of him.

The ride to Garvey's was one of the happiest hours of his life, Alistair thought. Maddie snuggled in his arms and chatted all the way. She pointed out a red cardinal flitting in the road ahead and told him all about how his crest meant that he was a royal bird and that mockingbirds were soldiers who guarded the cardinals against the rascally blue jays. He looked at Lily, wondering if this was a tale from a storybook, but Lily just smiled and shook her head.

When they arrived at Bickell's place, Alistair gave Maddie a hug and handed her down to Thomas. He dismounted quickly so as to help Lily out of the wagon. He was perfectly proper taking her hand, but he hoped it was also reasonable to lightly place his other hand on her waist as she hopped down.

He didn't mean to embarrass her, but she didn't meet his eyes, so he supposed he had.

Alistair just did not know how to act twenty-four or twenty-eight anymore. That's when he might have courted a woman, but instead he'd been in love with Nicolette, and then he'd gone off to war. Now here he was past thirty, and he committed one gaucherie after another.

Any young woman of his social circle would have smiled, maybe even simpered, at the familiarity. But Lily was not a Southern belle angling after a husband. In fact, she was the exact opposite, as she'd made clear.

But there had been a slight flush and a sudden intake of breath as she waited that instant for him to release her. In spite of her avowal she would not marry again, she was not indifferent to him.

While the women got dinner on the table, Alistair sat on the front porch with Garvey. Thomas sat on the floor, leaning against the post.

"Only a few months until the election, Thomas. You think you'll be ready?" Alistair asked.

"Not really, no sir. I wish we had another two months to organize, to make sure everybody knows where to go, how to go about casting a ballot. Major Bodell assures me his soldiers will be a presence at the polls and in the streets the day of the election. Still, I'd like to have our own men at each polling place to protect everybody."

"You're expecting trouble, then."

"Well, I want us to be prepared, that's all. There was another cross burning two nights ago. You hear about that?"

"Yes, I heard. The Knights of the White Camellia, I believe. They've been spreading out from harassing blacks in New Orleans, moving into the countryside."

"I didn't hear who they targeted this time," Garvey said, slapping at a mosquito.

"It was Martha Burnett."

"The widow? Why did they pick on her?"

"She's been teaching Negro children to read in her kitchen."

"Has she, by damn. Well, good for her." Garvey rubbed his chin. "Martha was the prettiest thing when she was a girl. Yellowest hair you ever saw. Like to broke my heart when she married Burnett." He grinned. "Course that was before I met my Lena."

"Reverend Tyrone told her to leave off," Thomas said. "At least for now. And I guess he's right. It's too dangerous, and she's all alone in that little house."

Alistair felt the sweat trickling down his ribs. He wished Garvey would take his jacket off. Just because it was Sunday didn't mean God meant for them to expire of the heat. But Garvey kept his jacket on and his tie tied, so Alistair did, too. "How many more speeches do you have scheduled before the 27th of September, Thomas?" he asked.

"One nearly every day, two on Saturdays. Having those guards there, on horseback, that helps, Major, thank you. The women feel a lot safer with them there. I guess we all do."

Alistair lifted his hand lazily. "Chamard hired some of them, too." And so had Musette DeBlieux, but he figured the less her name was spoken in connection with these dealings, the safer she was.

Little feet thundered through the house and burst onto the porch. The girls spoke over each other, breathless with their message. "Rachel says come on to dinner," and "Mama said dinner's on the table."

Thomas collected Fanny and the basket she'd been packing and took her for a picnic. Maddie chose to eat with Dawn and her family in the kitchen, so it was only Alistair, Lily, and Garvey at the table.

The dining room was mercifully cool with the sun on the other side of the house. Lily had set the table with a white damask cloth and Mrs. Bickell's best china. They passed the field peas, ham, fried chicken, boiled okra, sliced tomatoes and cucumbers in companionable silence.

"My mother sends her regards, Garvey," Alistair said as he accepted the biscuits.

"She spending the summer on Pontchartrain?"

"Not this year. I took her to stay with friends up on the Cane River. Chamard's first wife's second cousin, Euphonia Broussard. You know her?"

That explained the two weeks he'd disappeared, Lily thought. So his absence had nothing to do with hurt feelings, nothing to do with her at all. That was, strangely, disappointing. What nonsense, she told herself. She had to get over this infatuation with Alistair Whiteaker.

"Broussard? Don't believe I know any Broussards."

"Gracious, Uncle Garvey," Lily said. "There is a family in St. James Parish you don't know?"

"Ha," he said with a grin. "The Cane River isn't in St. James Parish."

"Ah, I see."

"Lily," Alistair said, "didn't your family come from Parkersburg in West Virginia?" She felt the heat flood her face. She hadn't thought about what it meant for Alistair to use her given name in company. She darted a glance at Uncle Garvey, but he seemed intent on his drumstick.

"I read about this new railway bridge they're building across the Ohio River at Parkersburg. Going to be the longest railroad bridge in the world when it's finished."

"That'll be a sight to see," Uncle Garvey said. "I believe I'll have to take a rail trip just for the pleasure of crossing over that bridge."

"Do you like railroad travel, Lily?" he asked her.

He seemed to delight in using her name. The way he said it, like a caress -- the man was presumptuous. And oh so seductive.

"When the weather is cool enough to close the windows against all the soot," she said, "I like it fine."

After lemon cake, Uncle Garvey excused himself to take a nap. Distant thunder had rumbled during dessert and Lily wondered if Alistair would make his goodbyes now. She wished he would go, and she wished he wouldn't. She wished she were not a fool.

Alistair held a finger up, asking her to wait a moment. He stuck his head in the kitchen. "Rachel," he said, his hand on the door jamb, "That was a fine meal. Best lemon cake in three parishes."

"For a compliment that good, I make you another one next time you come."

"I'll have to remember how you reward compliments, Rachel. Thank you."

"Aren't you the charmer," Lily said with a smile.

"I aim to please."

He stared at her a moment, and she let his gaze lock with hers. She should lead him to the sitting room instead of gawking at him.

The freshening breeze blew the window curtains into the room. "It's going to rain," he said. "I'll go on home while I still can."

"You'll get wet."

"I have a slicker."

So that was settled. And still the two of them stood on opposite sides of the dining room, her arms crossed over her chest, his loose by his sides.

"I brought something," he said.

"Did you?"

"A book. We can go out to my saddle bags for it. Then I'll go on."

"All right."

Lily smelled the rain in the air as the wind picked up. It whipped her skirts against her knees and rustled the chinaberry tree. "It's going to storm. You shouldn't ride when it's like this."

"I'll be fine."

They didn't speak again as they crossed the yard to the barn, Lily walking with her hands behind her back. She probably shouldn't have come out here, but there was Peep working a piece of leather near the barn door. They wouldn't be alone.

"I saddled your mare, Major, without pulling the cinches, so she'd be ready for you. It gone rain buckets here in a bit."

"Thank you, Peep. I'll take care of the cinches."

"I'll go on and see to those chickens. They need to be cooped so they don't blow off in the storm."

Lily drew in a breath. So they were to be alone after all. He held his hand out for her to precede him into the barn.

It was shadowed in here and smelled of clean straw and horses. Alistair unbuckled his saddle bag and brought out the book.

"*Alice's Adventures in Wonderland*," Lily read. She thumbed the pages open and saw drawings of a rabbit in a plaid coat and a grinning cat in a tree.

"For you to read to Maddie."

"What a beautiful book. And dear by the looks of it. Alistair, I can't accept such an expensive gift."

"It's really for Maddie, you know."

"Yes, but – "

"And she did let me hold her in church this morning." He waggled his eyebrows at her. "*She* likes me."

Lily could only laugh. "I daresay everyone likes you, Alistair Whiteaker."

She stilled. She felt as if her face were being painted as his eyes roved over her forehead, her nose, then lingered on her mouth.

He bent to her, his lips barely touching hers.

Lily closed her eyes. She felt his breath warm on her face. She leaned in.

"Alistair. I can't marry again," she said, her lips a breath away from his.

"You said 'won't' last time." His lips touched hers again, whispering across her mouth.

"What's the difference?" she murmured.

"That's what we're going to find out."

He wrapped his arms around her and claimed her mouth.

Lily had never in her life been kissed like this, as if she were precious. Her arms wrapped around his neck and he pulled her even closer, his kisses trailing across her jaw.

He returned to her mouth, hungry and urgent. Lily should step away. He wouldn't insist. But she didn't. She responded with all the hunger she had saved up, too.

Finally, breathless, Alistair pulled back.

"I'm glad we got that out of the way," he said.

"What?"

"Our first kiss. The first one is hard to ask for, but not the next one." He pulled her close again and kissed her till she was boneless.

"Alistair." She took in a ragged breath and put her hands on his chest.

"Lily," he said softly, his fingers stroking hers.

"I really . . . "

"What, Lily?"

"I really can't ever marry again."

The question was there in his face, but he didn't ask it. She couldn't have answered it anyway.

He wiped her cheek with his thumb. "Someday you'll tell me why."

She shook her head. "No. I won't." She gathered her skirts and ran from him, back to the house where she was safe.

# Chapter Twelve

Thomas spent his days talking to people, individually and in small groups. People heard so many things and so many of those things were contradictory or just plain wrong. They had questions, and he stayed to answer them as long as they wanted to ask.

Was it true the Freedmen's Bureau guaranteed freedmen a $10 a month wage? No, that wasn't true. What Mr. Witherspoon did was help the freedmen and the planters negotiate a fair wage. It was a give and take, both sides having to learn to compromise.

What if the boss promised a dollar extra for levee work, and then, when the job was done, refused to pay? That was exactly the kind of the thing the Freedmen's Bureau is meant to handle, Thomas told them. Take your case to Mr. Witherspoon and see what he can do.

All the while Thomas talked to people, he kept an eye on the white people who lolled about on the edges of the crowd, looking to see if they were the same men shadowing him every week. The U. S. Army couldn't be everywhere, and Thomas's people watched them, too, wary eyes keeping track of those who wanted the old days back, the days when any white man was better than a nigger slave. They weren't going back to that.

He returned to the house every night dusty, sweaty, tired and exhilarated. People were listening, they were talking. On September 27, they would vote. They would have a black man at the constitutional convention.

He and Mr. Bickell had talked to Major Whiteaker – the guards around the farm were not- needed, they thought. They hoped. At any rate, they couldn't live like they were under siege.

Jacques Valmar had not been seen since the town had discovered him tarred and feathered and tied to the post in the middle of the square. Thomas wished he could have seen him scurrying down the street like a feathered monster from a children's book, but he did see the picture a traveling photographer took of him and sold to the newspaper. The story was every man in town laughed and pointed. The women, most of them, turned their heads. There, in the middle of the man's body, was a bright red . . . well, they pretended not to know what the bright red was.

Of course Thomas knew who had done it, but no one was confessing and he wasn't going to tell anyone, not even Fanny. Someday, years from now, he'd get Cabel to tell him how they'd done it. They'd probably laugh themselves silly over it.

The only time Thomas could see Fanny was in the early morning. He rode over to the Whiteaker place first thing every morning so he could walk Fanny from the cabin to the ballroom where she was holding classes. He told her everything – except who had done the tarring and feathering. They talked over what he would say, what the news from New Orleans and Baton Rouge meant, what President Johnson was doing in Washington. Two years ago, they had assumed Johnson would continue with Lincoln's plans to rebuild the South and strengthen the Union. Instead, the president was working hard and fast to restore the rebels' lands to them, to cut the heart out of the protections put in place to make former slaves full members of society.

"My granny would have said, 'That man come here straight from the devil to do evil on this earth,'" Fanny told him. "I don't think I'd argue with her."

"When we have the vote, we'll get men like him out of office." And off he would go again.

Thomas knew he would be a bore to anyone else, but Fanny was as obsessed as he. She listened, and she contributed, too. She had a good head for strategy.

"Don't act like you the only black man got a head on his shoulders, Thomas Bickell. Let these others know they have an important part to play, too. It's going to take all of us, not just one brilliant, handsome orator."

"Handsome, huh?"

She poked him. "There's Marcus Deslondes – he's keeping up with the news, he can talk to people."

"Marcus," Thomas said. "I heard it was his great grandfather led that slave rebellion in 1811. Was that just gossip? Do you know?"

"My grandmother knew Marcus's granddaddy. It's true."

"I don't think Marcus is but fifteen or sixteen, Fanny."

"And how old were you when you ran off to Donaldsonville to join the Union Army?"

Thomas nodded. "All right. He's old enough."

"And he can read, Thomas. All the Deslondes can read. And there's Amelia Cassatt. She knows everybody, and she's smart as a whip."

"A woman?"

"Don't you dare tell me a woman can't think and talk as well as any man."

"Fanny, don't get all huffy. I just meant it's dangerous, talking out."

"We're all in danger if we don't get the vote."

He walked a few steps. "You're right. I'll go over all of it with Marcus. You talk to Amelia?"

There was an arbor covered over with grape vines this time of year about fifty yards from the main house. When they stepped into the shady nook, they put politics aside. Thomas took her into his arms, she wrapped hers around his neck, and they kissed until they barely had sense enough to stop. Struggling to get their breath back, they fixed Fanny's hair and Thomas's tie.

"You look mighty fine in this suit, Mr. Bickell," she said as she patted his lapel straight.

"I do, don't I?"

"You wipe that grin off your face."

"Or what?"

She stretched up and pecked him on the mouth. "Or I'll kiss it off."

He grabbed for her and she backed away, laughing.

"I'm going to work. And I don't want you messing my hair up again."

"They're just kids. They won't know why your hair's mussed."

"The older ones will know exactly why my hair's mussed."

They spent a few more moments smiling at each other. "All right. Let's get to work."

They emerged into the sunshine. "When's the school house going to be ready?" he asked.

"Major Whiteaker hopes we can move in next Monday."

"Already? I'm impressed."

"I dream about it, Thomas. About the way the light comes in the windows, how the soft gray of the walls makes us feel cool, how it sounds when the children come in excited and noisy in the mornings."

Her brown eyes shining, Fanny gripped his hand. "Thomas, this has to be the best time of my life. I'm so happy."

He didn't care if someone saw them from the house. He pulled her into a hug and whispered in her ear. "We're going to have lots of happy years, Fanny. You and me."

She tilted her face up to his and he kissed her, right in sight of the mockingbirds, the blue jays, and God.

"I love you, Thomas Bickell," she whispered.

He grinned at her. "I am brilliant and handsome, after all. You said so yourself."

"You thought I was talking about you?" She shook her head. "Men. Such foolish babies."

He gave her a grin and squeezed her hand. "See you in the morning."

Thomas strode back to where he'd tied the horse he had on loan from Major Whiteaker. Cabel was standing next to the mare waiting for him, his mouth set in a grim line.

"Peep said I might catch you here before you headed out."

"What's wrong?"

"They got Alfie."

"What? Who'd mess with an old man like Alfie?"

"They didn't mess with him. They killed him."

Thomas couldn't have heard right. "They didn't kill him."

"They did. Burned the cabin with him inside. Annie got out, but she's burned up pretty bad. Thomas, you need to hear what she has to say while she can still talk, but I came for Major Whiteaker as much as for you. She used to belong to him, and she wants to tell him who did this."

In twenty minutes Whiteaker had his mount saddled and a rifle in his scabbard, and the three of them were on their way to Alfie's cabin.

When they arrived, the cabin was still smoldering, still flaming weakly at the back wall. Most of it was simply gone, black soot and ash all that was left. Two women knelt beside Alfie's body laid out under a pine tree, a horse blanket covering him.

Alfie's aged wife was in the back of a wagon with Dr. Huggins bent over her.

"Whiteaker," he said, "you want to talk to this woman, do it quick. She won't take the laudanum till she's told who did this."

"Let me get up there, Doc," Alistair said.

"She said there were three of them," the doctor murmured to Alistair as he climbed down.

Alistair climbed up and knelt at the old woman's side. "Annie," he said. Her hair was burned off on the right side of her head. Half her face was blackened and oozing. Alistair was grateful a sheet covered the rest of her body. He'd seen wounds in the war – limbs blown off, blood spurting – but burns were the worst.

"Annie, I'm here." He didn't know where to touch her. She pulled her left hand out from under the sheet and he grasped it. "You must be in terrible pain. Let the doc give you the laudanum."

"In a minute." Her voice was raspy and breathless.

Alistair looked at Dr. Huggins. He shook his head. "I think she inhaled some fire."

"I seen 'em, Major."

He leaned over to catch her voice. "You know who they were, Annie?"

She closed her eyes tight. "One man didn't talk like he was from around here. From up North somewhere."

"All right. Just breathe, Annie. Let me hold you up some. You'll breathe better."

She gasped, her chest heaving, her eyes wide. "Don't move me. Please."

"Annie, take the laudanum."

"One of them had yellow hair," she whispered. "Down below his collar. A blue bandana."

"All right."

"The other one, the one with the torch . . . " She gripped his hand tighter. ". . . had new boots. Pointy. Red scarf."

She closed her eyes again. It hurt Alistair to take a breath listening to her try to breathe.

"All right, Annie. Rest. The doctor will give you something to help you rest."

"Pray with me, Major," she rasped.

Alistair wrapped both hands around hers and bent his head. "Our Father who art in heaven, hallowed be thy name . . ."

He continued the prayer as Doctor Huggins climbed back into the wagon and held a cup of laudanum to her lips. "Drink a little more," he said gently.

Annie's hand in his began to relax, then lost all its tension.

"She'll sleep now," the doc said. "Deep enough not to feel all this pain."

They climbed out of the wagon and one of the women climbed up to sit with her.

"She won't make it, will she?" Alistair said, not really asking.

"No. Her lungs are filling up."

"Thank you for being here, Doc."

"I've known these people all my life."

"Even so, not every doctor would have bothered."

Doctor Huggins grimaced. "Yes, I'm aware." He looked Alistair in the eye. "That's got to change, Alistair."

"Yes. It has."

Thomas had been gripping the side of the wagon, straining to hear what Annie said. He stepped away, feeling sick. He'd known Annie and Alfie all his life, too. It was going to be an awful blow to tell his mother and father they were both gone. Murdered.

"We got to talk," Cabel said.

Hands on his hips, looking at the dirt, Thomas nodded. "And Whiteaker. We need him if we have any hope of getting the sheriff involved. You're going to have to tell the major you were in on the tarring and feathering."

The three of them stood in the shade of a bay tree while Cabel told them Valmar had been wearing a pair of pointy-toed boots the night they temporarily abducted them.

"So how did Valmar know it was Alfie?" Thomas asked.

Cabel shrugged. "I guess there aren't a lot of black men as old as Alfie."

Alistair narrowed his eyes at Cabel. "Any way he can guess who the rest of you are? Valentine Chamard is uncommonly tall. We'll have to warn him. Anybody say anybody else's name?"

"We knew not to do that. Don't think we did." He paused a moment. "Hope we didn't." He looked at Thomas, a little shamefaced. "We were having a lot of fun, you have to understand." He grinned. "Funny as hell, in fact."

"You better come back with me," Alistair said. "Get you a rifle and some ammunition."

"And you'll have to move out, Cabel. You can't be at home with all those little brothers and sisters in the house."

"I know it. And we'll have to make it known I'm not there."

Alistair put his hat back on. "Let's go see Chamard."

Single file they directed their horses up the back roads toward Cherleu. Thomas's stomach roiled. The stench of burned flesh still clung to his clothes. The sight of Annie's poor burned body – he'd never forget that.

Half a mile from Chamard's place, Thomas's head jerked up – rifle fire. They spurred their horses on, but Alistair was the only one with a firearm.

They met Bertrand Chamard and Valentine running along the edge of a patch of woods toward Thomas's own home.

"I reckon they after you," Valentine panted.

"You stay back, Thomas," Bertrand Chamard commanded. "You aren't armed and you don't know how to shoot anyway."

"Cabel, you too," Whiteaker said. "You can't do any good without a firearm."

"Then give me one, dammit. I can shoot better than Valentine, that's for damn sure."

Valentine bent over, catching his breath. "All right then." He handed Cabel his rifle. "Don't shoot one of those little girls, for Christ's sake."

"Valentine," Chamard said, "take Thomas back to the house. Arm him, and then you stay home, you old coot."

Valentine straightened, every inch the insulted gentleman. "You are almost as old as I am."

"Yeah, but I'm not the one can't catch his breath." Chamard softened his tone. "We'll need someone to patch us up when we come back with our battle wounds. Valentine, please. I couldn't bear it if – damn it to hell, why am I explaining myself to you? Just stay home, Valentine."

Thomas ran for the Cherleu house for a firearm. He should have learned to shoot better. Cabel was deadly out in the woods when a deer bounded through the brush or a coon darted behind a tree limb. Thomas had never bothered to try – maybe he'd never been hungry enough to eat a raccoon. He mostly trailed along, Mr. Bickell's old rifle over his shoulder. If a possum chose to amble across his path, he'd aim and maybe even pull the trigger, but he couldn't remember that he every hit anything, not even a squirrel. But he could point the damn thing and make a racket with the best of them.

~~~

Alistair galloped another hundred yards before he slowed, then dismounted and tied his horse in the copse of bay trees. He crept ahead, Chamard and Cabel behind him.

At the edge of Cherleu's property, they darted across the lane onto Toulouse and crossed through the pecan orchard to Bickell's place. "Don't fire toward the house. There are two little girls in there, Rachel, Mrs. Palmer."

"Alistair, we are not stupid."

Alistair grinned at him and crouched down.

Three horsemen were circling the house, firing their weapons into the air, hooting and hollering like wild Indians.

Their faces were covered by bandanas, one red, two blue. Bandanas, a Yankee accent, a new pair of boots, and a head of yellow hair would not be enough to impress a judge, but if they could capture one of them, he'd give up the other two. Then they'd get somewhere.

A shotgun blast lit up the front window.

"Bickell! Hold your fire!" Alistair called.

"That you?"

"Yeah, it's me."

Damned fool conversation in the middle of a firefight. Alistair motioned to Chamard and Cabel to flank him and remembered he was the only soldier here. He mimed the maneuver more carefully and they moved into position.

The horsemen were still firing into the air, wheeling their horses around. Having the time of their miserable lives, he thought.

Wait, he signaled. He stood up and rested the barrel of his rifle on a knot in the pecan tree. He aimed, gently squeezed the trigger, and watched a man's thigh explode.

When he fell off his horse, the other two dug in their spurs and galloped down the back road to safety. That left the man on the ground, bleeding and writhing, his hands gripping his thigh.

Alistair ran for him, his rifle at the ready. He poked the gun into the man's chest and told Cabel, "Check if he's got a pistol."

Cabel kicked the man's rifle out of reach and frisked him, even rolling him over to see that he didn't have a firearm tucked in the back waist of his pants.

"Check his boots," Alistair said.

Cabel did that. "No knife. He's clean."

Bertrand Chamard reached down and unmasked the man. "Well, look who this is. Not a pretty face, grimacing like that, Valmar. You in pain?"

"I'm bleeding to death, you fool!"

Alistair sighed. He yanked the bandana over the man's head and fashioned a tourniquet out of it.

"Soldiering skill, eh?" Chamard said.

"Among many."

Thomas ran up, a rifle in his hand.

"Don't point that thing at me," Cabel told him. "You don't half know what end is what."

The man on the ground still had energy to sneer.

"You got something to say, fella?" Chamard said, kicking the injured leg with his toe.

Peep and Garvey Bickell came out of the house, both of them armed. "Who is the bastard?" Garvey said.

"None of your damn business," Valmar snarled.

"Give him another tap on the leg, Chamard."

"Glad to."

He kicked him just below the wound. "Tell Mr. Bickell your name. Least you can do, shooting up his house."

Their captive spent his breath gasping, his hands gripped around the wound in his leg. "Reckon he needs another one," Garvey said.

"No! Valmar. My name's Valmar.'

"Well, Mr. Valmar," Garvey said, "you're in a world of trouble. If you live."

Alistair asked Garvey, "Everybody all right inside?"

"Shot a couple of windows out. Flying glass gave Dawn a little cut on her chin. Everybody else intact. Now Thomas," he called as Thomas ran for the house, "it's not bad."

Thomas thundered into the house. "Dawn! Where are you?"

"We're in the kitchen, son."

Dawn was calmly sitting on the kitchen table while Rachel sewed up her chin.

"Hi, Thomas," she said.

Thomas heaved out a breath and pulled a chair up next to Dawn. "Got yourself a cut, huh."

She nodded solemnly. "It's going to make a scar. I won't be pretty no more."

"You got it all wrong. You'll be pretty with a very interesting scar. Not everybody gets a scar that is part of history. The reason you got this cut today? It's part of the war. It's not really over yet, and it's going to be in the history books. That scar proves you were part of it."

"Like a soldier, you mean." She winced as her mother put in one last stitch.

"Yeah. Like a soldier."

"They came for you," his mother said quietly.

Thomas stood up. "Yeah. Mama, I'm going to have to move out."

"I know it. But you got to find someplace safe. Where you gone go?"

"I'll let you know."

His mama opened her arms. He figured he needed a hug as much as she did. "Main thing is, keep yourself safe," she said into his neck.

"I will, Mama. I'll go talk to Papa."

Outside, Alistair said to Chamard, "You got this?"

Chamard raised his eyebrows and then glanced at the house. "Yeah. Go on."

Alistair strode into the house without knocking. "Lily!"

"In here."

She was watching out the window, Maddie at her side. He marched over and wrapped Lily in his arms. She tried to pull back but he wouldn't let her.

"We're all right," she said.

He touched his forehead to hers. "Scared the life out of me."

He opened an arm for Maddie. She stepped in and leaned against his side. "Miss Maddie, looks like you did a good job taking care of your mama. You can be very proud how brave you were today."

"I cried a little."

"A little girl is allowed to cry. You were still brave."

He led them over to the sofa. Maddie crawled into his lap and leaned against his chest.

"God, you don't know what it means to me she'll do that," he murmured to Lily.

"I think I do."

Alistair touched his thumb to Lily's lip and traced the smile on her face.

She grabbed his wrist. "Alistair, don't."

He took his hand away. "Tell me what happened."

"Those three came on at a full gallop, circling the house, firing into the air, yelling. They were calling out "Thomas, you . . . " She glanced at Maddie. "Calling for Thomas to come out. When he didn't, they shot out a couple of windows."

"Dawn has a cut? Is she all right?"

Maddie sat up and showed him on her chin. "Right there. She gets to have stitches, Rachel said. Will they get her drunk first?"

"I don't think so. I bet she'll get a spoonful of honey, though."

"That would be all right. She likes honey." Maddie leaned back into his chest.

"That man, did you shoot to . . . " Lily glanced at Maddie again.

"No. I aimed at his leg."

"Then you're a good shot."

"Yeah." He didn't want to talk about all the things the war had taught him to do.

Garvey stuck his head in the front door and hollered. "Rachel, will you come out here and look at this wound?"

She passed by the sitting room with a bundle of clean rags, a bottle of turpentine, and her sewing kit.

"I better go see if I've . . . " He didn't want Maddie thinking about killing. "If the man's going to . . . " Or dying either.

"I hope he will be all right."

"I do, too." He stood up and gently placed Maddie on the sofa. "You look like you're ready for a sleep."

"I don't take naps, Major Whiteaker. For goodness' sake."

"Excuse me. I know very little about young ladies."

"It's all right," she said. "You're only a man."

Alistair grinned at Lily. "Now where did she hear that?"

"I have no idea." She held her hands up in innocence. "Not from me."

Lily had just been through a siege, yet she hardly had a hair out of place, and she had her daughter feeling calm and safe before he ever got in the door. "You're quite a woman, Lily Palmer."

"All I did was a good job of hiding in the corner with Maddie."

"A very good job."

He should go see if he'd killed the bastard lying in the dirt outside. "I'm glad you're all right."

"We're fine, Alistair. Thank you."

Rachel had laid a cloth over the bloody sand to protect her skirt and knelt next to the man's thigh. She'd cut away his pants enough to get at the wound and was daubing at the blood.

"Bullet still in there?" Alistair asked.

"Yes, sir."

Alistair crouched and examined where the bullet had gone in. Missed the bone. Apparently missed the biggest artery or he'd already be dead.

"Can you get it out?"

"Any reason I should?" she said.

"What the hell's the matter with you?" Valmar growled, his face contorted with pain. "What kind of nigger woman won't help a man been gunshot?"

Chamard kicked him in the leg again and Valmar shrieked, but he hushed after that.

"You notice our friend has a red bandana and pointy-toed boots?" Chamard said.

Alistair nodded. "Rachel, we need him alive. We need him to tell who the other two are. They're the ones burned out Alfie this morning."

"Alfie? And Annie?"

"Alfie died right away. Annie, probably gone by now. I'm sorry, Rachel."

Rachel sat very still for a long moment. Then she opened the bottle of turpentine and with no warning poured it straight into the wound. Valmar howled.

"Whiskey!" he cried. "At least give me some whiskey."

"Nope," Rachel said. She gave Garvey a look like he better not offer any either. "No whiskey."

Peep and Thomas joined them as she leaned over the scoundrel. "This gets infected," Rachel said, looking him right in the eye, "they'll cut your leg off. Unless it's too late. Then your balls gone turn black and your cock gone fall off before you die."

Valmar's mouth hung open and his eyes bulged.

Peep touched his wife's shoulder. "Rachel, you are one scary woman. He gone live?"

"For now. Eventually, the devil take him back to hell with him."

"Get her away from me! Get her away!"

Alistair laughed out loud. "Use your biggest needle, Rachel. First we better get him out of this sun if we want to keep him alive for the sheriff."

Once they'd moved Valmar inside and laid him out on the kitchen floor, no pallet, no pillow, nothing, they left him to Rachel's tender care.

"Don't leave me alone in here with her!" he yelled at them as they filed out of the kitchen. "She'll kill me."

"Probably won't," she said. "Might though. You best shut up. Dawn, you go on and find Maddie. This creature stink too bad for you to be in here."

# Chapter Thirteen

Once Rachel had dug the bullet out and sewed him up, they loaded Valmar into the back of the wagon, again with no pallet, no cushioning at all. He was quite noisy about his discomfort on the way into town, but Thomas was unmoved.

Garvey drove the wagon, Thomas and Alistair rode their horses. As the feather master, Cabel, they agreed, had best not come. But Thomas had heard Annie's descriptions as well as the major had, and he could honestly say he'd had no part in the tarring and feathering.

"You stay out here with him, Mr. Bickell?" Thomas asked when they'd pulled up in front of the jail.

"Sure. You two take the honors. I'm happy to sit out here and watch the flies torment our passenger."

"You son-of-a-bitch," Valmar said. "You even parked this wagon so you're in the shade and I'm not. I'm a white man, by God, and you treat me like this."

"Second thought," Garvey said, "he isn't going anywhere. I think I'll go into Mason's over there and get a bag of butterscotch for the girls." He winked at Thomas. He used to bring him candy from town when he was a child, too.

Two minutes later, Thomas, Major Whiteaker and the sheriff came out to find Valmar trying to ease himself off the wagon. It crossed Thomas's mind that with one finger he could probably topple Valmar onto the hard-packed dirt. It was an entertaining thought, but of course he did not do it. Instead, he took his pleasure from the obvious pain on the man's face. Hurt that bad, and he'd thought he could sneak away? The man was either stupid or desperate.

"Well, that's handy, you already down from the wagon." The sheriff was a tall rangy man with a wrinkled red neck. His eyes were light gray and if he turned them on a man, he knew he'd been looked at. "Come right on in. I got a cell with your name on it."

Leaning on the wagon, Valmar pointed his finger at the major. "He's a damn nigger lover, and you know it. He and his trained monkey are lying through their teeth."

"And yet, here you are with a bullet hole in your leg," the sheriff said.

With Major Whiteaker and the sheriff on either side, they got him into a jail cell and swung the door shut with what Thomas decided was a satisfying clang.

"All right," Sheriff Paget said. "Let's get this written up."

Garvey came in then. There were only two chairs immediately in front of Paget's desk. Whiteaker raised an eyebrow at Thomas and, with a slight motion of his head, indicated Thomas should sit in one and Garvey in the other.

The sheriff was half into his seat when he noticed the major, tall and aristocratic, was still standing. He glanced at Thomas who carefully kept his face blank. Yes, he was in a chair. Yes, a white man was standing. Thomas understood perfectly. He was to offer no challenge to the sheriff but let the situation itself compel Sheriff Paget to find a third chair. He certainly would not allow a man of Alistair Whiteaker's consequence to remain standing.

Once all four of them were seated, the sheriff rummaged in his desk for paper, dipped his pen, and said, "Where and when did the incident occur?"

"My place, about ten o'clock this morning," Garvey said.

"I need a goddam doctor in here," Valmar hollered.

Paget lay his pen down carefully, walked slowly to the cell, and said, "Mr. Valmar, you are not bleeding. When I am finished taking statements, I will cross the street and fetch Doctor Millingham. Until then, you will please be quiet."

"The hell I will. I got rights. You get that doctor in here right now."

Paget turned his back on Valmar, resumed his seat, and picked up his pen. "Garvey Bickell's place, ten o'clock," he said as he wrote. "And what took place this morning?"

"Three hooligans came racing into the yard, on horseback, and started screaming like banshees, hollering for Thomas here to come out."

"And your name?" Paget said, looking at Thomas.

"Thomas Bickell, sir."

"I'm in pain, dammit. Call the doctor or – I'll get me a lawyer in here."

Paget seemed not to hear.

"And did you come out?"

"No, sir. I was near Major Whiteaker's place where three men burned a cabin this morning, murdering a man named Alfie, and severely burning his wife Annie."

"Why were you there?"

Thomas took an instant to consider how to answer without mentioning Cabel. "I was present when word was brought to Major Whiteaker that people on his property had been burned out. I accompanied him to see if there was something I could do to help."

"You know these people, this Alfie and Annie?"

"All my life, yes, sir."

Paget dipped his pen again. "Their last names?"

Thomas did not know. Lots of ex-slaves had taken their old masters' names, but they might have chosen something else. River was popular, since they all lived near the Mississippi, or Fields, sometimes even Cane. He'd wondered, the first time he'd heard of a man called Cane, how a soul could take the name of the bitter crop that had kept his family in bondage for generations.

"Call them Whiteaker," the major said.

Ah, Thomas thought. The white man claiming Annie and Alfie for his own even in death. Major Whiteaker was a good man, a friend to his people, but even he did not see the insult in providing them with his own last name.

"It was River, sir," Thomas said. He didn't look at Alistair nor Mr. Bickell.

They went through the morning's events, including Annie's description of the three men who'd burned them out.

"Dr. Huggins was there as well," the major said. "He will confirm what Thomas and I heard."

Paget put his hands together on the desktop. "What we have here is a charge of disorderly conduct, disturbing the peace, and destruction of property. He'll owe you for the two windows, Mr. Bickell."

"Why, he could have killed somebody, firing into the house like that. He ought to be charged with attempted murder."

"Have to establish intent for that."

"What about endangerment of women and children?"

"Hmm. That's likely included under disorderly conduct. I'll talk to the judge when he gets back from Baton Rouge."

"What about Alfie and – " Thomas began.

Major Whiteaker interrupted him. "Sheriff Paget, I intend to see Mr. Valmar answers to the charge of murder in the deaths of

Alfie and Annie . . . River. I wish to be present when he is interrogated about the identity of his two companions."

"Now Major, the grounds for that charge are insubstantial. A dying old woman, in great pain, says she heard a Yankee accent, saw a yellow-haired man and a pair of new boots. If I stepped out this door, I could probably rustle up a dozen men to fit those three descriptions."

"And the coincidence of their continuing their mayhem a short while later at Mr. Bickell's home?"

"Proximity is not proof of guilt, Major Whiteaker."

"Sheriff Paget, you are familiar with Mr. Valmar's recent humiliation?"

Paget did not even try to keep the smirk off his face. "I imagine every man in Donaldsonville could tell you who Valmar is, and just how he looked standing there with red privates and feathers from head to toe."

"Alfie was one of the men who provided the tar and feathers. And I believe Valmar had misinformation about Thomas Bickell," Alistair said.

"Well, this just gets more and more tangled,"

The tangle certainly put the sheriff in a tight spot. Major Bodell and the U.S. Army as well as Agent Witherspoon of the Freedmen's Bureau were watching him, pushing him to safeguard the black population. But the Army wouldn't be here forever. Paget had to think about all the whites he'd be answering to who wanted the old days back, men who expected a sheriff to teach the Negroes things hadn't changed so much after all.

"It is a tangle, Sheriff, but I believe we can tease out the various threads."

Alistair reminded Paget that Thomas had been whipped by Jacques Valmar at the ice cream social. Even though Thomas was not involved in the tar and feathering, it was natural Valmar would think he was. And if for no other reason, Valmar would target Thomas as a leader among his people.

"What of it, Major Whiteaker? Plenty of men in town want to bring a fellow like your Thomas down. Plenty of men with pointy-toed boots. All you got is supposition piled on supposition. Even if it's all true, it's not proof."

"That's why I would like to be present when Mr. Valmar reveals who was with him this morning when he besieged Bickell's home – and when he set fire to the cabin with two old people in it."

Paget cast a suspicious glance on Thomas. "And this young man took no part in the tarring and feathering?"

"Thomas had no part in it."

"And you know this for a fact, Major?"

Thomas was fascinated to see that Alistair Whiteaker could lie with the best of them. "The night in question, I was visiting Mr. Bickell and Thomas was present. In the room."

As Thomas would have a hard time proving he was innocent, he appreciated the major's lie. When a man perjures himself for you, you know he's a real friend.

"What a tangle," Paget said again, running his fingers through his thinning hair. "I will present your stories to the prosecutor, who is currently in Baton Rouge with the judge. But I don't have much expectation you'll get anywhere past disorderly conduct and destruction of property."

Valmar reanimated himself at that point. "I won't never be able to walk again you don't get the doctor in here," he blubbered.

"Major Whiteaker," Paget said, shoving paper, pen, and ink across the desk, "you write all this down so I'm sure I get it right. I'm going to see if Doc Millingham is in."

Paget put his hat on and paused. "Son," he said to Thomas, "you make bad blood between you and a white man you better know you ain't going to win."

Thomas looked the sheriff in the eye. "That's going to change."

Paget snorted and went for the doctor.

Except for Valmar's moans and pitiful sniffles, the only sound in the jail was the scratch of the pen across the paper as Alistair set out the chain of events and suppositions.

Thomas realized suppositions were not evidence. He'd read through four law books by now, and imagined the stack of those remaining must tower ten feet in the air. But if they got a confession, a witness to Valmar bragging . . . something could turn up, and then Alfie and Annie could have justice.

Bad as this was, Thomas appreciated how far they had come in just the last few years. Here he was, a black man in the white sheriff's office, without fear, adding his name to a complaint against a white man. And he was sitting down in the presence of other white men.

He had no illusions, however. Even now, free, decently dressed, well-spoken as he was, if he'd brought Valmar in without the major and Mr. Bickell, he would not have been heard. He might even have ended up in a cell himself, charged with shooting Valmar. A sharp pain in his molar stabbed into his jaw and

Thomas reminded himself not to grind his teeth. Major Whiteaker's pen glided across the page as he wrote. Mr. Bickell dozed in his chair.

Doctor Millingham might be delivering a baby or stitching up some poor sot. Or sitting at a dying man's bedside. Mr. Chamard had once suggested Thomas might want to pursue medical studies as his son Gabe had. He'd even offered to sponsor him. But Thomas knew he had no stomach for medicine. What had set him on his path in life had been the time Mr. Bickell had taken him with him all the way to New Orleans to consult a lawyer about a disputed sum of money. The office had bookshelves from floor to ceiling, every shelf filled with burgundy covered volumes, the whole room smelling of leather and paper and ink. The lawyer was content for young Thomas to sit at Mr. Bickell's side throughout the interview. They'd had brandy, the two men, adding to the rich scents of the place, and Thomas had marveled at the string of impressive sounding words that came from the lawyer's mouth. He knew everything. What to do, what papers to fill out, whom to talk to at the courthouse. Thomas had wanted to be that man.

And with emancipation and hard work, Thomas was on his way. He wasn't going to let men like Jacques Valmar stop him.

"Done," Major Whiteaker said. He straightened his many-paged account and set it in the middle of Sheriff Paget's desk with the pen placed squarely on top.

Mr. Bickell wiped a hand over his face, waking up.

"I don't think we need wait for the sheriff and the doctor," Major Whiteaker said. "Let's be on our way."

Thomas expected a loud whining complaint from Valmar about leaving him alone, what if he bled to death, and he a white man! Instead he heard a slight snoring from the cell.

They stepped into the bright afternoon sun. They'd be limp and wilted by the time they got home in this heat. Thomas settled his hat on his head and offered to drive the wagon back for Mr. Bickell. He could tie his mount to the back.

"I can still drive my own wagon, thank you very much," he said in mock annoyance.

"Yes, sir," he said with a smile.

"You got business in town, anyway, don't you?"

"I thought I'd see if Tafferty has my boots ready."

"Then I'll see you back at the house. Alistair, you come home for supper with me. Those women will want to fuss over you after your heroics this morning."

"I'll come for the food and the good company, no fussing required. Thank you."

Thomas saw them off and headed for Tafferty's. As he turned the corner, he collided with Musette DeBlieux. He grabbed her at the elbows, steadying her. She smelled of jasmine. Her straight black hair was done up in a shiny coil and she was wearing her blue dress, the one that showed off her tiny waist. He dropped his hands. "Miss Musette. Good morning."

She touched her fingers to her nose. "Good morning."

"Did I plow into your nose?" Should he move her fingers to have a look? No. He really needed to keep the touching to a minimum.

"Quite all right," she said. "I wasn't paying attention."

Carrie Ann was right behind her. He knew Carrie Ann from the Toulouse quarters when they were children. She was one of those who stayed on the place when the war was over, working for wages now. She had five packages clutched to her chest, one of them threatening to slip out from under her littlest finger, another tipping precariously under her thumb.

Thomas stepped quickly to gather the two about to fall.

"Thank you, Thomas," Carrie Ann said. "I was about to lose that one."

And there was Musette with her lacy bag and her parasol, unencumbered by brown paper parcels. Well, it was going to take time for people to adjust. He really did not want to criticize Musette even to himself after all she had done for black people. For him.

He smiled. "I've got it." He turned back to Musette. "Are you on the way to your carriage?"

"Yes, I've got everything I needed."

And now Thomas had a choice. If he offered to carry the packages and escort her to the stables, he could walk beside her, like a white man would, or he could trail along behind her with Carrie Ann like a two-legged beast of burden. Neither option was comfortable. Walking beside her would be noticed, of course. She would become a subject of gossip and it would not be kind. But his pride had legs of its own. He would not be her servant, however much she had done for him.

Carrie Ann solved his dilemma. "I've got them sorted out now, Thomas. Let me have them." She took the two packages from him and held them securely with the others.

"Carrie Ann, you may go ahead to the carriage," Musette said.

This was not a good idea, for the two of them to chat on the sidewalk where anybody could see them. Musette ought to know better than to show a black man any interest in town. He was not some gray-haired uncle in slave's clothing, dipping his head, saying Yesum, Yesum. Not good for her, and dangerous for him. He should tip his hat, bid her good day, and go on to Tafferty's.

"How are you, Thomas?"

He was rather startled. She had never before spoken to him with such cold formality. "Very well, thank you, Miss Musette. And you?"

She seemed uneasy, twirling her closed parasol, looking over his shoulder. He was sorry for it. He knew she was attracted to him. And what man would not be attracted to Musette DeBlieux? But he was not in love with her. Sometimes, at odd awkward moments, he thought she had been foolish enough to fall in love with him. Other times he couldn't credit such a foolish thing.

But she was lonely in that big house, her mother and sisters away.

He couldn't think of a thing to say. He put his hands behind his back, waiting. Finally, he said, "Not too hot today, for July."

"I saw you Sunday, when church let out. I was passing by on the road."

"Did you? You didn't want to stop and visit? Mrs. Palmer and Major Whiteaker were there, and of course Mr. Bickell."

"You've developed a friendship with that teacher. Fanny, is that her name?"

"Fanny Brown."

Her eyes seemed to glance at him and then away. She still had not really looked at him. She opened her mouth, then closed it. Finally, she met his eyes. "Are you going to marry her?"

"Yes. In the fall. After the elections."

For a moment, her face was stiff and her eyes unreadable. Suddenly, as if the sun had come from behind the clouds, her face brightened, her eyes shone, and she gave him an ear-to-ear smile. "Congratulations. What wonderful news."

"Thank you, Miss Musette. Thank you very much." That smile wouldn't have deceived a child. She was jealous? Hurt?

"Excuse me. I need to get home." And with that, she opened her parasol and strode off.

He watched her cross the unpaved street, striding so hard little puffs of dust shot out from behind her feet.

Was this his fault? What should he have done differently these past months? He walked on toward Tafferty's, thinking of all the time they'd spent together. Not just these past months – off and on for several years now. From his first lessons in reading to the days when they talked about Thomas Paine and John Locke and John Adams, then Wordsworth and Whitman. He had let his guard down, had forgotten to be the subservient black man and had just been . . . himself. And he guessed that was what had happened to Musette, too. She had forgotten to play her role as gracious white woman bestowing the privilege of her attention on a subservient. She'd just been a young woman with a man she could talk to.

He had heard his mother through his bedroom door that day she'd hissed at Musette. "You could get my boy killed," she'd said. It was still true. He didn't want to hurt her, but he'd have to stay away from her.

At Tafferty's he went inside to see if his boots were ready. He wished he'd told her about Annie and Alfie, about the men terrorizing his family that morning. Living so close, she needed to look out for trouble.

~~~

Musette marched on to the stables. What did she care if Thomas married that woman? She wasn't going to marry him herself. That would be ridiculous – she was rich, she was white, and he was only – she pressed her hand against her mouth. She was a fool. She hoped he married his little school teacher right away, that they had a baby together right away. Then she could put him out of her mind.

Two men stepped in front of her. She stopped so suddenly her hoop skirt swayed forward and back. They smelled foul and they leered at her. She moved to step off the plank sidewalk to get around them.

"Hold on there." A tall beanpole of a man held his hand up to stop her. The other man, with greasy yellow hair and bad teeth, side-stepped to keep her on the sidewalk.

"Stand aside, sir," she told the yellow-haired man. She had donned her cloak of superiority. She would not be afraid of this riff raff.

"Oh, look, Fisher, she's gone all hoity-toity on us."

"Don't see what she got to be hoity-toity about, a nigger-loving bitch like her. Not when she lie down with a black nigger."

Musette gasped.

"You will get out of my way at once," she said. She held her parasol up in warning.

The one called Fisher giggled at her. "Look at that. She gone whip us with that frilly little thing." He grabbed it right out of her hand.

The blond man ogled her. "We seen you with that nigger boy, smiling big, pushing your tits out – "

Musette slapped him hard as she could.

Fisher grabbed her arm and pulled it up behind her. That fine cloak of superiority slid right off her shoulders. Musette's heart pounded against her ribs and she cried out as he wrenched her arm further up her back.

"Hey hey hey!"

An Army officer rushed across the street. "Get your hands off that woman!"

Musette's assailants fled, the man Fisher throwing a last leer over his shoulder.

"Miss? Are you hurt?"

She was too stunned to object when the officer took hold of her arm and ran his hand from shoulder to wrist.

"Nothing broken, thank goodness," he said. But he didn't release her.

Musette stepped back, afraid she was going to be sick.

"Do you know who those men were? I could call out a squad and probably find them within the hour."

She shook her head. "I don't know them."

"Miss?" he said, bending his head as if he hadn't heard her.

Musette took in a breath. "I don't know them."

"Why did they accost you?"

"I have no idea . . . Lieutenant," she said, seeing the insignia on his collar.

"You're quite shaken, aren't you? Let me escort you to – where shall I take you?"

"That's not necessary. I'm only going around the corner to the livery."

"You are in town alone?"

"Oh, no. Of course not. My maid had packages to carry and went ahead to the livery stable."

The lieutenant placed her hand on his forearm with a rather direct informality. "This way, I believe," he said.

Amid the cauldron of shame and fear and anger, she was embarrassed this Union officer had witnessed her humiliation. But she could breathe more easily now.

"I should introduce myself," he said. "I'm Colin McKee, from Boston, First Lieutenant, U. S. Army, though that part you deduced on your own." He dipped his head in recognition that this was an occasion for a bow, however abbreviated. But the Yankees were notorious for their lack of propriety.

"How do you do?"

When she said nothing else, he said, "May I ask for your name?"

"Why?" she said, startled. Was he going to write a formal accounting of the incident?

He blinked at her. "Merely getting acquainted, Miss . . . "

"Oh, of course. Musette DeBlieux."

"How do you do, Miss DeBlieux."

After a few more awkward steps, she said, "I know a Finnian McKee from Boston."

The Lieutenant stopped right in the middle of the boardwalk. "Do you indeed?" he said with a big smile. "Finnian McKee, late of Boston, now a citizen of New Orleans, is my cousin and best friend in the world."

Now Musette had the wits to notice, she could see a strong resemblance. Dark hair, a dark moustache much like Finn's, tall and well-made. "This is quite a coincidence. Finn is married to my cousin Nicolette."

"Yes! I've just come back from New Orleans and stayed with them for the two days my business required."

Nicolette was well into her pregnancy and no doubt was suffering with the heat, but how did one ask a gentleman about a pregnant woman? Well, one didn't, that's all. "They are both well?" That should be acceptable.

"Quite, though of course Nicolette suffers from the heat in her condition."

Musette managed to retain a blank face in spite of the man's blunt impropriety.

"Here we are," she said. They were at the livery where Carrie Ann waited with the carriage.

"May I – "

"Thank you, Lieutenant. Let it never be said that Southern gentleman have the only claim to gallantry. Good day to you. I'm most obliged."

She left him quickly and hurried into the shady interior of the livery stable. He had been about to ask if he could call on her, and she didn't want to see him again, ever.

# Chapter Fourteen

Alistair came to supper on Wednesday. Dinner on Sunday. Supper again on Tuesday. Lily suspected Uncle Garvey, with Rachel's connivance, was matchmaking. And on her part, every time she saw him, she came that much closer to forgetting why she could not have him.

She was tormented remembering his kisses in the barn, but Alistair himself showed no sign he ever thought of it. Had it meant so little to him, kisses that had turned her inside out, that kept her awake -- could he just dismiss it from his mind? Had he always visited Uncle Garvey so often and now she was simply *also there?*

She was a young woman who had not been loved in a long time. But to allow him any closer, she would have to tell him what she'd done. And that she could not do. If anyone ever knew, ever found her or recognized her, they would take Maddie away. Besides, she did not want to see the look on his face when he realized what she was.

Running this farm, raising Maddie. That would be enough. She would be happy here, and oh so grateful to Uncle Garvey. She would simply have to accept that Alistair would be part of their lives – as a friend and a neighbor, nothing more.

Sunday, the family was arranged in their pew, Uncle Garvey was nearest the wall, then Maddie, then Lily. Alistair slipped into the pew just as Reverend Tyrone began the service. When Maddie peered around her, Lily placed her hand on her knee to settle her, but Maddie paid her no mind. She quietly, determinedly crawled over her and wedged herself next to Alistair.

The smile that lit his face put the sun to shame.

This would not do. Maddie was becoming far too attached to him. She was going to have to explain to Uncle Garvey that she didn't want him encouraging Alistair to visit. And she would have to tell Alistair not to come to church, not to come to dinner or supper, not to come at all.

That's what she had to do.

He came home with them for dinner. Afterwards, he and Lily and Uncle Garvey sat in the sitting room, the talk ranging from farm matters to the coming convention to gossip about Bob Andry's oldest boy heading to Brazil to study trees.

After an hour, Alistair raised himself out of the deep green chair. "I'd better get on."

Good, she thought. She couldn't relax with him sitting there, the light from the window catching the gold in his hair, his blue eyes finding hers much too often. And when he laughed in that rich baritone, she just wanted to cry.

She followed him into the hallway to tell him not to come back.

"Lily," he said as she handed him his hat.

She took a breath, determined. "We must go back to Mrs. Palmer and Major Whiteaker."

"Must we?" he said softly.

"And you shouldn't come here anymore."

Her eyes were back on his neckcloth. She heard him take in a breath and let it out.

"Why is that, Mrs. Palmer?"

She had to swallow before she could speak. And she still couldn't look at him. "You know why."

"I haven't pressed you, Lily. And I won't."

She covered her mouth with her fingers. If she cried now, she would despise herself for evermore.

He took her other hand. "Clearly there is something I don't know, Lily, something I don't understand. Maybe someday, you'll trust me enough to tell me. All I want now is your friendship." He gave her hand a gentle squeeze. "I won't press. I promise. Just don't shut me out."

He dipped his head to make her look at him. He had the dearest soft smile and his eyes were kind and very blue.

"Mrs. Palmer?"

She wanted him to wrap his arms around her. She wanted to pull his head down so she could kiss him. She was about to cry.

She turned on her heel and fled.

Upstairs, she flung herself on her bed and sobbed like an adolescent girl who's been jilted by her first love.

What a fool she was. When she'd run from Frederick lying on the floor, she'd been terrified. Then they didn't come looking for her, didn't find her. Even with the guilt, she'd been elated. A new life ahead of her, a place to call home. Peace.

And now this. She surely had been more miserable the last years of her marriage, but it had been a constant, nearly comfortable kind of misery with the occasional moments of violence to remind her it could indeed get worse. She had endured, she had kept trying, until the end when she'd decided to take Maddie and leave him.

This was a different kind of misery. She didn't know how it could hurt worse, but it did.

The bedroom door opened and Uncle Garvey stepped in without knocking. Horrified he should find her like this, she wiped at her face and sat up. "I just have a headache, Uncle Garvey. You don't have to worry."

"Not dying, huh?" he said. Sitting next to her on the bed, the mattress tilting her toward him, he opened up his arm and pulled her in to his shoulder.

"Sugar, Lena and I didn't raise any daughters, but I think I know what a headache sounds like. You're crying like you lost the love of your life, and far as I can tell, he keeps coming around here like he's just waiting for the littlest sign from you."

"I can't have him, Uncle Garvey, I just can't."

He patted her arm. He gave her a squeeze. "You're going to tell me it's none of my business, but Lily, I'm going to ask anyway. Is your husband dead or not?"

She closed her eyes and leaned against her uncle. "He is, Uncle Garvey. He's dead."

"Then what, Lily? Alistair looks at you like you're made of sunshine and honey, and you look at him like he's made out of, what, moonbeams?"

"I can't marry again, Uncle Garvey. Please, don't ask me anymore."

He kissed the top of her head. "All right, honey."

She washed her face and went downstairs. Maddie and Dawn were still having a tea party with their dolls on the back porch. To tempt their wooden-headed guests, Rachel had cut slices of cake into tiny little squares.

Lily feared Rachel would notice her reddened eyes, so she kept her head down while she tied her apron on.

"Miss Lily," she said. "I got a big slice of coconut cake for Miss Musette, you want to take it to her. These gals gone be busy with their dolls for a while yet."

She wondered if Uncle Garvey had said something to her, or maybe Rachel saw on her own how raw Lily was. Or maybe Rachel was just offering a piece of cake to Musette. She might not want

Musette to have anything to do with her son, but Rachel had known her since she was a girl. She wouldn't forget that.

"You go on. These gals get restless, I'll set them to cutting up cucumbers for pickles."

Lily walked up behind Rachel standing at the dry sink and put her arms around her. She gave her a quick hug and went for her bonnet.

In the hallway, Lily eyed that bonnet resting on its peg. She'd left off wearing it most of the time. What did it matter if her face turned brown as a walnut? She was free to do as she chose, wasn't she? But it was what women were supposed to do, wear bonnets, worry about their complexions. She snagged it off its peg and tied it on. She'd go see Musette and they could not talk about Thomas and not talk about Alistair. They'd have a fine visit. As long as they didn't talk about anything important.

# Chapter Fifteen

Musette came down the stairs of the back gallery with Lily so as not to say goodbye just yet. When she left, it'd just be her again in this empty, quiet house.

"When I finish it, I'll save it for you," Lily said.

"Wonderful. I've read all her other books, but somehow I've missed that one."

"See you soon," Lily said.

Out of the corner of her eye Musette saw a man moving erratically, like he was drunk. She squinted to see who it was, then broke into a sprint.

"Uncle Thibault!"

When he saw her, he started crying. His pants were stained down the front where he'd wet himself. His face was bloody and one eye was swelled.

Musette grabbed him in her arms and held him tight. Lily came running.

"He's been beaten?"

"Help me get him inside. Clementine keeps all our ointments. Johnson," she called to a man coming around the shed. "Get Mr. Gale."

"I don't know why they had to go and do that," Thibault cried. "I didn't do nothing, I know I didn't. I'd remember if I done something wrong, wouldn't I, Josie?"

At Lily's glance, Musette said, "I look like my mother." She squeezed him. "I'm sure you didn't do anything wrong, Uncle Thibault. You're the best man I know."

They got him to the cookhouse and Clementine set him down in a chair. She washed his face and his hands, and she told her girl, "Run get Calvin, honey."

"Lily," Musette said. "Will you tell Mr. Chamard, and your uncle?"

"Of course," Lily said and hurried out.

Musette knelt down next to Thibault. "Calvin will be here in just a minute. When Clementine gets you bandaged up, he'll take you down to the quarters and put you to bed. I'll bring you something to take the pain away, too."

Mr. Gale, the overseer, stepped in. "What happened?"

Musette had to steady her voice before she could answer him. "Somebody beat Thibault. I haven't asked him about it yet."

Mr. Gale crouched down so Thibault could see him. "You know me, Thibault? You know who I am?"

"Sure, I know you. Knowed you since you was a little feller."

"Can you tell me who did this to you? If I can find them, I'll . . . take care of them for you."

"One of them was that fella, hair yellow as a buttercup. Used to bring crawdads around here. And sometimes he'd have a mess of fish to sell – Ow, Clementine," he said, pushing her hand away.

Musette patted his hand. "Uncle Thibault, can you let Clementine get a little paste on your lip so it'll heal?"

Thibault gulped a breath and shook his head. "It makes it hurt worse, Josie."

"I know it does."

"Here," Clementine said, all business. "You let me get this medicine on you lip, I'll give you a biscuit with honey on it. Sit still now."

Thibault closed his eyes tight and grimaced, but he let Clementine smooth the ointment on his busted lip.

"Thibault, there was another one?" Gale asked.

He looked at Musette. "The other one skinny as a beanpole, and he stunk bad, Josie."

"So you recognized the blond man, but not the skinny one?"

"He ain't from around here."

"How do you know that, Thibault?"

"He talk funny, that's how. He ain't from around here."

Gale looked at Musette and frowned. "What's wrong? You know these men?"

"They're the ones who accosted me in town."

Mr. Gale stood up and scowled. "You mean to say you were accosted in town and you didn't tell me? Damnation, Musette." He never called her Musette, not since they'd been children. It was always Miss DeBlieux. "With everything that's going on in this parish – hell, you should have told me."

"I'm sorry, Andrew."

"Well, who are they?"

"One of them was called Fisher. He had a Yankee accent. That's all I know."

"Why did they bother you?"

Musette fingered the broach at her throat. "I have no idea."

"What about you, Thibault? Why'd they bother you?"

"They asked me where that boy Thomas staying. I told them wadn't he down at the Bickell place, and they say no he ain't, where he staying? Every time I tell them I don't know where, they just hit me again."

Calvin, a tall slender man, dark as night, came in and took it all in without comment. He walked over to Thibault and put his hand on his shoulder. "Daddy? You all right?"

"Don't tell your mama, Calvin." He started to cry again. "She fuss at me if she find out I got myself beat up." His mama had been dead for years, but Calvin didn't remind him. He just rubbed Thibault's shoulder and stayed close.

Clementine said, "He be right as rain soon as you all get out of the way and let me doctor him some. Ya'll get on now."

Mr. Gale and Musette shared a look and a smile.

"Clementine, what have I told you about your impudence?" Mr. Gale said.

"Don't know no big words like *impudence*," she said, pronouncing it perfectly. "Calvin, get your daddy's shirt off."

Once Clementine had finished and they got Thibault in bed, Musette gave him a spoonful of laudanum diluted in a cup of water.

"You sleep, now, Uncle Thibault. You staying with him, Calvin?"

"I'll be here when he wakes up. Me or my wife."

Calvin was another man on the place she'd known all her life. She was grateful he'd stayed when the war was over. He could have gone anytime in the last two decades – her mother had given all Thibault's children their papers soon as they were old enough to make a living on their own. Calvin had set up a carpentry shop on his Aunt Cleo's little plot of land next to Toulouse and made furniture for everybody in the parish. His two brothers were both in New Orleans, one a musician, the other an accountant.

"Call me when he wakes up?" Musette said.

Calvin nodded, his eyes on his father lying in the bed, bruised and half asleep.

"Andrew, you need to be there when I talk to Mr. Chamard."

"Certainly, Miss DeBlieux."

She smiled at him. "So we're back to that. Very well, Mr. Gale."

~~

They convened in Musette's sitting room, Mr. Chamard, Mr. Gale, Alistair Whiteaker, and Garvey Bickell.

"Thomas needs to know they're after him," Musette said.

"He knows."

"He doesn't know about Thibault."

"I'll go by and tell him," the major said.

Musette poured a brandy for Mr. Chamard and hoped she seemed only mildly curious. "Where is he staying?"

She caught Chamard exchanging a look with Alistair Whiteaker.

"The fewer people who know where he is, the safer he is," Chamard said.

She bristled at that. "You can't think I would tell anyone."

"Of course not." He sipped the brandy. "Very nice. Gran Reserva?"

"Yes," she snapped. She stepped close and spoke only to him. "Don't treat me like a child, Mr. Chamard."

He raised his eyebrows. "Musette, my dear," he said quietly, "I know you are not a child. You are running Toulouse with the same shrewd wisdom as your great grandmother, whom I much admired." He raised his glass in salute.

"But you're not going to tell me where he is."

He sniffed his brandy before he looked her in the eye. "No, I'm not."

She crossed her arms. The others were talking, not paying any mind to her little drama. She could stare at him and wait him out.

"He's safe enough where he sleeps, Musette. But he can't stay there all day. He has his speeches and his campaign, talking to people, riding all over the parish."

Chamard knew her as well as her own mother did, Musette thought. He knew why she asked.

"He's armed," Chamard said. "Let it go."

He meant let Thomas go. And he was right. He was marrying Fanny Brown. He had his life, she had hers.

"That scum Valmar still locked up?" Bickell asked.

"Yes, he is. Claims he can't make bail, can't get around yet with that hole in his leg. But he won't give up his friends."

"You're surprised, Alistair?"

"I am. I expected him to sing loud and clear if it meant he'd get a break from the prosecutor."

"And you're thinking these two, whoever they are, helped Valmar burn out Alfie and Annie and attacked Thibault?"

Gale said, "I know who they are."

Chamard looked at him in astonishment. "We've had men slyly asking questions all over this end of the parish, and all we had to do was ask Andrew Gale?"

Gale laughed. "Thibault said the blond is the man comes round sometimes selling crawfish. That's Harry Shipton. The other one is Otto Fisher, down here from New Jersey to make easy money. I met him when I played poker with him and Shipton at the Blue Bird."

"If they're the ones helped burn out Alfie and Annie, then they've murdered two people. They don't fear the law."

"We need to *do* something," Musette said.

"These men are not blessed with big brains, Musette," Chamard said. "They'll do something else, something stupid, and we'll have them."

"At least we have to get Thomas some protection. Get him armed."

"He's a terrible shot," Garvey said. "Don't know what's the matter with the boy."

"He's not blind," the major said. "I'll take more ammo and he can shoot cans till he gets the knack."

# Chapter Sixteen

Thibault, that poor old man, was laid up, beaten and confused, because two men wanted Thomas Bickell. Alistair felt anger and helplessness in equal measure. He couldn't stomach going after Fisher and Shipton himself – even if he could find them -- and violently exacting vigilante justice. The country had had enough of that kind of retribution. He wanted the law to make things right – but the level of proof required had to be unimpeachable. They didn't have it yet.

At least Thomas would be safe in the dilapidated cabin at the very far end of Bertrand Chamard's plantation. They had made a party of four to go have a look at it. Weeds obscured the old paths, and the roof looked like it could slide off given a good push.

"How old is this place?" Thomas asked. He looked to Chamard with his question since it was his property.

Alistair saw Chamard had tears in his eyes before he turned abruptly, "I'll see you back at the house," he said, his voice thick. He mounted his horse and headed home.

Alistair looked at the old shack and back to Valentine. Thomas was less discreet. "What happened?"

Valentine shook his head. "Bertie had this cabin built for a place to meet the woman he loved most in all his life. Still loves her, in fact."

Thomas looked at the ramshackle cabin. "Here?"

Valentine laughed. "This cabin old now. Built about the time you was born, Major."

Alistair knew who Valentine meant. Bertrand Chamard and Nicolette's mother Cleo had been talked about even when he was a young man. One of the great romances in Louisiana, his Aunt Adeline had told him -- when his mother was not in the room to hush her.

"I guess she was a slave," Thomas said. Alistair could hear the disappointment in his voice that Bertrand Chamard, his mentor, had been one of those planters who took his pleasure from among the women in the quarters.

"Not like you thinking," Valentine said. "She was a slave, but she wasn't Bertie's slave. She'd meet him at this cabin because she wanted to, but finally she run off and lived a free woman. When Bertie found her in New Orleans, they made a life together, raised two children."

Yes, Gabe and Nicolette, all the while Chamard had a first, then a second wife and a son with each of them. Alistair knew the story well because one of those sons was his best friend. But Cleo was with someone else now. She'd wanted a real home, a husband who was with her every night. According to Alistair's friend Marcel, Chamard took it hard.

Valentine gave his head a shake. "What am I doing telling any of this? Ain't none of ya'lls business. And ain't mine to tell."

He stepped onto the weathered porch and scraped the warped door open.

Alistair jumped aside when a raccoon scooted out. Inside they found a dried up snakeskin, a rat's nest, and droppings of who knew how many animals. Didn't smell very good, and they could see daylight through the ceiling.

"I've got a tent you can set up in here," Valentine said. "Nobody will see it, and it'll keep the rain off you."

"Thank you, Valentine. I won't be here except to sleep some of the time, anyway."

Alistair stared at him, wondering whether he appreciated the danger he was in.

Thomas put his hands on his hips. "Major, you didn't think I was going to hide out here indefinitely?"

"Course not," Valentine intervened. "But you doing the right thing to get out of the house where you got women and children."

"Should have done it before now," Thomas muttered.

Alistair had agreed.

The day after Thibault was beaten, Alistair wrapped two rifles and two handguns in oiled cloth and placed them in the back of the wagon.

Valmar still sat in the jail, but he hadn't talked. Even if they could prove Valmar knew Fisher and Shipton, neither the sheriff nor the prosecutor accepted acquaintanceship as evidence. "My Uncle Bob knows Valmar, too," the sheriff had said. "That don't mean he's guilty of a crime."

And why were these two making it their business to take up mischief for Valmar's sake? What did they care if Thomas, or Thibault, had made an enemy of Valmar?

He guessed he knew why. He had known men in the army, weak men, who'd follow a bully around, laughing when he wanted them to laugh, punching somebody if the bully wanted them to. Like they had no sense of themselves except as the bully's creatures. Sometimes they'd been more dangerous than the bully. So even if Valmar was locked up, Shipton and Fisher could do a lot of damage.

Alistair joined the Bickells for supper even though Lily had asked him to stay away. But this wasn't about the two of them.

Rachel fed them a feast, everything fresh picked from the garden, the chicken plucked an hour before supper.

"Rachel, how good a shot are you?" he asked as she set a bowl of beans on the table.

"Tolerable, Major Whiteaker. I can hit what I want to."

"With a rifle?"

"Yes, sir. Rifle or shotgun. Course with a shotgun you don't have to do nothing but point it and pull the trigger."

"And you, Mrs. Palmer?"

"I've never shot a gun."

"After supper, I'd like to teach you how."

He watched thoughts flit across her face. This wasn't courtship. Lily would understand that. She knew what was at stake.

She nodded. "Thank you. I would like to be prepared."

After supper, Lily walked with Alistair to the end of the lane where the woods began.

"You aren't nervous about this, are you?"

"A little, but I'll do my best. If those men come again, I want to be ready."

"Well, they may. The Knights are stepping up their dirty deeds the closer we get to the election."

"The Knights? I thought you said they weren't the ones who attacked us."

He shook his head. "The Knights of the White Camellia won't have riff raff like Valmar with them, but they no doubt inspire them and even offer some cover for their activities. What's more, the Camellias get up to their own mischief." He held the pistol up. "So. You'll learn how to shoot."

He loaded the pistol with one bullet and handed it to her.

Lily looked it over, weighing it, fitting her finger in the trigger guard.

"Alistair."

He smiled. She had forgotten the Major Whiteaker edict.

"I don't know if I can shoot a man."

"I understand. But we're not talking about killing in cold blood, Lily. We're talking about protecting you and Maddie."

She didn't look convinced.

"All we need do now, Lily, is teach you how not to shoot yourself in the foot. Let's don't think past that today, all right?"

"All right." She raised the pistol with one hand and pointed it toward the woods, the barrel of the gun drooping.

"Wait!" he told her. "There's going to be a kick. You have to allow for that. Number one, hold the gun with two hands. Higher. So your eye can sight on the notch. See it?"

She took in a deep breath, steadying herself.

"Good. You'll want to be still, not even breathing, when you pull the trigger."

He stepped behind her and put his arms on hers. "Because the gun will kick up, you want to aim just a little lower than where you want to hit. You see the gourd? Close one eye. That'll help."

"All right."

He stepped away from her. "Fire away."

She jerked the trigger. The gun fired, flew up and knocked her back a step.

"I brought the smallest pistol I have, Lily."

"I'll get used to it. Where did my bullet go?"

Alistair squinted down the lane. "See that pine tree about ten feet to the left of the gourd? The one with the branch hanging on?"

"That's what I hit?"

He grinned at her. "That branch wanted lopping off anyway. You aren't near sighted are you?"

"Alas. No excuse in that direction."

He took the pistol and loaded in another single bullet. He'd been a soldier for four years. He knew too much about what a raw recruit could do with a weapon without meaning any harm at all.

He adjusted her grip on the butt, put her right forefinger at the trigger. "You're going to squeeze, not yank at the trigger. And this time, don't lock your elbows." He had his arms around her again, loosening her arms, straightening her wrists.

Her hair smelled of rosewater. His mouth was only inches from the tender flesh below her ear, the skin dewy and inviting – but he'd promised not to press her. He dropped his arms and stepped away.

"Now, put one foot back a bit. Like that. Bend your front knee a little."

She took her time, adjusted her stance, sighted, drew in a breath, and fired. This time they heard the bullet thunk into the tree. Alistair walked down to check – she'd missed the gourd by a foot or so, but she was getting there.

On Lily's eighth try, she blasted that gourd into a thousand pieces.

She whirled to him, triumphant and grinning. He grabbed her up and whirled her around.

He meant to let her go when he set her down. But once her feet were on the ground, her arms still circled his neck. Her face, glowing and happy, was still turned up to his. He could see it in her eyes. She wasn't thinking about pushing him away. She wasn't thinking about how he shouldn't come here anymore.

She leaned into him, and he wrapped her in his arms. Her fingers slid into his hair as he kissed her. Whatever had made her tell him no, she'd forgotten it because she relaxed against him and opened her lips to him.

"Ah, here you are."

They broke apart, startled.

Lily staggered back, three, then four and five steps. "No." The word seemed forced from her lungs, hardly any sound behind it. "No." Her face was white as bone, her mouth hanging open.

"Lily?" Alistair started for her.

"No need for you to comfort my wife. I believe that will fall to me. Hello, Lily."

Alistair grabbed her, to keep her from falling. Both of her hands were stretched in front of her, palms out, like she could stop disaster from coming.

He had said *my wife*. Alistair put his arm around her waist. "I've got you," he whispered. "I've got you."

The man stared at them, a smirk quirking his lips. He was tall and dark, neatly dressed if a little travel worn. "Come, Lily. Doesn't your husband deserve a better welcome than this?"

He spread his arms out as if to welcome her into his embrace.

Clinging to Alistair's arm, Lily opened her mouth, but nothing came out. Her breathing was fast and erratic. She was going to faint if she didn't get her lungs under control. "Easy, Lily. Just breathe. I've got you."

"Well, I'll introduce myself to your gallant friend if you are disinclined. I am Frederick Palmer. That is my wife you're handling."

The man expressed no indignation at having found his wife embracing another man, kissing another man, but there was a nasty gleam in his eye.

Lily turned her face to Alistair. Her eyes teared and her mouth trembled. She still clutched his forearm. "Oh, God. Alistair."

Garvey came up behind Palmer. "I suggest we go back to the house. Mr. Palmer, after you."

Palmer gave his wife and Alistair another look, amused if anything, Alistair thought, but there had been that glimmer of rage.

Alistair bent to her ear. "Can you walk?"

Her whole body shuddered as she let out a breath. She took hold of his hand and gripped it with both of hers as they followed her husband to the house.

"You thought he was dead?" Alistair asked quietly.

"I thought I'd killed him." She let his hand go and wrapped her arms around her middle, a declaration that she would not lean on him.

But he wanted her to. "Lily." He stopped and waited until she looked at him. "You are not alone."

She squeezed her eyes shut and shook her head. Shoulders hunched, she hurried on ahead of him.

When Alistair entered through the kitchen, he heard Palmer saying, "And here is my beautiful little girl."

Alistair stepped into the sitting room where Garvey had a hand on Maddie's shoulder.

"No kiss for your father, Maddie? Come here, darling."

Maddie turned her whole body into Garvey's. So even his own daughter was not glad to see him. What kind of man was he?

"Mama?"

Lily seemed to grow three inches as she straightened her back. She took Maddie's hand and drew her close. "You may recall the last time you greeted your daughter it was with a blow."

Of course. Now Alistair knew everything he needed to know.

Palmer gave a sort of baritone giggle, like nothing Alistair had heard before.

"You misunderstood, Lily. As you so often do." He looked at Garvey, even glanced at Alistair. "Lily, her imagination gets away with her. At least I have always preferred to call it imagination. Mad is such a frightening concept." Now he looked directly at Lily. "They lock up mad women, don't they, dear?"

What little color had returned to Lily's cheeks drained again.

"What do you want, Frederick?"

He held his hands out. "Why, I want a little time with my family. It's been months since I've seen either of you."

Palmer looked at Garvey and then pointedly at Alistair. "Gentlemen, perhaps you would give a man a little privacy for such a poignant reunion."

Alistair watched Lily. She lifted her chin and gave a slight nod to Garvey. "Maddie, go with Uncle Garvey."

Then Lily looked at Alistair, her chin still up. Her mouth was firm and her stance tall and straight. That she kept her hands clasped together to hide their trembling Alistair didn't doubt.

"I'll stay," he said.

"Thank you. That isn't necessary."

He stayed rooted, his eyes on her.

"He is my husband, Major Whiteaker."

So final. So resigned. She meant for him to leave her with him.

"I'll be in the kitchen," he said.

~~~

Lily stood while Frederick sat on the settee and stretched his legs out.

"So," he said.

"What do you want, Frederick?"

He patted the sofa beside him. "Come. Give me a proper welcome. You're free enough with your kisses, it seems. I'll have one of my own."

"No."

His eyes narrowed. "Do you have any idea how much trouble you're in, Lily Palmer? You stole from me. You knocked me out. You ran away -- with my child. What do you suppose a judge would make of all those un-wifely deeds?"

"Maddie remembers what you did. To her, and to me. I have scars to show for being wifely, as you say. What do you suppose a judge would make of that?"

He spread his arms along the back of the settee, at his ease. "He would say, my dear Lily, that I am your husband. Your lord and master. No law against a man disciplining a wayward wife."

"I want a divorce."

"Well, you can't have one."

"Why not? You don't love me. Or Maddie. You don't even like us."

"I like you fine, Lily." Palmer looked around the room. "Your brother-in-law said you are to inherit this tidy little farm. Is that right?"

"Gillian's husband told you where I was?"

"Had to. For some reason he thought I was dead. When he saw I wasn't, well, it's like I said. Your lord and master."

"There's no place for you here. I want you gone."

He glanced out the window. "Be dark soon."

"Then sleep in the barn."

"I'll be much more comfortable in your bed, my darling. Why I don't I have a wash-up and a little late supper. Your woman in there won't mind heating something up. I'm not particular about what."

She stared at him. All those nights she'd lain awake, sorry she'd killed him. Having him alive was not as gladful as she'd imagined. "You can wash on the back porch. There's a cistern there and a basin."

"Towels, soap, privacy? Nothing like that available down here in the wilds of Louisiana?"

She stared at the dark hair falling over his forehead, at the glossy moustache she had once thought so very dashing. She had thought him handsome. Romantic, even. And then he'd started drinking.

"The bedroom is the second on the right," she told Frederick.

"Aren't you going to show me the way? Do all the wifely things a woman should do, collect the towels, loosen my tie?"

If he touched her, that way, she would be sick. She would not be in a bedroom with him ever again.

"I trust you can loosen your own tie."

In the kitchen, her friends, her new family, waited. And Alistair. She hesitated at the door. Every face turned to her, but she couldn't look at them. She'd lied to them, to all of them.

"Mama." Maddie ran to her and wrapped her arms around her waist.

"It's all right, sweetheart. Everything will be all right."

"Do we have to go away?"

"No, Maddie. This is home. I promised, didn't I?"

A huge shuddering sigh shook Maddie's little shoulders.

"All right then, Miss Maddie," Rachel said. "You come on with me and let's get Dawn ready for bed. You can snuggle up with her tonight."

When Maddie let go of her, Lily swayed. Uncle Garvey took her by the elbow, sat her at the table, and poured her a glass of sherry. "You don't have to say a damn thing. You just get that down and catch your breath."

She picked up the glass but her hands trembled and she had to set it down again. Alistair sat at the end of the table on her right, his hands turning his pocket watch over and over.

Uncle Garvey pulled a chair next to hers and rubbed the back of her neck. "Whatever you want to do, that's what we'll do, honey."

It would be easy to turn in to his big chest and sob out all her fear. She couldn't do that.

"What do you want to do, Lily?" Alistair asked, his eyes on his pocket watch.

She swallowed. No more lies. "I want a divorce. But he says no."

"He can be persuaded," Alistair said.

She jerked her head up. "Alistair, no. You can't shoot him."

His eyes widened. "Lily. Of course I can't shoot him." The sound he made was almost a laugh. "Though I think maybe he needs killing."

She shook her head. "I've lived with his death on my head for three months now. It's a terrible blight on your soul, you told me that, Alistair."

"What do you mean, 'on your head,' Lily?" Uncle Garvey asked her. "No, I said you don't have to tell us a damn thing, and I meant it."

She put her hands in her lap and focused on them. "You need to know why I lied, Uncle Garvey."

"Then tell me, honey, if you want to."

She drew a deep breath. "He had a hangover that morning. He was irritable. He hit Maddie." She pressed her fingers against her lips until she could go on. "He'd never done that before, but there had been a first time for hitting me, too. So when he left for work, I took the money he kept in his bureau drawer and packed a valise for Maddie and one for me. He found me closing up the bags. I don't know why he came home. He never came home until supper." She looked at Uncle Garvey, wanting him to understand. "Maddie didn't see – she was in the front room choosing a book to take with us. She didn't see."

"All right," he said.

She squeezed her eyes shut. "He hit me. This time . . . this time, I fought back. I shoved him, as hard as I could. Then he came after me. The look on his face – I thought he meant to kill me this time."

She leaned into her hands, covering her face. Uncle Garvey put his hand on her back, blessed man.

"He knocked me down. The door stop, an iron rooster he gave me when we moved into our first home. I grabbed it. I hit him with it as hard as I could."

"And you thought you'd killed him," Alistair said. He reached for her hand and gripped it. "I'm glad you're free of that burden, at least."

She nodded. Then she gave the same sort of half-laugh he'd made. "Yes. At least I'm not a murderess."

Alistair stood. "I'm going to New Orleans in the morning. Garvey, you see to teaching Lily how to handle that pistol?"

Garvey followed Alistair on to the back porch. "Hell of a thing."

"He's not going to ruin her life."

"The man is her husband. Lawfully wedded."

Alistair settled his hat on his head. "I'll be back in a few days."

# Chapter Seventeen

Lily sent Rachel to bed, laid out a cold supper for her husband on the kitchen table, and sat waiting with her hands in her lap. Alistair had every right to walk away. She was a liar, letting him think she was a decent woman who was innocently widowed by a traffic accident. And he'd wasted his time with her, a married woman. She had managed not to run after him when he left. She'd had that much control, at least. And now she was steeled to deal with Frederick.

Frederick came down freshly brushed and washed. "And here you are again. I find I must hunt for my wife to have a few moments of her time."

She didn't answer him.

He sat down and dug into his supper. He'd always been a good eater though he was as slim as the day she'd met him eight years ago. The alcohol, she supposed, kept him lean.

"Aren't you going to ask after your dear sister?"

When she didn't answer, he didn't seem to mind. "She cried many a tear over her resurrected brother-in-law. So glad I'm alive, you see. Don't know where she and her husband got the idea I was dead."

"I told her you were."

Frederick paused. "I see. That would mean – you had killed me yourself. Was that what you intended, Lily? To kill me?"

She shrugged. "I found I could live with it."

He didn't like that, but the nasty glint in his eye lasted only a heartbeat. Then his smile reappeared.

"Why, Lily Palmer. I believe you've developed a spine."

"You needn't expect me to cower, Frederick. I'm through with that. I'm through with you."

He grabbed her hand quick as a snake and squeezed. "You are my wife. Mrs. Frederick Palmer."

"You're hurting me. Again."

He pushed his chair back and stood. "Come up stairs."

135

She shook her head. Even as he ground the bones in her hand together, she said, "No."

"You are my wife."

"Only by law."

He gave her an oily grin. "And by law, you belong to me. Your body belongs to me. And we're going upstairs so I can exercise my rights."

She shook her head again. She was not going upstairs with him. Ever.

He jerked her body to his and mashed his mouth against hers, bruising her lips against her teeth.

"Lily," he breathed, and almost gently, he kissed her again. "I want you, Lily. I've always wanted you."

He was bigger than she was. Stronger than she. If she had to fight him, she would, but for now, she simply became inert.

"Dammit, you're my wife." He gripped her arms until they ached. "Kiss me, Lily."

She made her mouth, her whole body, relax.

Frederick changed tactics. His hands loosened so that he could gently stroke up and down her arms. "I'll make you want me. Like I used to. You remember, don't you, Lily? How I'd wake you in the night, kissing and stroking until you were hot and ready for me. Remember how sweet it was?"

"That was a long time ago, Frederick."

Holding on to her he began pushing her toward the door. "We're going upstairs and I'm going to remind you what a husband does with his wife."

"No."

"No no no me all you want. The law says I can take my wife whether she likes it or not. But it's so much more fun when she likes it. Remember?"

He pushed her up against the wall and shoved her skirt up to her waist. His mouth opened over hers, hot and demanding.

She was the Lily hovering near the ceiling, watching her husband maul her. She hardly felt his hand fumbling between her legs, hardly felt his hot breath on her cheek.

He released her mouth to ravish her neck.

"You will add rape to your abuses, Frederick?" She sounded calm, even cool, this Lily with her back to the wall.

He palmed her breast, pinched her nipple through the fabric.

It wasn't time to fight yet. Soon, maybe. She would know when. Now she kept her hands at her sides and made her body limp.

He took hold of her shoulders and banged her head against the wall. "Damn you, Lily."

She didn't know what came over her. A kind of joy welled up inside her. She was Lily. She was not Frederick's *thing*. It didn't matter if he hit her, she would never be his again.

She smiled. Frederick raised his hand to her. And he held it there, poised.

She stepped away from him. She walked into the dark hallway, down to Thomas's empty room, and closed the door.

~~~

The next morning, Frederick did not appear for breakfast. Once the dishes were done, Lily sat at the kitchen table with Uncle Garvey learning how the revolving mechanism worked and how to load the pistol.

"Alistair only loaded one bullet at a time."

Uncle Garvey laughed. "Sounds like a soldier who had a bad experience teaching a young fellow to shoot."

"I want to keep the pistol with me. I want it loaded, all the way."

"Nah, honey. That's dangerous. Nobody walks around with all six chambers filled lessen they're about to go into battle. You drop it, you knock the hammer on something, it'll go off and . . . " He heaved a breath. "We got two little girls on the place."

She caught her lower lip in her teeth, thinking. "If the hammer hits on an empty chamber, nothing happens. The revolver part just moves on to the next chamber and waits for the trigger to be pulled again, right?"

"That's right."

"So if I put the bullet in say, the third chamber, I'd have to pull the trigger twice before the bullet was up for the next trigger pull."

"Yeah."

"Is that as safe as it sounds?"

"Well, I suppose it is. Yeah."

"I can't be out in the garden, have the raiders charge onto the place, and me with an empty gun."

Uncle Garvey eyed her. "You're not thinking about putting a bullet in your husband, Lily."

Her mouth quirked up. "I killed him once. That will have to do."

"Then let's go shoot some gourds."

After practice, Lily watched Uncle Garvey clean and reassemble the pistol at the kitchen table.

"Think you can do it next time?" he asked.

"Probably. But I'd hate to put the thing together backwards and end up shooting myself. I'd appreciate another lesson or two, Uncle Garvey."

"Then that's what we'll do. Alistair will be pleased at how well you shot today."

Lily turned away. Alistair wouldn't be pleased with her ever again. He'd left for New Orleans as soon as she told the truth, getting as far away from her as he could. She didn't blame him, but it hurt.

Frederick ambled into the kitchen. "What's all the shooting this morning. You aiming to do me in again, Lily?"

Uncle Garvey scowled at him. "That is in poor taste, Mr. Palmer."

Frederick laughed. "A Southern gentleman, chivalrous to the end."

"Yes, by God." Uncle Garvey scraped his chair back, collected his pistol and the chamois. "I'll be just upstairs, Lily, you need me."

Lily wanted to slap the smirk off Frederick's face. When had he become so smug, so superior? Toward the end of the war, she thought. The shoe manufacturer he worked for saw the orders from the U. S. Army drying up, no longer any need for thousands upon thousands of shoes for soldiers. Frederick had made good money during those years he took orders from the government, not just for shoes, but for leather harness, saddlebags, holsters. He'd bought the house on Cavendish Square for her, had put some money in the bank. And then the factory closed. All those soldiers came home and there were not enough jobs for all of them. Frederick began to drink their savings up as he looked for work. When he finally found a job as a salesman in a shoe store for a fraction of what he'd earned before, he'd drunk even more.

She didn't excuse him. Plenty of men had come down in the world because of the war. Some of them had lost limbs, some of them had lost sons and fathers. They didn't drown themselves in self-pity and liquor. They didn't bully their wives and children to make themselves feel powerful.

She put the cap back on the oil can for Uncle Garvey. "I have work to do in the garden." She hooked her apron on the peg and walked out the back door.

An hour later, she came in, her hands prickly from picking okra. She washed up and went to find Maddie. She was in the sitting room in her father's lap. He was being charming, his voice smooth and full of good humor as he told her all about some pipe dream of his. Something about streams full of gold. He could spin a dream, Frederick could.

Lily's heart squeezed. What if he made Maddie love him again? Made her forget how frightened she'd been the last months they were all together? She realized suddenly how Frederick could get back at her. He could make Maddie want to be with him. The law would allow it, no question about that.

"Maddie, come here," she said.

Maddie slid off her father's lap and Frederick let her go. *This time*, his eyes told Lily.

How many weeks, or maybe only days, before Maddie chose to stay cuddled on her father's lap?

~~~

In New Orleans, Alistair made an appointment with Gordon Smith, a man who'd been imprisoned with him the last months of the war and who had rejoined the law practice he shared with his father. After the niceties, the pouring of whiskey and lighting of cigars, Smith said, "What can I do for you, Alistair?"

Alistair laid out Lily's situation for him. "What would it take for her to be rid of her husband?"

Smith eyed him shrewdly through a puff of cigar smoke.

"Your interest in this personal?" he asked.

"Yes. And no. Whether I have any future with Lily Palmer is beside the point. The man is a wife-beater and even hit his little girl."

"A man may spank his child, Alistair."

"A spanking delivered in correction does not make a child afraid of her father. I saw how Maddie recoiled from him when she saw him again."

Smith smoked for a while. "It doesn't look good for Mrs. Palmer, I'll have to tell you honestly. A woman may divorce a man who beats her, this is true. But she beat him back, hard enough that she thought she'd killed him. Do I understand that correctly?"

"Yes."

"He could claim desertion, abandonment. He could claim she stole his child from him."

Alistair closed his eyes and inhaled.

"Any chance he could claim adultery?" Smith asked.

Alistair's eyes snapped open. He felt heat rise up his neck and over his face. There had been those kisses. But Lily had thought she was a widow. "No."

Smith focused on his cigar. "Could you prove that?"

How did one prove a thing did not happen? But he and Lily had never been alone more than a few minutes, and even then it was in plain sight of anyone glancing at the orchard. Or into the barn. Or . . . "Garvey Bickell will swear there has been no adultery. As will I."

Smith leaned forward, his elbows on his desk. "I'll tell you straight, Alistair. This man has a better chance of divorcing his wife than she has of divorcing him. And on his terms. There is the child to consider, as well. I assume she will not risk losing her little girl. All she'd get from a divorce petition is notoriety and her husband's enmity. You'll need more than this to wrest her free of this marriage."

Alistair didn't let himself think. Didn't let himself feel. He drank his whiskey to be polite, then collected his hat.

He walked the streets, thinking, trying not to feel. Lily was stuck, with a man she didn't love. She loved Alistair, or she would, given a chance. They could have a life together. He would be a father to Maddie, and he and Lily would have more children. To lose that future – he stumbled on, his heart and his mind both gray and dull.

When he thought he could be civil, he returned to his friend Marcel's house for supper. Deborah Ann expected polite conversation, and he managed that. After she retired, he and Marcel drank too much and talked about the war.

# Chapter Eighteen

How quickly despair became routine, Lily thought. She didn't fear Frederick would abuse her, not here in Uncle Garvey's house. But she worried about what he wanted. About how he tried to get close to Maddie. But that she would not allow. She kept Maddie at her side from the time she woke until she was tucked into bed with Dawn. Lily herself slept in what had been Thomas's room.

She watched, waiting for Frederick to reveal himself with impatience or even boredom. Instead, he seemed quite content to relax and enjoy Rachel's cooking and the quiet life of Uncle Garvey's farm. Not that he offered to contribute a moment's work in the garden or the barn or even in the simplest tasks like drawing water from the well.

But a week after his arrival, a week after Alistair had gone to New Orleans to get away from her and the mess she'd made, Frederick politely asked Uncle Garvey for the use of a mule to ride into Donaldsonville.

"These are work animals, Mr. Palmer. Peep needs one in the field. I need one to pull the wagon to the levee with my produce."

Frederick smiled. "That's fine, Uncle. I'll wait until you have made your delivery to the steam boat."

Uncle Garvey glanced at her. She only shrugged. They were Uncle Garvey's animals.

"You can borrow Rosie," he said. "Have her back in the stable before dark, rubbed down and fed."

Frederick gave him a mock salute and another oily smile.

Lily stood on the back porch, Maddie at her side, and watched him ride away. She drew in a huge breath. He'd be gone the rest of the day.

"Where's Daddy going?" Maddie asked.

"Into town." Lily watched her closely. "Will you miss him?" She had allowed Frederick to see Maddie only in her own company. She didn't think he would hit Maddie, but making her love him again would be hurt enough.

"Is he coming back?"

141

Maddie's little face was far too solemn. "Yes, he'll be back."

"Can I go play with the kittens?"

Lily let her go and sank into the ladder-back chair with a sigh. Uncle Garvey joined her on the porch.

"That man a gambler?" he said.

"Sometimes."

"He got any money?"

"He sold the house, he said."

Uncle Garvey pulled a chair over and sat with her. "I been thinking, Lily."

"Me, too, Uncle Garvey. I don't want you to give me the farm. Not now."

"Well, honey, I think you're right. Transferring the deed to you now would be like tucking it in that man's pocket. There's no hurry in my getting to San Francisco. It'll wait. And there's other ways to make this a home for you and Maddie."

"So you think that's why he's here, too? For the property?"

"He knew all about our arrangement before he got here, didn't he? Your sister told him. Not that I blame her. He's your husband."

"I don't blame her either, Uncle Garvey. Frederick can charm the ants out of a honey jar."

They listened to the sounds of the farm, Rachel's hoe chopping into the ground, a blue jay squawking.

"Might be, Lily, that he just wants you back, you and Maddie."

For a short time, lying awake that first night, she'd almost softened toward him, thinking he'd missed them, that in spite of everything, he loved them. But he hadn't promised things would be better, that he would treat her right, that he would stop the drinking. "I don't think so. I don't trust him, Uncle Garvey, and I'm glad you don't either."

"Well then, we'll go on as we are for a while. I'll write Avery and tell him I'm needed here for now."

"Thank you, Uncle Garvey. You are the truest friend I've ever had."

Alistair arrived that afternoon, P.G. trotting along beside his horse. Maddie and Dawn came running out of the barn, yelling. "Major Whiteaker, Portia had kittens!"

Lily came onto the porch wiping her hands on a dish towel. So he had come back. He threw her a smile and let Maddie pull him along by the hand to see the kittens.

What was he doing here? He'd left quickly enough the night Frederick arrived. Once he'd satisfied himself she was a liar, he'd taken himself off to New Orleans, a city famous for its beautiful women, and for its brothels. She wondered if he had spent his time with one of those renowned quadroon beauties. But here he was, looking at kittens.

It was none of her business, what Alistair Whiteaker did, but she followed to the barn anyway.

He was kneeling in the clean straw where six kittens dozed near their mama.

"You can pick one up if you're careful," Maddie said. "Like this, so his baby head doesn't flop over."

Alistair slid his fingers under a sleepy tan and white. "Like this?"

"He knows how to hold a kitten, silly," Dawn whispered loudly.

P.G. nosed in beside Alistair's knee and sniffed at the pile of kittens.

Alistair looked up to share a grin with Lily, but his smile faded as he held her eyes. They really didn't have much to smile about, she and Alistair.

Maddie squealed. "P.G.! Don't eat the kittens!"

Alistair placed a gentle hand on P.G.'s head. "He won't hurt them, Maddie. He likes kittens, don't you, P.G.?"

Alistair stood, the kitten still cradled in one hand.

"You want a glass of tea?" Lily asked.

He gave his kitten to Dawn. "You look after P.G. for me?"

He shortened his stride to walk across the yard with her. She kept her distance, careful not to touch him. But she wanted to.

"Sit out here where there's a little breeze. I'll be right back."

He held himself very still while she was gone. He couldn't let himself feel anything, not even hope.

She came back with glasses of tea, cooled in a bucket of well water all morning. "How was New Orleans?"

"Hot. Have to wear a coat and tie in town. Don't know how the city folks bear it."

They drank their tea in silence, their glasses half empty before he spoke. "Where's your husband?" he said quietly.

"He rode into Donaldsonville."

"Are you all right?"

"Of course." She didn't meet his gaze. "Really, we're fine. Thank you."

"I saw a friend of mine, in New Orleans. A lawyer."

She turned to him. Was that hope in her eyes? She was stronger than he, then. "What about?"

"Lily, a divorce will be difficult to get."

That little flame in her eyes was gone. "Yes. I thought it would be."

"Lily, I know people all over this state. A lot of them owe me favors. I'll find a judge, one who understands, who'll –"

"You can't fix this, Alistair."

He pulled back in his chair. "Then you're -- " He looked toward the barn where he could see the girls moving in the shadows, he looked toward the fields, anywhere but at her. "Are you --?"

She would know what he was wondering. Was she sleeping with her husband.

"No, Alistair. I will not be his wife again. The law may define me that way, but it is not who I am. I am not his."

He took her hand. "But Maddie is his."

She closed her eyes. "Yes," she whispered. "Oh, Alistair, I'm terrified. What if he tries to take Maddie?"

"We won't let him."

She held on to his hand with both of hers. "The law . . . "

"I am a very rich man, Lily. It isn't right, but for once, I will be glad to bribe and coerce any judge or attorney to keep you and Maddie together, to get you free."

"You'd do that?"

"Palmer can get a divorce much more easily than you can. I came so I could talk to him today. To see how much he'd take to let you go. But, yes, I'm prepared to bribe judges if he doesn't want money more than he wants you and Maddie."

Every man has his price, isn't that what the adage says? Alistair had seen Frederick Palmer only the one time, but it was also the first meeting between Palmer and Lily. There had been no evidence of love. Not even of regard or respect.

In spite of the years spent killing Union soldiers, Alistair was not at heart a violent man. But if Lily were his wife and he'd come upon another man kissing her, he would have pounded that man into the ground. And if he'd seen her kissing that man back, his heart would have cracked. He would not have said with cool indifference, "That is my wife you're handling."

The man would have a price. Alistair would pay it. And then he and Lily would plan their future. He was profoundly grateful in that moment that he'd invested in steam ships and railroads before the war. Whatever Palmer wanted, he could afford it.

She brought his hand to her face and pressed it against her cheek.

"Lily," he said, his voice hoarse. "Darling." He gently pulled his hand from hers. "I can't . . . I better go."

# Chapter Nineteen

Thomas and his supporters had put up fliers all over town to announce the rally. They had a good crowd here on the western edge of Donaldsonville. He climbed onto the back of a wagon and looked over the people who'd come to hear him speak. Saturday afternoon, they'd mostly come straight from the fields on their half day off. They were dusty and their clothes had patches on patches, but they were men and women who meant to take control of their lives, who needed only information. Considering the posters announcing the rallies were usually torn down the same day they were put up, Thomas was always surprised as many showed up as they did.

Cabel climbed onto the wagon and leaned in to speak into Thomas's ear. "They gathering at the Blue Bird Tavern, like we thought. Most of them on horseback."

Thomas glanced around the perimeter of the growing crowd. Musette DeBlieux sat in her carriage with Carrie Ann under a chinaberry tree. She should not be here, certainly not with only Carrie Ann for protection. The woman had no sense. She put herself in danger, and did her reputation no good, to be hovering around these rallies.

Major Bodell had sent half a dozen cavalry to monitor the rally, for which Thomas was grateful. Thomas also had his own guard, four mounted black men, rifles at the ready, placed around the edge of the crowd. Whether they'd be enough to keep the White Camellias from disrupting the rally, well, they'd just have to see.

They'd had heated discussions well into the night the past week about whether to arm their own sentinels. Mr. Chamard, Major Whiteaker, even Garvey Bickell argued for unarmed guards. Thomas understood -- if trouble erupted and they killed white men – that would not help them win the election in September.

But Thomas had decided Cabel and Reynard were right. They were men, and they would not allow other men to intimidate or prevent them from acting. If they wanted the vote, they had to be prepared to fight for it. Even so, Thomas had insisted the four guards keep their fingers off their triggers. They were not to shoot at anybody unless they were shot at themselves – mere firing into the air by the raiders was not enough provocation to shoot back, he'd warned.

Cabel hopped down from the wagon, and Thomas addressed the people. "Friends," he called, his voice carrying over the mild wind and the shuffle of feet. "Five weeks from now, we elect our delegates to the state convention. Once we have our people represented, fully represented, by people we ourselves have chosen, we will march on into full, unabridged citizenship in this country. We will have the vote!"

The Knights were here, as always, engaged in their usual tricks, trying to intimidate people who dared come to these political rallies. One of them made a show of looking at faces and then writing on his clipboard, taking names of those he would not hire for a season's work. Two stood near the wagon, their heads together. Now and then one would point at a face in the crowd and murmur. Thomas saw one black man, then another, leave the rally after being singled out. Sometimes intimidation worked very well.

The soldiers saw all that, but there was little they could do about that kind of harassment.

"What will that mean to you and me?" Thomas asked the crowd. His complete attention was on the faces below him now, on his fervent desire that they understand this was their chance.

When the first shots rang out, he was as startled as the people with their backs to the oncoming horsemen. These were not the ragged scoundrels who'd raided the ice cream social – these men had fine mounts, their boots were polished, their rifles gleamed. Knights of the White Camellia.

The Camellias' rifles were pointed into the air. The real danger was from being trampled as the men masked with white kerchiefs spurred their horses into the crowd. People screamed and dodged the horses, dust rising thick into the air.

A black man grabbed the reins of a horse and was lifted off his feet for a moment, but he dragged that horse to a halt. Other men pulled the raider off his saddle.

Thomas leapt from the wagon, pushing his way to the downed man. If his people killed him, there would be hell to pay. "Stop!" he shouted. "Hold on – Stop!"

The soldiers were using their horses to herd the Camellias like cattle, shouting and jostling the raiders. Through the dust, the confusion and noise, Thomas shoved through the churning crowd and grabbed the collar of the black man bent over his captive, pummeling him with his fists. "John Berry, stop, I say!"

Berry, his chest heaving, a wild look in his eye, reined himself in.

Thomas recognized the man John Berry had been about to knock out -- Moltrey, the tailor who had refused to make Thomas a suit.

"Thomas!"

He raised his head, spied Cabel pointing toward the chinaberry tree. Two men on horseback were charging round and round Musette's carriage, yelling at her. Thomas sprinted through the crowd to reach her.

"Nigger loving whore!" they shouted.

Carrie Ann screamed. When two soldiers peeled off from the main fracas and headed for the carriage, the raiders sped down the road with the rest of the Camellias, hooting and yelling from behind their white masks. The soldiers followed them, not bothering to spur their horses enough to catch them.

Musette's hands were clutched around the reins as her horse stamped, rattled by all the confusion. Cabel grabbed its halter to settle it down.

Thomas gripped the hand rail of the carriage. "What the hell do you think you're doing here?" He heard the snarl in his voice, hardly the respect he owed her, but he was angry and scared at the same time. Stray bullets didn't care if they pierced black hide or white hide.

"I am a citizen, am I not, even if I cannot vote." Her face was pinched and gray, but she had on her pointy-nosed superior air.

"These rallies are opportunities for mayhem, you know that! And now the White Camellias have seen you here, what do you suppose they will tell everyone about Musette DeBlieux mingling with the coloreds?"

"I am here in my carriage, come to town to shop. The coloreds, as you so astutely call them, are gathered over there."

"Don't split hairs with me, Musette."

"Don't tell me what to do."

He dropped his hands from the rail, startled by the venomous flash in her eyes. "Miss DeBlieux, please don't come to another rally," he said, coldly formal. "I cannot protect you."

She opened her mouth to spew a retort, but Carrie Ann gripped her arm. "We're going, Thomas. Right now. Miss Musette, you let me have them reins and I get us home."

Musette turned her face forward, chin held high. With a stiff back, she allowed Carrie Ann to drive them away.

The raiders were gone. People began to disperse, except for those around the man John Berry had been punishing. Reynard had a grip on the white man, who could hardly stand on his own from the beating he'd taken.

"Sheriff will just let him go, you know that," Cabel said.

"No," Reynard argued, "I don't know that -- "

Thomas interrupted. "He hurt anybody, his horse hurt anybody?"

"Knocked my woman down."

Good, Thomas thought, aware how callous that was, and how necessary if they were to get the law involved. "Where is she? She back on her feet?"

"Come here, Sarah. Show him."

A slight woman of middle years stepped boldly around her husband and spat at the masked man. She held her arm close to her side and already the wrist was swelling. "He broke my arm, the devil." She spat at him again.

"Then you come with me to the sheriff. Fill out a complaint. Then the law has to charge him." He shouted to the crowd. "Anybody else hurt?"

Another woman, bent with age, and a boy nearly grown were brought to the center. The woman's face was covered by a sheet of blood still pouring from the gash on her forehead. The boy was merely dusty and bruised.

"You three, and as many of you as can, come as witnesses, come with me to the jail. We have the right not to be assaulted, and the law will be on our side."

"You a dreamer, Thomas Bickell!" someone shouted.

"Yes. I am a dreamer," he shouted to the crowd. "And we're going to make that dream come true! Together!"

Sheriff Paget didn't seem surprised to see them filing into his cramped office. Agent Witherspoon from the Freedmen's Bureau was already there.

"Mr. Bickell," Mr. Witherspoon said. "Are you harmed?"

"Not me, but others are. You can see we need more than six soldiers at these events, Mr. Witherspoon."

Thomas watched the man think. This should not have happened – it was the Bureau's responsibility to see that elections were conducted fairly.

Witherspoon nodded. "I will speak to Major Bodell. In the future, you can count on a dozen soldiers, Mr. Bickell."

"All right," Paget said. "Let's hear it."

"Sheriff, this man was directly involved in injuring these people. They wish to press charges against him."

The sheriff eyed the White Camellia. The pristine white mask he'd worn hung around his neck, grimy with blood and dirt. His face was swollen and his eyes were already black.

"Mr. Moltrey," Sheriff Paget said. He shook his head. "You're a sorry sight."

"You see what they did to me, Sheriff. I'm pressing charges against every one of them."

Thomas didn't blink. "Unfortunately, Mr. Moltrey was somewhat battered when he fell off his horse in the midst of a stampede of frightened people, a stampede he is responsible for. Also, most unfortunately, there is no knowing who among the hundred men attending the rally accidentally rammed his fists into this man's face. Purely in reaction to the damage Mr. Moltrey caused these two women."

Paget gave him the eye, but Thomas had not grown into his leadership without courage.

"That's the same nigger come here with Chamard, ain't it?" This was Valmar shouting from his cell, the same cell he'd been in for weeks, ever since he'd set fire to Alfie and Annie's cabin.

If not yet tried, at least the man was still locked up. Getting free room and board while his leg healed.

"Charge your pretty boy with something, why don't you, Paget," Valmar yelled. "He causing a lot of damned trouble. Damned nigger getting away with everything and Moltrey there an upstanding citizen."

"Pipe down, Valmar," the sheriff said. "All right, let's get on with it. Deputy?" At his nod, the deputy helped Moltrey into a cell and stowed him on a cot before he clanged the barred door shut.

"You're going to cost the parish another doctor bill, Thomas Bickell."

"Yes, sir."

Paget sat down, rummaged through desk drawers, and came up with the forms he needed.

"Sheriff," Witherspoon said. "I may be able to save you the trouble of all that paperwork. This man is accused of interfering with an election. The Freedmen's Bureau and the U. S. Army are charged with preventing just such an action. We will take the responsibility of trying him and meting justice if that is appropriate."

The sheriff thought that over. Thomas wondered if Paget resented Witherspoon looking over his shoulder all the time. Maybe not – he wouldn't be sheriff if the Bureau's agent and Major Bodell hadn't approved him.

Paget passed a hand over his mouth, but Thomas detected the beginnings of a smile under that hand.

"Mr. Witherspoon, that's the best offer I've heard in many a day. Mr. Moltrey is all yours."

"Thank you, sir. I will arrange to transport him to New Orleans and see that our clerk comes promptly to take statements."

Thomas saw Reynard giving Cabel a triumphant look, which of course made Cabel scowl. As for himself, Thomas smiled.

~~~

Musette arrived home shaken and dusty. She bathed and changed, and still her hands shook. The raiders had frightened her. They'd shamed her. And then Thomas had treated her like a stupid child.

She hated him. He was the one who was stupid. He'd come striding from the melee like some avenging angel, unarmed against wild men with horses and rifles.

He'd been splendid. He'd been frightened for her. And he'd called her Musette again. Before he turned cold and ugly and called her Miss DeBlieux.

She pressed her forehead against the window glass. She never wanted to see him again. She could go into the convent. The Ursalines would take her. She'd never marry anyway. Now her reputation was ruined, and there were hardly any men left to marry after the ravages of war anyway.

What would her mother think about having a nun for a daughter? She was a good Catholic. She ought to be proud of her. But she knew her mother would not be pleased. She expected her daughters to make happy marriages, as her own had been with Papa. That wasn't going to happen though. There would be no happy ending for her.

If she were a man she'd go into Papa's study and get drunk. As it was, she sipped a glass of sherry and lay down on her day bed.

She wakened when she heard voices in the parlor. Mr. Chamard had come to call. What time was it? Nearly dark. Carrie Ann had let her sleep through supper time. She splashed water on her face and tidied her hair.

Mr. Chamard stood when she entered the room.

"I see Carrie Ann has taken care of you," Musette said, nodding at the whiskey decanter at his elbow.

"As always. How are you, my dear? I hear you had a trying day."

She tried a small smile. "Yes. It was trying."

She sat on the sofa. He settled back into his favorite chair, the same one her papa had used to sit in after supper.

"You may as well tell me," she said. "What are they saying?"

"They? The mysterious, ever-present 'they'?" He sipped at his whiskey. "Well, let's just say the gossip is not sympathetic. You couldn't have expected it would be."

"I did nothing wrong. It was a public gathering, a political assembly. Why shouldn't I be there?"

Chamard idly rubbed at his temple. "Musette, have you been to any political rallies at which Thomas did not speak? Have you talked parlor politics with your friends? Have you a reputation for serious political involvement?"

She hardened her jaw. She had not expected a scolding from him, of all people, the most indulgent man she'd ever known. He'd been like a second father to her since Papa died.

"I'll answer my own questions. You have not. You are becoming conspicuous, my dearest Musette. It must stop."

She lifted her chin and stared over his shoulder.

Chamard left his comfortable chair to sit on the sofa beside her. He reached for her hand, but she pulled away from him. "None of that now," he said, and took her hand anyway. "Look at me, sweetheart."

She turned her face to him, but she kept her gaze on his necktie.

"Your mother knows you're headstrong and she might forgive me for the trouble you've made for yourself so far, but she will shake me by the scruff of the neck if I let you dig yourself any deeper."

She couldn't bear to look at him. She tried to tug her hand free, but he wouldn't let her.

"You see, don't you, that you endanger Toulouse as well as yourself? This bunch, the Knights of the White Camellia. They're a new group. I don't know what they're willing to do, but they are determined to restore the life they lost during the war. They will not let a woman, a Negro-sympathizing woman, stand in their way. You must keep your head down – I repeat, I do not know what they are capable of, but I know you endanger yourself going to these rallies."

She had to swallow and blink to control herself.

"And you endanger Thomas."

Startled, she looked at him then.

"Your partiality for him has also become a subject of gossip." He held his hand up as she began to protest. "Darling girl, it is very difficult to hide one's feelings when they are as strong as yours. White men have done terrible things to black men when they thought -- You know this. Black men must be seen to be sexless creatures in relation to white women."

She leaned into her hands, hiding her face. "I don't want him hurt."

When she gasped and gulped for air, Chamard wrapped an arm around her and pulled her close. "Of course you don't."

He rocked her as she sobbed. "Let it all out, sweetheart. Just let it out. I've got you."

She wept until her head throbbed and her diaphragm spasmed with hiccups. When she calmed enough to accept his handkerchief, Chamard told her quietly, "No one ever died of a broken heart, my dear. It will get easier."

"That's absurd. My heart is not broken. I'm merely overset."

"Of course you are, after such a day. Now. When the convention begins in the fall, I will take you to watch the debates if you like. But, Musette – " he took her by the chin and made her look at him – "you will not go to any more events where Thomas is present without me, understand? Josie will skin me alive if she finds out you were at the rally today. You have no consideration for an old man's dignity."

"Let's don't tell her then," Musette sniffled.

# Chapter Twenty

"I believe I hear our guests arriving," Garvey said.

"Yes, sir. I'll get the door."

Late as it was, Thomas opened the door to Valentine, Chamard, and Whiteaker. They settled in to talk over the debacle at the rally and Agent Witherspoon's response to it.

"He's a good man. It's just he's got to juggle the rights of the freedmen with the planters' demands for their own justice," Garvey said.

"I hate to think what this electioneering would have brought down on our heads without him and Major Bodell," Valentine said. "Every black man stuck his head up likely been killed."

Nobody contradicted him.

"So my tailor is off to New Orleans," Chamard said.

Valentine put on a doleful face. "With Mr. Moltrey gone, I don't know where we gone get your vests no more."

"Maybe we'll put a needle in your nimble fingers and see how you do," Chamard teased.

Long accustomed to the good-natured bickering of those two, Garvey cut in. "And Valmar is still moldering in a cell."

"Yes, sir," Thomas said. "At least he's still in jail. What is his legal status, Major Whiteaker. Do you know?"

Alistair nodded. "He's been arraigned, but Valmar's attorney has asked for more time to prepare his defense, and as far as the prosecuting attorney cares, he can have as long as he likes. Meanwhile, Valmar pleads he's too sick to be put out. The hole in his leg festered, you know, and as long as he's in jail, he's got the doctor and a deputy looking after him at parish expense."

"He's said nothing about his cronies, is that right?" Garvey said. "Hell of a thing, when you know a man is guilty as sin and can't do a thing about it."

If he had been inclined to bitterness, Thomas thought, the gall would be rising in his throat at the irony of these white men feeling helpless at an injustice. But these men were the good ones, the ones who tried to be fair as far as they could see it. Slave owners, yes, they had been. But they were trying.

"We are doing something about it, Garvey," the major said. "The judge will set a court date eventually. He won't be able to let this go, not with Witherspoon and Modell watching him. Chamard and I, we'll have a word with him, too."

"And the other men?"

"Fisher and Shipton are hiding out, or they've left the parish. Either way, nobody knows where they are."

"Shipton can't stay away forever. He's got family here, a few acres to tend," Garvey said.

Thomas wove his fingers together and leaned on his knees. "I don't mean to be cynical, but I don't have much expectation of justice for Annie and Alfie."

"I appreciate your acuity," Chamard said. "But don't give up hope. You have to play the long game, Thomas."

"Yes, sir. I understand. Change will take time."

The door to the sitting room swung open and Frederick Palmer stepped inside. "Gentlemen," he said, looking around the room. "It seems we're having something of a pow wow here." He sauntered in and took a chair. "Lily tells me you're all worked up about the to-do in town today."

Thomas kept quiet. It would be up to the white men to handle Palmer.

"Did you see the rally?" Garvey said.

"Rally? I thought it was a riot. Bunch of rabble, jawing low-lifes complaining, getting ahead of themselves."

"And the charging into the crowd with horses, the rifles firing?" Alistair asked quietly.

"Glad to see you got concerned citizens willing to keep the community in line."

"By assaulting innocent people."

Palmer snorted. "Don't know how innocent they were. Rioting in the streets."

Thomas stood up. He'd heard all he could take. "Good night, gentlemen."

"Don't rush off on my account, boy. I know you're something of a favorite around here. Everyone's pet nigger."

The silence was as intense as the cold hostility radiating from Thomas and his friends.

Palmer laughed. "Sorry. I see I've stepped on someone's toes. Next you'll tell me a Yank like me can't understand how you all get along down here. I'm sure you're right. Garvey, you got the good stuff hidden somewhere?"

"Good night, Thomas," Alistair said, releasing him from the awkward moment.

"I'll come out with you," Valentine said.

Garvey got out his bottle of scotch from behind a row of books and poured each of them a glass. Surely not Palmer's first of the day, Alistair thought, judging by the glaze in his eyes.

"So you were there," Alistair began. "As a stranger in town, I don't suppose you know who the 'concerned citizens' were."

"Oh, I met a few. They bought me a drink, I bought them a drink. Friendly fellows. Upstanding."

Lily stepped into the room, a line between her brows. Anxious, Alistair thought. Her husband had been drinking, and she knew what that could mean.

"Anything I can get you, Uncle Garvey?"

When she glanced at Alistair, he gave her the merest shake of his head. He didn't want her in here.

"Nothing, Lily darling," her uncle said. "Why don't you go on to bed."

She gave her husband a piercing look before she told them good night and closed the door.

They sipped in silence for a moment. Palmer grinned. "You're just dying for me to tell you their names, aren't you? Well, I don't mind. And neither do they, I reckon. Let's see. Pete Kresky. Charlie Dillinger. Michael something or other. Can't remember all of them. They're recruiting, you see. Thought I'd make a fine addition to their numbers."

"Recruiting." Chamard said. "Into the White Camellia, I suppose."

"Camellia, chrysanthemum, something flowery."

"And these are the men who rampaged on horseback through men and women on foot. Two women were seriously injured, Mr. Palmer."

"Oh, I doubt the fine fellows I met were involved in any rampage. The horsemen all wore masks, I understand," he said with a sly grin. "No idea who they were."

Garvey Bickell stood up. "Mr. Palmer -- "

"Oh, you must call me Frederick, Garvey. We're family after all."

Very deliberately, Garvey began again. "Mr. Palmer. You are new to St. James Parish. I appreciate you do not yet understand the tensions here. As long as you are lodged in my home, I will take it amiss if you consort with these criminals calling themselves the Knights of the White Camellia."

"Criminals?" Frederick laughed. "That's putting it rather strong, isn't it?"

Whiteaker stood up. In spite of this fascinating look into the mind and heart of Lily's husband, he'd had enough of the man's company.

Chamard stood too. "Some people would agree with you," he said quietly. "But you are in the home of a man whose principles do not extend to bigotry and injustice. Racism, I'm forcefully reminded tonight, is not confined to Southerners."

Chamard followed Alistair into the hallway where they found their hats on the side table. "See you tomorrow, Alistair," Chamard said and let himself out.

Lily was waiting for him in the shadows. "He's drunk, isn't he?"

"Close to it."

"He doesn't know anyone. He couldn't have anything to do with what happened at the rally."

"No. He didn't."

The light from the hall lamp was behind her and he couldn't read her face, but she must have seen something in his.

"What then? Something? Tell me."

"Only that he's become acquainted with some of the men in the White Camellia."

"Acquainted." She held his eyes a long time.

"They've asked him to join them."

She shook her head, disturbed. "He doesn't understand, that's all. I'll talk to him tomorrow."

Alistair touched her arm, the merest touch. "Lily. He does understand."

Lily pressed her fingers against her forehead. It must be difficult for her, finding new things at this late date to dislike about her husband. "It's not your fault," he murmured.

"No." She tried to smile for him. "Of course not. Alistair?"

"What is it?"

"About church tomorrow."

He'd dreaded this, that she'd insist on cutting off all contact with him, even in church. "You don't want me to come."

"Frederick mustn't think, he mustn't know . . . "

Alistair chucked her under the chin. "Lily, when he saw us together the first time, we were kissing. He knows."

She laughed on a sad little exhalation. "Of course."

He wanted to dip his head and kiss her on the forehead, just for that smallest contact. But it would not do.

"I won't come, Lily. Good night."

As he grasped the front door knob, she came up behind him and turned him to her. Quickly, lightly, she grasped his face and touched her lips to his. "Thank you."

He nodded, too moved to speak, and had to leave her standing in the doorway.

~~~

Monday morning, Thomas filed into the courtroom behind Whiteaker, Chamard, and Garvey Bickell, Valentine bringing up the rear. They seated themselves in the second row behind the prosecutor's table so that they could see Jacques Valmar on the other side of the room.

The benches filled, then men stood around the perimeter of the public area. Mostly white, as Thomas expected, but no longer all white as there would have been only two years ago. Cabel, Reynard, Smithy, John Carpenter, half a dozen other black men stood in twos and threes among those who'd arrived too late to get a seat.

Whiteaker had done the impossible: Valmar was to be tried for the murder of Alfie and Annie. Sheriff Paget had made it clear he thought there was no case for charging Valmar with murder. Insufficient evidence, he'd said. But Whiteaker had persuaded Major Bodell and the prosecutor John Marshal otherwise, and here they were.

A white man, black victims. A conviction was unlikely, Thomas knew. Plenty of white men were enraged charges had even been brought against a white man. The tension in the room showed in all the clenched jaws, the grim faces, the crossed arms.

"How did you do it?" Thomas whispered to Major Whiteaker as they waited.

"Well, the Army is here to see the law is exercised justly. That is there mission. That, and I called on Mr. Marshal at his second home and laid it all out for him, step by step."

"His second home?"

"The one up the road a piece where he lives now. Since his wife died, he stays there with Melanie Jane, the woman he raised five children with."

No doubt one of his slaves, ex-slaves, Thomas thought. "Black woman, black children."

Major Whiteaker nodded. "Freed her years ago and made sure their children went to school. He's sympathetic, Thomas, and Melanie Jane was a niece of Alfie and Annie's."

The jurors filed in, all white men. The deputies brought Valmar into the courtroom to sit at the defender's table. His hands were cuffed, and he limped heavily, the leg the major had sent a bullet through weakened, probably forever. Thomas did not grieve for him.

Before Valmar sat down he cast his eye over the citizens gathered to hear his trial and bestowed a cocky grin on some of the audience. Then he narrowed his gaze to Thomas and sneered.

"All rise," the bailiff called. Everyone stood, and the judge entered.

Judge Lafitte decreed that he would consider both charges against Valmar, disorderly conduct for the rioting around the Bickell house, and murder setting the fire that killed two old people. He explained that, and then observed, "I doubt considering the two events will confuse the jury. I have faith in them to sort it out," he said. "Let's proceed."

The disorderly conduct charge was dispatched first. Garvey Bickell was called for the prosecution to testify to having seen Valmar shot off his horse, prior to which he'd been rioting with two other men, shouting and firing their rifles into his house.

"Who was in the house at that time, Mr. Bickell?" Marshal asked.

"My niece, Lily Palmer, and her daughter Maddie, six years old, Dawn Bickell, also six years old, and her parents Rachel and Peep Bickell."

"Yet no one in your household was injured. I understand there was a lot of commotion, a lot of confusion during this episode. What evidence did you have to convince you shots had been fired into the house?"

"Broken window glass, Mr. Marshal. And two lead slugs in the dining room wall."

Mr. Chamard confirmed Garvey Bickell's testimony. Alistair Whiteaker then took the stand.

"I noticed Mr. Valmar walks with a limp, Major Whiteaker. Can you explain that?"

"I shot him."

Judging by the buzz in the room, some of the audience had not known that. Whiteaker continued with his account of the events of that afternoon.

Eventually, the defense began cross-examination. Valmar's attorney Mr. Pickering went over Garvey's testimony, then asked him, "That's a lot of Bickell's in the house, sir. They all your kinfolk, we may assume?"

"Not by blood, no sir."

Mr. Pickering pretended to be amazed. "All those Bickells and no blood kin?"

"Don't go acting stupid, Jacob. You know as well as everyone here it was common for the black folks to take the name of their master. You probably got a few dozen Pickerings in your neck of the woods. They all your younguns?"

Plenty of folks tittered and the judge mildly tapped his gavel. "I assume you're playing to the reporters here from New Orleans, Mr. Pickering. Please keep to the point."

They disposed of the charge of disorderly conduct and reckless endangerment of women and children that afternoon. The judge gave his instructions to the jury and sent them home for the night.

Nine o'clock the next morning, the charge of murder was tried. Whiteaker testified again, Dr. Huggins swore to hearing the same accusations from Annie, and then Thomas was called. This, a black man testifying in court as a witness, was one of the new wonders in the world. Not even a year had passed since the Civil Rights Act had determined a black man's eyes and ears worked as well as a white man's. And was as likely to be truthful.

Pickering tucked his thumbs into his suspenders. "Don't want you feeling nervous up here on the stand, boy. You ever been in a court of law in your life?"

"Yes, sir."

Pickering raised his eyebrows. "Oh. You mean to say you have been charged with a crime yourself."

"No, sir. I mean to say I was here yesterday."

Somebody snickered. If Thomas had to guess, he'd figure it was Cabel. But he could see the tight white faces of the jury. *Uppity*, that's what they'd be thinking. An uppity black boy talking back to his betters. But even Thomas knew the first rule in courtroom proceedings – don't ask a question you don't know the answer to, so if Pickering was embarrassed, he'd done it to himself.

When it was time for the summations, both sides were succinct.

"The evidence is circumstantial, yes," Mr. Marshall, the prosecutor, admitted. "But compelling nonetheless. We have the testimony of a dying woman that three men lit the fire that killed her husband Alfie and a short time later, Annie herself. She described three men wearing bandanas, one red, two blue. One with long yellow hair, another with a Yankee accent. Neither of those two is our defendant. No, Jacques Valmar is the arsonist who wore a red bandana that day."

The prosecutor walked to the evidence table and held the bandana aloft. "Furthermore, everyone who saw Mr. Valmar tied to the bell post covered in tar and feathers remembers how neatly his shiny new boots were placed next to him. Boots poor Annie Rivers described with her dying breath."

Marshall looked directly at the jurors. "Not two hours later, three men terrorized the home of Garvey Bickell. One with long yellow hair and a blue bandana. Another in a blue bandana. And Jacques Valmar, wearing a red bandana – and pointy boots.

"No question Mr. Valmar was at Mr. Bickell's home, recklessly firing shots into a house where women and children live. He has a ruined leg to prove it. And, gentlemen, there is no question that Valmar came to the Bickell's straight from burning a cabin to the ground with two old people in it. That man," he said, pointing to Valmar, "is a murderer."

Next Mr. Pickering delivered the defense's summation, hitting the points just as Thomas expected. "How many of you men got a bandana in your pocket?" he asked the jurors. "Any of them red or blue?" He pointed to juror number three. "Henry Spade, I notice you got long blond hair. You been setting any cabins on fire lately? As for the accent, maybe you good folks have noticed, our town is overrun with Yankees down here to take advantage of our difficulties. You've heard them on the streets, in the taverns; how many men you think are in this parish this very day with a Yankee accent?

"That leaves Mr. Valmar here. Anybody in the courtroom bought a pair of new boots the last few months? Got pointy toes, like the Texans sport?" Pickering himself raised his hand. "I got a pair like that myself. Oh, in the back – thank you, Fred – you got a pair like that, too."

The defense rested and Mr. Pickering returned to his seat with a smug smile directed at the prosecutor. The jury was sent into deliberations, then everyone stood as Judge Lafitte left the courtroom.

"Well," Major Whiteaker said. "Now we wait."

Thomas nor Valentine could go into the tavern or the café with their white friends. To try it would be like throwing matches into a puddle of kerosene with the town so riled up. They split up, Thomas and Valentine going to their own tavern on the other side of town.

Hours later, a boy sent by the bailiff ducked into the tavern and announced that the jury had been sent home for the night, court to commence at ten o'clock in the morning.

"Well, lets us go then," Valentine said.

"I'll come with you," Thomas said. "Fanny promised to meet me at mama's."

"Then Cabel and I are inviting ourselves to supper," Reynard said. "You ain't going nowhere on your own, not tonight, nor tomorrow night or the next neither."

They arrived just as dark fell. Thomas took Fanny to the back porch where he could put his arms around her in the shadows.

"Ahem," Mr. Chamard said tactfully. "Thomas, I'll stop by and tell Miss Musette how it went today."

Thomas quickly released Fanny and stepped away. "Yes, sir. I know she'll want to hear."

"Good night, then." He peered at Fanny. "Don't neglect your supper now."

She grinned at him. "No, sir. We're going right in."

Major Whiteaker stayed, along with Reynard and Cabel. Lily had finally convinced Rachel to set one table – no sense separating when they'd all spent the entire day together, had breakfast together, labored together. So they were a big crowd at the big table. After supper was cleared away, they re-convened.

Fanny acted as secretary and took down the names of the twelve jurors, most of them known to one or more of the people around the table.

Lily put Maddie to bed and returned to the dining room to sit with her hands in her lap. Her eyes kept straying to Alistair. Now and then they'd catch each other staring. Alistair would stare on, unblinking. Lily would give him a tense smile and look away. She had no business looking at Alistair Whiteaker. Married women did not look on other men like she looked at Alistair.

"I'm thinking Joe Jackson gone vote to convict," Reynard said. "He got him some brown children over to Vacherie."

"That don't persuade me," Cabel said.

Fanny dipped her old-fashioned quill in the ink. "I'll put a question mark next to his name."

"Ronald James. No question he'll vote to acquit."

"Agreed. Mickey Thorpe?"

"He'll acquit."

When they'd finished their tally, they had two question marks and ten definite acquittals.

"Likely those two will have visitors tonight," Alistair said.

Thomas nodded. It took Lily longer to understand. "They'd do that? Isn't that against the law, intimidating a jury?"

"Yes, ma'am," Thomas said. "It's against the law."

"But if they wear masks . . . " Garvey said.

"And they will." Thomas stood up. "I'll take you home, Fanny."

"No," Garvey said, shaking his head. "Fanny can sleep here tonight. You and Reynard and Cabel too. Not having any of you out there with all this going on."

The young men went out to the barn to bunk down. Garvey showed Fanny where she could sleep. That left Lily and Alistair alone. She should go to bed, too. In just a minute, she would.

"Did you see Frederick in town?"

"I did," Alistair said. "Having a drink with Charlie Dillinger and Pete Kresky. They're both in the White Camellia."

"And you're expecting trouble? That's why Uncle Garvey told Thomas and his friends to spend the night?"

Alistair's gaze was on her mouth as she talked. She was past blushing. She knew exactly what he was thinking because she wanted the same thing. But they were not going to be together, she and Alistair. Not without a divorce, and even then -- Alistair had a mother and a younger, unwed sister. They would not welcome a divorcee into the family.

She forgot to talk. He was silent. Her gaze ranged over his face from brow to chin. His eyes focused on hers, then again on her mouth.

Lily had never known a better man than Alistair Whiteaker. She'd never wanted a man as much as she wanted Alistair. And she might never kiss him again. Never touch him again.

Rachel passed through the room on her way upstairs. "Goodnight, Major, Miss Lily."

"Good night, Rachel," Lily said.

Alistair brought himself back to her question. "It would be decent tactics, for the Camellias to be up to nasty tricks tonight. If anyone on the jury is wavering, he'll probably change his mind if he sees a horde of men masked in white tearing around his house in the middle of the night."

"But no one here has a vote. There's no reason for them to come here."

"Don't expect so, but Thomas, the others and I will take turns patrolling out around the house so we don't get surprised. Probably nobody coming here, though, you're right."

"Alistair." She wanted to tell him so much. Thank you, I love you, I'm sorry . . . But she couldn't say any of those things.

Alistair let out a breath. "I better get outside. We'll be around if anything happens. I promise."

A short while later, Lily had stripped down to her slip to endure the heat of the night and was brushing out her hair when she heard the back door slam and heavy steps crossing the floor "Lily!" Frederick clomped through the house to her door and pounded on it. "Lily."

She grabbed a shawl to put around her shoulders and opened the door a crack. "Shhhh. You'll wake the whole house."

"Come out here, Lily."

He reeked of whiskey and stale sweat. "Go to bed," she hissed.

He leaned against her door. "I want to talk to you. You want, I'll be glad to come in there and talk. In fact," he said, and pushed the door open, "I think it's a fine idea. I'll come in there."

Lily ducked under his arm into the hallway. "Come on, then," she whispered. "We can talk in the kitchen."

She lit the lantern and gathered what she'd need for the coming hangover. She cracked an egg into a coffee cup, added salt, pepper and hot sauce, and handed it to him. "Drink this."

He poured it down his throat and gagged. "How much hot sauce you put in this, woman?"

She sat down and folded her hands on the table. "Frederick. These men you've taken up with. The Knights of the White Camellia."

"So your little friends been gossiping, have they? Well, what about them. Fine, upstanding members of the community, every one of them."

He wasn't drunk enough to slur his words at least. "No, Frederick, they are not. They are a bunch of mean-spirited juveniles, charging into people with their horses. They're reckless, and they think they don't have to answer to anyone."

"What rot, Lily. One of them is a lawyer, for Christ's sake."

"They're trouble, Frederick. They wish trouble on the people in this family."

"This family? You talking about the black boy you got all dressed up so he can spout nonsense to his people?" He leaned toward her and jabbed a finger at her. "What the hell's got into you, Lily?"

She quailed at the ugliness in his face, but she wouldn't back down. "These are good people, Frederick. Don't bring trouble here."

"They're not your family. They're Negroes. And here you are letting Maddie sleep with that little pickaninny – what kind of mother are you?"

Lily pushed her chair back and stood toe to toe with him. "The kind who has never struck her daughter in the face."

"I never did that."

"Yes, you did. And Maddie has not forgotten it."

"Is that what this is all about? This is why you scurried off, dragging Maddie with you to come down here and live with white trash and Negroes?"

Lily wanted to slap him. She could almost feel the impact of her palm on his face. Instead, she gripped her hands together.

"You don't belong here, Frederick. I want you to leave." Now he would hit her, she was sure of it. He was drunk, and she'd riled him. Well, let him. This time she would not take it quietly. She had two hands, two feet, fingernails. She could bite him if she had to.

"When I'm ready, we'll leave. You, me, and Maddie."

"I told you. I'm staying. Maddie's staying."

Frederick smiled at her, and that scared her. "You're my wife, Lily, darling. And I've missed you. I'll make it up to Maddie if she thought I was rough with her. When it's time, we'll leave and we'll be our own little family again. Tell me you don't want that, sweetheart, don't want to be happy like we used to be?"

He stepped close and put his hands on her arms. "Remember how happy we were?" He blinked his eyes slowly. Just how drunk was he?

"What are you doing here, Frederick? What do you want?"

"Right now I want to come back to that little bed you been sleeping in and remind you how good I can make you feel. That's what I'd like." He trailed his fingers across the side of her neck.

She shivered. "That's not going to happen. Sit down, Frederick."

Here was the Frederick she'd come to know. His face darkened and his mouth pursed. The handsome, dashing Frederick disappeared and this bully emerged.

"You little slut." He tightened his hand on her neck. "You been fucking that Whiteaker."

"Don't be vulgar, Frederick. And I have not been sleeping with Major Whiteaker."

"But you want to, don't you? You always liked a good fuck."

Lily pushed his hands away. "If that's the language you're going to use, I'll tell you good night."

Frederick raised his palms, immediately changing tactics. "No, no." He slid into a chair with the care of a man who knows his balance is impaired.

"I want you to leave, Frederick. I want a divorce, and I want you to leave."

He grinned at her. "No. I told you once. No."

"I won't be your wife again."

"So you said."

"Then what do you want? An easy life, living off Uncle Garvey?"

He snorted. "As if I'd stay on a little pissant farm like this, nothing but cows for company."

She waited, knowing what was coming.

"Soon as Bickell leaves you the property, I'll sell it. Then I'll have a stake. You and me and Maddie, we'll make a fresh start."

It was as Uncle Garvey – and she – had expected. She'd tell her uncle in the morning – he could not leave her the farm. Legally, that would be the same as handing it over to Frederick.

"Uncle Garvey has changed his mind."

"What do you mean? You're his kin."

He reached over the table, grasped her upper arm, and squeezed. "You better change his mind back, Lily Palmer. I want that stake."

"To do what with?"

"There's still gold in those California hills. Or I might buy myself a saloon in San Francisco. Make a fortune selling whiskey and playing cards."

Lily jerked her arm free. "You're not getting your stake from Uncle Garvey, Frederick. You might as well take yourself to California right now and try your luck at the gambling tables."

She didn't tell him she knew how to get him his stake. She didn't want him to have Alistair's money. She wanted him to just go.

Frederick scraped his chair back and grabbed her arm again. The pain was nothing. He was only bruising her, and she'd been bruised before.

"I told you. Change the old man's mind."

"I won't."

As soon as she heard the steps on the back porch, she knew it was Alistair. Her face burned. She hated for him to see her like this, her husband drunk and looming over her, hurting her. And she in only her chemise and a summer shawl.

"Mr. Palmer. You're home," Alistair said as he came in.

Frederick dropped Lily's arm. "As you see," he said with a smirk.

"I saw you in the courtroom today. What do you think of Valmar's chances?"

"So we're going to make polite conversation? I don't think so, Whiteaker. I'm having a talk with my wife. Nothing here any of your business."

Whiteaker walked over to the table and pulled out a chair. "I think this is very much my business."

Frederick scowled. "Lily, tell your lover-boy to get lost."

Alistair sat down. "If you'll take your seat, Mr. Palmer, we have business to discuss."

"Business."

"Yes. I was eavesdropping outside the window," Alistair said without a trace of embarrassment. "You want a stake. I want something, too."

"You want my wife. Well, you can't have her."

Alistair glanced at her. "Maybe, maybe not. Depends on Lily."

"You're talking about my wife," he snarled. "When I leave, she's going with me."

Lily turned to look him fully in the eye. "I am not, Frederick. You will leave here alone."

He gripped a handful of her hair. "Maddie is mine," he snarled. "I can take her anytime."

Alistair leapt up and started around the table. Frederick released her and stepped back, wary, maybe a little frightened.

Lily clasped her elbows to keep her hands from trembling. "We'll sit down now, all of us."

Alistair gave Frederick a look that would give any man cause to think twice about what he did next. Then he calmly returned to his chair as she and Frederick sat.

"You won't take Maddie," Alistair continued in a conversational voice, as if he hadn't just tacitly threatened Frederick. "I am going to make it worth your while to leave here, alone."

There he was, sitting at his ease, a day old beard on his face, his collar off and his shirt rumpled, but he was as cool and calm as if he were talking about buying a pig or a goat instead of a woman and her child. Lily felt a hysterical laugh bubbling up inside her and pressed her fingers to her mouth.

"What kind of man do you think I am?" Frederick's face flushed. She knew from experience he was going to get louder from here on.

Alistair answered quietly. "I think you're a man who wants to start a new life. California, Texas, Mexico. With money in your pocket."

"That's ridiculous. I'm not selling my wife and daughter." He flung his arm wide, making his point. "They're mine, and you're a damned scoundrel for suggesting they're for sale."

Alistair nodded. If he felt any shame at offering to buy her and Maddie, it didn't show.

" 'Sell.' That's one way to put it. I prefer to think of it as an incentive for you to leave Lily to live her own life while you go off and explore the possibilities of being a single man. With money in his pocket."

Lily watched Frederick's jaw clench. He had his pride, oh yes, Frederick had plenty of pride. Maybe the anger was burning off some of the alcohol. His eyes were furious, but they were clear now. Maybe he was seeing possibilities.

"Please, Frederick," she said softly.

Frederick snorted. "Please, Frederick," he mocked. "Please sell me to this man, and our daughter, too. What happened to the little mouse I married? You a strumpet now, Lily Palmer?"

Alistair leaned back in his chair, his hands seemingly at ease on the table, but she could see how white his thumbs were pressing into the wood.

"I'll thank you to be civil to Lily, Palmer."

"Or what? You'll play the hero?"

"Yes. I will. Here's the offer. You give Lily a divorce, sign over your rights to Maddie, and I give you $5,000."

Lily was stunned. Frederick was, too, his mouth open. Five thousand dollars.

Alistair stood up then. "Lily, you look dead on your feet. I think we're finished here."

She bobbed her head up and down. "Yes," she whispered. She quickly and quietly left the room, but she heard Alistair's last words.

"I'll give you a few days to think about it, Mr. Palmer. It's a big decision."

Dear Lord, she thought. He's really done it. He's offered to buy Frederick off. It was horrible, dishonorable, thrilling, and confusing.

# Chapter Twenty-One

It was a night to be abroad. The sky was clear, the moon full and bright. In groups of four and five, respected citizens of St. James and Ascension Parishes donned their white masks and knocked on the doors of those jurors who might be planning to convict Valmar of murder. The Knights of the White Camellia would not let that happen.

One of these visits was civil. "You got a nice place here, Mr. Banks. Two girls, a pretty wife. Know you want to keep them safe." In the same soothing tones, the masked leader said, "See you in court tomorrow. Know you'll do the right thing."

The Camellias visiting Joe Jackson however found him obstreperous. When they departed, they left Mr. Jackson in a heap out in front of his house, doubled over and bleeding.

~~~

Lily rose early, got Maddie up and dressed, and went downstairs to help Rachel fix breakfast for Thomas and his friends.

"Is Major Whiteaker coming in?" Lily asked when the men came into the kitchen, their hair still wet from washing up.

"Left about two this morning, Miss Lily," Thomas said. "After he woke Reynard for the next watch."

"In the dark?"

"Bright night, big moon," Reynard volunteered around a mouth full of cornbread.

Once everyone was fed and had left for town to await the verdict on Jacques Valmar, Lily wiped the table and emptied the dish pan. Her hands stilled as she hung her apron on a peg – those were Frederick's footsteps coming down the stairs. She dreaded seeing him this morning. Even Frederick, as much as he'd changed, would feel the humiliation of last night's offer. She wondered if he'd be hurt, or merely angry. Was he tempted? Five thousand dollars was a lot of money. A fortune. He could pay his passage to San Francisco and still have a very large stake to pan gold, or buy into a saloon, or just gamble.

What if he wouldn't go? What if he tossed Alistair's offer back in his face? Did he even think about what would be best for Maddie?

She put her apron back on, resigned to fixing his breakfast, but she heard him cross the hallway and go out the front door.

She let out a breath. He didn't want to see her this morning either. So maybe he was thinking about Alistair's offer. She put her hand on her forehead. If only, she thought.

~~~

Alistair tried not to fidget, waiting in the courtroom for the jury to return its verdict. Many of the men stood outside, smoking and debating. He preferred the quiet murmurs of the few men who sat around the courtroom, leaving him to his own thoughts.

His offer to Frederick Palmer might backfire. It was a terrible insult, after all, to give a man money to leave his family. That's why he'd offered him a fortune. If it'd been less, it might have been too easy to turn down. A man had his pride, and maybe, in spite of indications to the contrary, Palmer had some honor. What knotted his gut was the possibility that Palmer truly wanted Lily and Maddie with him, out of love, not possession. Alistair could hardly bear the tension of waiting him out, giving him time to imagine what five thousand dollars could do for him.

The bailiff strode through the courtroom to the outer door and hollered, "Ya'll come on. It's time." It wasn't even eleven o'clock. They hadn't deliberated long.

The room filled with surprising quiet and order, everyone having already said all they had to say. Now they'd hear what the jury said.

Valmar was brought in, cuffed, but smiling and cocky. Everyone rose and the judge took his seat.

Alistair eyed the faces of the jurors as they were brought in. Joe Jackson, one of the men Fanny had labeled with a question mark, had a bruised jaw, a split lip, and sore ribs judging by how stiffly he took his chair.

The judge polled the jurors, On the charge of disorderly conduct and reckless endangerment – twelve guilty votes. On the two charges of murder – twelve to acquit.

Alistair of course was not surprised. Thomas gripped his pencil tightly, but Chamard leaned over and spoke in his ear. Thomas took a breath and nodded, the pencil going in his pocket.

The judge had his sentencing already prepared, for he surely was not surprised either. "For disorderly conduct and reckless endangerment, Jacques Valmar, you are sentenced to time served and the fine of $20. Since you are acquitted of all other charges, you are free to go." He pointed his gavel at Valmar. "Do not let me see you in my courtroom again."

Valmar turned around and found Thomas. "Hey, boy. Now you see what messing with a white man gets you." He laughed, showing his yellow teeth. "Nothing!"

The judge called to the bailiff over the noise of the courtroom. "Get him out of here."

The bailiff and the deputy took Valmar by the arms and hustled him out.

There were a lot of pleased faces and satisfied grins among the men making their way out of the courtroom. Alistair saw Percy Randolph, the white candidate for the convention, pull Chamard aside and talk earnestly in his ear. Randolph thought Chamard might vote for him for the convention, did he? That was certainly a miscalculation on Randolph's part. Or maybe he was inviting a fine upstanding citizen like Chamard to join the White Camellia.

Alistair smiled grimly, aware he would not be invited into their pure white ranks. His lineage was as white as any of theirs, whiter than some, he supposed. His service as a Confederate officer was lauded. But he had built a school, hired a black teacher, supported Thomas Bickell, and occasionally gave his opinion that the old ways had to change.

Chamard smiled, patted Randolph on the back, and offered him a fine cigar out of his breast pocket. Chamard never made an enemy if he could help it, so he left Mr. Randolph feeling benignly disposed with his opinion of himself as a mighty fine fellow intact. But he would not have persuaded Chamard, Alistair was sure of that.

Outside, the sun was blinding. Alistair put his hat on, thinking how good a glass of whiskey would be right now.

Thomas came to stand at his elbow. "Thank you. It meant something, bringing the man to trial even if he was acquitted."

"Yes. It's a step," Alistair said.

Thomas inclined his head toward his friends. "We're going back to campaigning. No speeches scheduled today, just seeing people where they work, talking, listening."

"You three stick together, Thomas, at least until after the election," Garvey said. "A lot of people resent a black man being involved in Valmar's troubles. And the way Valmar was taunting you – you be careful."

"Yes, sir. I'm aware."

"Kind of funny, considering Thomas wadn't even there the night we tarred and feathered the man."

Thomas glared at Reynard. "Your big mouth," he muttered.

Reynard bit his lip and looked at the dirt.

Alistair laughed out loud. "I didn't hear that."

The River Queen, the least seedy bar in town, buzzed with talk of the trial and who said what and why. Alistair and Chamard and Garvey took a small table in the back, lucky to get a chair at all. Garvey wanted coffee, it not yet eleven o'clock. Chamard ordered brandy, and Alistair had a small carafe of red wine. They'd do precious little talking in here with the noise level so high.

They sipped their drinks, listened in on their neighbors' too-loud conversations, and looked around.

Alistair's gaze fell on Frederick Palmer at the poker table. He had sold his house, word was, so he had money burning holes in his pocket. He couldn't have got more than a few hundred for that little house, according to Garvey. If Alistair was lucky, Palmer would lose every dollar and be desperate for the "incentive" money dangling in front of him.

Next to Palmer sat a pretty woman with dark hair and white shoulders displayed in a revealing red dress. She leaned over and spoke into Palmer's ear. He laughed and put his arm around her. Not new acquaintances then? Maybe she'd like a man with five thousand dollars and big plans for California.

"I said, it's too loud in here for me. You ready to go?" Garvey asked.

"Sure."

Outside Alistair heaved a breath in relief to be out of that din.

"Our Mr. Palmer was in there, did you see?" Chamard asked.

"Must have walked all the way in to town," Garvey said, "cause he didn't borrow any of my stock."

"He planning to stay?" Chamard said.

"I'm sure as hell not giving him any reason to," Garvey said. "Lily neither."

Alistair did not offer an opinion.

~~~

Not so many hours later, Alistair arrived at the Bickell place just before dusk, sick at heart and dreading the moments to come. Lily, Rachel and the children were busy on the other side of the barn chasing fire flies and didn't see him. Peep was just inside the barn putting tackle away. Garvey was tending to his mule at the trough.

And there was Thomas on the porch, sharpening knives.

"Evening, Alistair," Garvey said as he set a bucket of water down. And then he gave Alistair a keen look. "What's wrong?"

Alistair glanced over his shoulder at the women and kept his voice low. "It's Fanny Brown, Garvey. Somebody got her on the way to your place after school."

The old man sagged against the mule. "My Lord. She's dead?"

"No. There are some who'd say this is a worse fate for a woman than being dead, but I don't hold with that."

"Raped, then."

Alistair nodded. "And beaten."

"Good God, Alistair." Garvey wiped a hand across his face. "Why would anybody do such a thing?"

"Thomas had body guards, and Fanny didn't."

"So they went after her to get to him."

"You want me to tell Thomas, or would you rather?"

Garvey breathed in and out. "I think we better tell Peep."

Garvey called Peep over. When he told him, Peep reared his head back like he'd been slapped.

As Peep walked to the back porch to tell Thomas, Garvey said, "She wasn't supposed to come out on the road by herself. We told her and told her. Not with things riled up like this."

"She wanted to know about the trial, I expect. Thomas not staying out at the old cabin anymore?"

"He is, but he come by here late, and Rachel wanted him home for a night."

Thomas set the blade he was honing aside when his father came up on the porch. A moment later, he leapt to his feet, knocking his chair over backwards.

Peep held his hand up to slow him down, but Thomas was off the porch and striding for Alistair. Rachel was running by now, running for Peep. When she knew the worst, she leaned into Peep and he held her close.

"Where is she?" Thomas demanded.

"My house. Musette is with her. She's being taken care of."

"I need the wagon," Thomas said to Garvey as he strode for the barn.

"I'll go with you," Rachel said. "Mr. Bickell, we're bringing her back here. Son, let your daddy hitch up the mule. You put your shoes on. I'll get blankets for the wagon." Thomas sprinted for the house, Rachel hurrying behind him.

"Thank you, Garvey. With Rachel here, I figure this is the best place for her."

"She ought to be here, Alistair. She and Thomas, well, you can see how Thomas feels about her."

Garvey went in the barn to help Peep with the wagon. Alistair turned and found Lily staring at him. "What's happened?"

Alistair heaved a sigh. He did not want to tell her this. He didn't want to tell anyone this.

"It's Fanny. She was attacked after school, probably on her way here."

Lily's hand flew to her mouth.

"She's hurt bad, Lily, but she can get over this. She's alive. She's young."

Would she let him take her in his arms? He could hold her, smooth the hair off her forehead. But it was not his place to comfort another man's wife. "Thomas and Rachel will bring her here."

"Where did it . . . Who found her?"

"Musette DeBlieux. She stayed in town visiting friends after the trial. She came back late in the afternoon and found her on the road, not far from the schoolhouse. Musette's with her at my place."

She put her hand on his forearm. "Thank you, Alistair."

He slid his arm through her grasp to take her hand. "For bringing bad news?"

"For being kind. For caring."

She squeezed his hand. "I'll get a bed ready."

He watched her take the girls inside before he mounted his horse. It'd be dark by the time Thomas and Rachel got to his place. He'd go ahead and collect some lanterns to light the way.

He'd seen no sigh of Palmer here on the farm. Had her sorry husband not come home? Did she wonder where he was?

He'd give the man another couple of days. By then, Palmer should have made up his mind. Lily could be free of him as soon as they got the papers made out, signed, and registered.

After that -- he'd have to give her some time before he asked her to marry him. He didn't want her to feel as if he'd bought her like a pig in a poke.

~~~

Musette lit the lamp on the other side of the room from where Fanny lay. The girl was awake, but she would not talk to either her or Carrie Ann.

They had washed her face and hands, took off her shoes and the ruined dress, and put her to bed. Musette had insisted she drink a cup of strong coffee with plenty of sugar in it. She didn't know if that was the right thing to give her, but women were not accustomed to brandy, her father's and Mr. Chamard's favorite remedy for anything from a summer cold to snakebite. Since the coffee, Fanny had rolled away from them on the bed and turned toward the wall.

They'd found her on the way back from town. Musette had taken Carrie Ann along as usual, and because Mr. Chamard insisted these days, she also had Cicero with her. And they had needed him.

Musette had spied a bump in the road ahead and squinted. "What is that?" she'd said.

Cicero jerked the horses to a stop and leapt out of the wagon. "Lord, Miss Musette," Carrie Ann cried. "That's a body."

Musette approached cautiously, afraid it was a dead body, and ashamed of herself for not rushing forward to see for herself.

"She's alive!" Cicero shouted.

Musette rushed on, Carrie Ann at her heels. The woman was folded in on herself, her skirts spread around her. Cicero knelt and gently turned her over.

"Oh no. Oh no. It's Fanny Brown," Carrie Ann said.

Her face was swollen. Her bodice was ripped and her petticoat was stained.

Musette knelt close to her and took her hand. "Fanny, can you hear me?"

Fanny didn't even look at her, at any of them. "I think she's in shock," Musette said.

"I reckon you right," Cicero said and picked Fanny up out of the dirt.

The three of them had gotten Fanny into the carriage and taken her to the nearest home, which was Alistair Whiteaker's.

Musette sat by the bed, wondering how long it would take for Thomas to get here. She had hated Fanny Brown, but this was heartbreaking. She seemed so young, so small, lying there in the bed. Everything ahead of her – a woman of accomplishment, to be married to an extraordinary man – a future full of promise. Who knew how this would change everything? She couldn't hate her, not anymore.

She got up to stare out the window at the setting sun and thought, But why should it change everything? Fanny had done nothing wrong. Musette couldn't believe Thomas, not Thomas Bickell, would turn from a woman he loved because she'd been raped.

She looked back at the still form under the sheet and found Fanny trembling. She strode the few steps to the bed. "Are you cold, Fanny?" She pulled up the counterpane and tucked it under Fanny's chin. "I could ring for another cup of hot coffee. Would you like that? Fanny?"

Fanny shook her head and closed her eyes. Musette understood Fanny had no family, but she had Thomas, and she'd have Rachel and Peep, and little Dawn. "Fanny, Major Whiteaker has gone to Garvey Bickell's. Thomas is coming for you."

Fanny shook her head violently. "No!"

That was the first word she'd spoken since they'd found her crumpled on the road.

"Not Thomas. Don't let Thomas in here."

Musette straightened up and sighed. "I'm sorry," she murmured. "I truly am, Fanny." She sat on the edge of the bed and took Fanny's hand.

"Everything will be all right. In the long run, everything will be all right. I'm sure of it." She squeezed Fanny's hand and because Fanny didn't pull away, she stayed on the bed and didn't let go.

# Chapter Twenty-Two

Thomas strode into the guest room to see Musette on the bed holding Fanny's hand, but Fanny immediately turned away and struggled to pull the covers over her head.

But not before he saw -- her entire face was swollen, her eyes blackened, her lip torn. Thomas reeled, the rage so strong in him that for a moment everything went black.

It took a few seconds for Musette to get out of his way, and he took that time to calm himself. No need to scare her. "Fanny." He put his hand on her shoulder.

She stiffened.

"Fanny, it's me." Gently he tugged at the sheet.

"Go away, Thomas."

He knelt at the side of the bed. "I'm not going away, Fanny. Mama's here, and Daddy. We're taking you back with us."

Fanny clutched the sheet, pulling it tightly over her head.

Rachel touched his shoulder. "Let me do this, son. You go on downstairs. I'll call you when I need you."

Outside the bedroom, Musette waited for him. "I'm sorry, Thomas."

He nodded, hardly seeing her. He waited in the hallway with his father and felt about as useful as a broken wheel. At first he heard his mother's voice murmuring, soothing. Then he heard a single wail from Fanny and whirled around to go in, but his daddy stopped him.

"She don't want you in there now. Just wait. Give her time."

Rachel called out, "Peep. Get me a basin of water."

"I'll get it," Musette said.

Thomas paced. Alistair Whiteaker came in from the stables and put his hand on his shoulder. "Come downstairs. We'll have a brandy while we wait."

Thomas sat in Major Whiteaker's study, sick with helplessness, the cut glass snifter forgotten in his hand.

Finally, Rachel came to the door. "Let's get her home. I can't do more until I got my needle and my ointments."

Thomas's stomach flipped over when she said needle. Where did Fanny need stitches?

Fanny stood behind Rachel, wrapped in a blanket, her head bent. Thomas rushed to her so she could lean against him, but she drew back.

"Fanny?" he said softly. She wouldn't look at him, wouldn't even raise her head. He didn't know what she was feeling -- what man could? -- but he knew she was hurting. He put his arm around her shoulder and kept it there even as she stiffened. She didn't have to look at him if she didn't want to, but he wouldn't let her push him away.

Alistair sent three men with lanterns to escort them all the way back home.

When they got there, Fanny stumbled getting out of the wagon. Thomas caught her up and carried her in. Her weight pulled at his bayonet wound, but he didn't care. She wasn't fighting him, and he thought that was a good sign.

"I made up the bed in Thomas's room, Rachel," Lily said. "And there's hot water on the stove."

Thomas carried her through the kitchen to his room where the window was open and the breezes brought in the smell of roses planted on the side of the house. He set her down gently and pushed the hair off her forehead.

Fanny put her hands over her face. "Go away, Thomas. Please."

He bent over and kissed the fingers covering her bruised eyes. "I will, Fanny, for now."

Lily and his mother crowded him out then with basins and water and clothes and the bottle of whiskey and the sewing basket. "Go on, son."

He waited in the kitchen with his father and Mr. Bickell. Nobody had a thing to say. They sat with their hands on the table, each lost in his own thoughts.

When Rachel came into the kitchen, Thomas jumped up.

"No, Thomas. She doesn't want to see you tonight. Let her sleep. Tomorrow is soon enough."

"Mama, I just want to – "

"No, son. Leave her be."

Thomas looked to his father. Peep nodded. "Let her alone tonight, son."

"I'll stay with her, Thomas. If she wakes in the night, I'll be right there."

Mr. Bickell stood and stretched his neck. "Rachel, where you putting Lily tonight?"

"Miss Lily gone sleep in our bed. Peep, you put up that old cot in Mr. Bickell's room for you to sleep on."

"All right. I'll see to it."

Thomas made himself a pallet in the hallway outside the room where Fanny lay. He didn't sleep much, but not because the floor was hard and the hallway airless. When his Mama came out of the room to see to breakfast, Thomas played possum. When he heard her rattling around in the kitchen, he opened the door carefully and slipped in.

Fanny was lying in a shaft of early morning light. The window was open, the curtains moving gently in the breeze.

Fanny clapped her hands over her face. "Go away. I told you. Please."

Thomas knelt next to the bed and gently pried a hand away from her face. She tried to tug free, but he didn't let go. "Fanny. It's me. Why do you think you have to hide from me?"

"You know why."

"I admit I've seen you looking prettier than you do right now." That attempt to lighten the mood fell flat.

"I'm not talking about my face." Her voice was so low he had to bend closer to hear her.

Thomas took both her hands in his. "I won't pretend I don't know what you mean, Fanny, but listen to me. It doesn't matter. I'm still going to ask you to marry me."

She stared at him from her swollen eyes. "You were going to ask me to marry you?"

"Didn't you figure that out? And there is no past tense to it, Fanny. I am going to ask you to marry me. Soon as the election is over in September."

"Thomas, I might be . . . I could be . . . "

He'd already thought of the worst. No, if Fanny had died, that would be the worst. But it could happen – Fanny could be pregnant. It had taken him most of the night to get the bile out of his throat thinking she might have to carry a white man's child. She didn't have a single bit of family left in this world, but Fanny would not have to raise a child alone.

"You might be carrying a baby, I know. Well, if you are, then our first child's going to be a little white-skinned savage. We'll have to fuss at him to eat his peas just like we will the rest of the children we'll have together. He'll be a child with a mama and a daddy who love him."

Fanny began to cry and he gathered her into his arms. "Scootch over so I can hold you." They lay side by side in that patch of sunlight, Thomas still except for the occasional kiss to the top of her head. After Fanny fell asleep, Thomas couldn't keep the fear from creeping in.

He'd made a hell of a promise just now. Raise the child of some man who'd raped Fanny? He'd have to grow a bigger heart, that's all there was to it. Just as Fanny wouldn't be the first black woman to bear a white child she didn't want, he wouldn't be the first black man to find room in his heart for the poor child that nobody, *nobody* else, wanted.

~~~

Thomas closed the curtain so the sun wouldn't beat down on Fanny and eased off the bed, careful not to wake her. He could hear Cabel and Reynard in the kitchen, waiting for him. They had to ride to the south end of the parish today where he'd talk and shake hands and talk some more. Only four more weeks.

He came home about dusk, sweaty, itchy, and grimy. He didn't care about that though and went straight to Fanny's room.

"Hi," he said.

"Hello, Thomas."

He stood there a moment, uncertain, because there was no welcome in her face. He stepped into the room. "Are you in pain?"

She turned her face to the window. "A little."

He pulled the chair up to the bedside. "You want Mama to get you something? She probably got some laudanum, or something."

"I don't want anything."

Her hand remained inert in his.

"Fanny?"

He'd thought they were all right when he left this morning. He'd told her they'd be married, they'd raise a white child if they needed to. What else could she want from him?

"I'm tired, Thomas." She scrunched down in the bed and turned toward the wall.

"Fanny?"

When she didn't answer him, he bit his lip. He had no idea what to do now.

"I'll check on you later, then."

Rachel had him a plate waiting when he went to the kitchen. "You gone be traveling in the dark again, son. I don't like that."

"Mama, I'm not leaving Fanny tonight."

His mother looked at Peep sitting at the table with a piece of pie in front of him. "It's all right, Mother," Peep said. "Cabel and Reynard out in the barn, and we armed like we ready to fight off a whole army. He can stay one more night."

"Wash up, then, son, and eat your dinner."

He came back scrubbed and hungry and sat down across from Peep.

"Tell me where all you been, who you talked to," Peep said.

Thomas pulled out his list of plantations and farms and together they checked off the ones he'd visited today. They talked over the questions people were asking, totted up the numbers of voters they could expect on election day.

"Word is, Daddy, that if you think you got a hundred votes promised to you, you better cut that about in half because people don't go to the polls like they say they will, or they get sick, or the mule throws a shoe."

"Half? That can't be right."

"I hope it isn't. We got more black people in these two parishes than white. If we can just get them to the polls, we'll beat Percy Randolph."

# Chapter Twenty-Three

It was getting late. Frederick should have left town much earlier to walk all the way back before dark. But he didn't really want to see Lily. She looked at him like he was some kind of insect that crawled out from under a rock. He didn't deserve that. Why, he hadn't said a word to her about braining him over the head so hard he'd had a fierce headache for days and his ears had rung for weeks.

"Oh no no no," she'd said when she saw him, like she'd seen a ghost.

Maybe she'd thought she killed him. He hadn't thought of that. And then didn't waste any time snagging herself another man. Alistair Fucking Whiteaker.

So, he decided, this would be the second night he didn't go home. Let her think about that.

He wrinkled his nose. He'd slept in his clothes last night in the hotel across the street. Didn't matter in the River Queen Saloon whether he smelled or not – the whole place smelled of spilt liquor, cigars, and working men.

"Deal me in," he said as he took his seat at Juliana's table. Poker went on around the clock here. He kept his hand in the game and sipped James Pepper whiskey.

He'd thought the liquor would settle him down, but it only burned deep in his gut. That damned Southern blue-blood and his money. The gall of the man, trying to buy Lily and Maddie from him. What kind of man did he think he was?

And Lily. She'd probably put him up to it. What had happened to her? She used to be so sweet. Biddable, that's what she'd been when he married her. And back when Maddie was small, there'd been nothing too good for her husband – she'd actually said those words to him. And cooked him his favorite meals, kissed him when he came in after working all day, sang while she washed the dishes.

Frederick's heart squeezed for a moment. It hadn't been like that in a long time.

She'd changed, Lily had, that's what the problem was.

"Card, Mr. Palmer?" Juliana said. He eyed her through the cigar smoke, pretty as a picture in her red satin dress, her bosom hardly covered by the black lace of the bodice.

"Two," he said and looked over his new cards.

He wasn't blameless, he supposed, but it does something to a man to have his livelihood pulled out from under him. The company should have seen it coming, the orders for shoes drying up with the war over. They should have made provisions for him, one of their top salesmen to the U. S. Army.

He'd drunk too much, he'd admit it. But dammit, Lily was his wife. She knew he was upset about taking a cut in pay, damn near laid off completely. "You're drunk," she'd say and get all stiff when he touched her.

"You win again, Mr. Palmer." Juliana gave him a smile and a wink as she shuffled the cards for the next deal.

"You're pretty good with those cards, Miss Juliana," he said.

She raised her eyebrows at him. "I'm pretty good at lots of things."

He laughed. He had no doubt she was as professional upstairs in the little bedrooms as she was here at the poker table.

After a couple more hands, Juliana stretched her arms overhead, displaying her bosom to good effect. "That's it for me, gentlemen," she said. "Thank you for such challenging play." She smiled at every man at the table and pushed her chair back.

As she passed behind Frederick's chair, she leaned in to his ear. "You played enough, Mr. Palmer? I'm mighty thirsty."

What could it hurt to buy the lady a drink? He had a pocket full of money from selling the house; he could afford to be generous.

They sat at a little table in the corner where they could hear each other over the usual din of men happy in their cups.

"Let's get acquainted," she said as he sat down.

"I thought I knew you pretty well," he said, giving her bosom a look.

She laughed. "Not as well as I'd like. There's more to me than a red satin dress, however little it leaves to the imagination."

Frederick held two fingers up to the bartender.

"You've certainly stimulated my imagination."

"Any time you want the real thing, Mr. Palmer," she said, her voice the sultriest thing he'd ever heard.

"Let's just have a drink," he said. "Get acquainted, like you said." He was not a whoring kind of man. Never had been. But it would serve Lily right, looking at him like he was a bug. And turning Maddie against him, too.

"I'll tell you something, you tell me something," Juliana said.

"All right. Tell me something."

She leaned in as if she had a great secret to share. "I'm going to California," she whispered in his ear." She sat back and added in a normal voice, "Soon as I get enough money."

He leaned forward in his chair, his eyes on hers.

"I got a friend in San Francisco," she said, "wrote me there ain't enough bars in town for all the men pouring in with money in their pockets. I aim to start my own place."

"What do you know about running a bar?"

"I been around bars all my life. I know everything I need to know and then some."

She smiled at the bartender when he brought their drinks. He gave her a wink and retreated to the bar.

"Now you. Tell me something."

"I'd rather hear about your bar."

Juliana beamed at him. A genuine smile this time. "All right. What would you like to know?"

He didn't know where to start. He wanted to know everything. Could she run all the gambling tables, did she know all the games, all the tricks? Would she keep girls for the rooms upstairs? And how much money did it take to buy a saloon and stock it with every kind of whiskey.

"You talking about a bar like this one?" he asked.

She looked around. "The River Queen ain't a bad place. I can do better though." She waved a hand in front of her face. "At least keep the place aired out."

They'd finished their third drink when Juliana stood and held out her hand. He followed her up the stairs into one of the little rooms.

# Chapter Twenty-Four

Thomas came back to the house every evening just before dark. He knew he should go on to the old cabin, but he had to see Fanny. Somebody had shot at him two days ago when he was on the other side of Donaldsonville. It was just a pot shot, didn't even come close to him or to Reynard or Cabel. They could have shot him easy any day for weeks now. They just meant to scare him.

And they had. He was cautious now, waiting in the bushes for half an hour before he took the turn off to home rather than going on to the cabin. Nobody followed him. Nobody knew he was here.

He wished he could stay with Fanny during the day. He wanted to, but he only had three more weeks to campaign. Besides talking the live long day, he had to keep up with the proposals coming from the Republican Party as well as keep an ear open for dirty tricks and last minute strategies coming from Percy Randolph.

If Fanny had smiled since the attack, it hadn't been when he was around. Give her time, his mother said. Well, he would.

He sat with her in the evening. Read to her. Told her everything he heard about the convention coming up. Now and then she'd say, "I see." That's all. And she wouldn't even let him sit next to her much less let him touch her. What else was he supposed to do?

Well, he hadn't tried flowers. He could do that.

"Where you going, Thomas?" Rachel said Sunday morning.

He ran a hand over his hair. "I'm going out to pick flowers. You don't mind me cutting your roses, Mama."

She tipped her head to the side. "Roses are nice."

"What?" he said. She was looking at him like maybe they weren't so nice.

"Fanny's been hiding in that room a solid week. Might be she'd like to go out and look for wildflowers. With you."

"Hiding?"

"Why you think she didn't go to church this morning?"

The heat rushed into his face and he looked at his shoes. "I thought maybe it hurt her to walk."

Rachel tipped her head to the side, looking at him. "I didn't think I raised a stupid child."

Thomas lifted his hands, helpless, mystified. "Just tell me, Mama. What am I supposed to do?"

"Get her out of this house. Make her smile."

His hands on his hips, he contemplated the floor. "All right."

Before he turned to go get her, Rachel handed him a basket. "Here. Let her fill this. Don't matter with what – flowers or butterbeans. Just get her doing something."

Thomas tapped on the door. "Come in," he heard.

Fanny was sitting in the chair, facing the window, her hands in her lap.

"Hi," he said. Should he come in and sit a while? Ask her what she was thinking about just sitting there?

He perched on the side of the bed. "What are you thinking about?" Was his voice gentle enough? Too gentle?

Fanny looked at her hands and then back out the window. "Nothing."

"I don't see how it could be nothing."

She kept a steady gaze on something outside. In spite of himself, he was getting annoyed. "You have to talk to me, Fanny. We're going to be married. We're going to spend the rest of our lives together. You have to talk to me."

"I'm not marrying you, Thomas."

"What?"

Now she looked at him. "I'm not marrying you. I'm not marrying anybody."

"That's ridiculous."

Well, that was a mistake. He could see that immediately by the way her face went hard and blank. He shook his head.

"Fanny, please explain this to me."

She breathed in and out. "I'm not marrying anyone."

"You said that. This is because of what those men . . . did to you?"

"You can't even say it, Thomas. Rape. That's what they did."

"Why does that mean you can't marry me? I told you it doesn't matter. I meant it."

"It matters to me."

Her back was straight and stiff. He was not doing this right.

He had their future all mapped out. He would be a delegate to the state convention. They would marry. He would become a lawyer. They would have kids, and if the first one was from . . . this, then they'd handle it, together. All of that future had Fanny right in the middle of it.

He closed his eyes. He breathed in. Fanny was going to marry him. They just had this bad patch to get through.

He reached for her hand. She resisted, but he insisted. "Fanny. I'm just a man. I don't know what to do for you. All I know is that I love you and you love me. For now, will you please just – let's just enjoy the morning. Come outside. Mama needs that basket filled up."

The tension in her arm relaxed a bit. She quit tugging her hand away from his.

"Filled up with what?"

"Butterbeans, I think."

She blinked. He'd made her tear up. But at least she wasn't so stiff.

"Well, then," she said. "Let's go pick butterbeans."

It wasn't the best time of day to be out picking beans. The sun was hot enough to fry an egg, but it was a little basket. They had it filled up pretty quick.

"Come on down to the river," Thomas said. "We can get a breeze, maybe find a patch of shade."

They left the basket on the back stoop and ambled down the lane. Thomas offered his arm like he was some grand gentleman and she took it.

He didn't feel any need to make conversation. It just felt good to have her walking along beside him. She seemed more herself this last half hour. Mama had been right. She'd needed to get out.

He squeezed her arm next to his ribs and tried a smile. Instead of an answering smile, she teared up and looked away. He slid his hand down to grip hers and held it tight as they walked along.

They were in the lane that divided Toulouse from Cherleu, Mr. Chamard's property. Shade from the sycamores and bay laurel kept the sun from baking their brains. Ahead of them, where the lane met the stables behind the DeBlieux house, Mr. Chamard and Musette DeBlieux were walking their horses toward the stables.

"Good afternoon," Mr. Chamard called. "Thomas, Fanny," he said, his horse's nose companionably hooked over his shoulder.

"Miss Musette, Mr. Chamard, how do you do?" Thomas said.

Fanny's grip tightened on his hand.

"I am glad to see you recovering, Fanny," Musette said.

"Thank you for the flowers, Miss DeBlieux."

"You're welcome, of course."

"We're just coming home from a ride," Mr. Chamard said. "Went as far as Alistair's but he wasn't home to offer us a lemonade."

"I won't keep you, sir. You'll be thirsty."

"I am indeed," Chamard said. He turned his horse to take her to her oat bag. "Come on, Sugar."

"How are you, Thomas?" Musette blurted.

He smiled at her. "I'm fine, Miss Musette. We're headed for the river to catch the breeze."

She gave him one of those over-bright smiles. "Give me a hand up, Thomas?"

It was only a few yards to the stables, but if she wanted to ride. "Of course."

He stepped up to Musette's horse and cupped his hands for her foot. She placed her hand lightly on his shoulder and he lifted her into the saddle.

"Thank you," she said. She hesitated before she rode off. "Fanny, I'm very glad to see you out and feeling better."

Thomas took hold of Fanny's hand again. When they were nearly to the river, Fanny said, "She's in love with you."

When he didn't answer, she said, "You know that, don't you?"

He shook his head, uncomfortable. "She's just lonely. She'll get over it."

"Maybe."

They walked a few steps. "She should marry Major Whiteaker," Fanny said. "I think he's lonely, too."

Thomas smiled. "I think Major Whiteaker has designs on our Mrs. Palmer."

"But she's married."

"Yeah. He knows that. At least his head does. His heart, though." He gave her hand a squeeze and smiled at her. "You women, niggling your way into a man's most private organ."

"That's your most private organ?" Fanny said and laughed at him. Maybe he'd get another laugh out of her before he took her home.

# Chapter Twenty-Five

Alistair couldn't sleep. What if Palmer turned the offer down? What if he really cared for Lily and Maddie? What if he had some honor after all?

He stayed away. It was what Lily wanted. What he ought to do. And if he didn't press Palmer for an answer, well, then, he wouldn't get a no, would he?

He kept up with Fanny, getting reports from his own servants and from Chamard. But Fanny didn't know that. He wanted her to be well, to know she had friends. He really should stop by to see her.

Anxiety gnawed at him as he hitched his horse to the rail behind the Bickell's house – maybe he should have offered Palmer $8,000.

"Settle yourself in the shade, P.G." He waited while his hound circled a couple of times before he lay down. "Good boy."

He retrieved two books from his saddlebag and knocked on the front door.

Lily answered his knock. He took his hat off. "Hello, Lily."

She looked worn down. Like she wasn't sleeping well, either. And she wasn't used to this infernal heat.

"He isn't here."

"I didn't come to see Garvey."

"No. I mean my husband isn't here."

He didn't like her calling him 'my husband.' She could just say 'Mr. Palmer,' couldn't she?

"I came to see Fanny."

Lily's face flushed. "Of course." She opened the door wider. "I don't know what I was thinking keeping you on the porch. Come in, Major."

Ah, back to Major and Mrs. "How is she doing?" he asked.

Lily sighed. "Her body is healing, but she is still quite, well, morose. Which of course is understandable."

"Yes. Of course."

How long would it be before she knew whether her rapist had impregnated her, he wondered. Six weeks? Two months? It was unlikely, but she must be miserable, waiting.

"Go on into the sitting room, Alistair. I'll get her."

'Alistair' that time. He had to admit, it was damned confusing. They were – what were they to each other? Not sweethearts, not really. Almost though. They had taken steps down that road, certainly.

He was at the window looking at the red petunias wilting in the afternoon heat when Fanny came into the room, Lily with her.

"Hello, Major Whiteaker. It's kind of you to come see me."

"I was worried. I mean, Mr. Chamard kept me apprised of your health. But it . . . " It was what? What did you say to a young woman, a virgin, he thought, who'd been raped? All over now? Cheerful again? "I wanted to see for myself."

"Rachel made lemonade earlier. I'll get us some," Lily said.

"Please, sit down, Major," Fanny said. The colored women's academy in Opelousas had done well by her. She had the manners and the poise of a society belle, and a far better education than most of them.

Alistair made a vague circular gesture around his face. "You look much better, Fanny. The swelling is all gone."

"Yes. I'm healing fine."

"Good. I brought you these."

She turned the books over in her hand. "*Oliver Twist*. One of my favorites. I shall be glad to read it again." She looked at the other book. "*The Celebrated Jumping Frog of Calaveras County*. Mark Twain. I don't know him."

"Twain is lots of fun. You should read it aloud for the family, Fanny. You'll all be snickering before you get past page three."

Fanny crossed the room and kissed his cheek. He swallowed, oddly moved. "Thank you, Major. You're the kindest man I know."

He didn't know if bribing Frederick Palmer to leave his wife and child could be counted kind. Kinder than killing the man, he supposed.

"You're very welcome."

He should go now. He'd done what he came for. It wouldn't do for Palmer to come in while he was here. Really, he should just go.

Lily came in with a tray of lemonade, so of course he couldn't leave yet.

They talked about Dickens. About where Rachel got her lemons. And about the school.

"Fanny, take your time," Alistair said. "Most schools are not open at all in the summer, so you've earned your time off."

"But the reason we were open was because our need is so urgent. The Negroes have got to learn to read, fast as we can teach them."

"Yes. I agree. But teachers are remarkably human. They need a break now and then. Give yourself this time, Fanny."

Lily got up to pour more lemonade. "No thank you, Lily. Please tell Rachel how much I enjoyed it."

When he stood up, he was very close to her. There was that fine sheen of perspiration on her upper lip again, and she smelled of soap and starch. He dragged his gaze from her mouth and picked up his hat.

"I'll come back to see you in a week or so, Fanny. Please don't push yourself. Just rest."

"Yes, sir. Thank you."

"I'll show you out," Lily said.

At the front door, he asked her, "Palmer in town?"

"I assume so."

He raised his eyebrows.

"I haven't seen him since, well, since you were here last."

Alistair counted up the days. Well, that was interesting. "His things are still here?"

He could see she knew what he was thinking. But if he were going to leave, he would want the money.

"They're here."

He could so easily lean over and kiss her. But he wanted more than a stolen kiss in the hallway.

Maybe it was time he went to town himself. Time to see what the man was up to. Alistair could sweeten the offer if that would nudge him to take the leap. Whatever it took to make her free.

If that's what she wanted.

"Lily, I don't mean to push you if you don't really want me to interfere. Do you truly want him to go, to leave you and Maddie here?"

She took her time, thinking, her eyes focused on his shirt front. "Alistair, I want to be free, but you mustn't feel it's because of you, of us." She hesitated. "I've found myself again here. I'm not ever going to be the frightened, subservient wife again." Finally she looked into his eyes. "I won't take him back, even if I remain his wife."

And that could be the way it played out. Palmer claiming her and Maddie, not letting go. And Lily might have to live with that.

But not if he could help it.

# Chapter Twenty-Six

Fanny no longer kept to the little bedroom staring out the window. She helped Rachel in the garden and in the kitchen. She played with Maddie and Dawn and taught them their letters. And she was grateful Thomas did not sleep at the house every night.

In the final days of the campaign, he couldn't make it home when he might be twenty miles away come dark. But when he did manage to stop in for an hour or two, the hardest moments were the hello and goodbye. Every peck on the cheek or caress of her shoulder made her want to wail. Because Thomas did not understand.

It was all very noble and loving of him to say he'd marry her anyway, but he was too preoccupied with the campaign to have thought it through.

He had no idea what it would be like, marrying a woman who'd been despoiled. On their wedding night, he would not be taking a virgin to bed. She was quite sure Thomas would be kind and reassuring, but he'd be reminded. Every time he made love to her, he'd be reminded. How long until he didn't want to be reminded anymore, until it was easier just to not touch her. Better to be alone than to wake up one morning and see him looking at her with a cold glint in his eye.

And what if she never got over this feeling of being dirty, inside and out? What if she never got over cringing whenever Thomas touched her? He didn't deserve a wife like that.

And if there were a child on the way, well they said God didn't send you more than you could bear. She wouldn't be the first woman to raise a child of rape, all by herself. At least she wouldn't have to live with a man who'd thought he was good enough to love this child and then discovered resentment eroding his good intentions. Another night of the baby keeping him awake, of paying for a doctor or a new pair of shoes? Thomas was a good man, and she didn't want resentment undermining his goodness.

No, she wouldn't marry him.

She'd teach school. She'd raise this child, if there was one on the way. And that would be her life. Thomas could marry someone else, someone who wouldn't embarrass him in his political life.

She didn't even cry about it anymore.

As for justice? She didn't expect any. She'd recognized Valmar – she'd seen him when he was caught at the ice cream raid. She'd described the others, though she'd told the sheriff the other two had only stood nearby, not helping her but not touching her either. Sheriff Paget, outraged Valmar had committed another crime the very same day he'd been acquitted of murder, promised to get them. But it had been weeks, and he had not yet arrested anyone.

Fanny decided she didn't care about sheriffs or courts. If she couldn't put a bullet in Valmar herself, then she wouldn't be satisfied with legal justice anyway. She could spend hours without thinking about vengeance, then at odd times, the rage would boil up inside her and she'd want to kill. Instead, she'd chop weeds like they were Valmar's face, wring out a dish towel as if it were his neck. He'd taken everything away from her, and she wouldn't be appeased by putting the man in jail. She wanted him dead.

"What are you scowling about, Fanny Brown?" Miss Lily asked her. They were shelling peas together on the back porch, Maddie and Dawn playing on the porch steps.

Fanny forced a smile. Miss Lily had her own troubles with Mr. Palmer. She didn't need to be dragged into Fanny's pit of woe.

"That God ought to have made it easier to get peas out of the pod," Fanny answered. "Don't you think?"

"Absolutely. And why didn't he make corn so it doesn't have all those tassels. I hate corn silk in my teeth."

"And why'd he make pigs smell so bad?"

"I know why God makes pigs smell bad, Miss Fanny," Dawn said.

"Oh? Why's that?"

"So the foxes won't come get the baby pigs. Them old foxes just wrinkle up their noses and go for the chickens instead."

"But the chicken house doesn't smell good, either," Maddie pointed out.

"Well, you know what Preacher Tyrone says," Dawn told her, her nose in the air as she imitated the preacher's superior manner. "The Lord works in mysterious ways."

Sheriff Paget interrupted their philosophical discussion, riding around the house and dismounting at the back porch.

Lily reached over and squeezed her wrist before Fanny stood.

"Afternoon, ladies."

"Good afternoon, Sheriff. Let me get you some cool water. Come on up and take a chair."

"Thank you, Fanny. I could use a cup of water."

"No, you sit with the sheriff," Lily said. "I'll bring us out some water."

Paget took Lily's chair. "Hot as Hades out there, Fanny."

"It might rain this afternoon. That'll cool us off."

"How are you little ladies?" Paget said to the girls. "What's that you're playing?"

"We're practicing spinning," Maddie said, holding up an acorn. "Peep promised to carve us a wooden top if we learn to spin an acorn."

Paget sat down on the top step. "Let's see if I can still do it."

Dawn handed him her acorn and the sheriff gave it a go. "Wait. Let me try again." He couldn't manage it. "Used to do these when my girls were little ones," he said to Fanny.

"Here we are." Lily came out with three glasses and two cups of cool water.

After he'd downed the water, he looked Fanny in the eye. "I came to tell you, Fanny, I haven't caught the bas . . . excuse me, the men who attacked you. I'm on my way from Vacherie. Deputy down there thought he had Valmar in his lockup, using a different name, but it wasn't him."

The Sheriff sighed. "I don't know where the hell – excuse me. I don't know where they've got themselves to. I have every man I know between Baton Rouge and New Orleans on the lookout for them."

When Fanny didn't answer him, Lily gave her foot a nudge with her toe. "Yes, sir. Thank you for going all that way."

"The man's done enough damage in this parish. I'll look till I find him."

"And the other two men?" Lily asked.

"I'm pretty sure I know who one of them is. Don't want to say, but you probably know, too. The third one, I expect we'll find him when we find Valmar. Meanwhile, all three of them are making themselves scarce. But the one, well he has a wife, children. He won't stay away. And likely when he comes back, I'll get him and he'll tell us where the other two are."

"Yes, sir," Fanny said. "I appreciate your going to so much trouble."

Sheriff Paget frowned at her. "Fanny, I'm trying to tell you. It is not a trouble to me. I'm not stopping until I hear they've run off to China. Understand?"

"Yes, sir. Thank you."

Again Fanny thought, I don't care. Unless I pull the trigger myself, I don't care.

~~~

Thomas met with a group of wealthy free black men who supported him with money and influence. The meeting ended with handshakes and assurances on both sides that they would win on September 27th. Then Thomas headed for the sheriff's office like he did every time he was in town.

"Good morning, Sheriff," he said. "Just checking if you had any information to share." There, wasn't that polite? He hadn't snarled or said *when the hell you going to catch the bastards.*

Paget put his hands on his hips. "Thomas Bickell," he said impatiently, "I am looking for the scoundrels. When I find them, I will let you know."

Jaw clamped, Thomas strode back down the street to where Cabel and Reynard waited with the horses. Reynard leaned against the rail with his arms crossed. "Thomas."

"What?" he snapped.

"We got a sheriff seems to be doing his job best he can. You got your own job. Winning this election gone decide a lot more than whether one or two bad guys get what's coming to them."

"It's not your woman got torn up."

"As you might have said once yourself a while back, maybe that's why I see this better than you. We close to Election Day. You got to keep yourself thinking on whether you or that fat old white man gone be the delegate to the convention."

Thomas ground his teeth and glared. Reynard met his gaze with cool detachment.

Thomas looked away first. He nodded. "All right. What's next on the schedule?"

"This something of a rest day. To keep from killing you before we even get to the election. Alls we really got to do the rest of today is keep the appointment with Witherspoon, Major Bodell, and Percy Randolph about where to set up the polls. But that ain't till five o'clock."

Thomas checked the time on the pocket watch Garvey Bickell had given him. "Can't have the Shining Light of your people showing up late," he'd said. "You take it, son. If I need to know what time to do something, I'll just ask Rachel. She loves telling me what to do." He'd winked at Thomas's mother and clapped him on the shoulder.

Thomas flipped the lid open. "One o'clock," he said to Reynard. "We have time to ride down to the house for a little while and still get back here on time."

"Major Bodell will not be best pleased if we late getting to him," Cabel said.

"We won't be late," Reynard said. "And I need a piece of Miss Rachel's pie. Or cake. Whatever she got, I need it."

"Come on, then," Cabel said. "Mount up."

Riding home, Thomas worried at the knot in his chest. Fanny continued to be glum. And she didn't act like she was glad to see him when he managed to get home. The last weeks, he'd gone from worry, to compassion, to impatience, to compassion, and back to worry. Today he was feeling downright anxious.

Why didn't Fanny believe him that he loved her whether she'd been – he always stumbled over the word, even talking to himself. Even though she had been raped. As if the word were writ in red paint, it brought the rage bubbling through his blood.

It was not with a glad heart that he rode into the back yard and tied his horse to the rail.

He stepped into the kitchen. "Mama?"

She came to him from the front of the house. "Thomas!" She opened her arms and hugged him hard. "You got time to stay the rest of the day? I'll kill us a chicken and fry it up."

"No, Mama. We're just here for half an hour. We got to get back to Donaldsonville."

Cabel and Reynard came in from watering the horses. "Afternoon, Miss Rachel."

"Good afternoon, boys. Why don't you sit down at the table and let me cut you a piece of cake. You got time for that."

"Hoping that's what you'd say, Miss Rachel. This listening to Thomas jaw at people the live long day wears a man out."

"Reckon we could give the speech ourselves by now, don't you?" Reynard said.

"Ya'll stuff something in your mouths. Where is she, Mama?"

"She's sweeping the floor upstairs."

"Save me some of that cake," he called over his shoulder. He took the stairs two at a time and found her in Garvey's room with her broom.

"Fanny."

She stabbed the broom into the corner chasing the last tiny mote of dust. She didn't even look at him.

He closed the door behind him. Fanny continued to concentrate on sweeping out that corner. He gently took the broom from her.

"Can you stop and tell me hello like you're the woman I'm going to marry?"

"I told you. I'm not going to marry you."

"And now there's your six-year-old stubborn face. I bet you used to stick that lip out at your mama when she scolded you."

He put his hands on her upper arms. She tensed, so he let go.

All right then. He'd slow it down. "Fanny, will you please take my hand?"

She looked at him suspiciously.

"I just want to hold your hand, Fanny. Is that so hard?"

She gave him her hand. He led her to the bed to sit down.

"I'm not getting on a bed with you, Thomas Bickell."

"There's no place else to sit, Fanny. Look, we'll lay the broom between us."

He kept hold of her hand and settled the broom on the bedspread.

"I've been thinking," he began.

"I don't doubt it. What does Mr. Witherspoon say about setting up the ballot stations?"

"I'll see him this afternoon. That's not what I've been thinking about."

Fanny tugged to free her hand but he wouldn't let her go.

'I've been thinking that I need to know what you're thinking. 'Not going to marry you, Thomas' does not make me understand what's going on in your mind. Talk to me, Fanny."

"Let go of my hand. I can't think with you touching me."

Thomas considered it. Decided against it. "No, I'm keeping your hand. Talk."

She looked away, her face turned down. The circles under her eyes were huge and dark and her dress hung on her. She wasn't taking care of herself.

"Did I do something wrong, Fanny? Is that what this is about?"

"You know what this is about."

"You don't love me anymore?"

She looked at him sharply. "Maybe I don't."

Thomas laughed. "You're a liar."

She jerked her hand out of his. "Go away, Thomas. I'm not marrying you." Fanny grabbed her broom and attacked the corner she'd already swept.

Thomas took a deep breath. The longer this went on . . .

"Let me see if I understand this. If I were attacked and beaten half to death, then I wouldn't love you anymore?"

"Don't be ridiculous."

"That's the logic you just used. Or maybe what you really mean is that if I were attacked, you wouldn't love me anymore."

She bent over and swiped the broom under the dresser drawers.

Thomas crossed his arms and stretched his legs out. "Fanny, will you please do me the courtesy of putting that damned broom down."

She straightened up, leaned her broom against the dresser, and crossed her own arms, her chin jutted out.

"If I lost a leg. Or an arm. Or a leg and an arm, you wouldn't love me anymore?"

She was furious with him, her eyes full of fire. "Losing a limb is not the same thing as being raped, and you know it."

"All right then. What if I were the one who got raped. That happens. Men get raped, too."

She blinked. "What?"

"You didn't know that?"

"That's absurd. There's no way – " She gestured vaguely at her skirts.

"Think about it. Or don't think about it. It can happen. Say it happened to me. I'd be every bit as terrorized as you have been. I'd be 'despoiled,' as you put it. And, by your thinking, I would therefore be unlovable forever more. Is that correct?"

She threw her hands up. "Just like you to turn this into an analytical discussion of logic. Logic has nothing to do with it – I'm talking about how I *feel*, Thomas!"

"Then tell me how you feel."

"Dirty, Thomas. I feel dirty. And useless. And ugly. And, and afraid – " She slapped her hands over her face, and gasped.

Carefully, gently, Thomas wrapped his arms around her and let her cry. Her whole body shook and it felt like his heart was being torn out. Those men – if he found them, he would make them suffer before he killed them. He tightened his arms around her and swallowed at the enormity of what he would do – it was not an idle boast to make himself feel better. He talked to people all day long. Someone would see Valmar and his pals. And if Thomas found them before the sheriff did . . .

He kissed Fanny's hair and rubbed her back. When she calmed and put her arms around his waist, he whispered in her ear. "You are beautiful. Desirable. Smart. Useful. And I love you."

"How can you, Thomas?"

"I don't know. You are also ornery and stubborn."

"People will know. They'll look at you and think, there's that man whose wife was – " She gulped air instead of saying it.

"They'll say there's the man who married that brave woman who was attacked, got up, and went back to work."

"Is that what I should do, go back to work?"

"I think so."

"Thomas. If there's a baby, I don't expect you to -- "

"Hush." He kissed her, just the merest brush of his lips over hers. "If there's a baby, we'll take care of it together. We'll make that baby ours, Fanny, yours and mine, because we'll be the ones who'll wipe his snotty nose and give him a puppy and make him eat his turnips."

"I don't deserve you," she said into his chest.

"Well, who does? But I'll settle for you."

"Thomas!" Cabel hollered from downstairs. "We got to get going."

"All right," he called.

He gently touched his forehead to hers. "You know what this means, Fanny Brown?"

"What?"

"Next time I come, I get a smile. And I'm going to want a hug."

"A smile and a hug. Yes, sir."

"Will you kiss me goodbye? Just a peck if that's all you feel like."

She held his eyes as she dropped her arms from his waist. "You are a kind man, Thomas Bickell." She put her hands on his shoulders for balance, stretched up, and kissed first one cheek and then the other. "Go on, now. You got to see Mr. W."

He touched her cheek. "I'll try to come by Friday."

He clattered down the stairs and blew into the kitchen full of energy. "Let's go."

His mama handed him a slab of pound cake to take with him and waved the three of them off.

# Chapter Twenty-Seven

Alistair took the steam boat to Baton Rouge and called on his old commander, Colonel Beauchamp. The colonel had interrupted his career on the bench to become a Confederate officer, and was now back in his judicial robes. They had noon dinner at Beauchamp's home on the bluff overlooking the Mississippi.

"Finest damned action I ever saw," Beauchamp reminded Alistair. They'd had this conversation before, and it always embarrassed him.

"Plenty of scenes just like it on every battlefield, Colonel."

"You always say that, but I must disagree."

And they ever would disagree. With an injured corporal over his shoulder, Alistair had rallied a platoon of panicked soldiers and led a counterattack that routed the Union assault. The colonel had commended him for bravery and insisted on presenting him with a letter extolling his actions, but Alistair still maintained that there was no dearth of courage on any field of battle, men of all colors and creeds charging into a barrage, the odds of their survival terrifying. And yet they did it, battle after battle. This was why Jefferson Davis had decided the Confederacy would not award medals – they were all heroes.

Over coffee, Alistair explained Lily Palmer's dilemma. And Alistair's solution. "Would formal, signed documents be enough for a divorce and for waiver of custody rights without the man appearing in court?"

"You want the man gone as soon as you get him to sign the papers, is that right?"

"Exactly."

The judge had to think about that for a while. "And your intentions after Mrs. Palmer has her divorce?"

"I imagine Mrs. Palmer will need some time to adjust to having the freedom to choose her own life."

"And you hope she'll choose to live it with you."

"Yes, sir, I do."

Beauchamp played with his spoon, thinking. "This money you've offered Palmer. It's a bribe, no getting around it."

"Yes, it is."

"Rather distasteful, that."

"Yes."

Beauchamp lit a cigar, puffed to get it drawing, and then he asked, "How much you offering him?"

"Five thousand dollars."

The judge's brows shot up his forehead. "You may be the only man in Louisiana who can come up with that kind of money."

"I sold my interest in the foundry in New Orleans. Marcel Chamard's. You know him."

"Of course I do. Fine boy, Chamard was, but he had a brother, didn't he, who – well, I'm not one to call him a traitor – let's just say he followed his conscience north."

"Yes. Yves, you mean."

"Well, the Chamards are neither here nor there." The judge blew a smoke ring, thinking. "That's a hell of a lot of money, Major."

"Yes, sir. I mean for it to be too much to walk away from."

"Does Mrs. Palmer know about the money?"

"She knows."

Beauchamp gave Alistair a shrewd look. "Did she ask you to do this?"

Alistair raised his chin. "No. She did not."

Beauchamp held a hand up. "All right. Don't get hot under the collar. I just want to know what I'm dealing with here."

The maid refilled their coffee cups and glided back out of the dining room.

"You have any proof the man was abusive?"

"There are scars, I understand. And neither his wife nor his daughter were glad to see him when he showed up."

"It speaks well of her that she discouraged you, a rich man, even when she thought she was widowed."

"She's a fine person, Colonel."

Beauchamp looked at him over his coffee cup. "What did you ever do with that fancy letter you earned, Alistair?"

"It's in a drawer somewhere."

"There are men who would have it framed, under glass, and proudly displayed on their parlor wall."

"I suppose."

Beauchamp rose and stood at the French doors looking out over his lawn, the Mississippi rolling along beyond that.

Maybe he should have approached someone else, Alistair thought. Someone who would be interested in an envelope full of cash. He understood the colonel's colleague, Judge Spooner, was not above a little favoritism in return for remuneration. But he wanted Beauchamp's name on the documents, a name that everyone would accept as representing a fair judgement.

"It's irregular, what you ask."

"I understand that, sir."

"But not illegal."

Alistair drew in a breath, his chest loosening.

"Entertain yourself this afternoon. You can stay here and read if you like. Come by my chambers at six o'clock. The clerk will have the documents you need waiting for you."

Alistair stood and straightened his coat. "Colonel." He had to swallow before he could go on. "Thank you, sir."

~~~

Two days later, Alistair stood at the open doorway into the River Queen Saloon and waited for his eyes to adjust. Then he stepped over to the bar and leaned his elbow against it while he scanned the place.

There he was at the far poker table, a haze of cigar smoke hovering overhead, a brunette in a red satin dress leaning into his shoulder.

Alistair wondered what kind of poker player Frederick Palmer was. He got himself a whiskey and threaded his way through the tables.

"Mind if I sit in?" he said, gesturing to the empty chair at Palmer's table. He knew each of these men. They wouldn't turn him away.

Palmer scowled, but Ed Young sitting to his left smiled warmly. "Major. How you doing, friend?"

"I'm well, Ed. How's that leg of yours?"

"Long as it's not raining and not cold, I'm good. Yankees can't shoot straight, that's the truth, or I'd be clomping around on a crutch instead of walking."

"Glad to hear it." Alistair sat. "Good evening, Lawrence. What's the game?"

He took in the piles of chips at each man's place. Palmer had been winning – his stacks were the biggest on the table. So the man knew his cards.

"What are you doing here?" Palmer said.

Alistair put on a surprised air. "Looking for a game to while away an afternoon, same as you."

Palmer shrugged Juliana off him. Alistair had seen the girl around. Very pretty with her black hair and dark eyes and skin just a shade darker than, say, an English brunette's would be. He wondered if the bigoted Mr. Palmer realized his gal was probably an octoroon, white enough to pass the inspection of a man from Pennsylvania.

"Juliana deals," Palmer declared.

Ed and Lawrence said sure, they were happy with Juliana.

She moved her chair away from Palmer and shuffled the cards with finesse.

"Five card draw?" she asked.

"Fine with me," Alistair said.

She looked pointedly at Palmer.

"Just deal," he said.

"Ten dollar ante, gentlemen."

Alistair fished out his purse and added his ante to the pile. A fairly serious game if they were starting out with a $50 pot.

As Juliana dealt, Alistair added up the value of the chips at Palmer's elbow. About three hundred dollars. The man had been playing very well indeed.

Palmer's body vibrated just the littlest bit. Alistair realized the man was pumping his knee under the table. Not the behavior of a man who had amassed all those chips. Alistair smiled to himself. He was making the man nervous.

Juliana gave Palmer a quelling look and he stilled.

Alistair took two cards on the draw. Palmer took one.

Juliana said, "Gentlemen, show your cards."

Palmer had a full house, sevens and threes. Alistair had four sixes, better than anyone else at the table. The pot went to Alistair.

Juliana dealt and they began a new round. Alistair had played poker of all sorts every day for nearly a year when he was a prisoner of war. The cards were so worn they were limp by the time the war was over, and by then, Alistair had learned a thing or two. He watched Palmer without ever directly gazing at him.

Juliana had a hold over him. Palmer had snapped at her when they began the play, but he also glanced at her at every point he had to make a decision. Take a card or don't? As far as Alistair could tell, Juliana never gave him a sign. She acted the professional here, but Palmer feared her displeasure.

He supposed it made sense, a bully being attracted by a stronger personality. And Alistair had no doubt Juliana, sitting there regally in her tawdry satin and lace, was a determined woman.

Palmer had not been home in nearly two weeks, yet he looked fresh. New shirt, shaved and barbered. Alistair could almost feel sorry for him, afraid to go home and face Lily. Maybe afraid to face his own sorry self.

Alistair stretched his legs out under the table. Palmer was here with Juliana, not home with Lily and Maddie. Palmer just needed a nudge, and he'd take Juliana.

"Ed," Alistair said, "how's that boy of yours? Still out in California?"

"San Francisco," Hank said, sipping his whiskey. "Hear him tell it, the streets are paved with gold and silver."

Alistair didn't miss the look that passed between Palmer and Juliana. Bless you, Ed.

"Anywhere out west got to be better than here," Lawrence Mayfield said. "Lawrence Junior, he's out in Texas now. Got him a little spread near Fort Worth, raising cattle."

Ed won that hand, Lawrence the next. Then Alistair took a pot, and Ed again. Palmer's pile of chips was dwindling, his knee pumping under the table again. Juliana's mouth was a grim line.

If Palmer had chosen to show his cards each of those times he lost, Alistair would have a better idea of how reckless or conservative a player he was, but he was not required to show a losing hand.

"Will you take another card, Mr. Mayfield?" Juliana asked.

"I'm good."

"Mr. Young?"

"Two."

"Major Whiteaker?"

"I'll take one, thank you."

"And you, Mr. Palmer?"

There was that nervous glance at Juliana again. It was overwarm in here, of course, but Palmer was the only one with sweat popping out on his brow.

"Three."

She gave them a moment, then called for their tallies.

"I'm busted," Ed said, displaying his hand. "That queen I was after chose to favor one of you gentlemen."

Lawrence Mayfield slapped his down face up and smiled. A full house, three eights, two sevens.

Alistair laid his down, three jacks, two tens, a full house to beat Mayfield's. The pot was his, unless Palmer could beat him.

Palmer slapped his hand down in disgust, cards face down.

Alistair had watched Juliana's hands since she'd shown off her dexterity shuffling the cards. If she were a man and got caught cheating, somebody would likely shoot her. Might not want to shoot a pretty woman, but it wouldn't go well for her either. She certainly had not fed Palmer any winning hands. As far as he could tell, she was an honest dealer.

But not a disinterested one.

"I believe it's time for a break, gentlemen. Shall we come back to the table in ten minutes?"

"Certainly, my dear," Ed said.

They stood, stretching their limbs. Lawrence and Ed involved themselves in the usual complaints of planters these days. The workers wanted too much, they didn't understand the basic economics of the plantation system, they thought they could get something for nothing now they were freedmen.

"They got themselves all riled up with this voting business. Got a political club they think I don't know about." Lawrence shook his head. "Meet late at night, talk about voting and that nonsense. Just keeps them confused. Politics is white men's business, I told them, the business of Negroes is to go into the fields and work."

Alistair watched Palmer over by the staircase with Juliana. They were standing very close, Palmer's head down as Juliana spoke. She wasn't whispering endearments in his ear, not with that look on her face. Alistair hoped she was telling him how little use she had for a man with no money.

"Course they don't listen to me when they've been taken care of their whole lives," Lawrence said.

Alistair hardly listened. He had heard it all before.

He supposed it was to Palmer's credit that he couldn't bring himself to accept the bribe. Awful thing, to take money to leave his wife and child. But losing that stack of chips, maybe losing Juliana – that might be enough to overcome his reluctance. Lily wasn't taking him back, she'd made that clear. He ought to take the stake and Juliana and be gone.

Alistair touched his breast pocket, the fabric stretched over the documents and an envelope containing $5,000.

Juliana seemed to have changed tactics. Through with her scold, she tenderly lifted Palmer's chin with her forefinger. He grabbed her hand and kissed her fingers.

Well then.

Juliana sashayed her way back to the table, Palmer trailing behind her.

"Gentlemen?" she said.

They took their places. Juliana dealt.

Palmer won the first hand with four jacks. He flashed a grin and raked the chips in.

Ed won, then Lawrence. Palmer again. Then Alistair. Slowly, Palmer's chips dwindled. His knee was pumping, and Juliana's face was tight. At some point she had quietly shifted her chair away from him.

Palmer's face shone with perspiration. He licked his lips. As often happened with desperate men, he became reckless. "Winner takes all," he said, and shoved all his chips into the center of the table.

"Well, I don't know about that, Palmer. I got me a nice little pile here, and yours is about a quarter what mine is."

"I'll sit this one out, too," Lawrence said.

"I'll see you," Alistair said and pushed his neatly stacked chips into the pile.

Palmer's eyes on Juliana reminded Alistair of a pup who's chewed the master's slippers. But aren't I loveable, the puppy was saying.

Juliana dealt.

"Card, Major Whiteaker?"

"I'm good."

"Mr. Palmer?"

"One."

Palmer didn't grimace or wince or whimper, but his face went pale.

"Straight flush, nine high," Alistair said.

Juliana quietly took the cards from Palmer's hand, looked at them, and placed them face down on the table.

"Congratulations, Major Whiteaker. If you gentlemen will excuse me, I have business elsewhere." Juliana rose from the chair and without a glance at Palmer, she left the table.

"That's it for me," Ed said. "Missus will be wanting me home for supper."

"See you Sunday," Lawrence said. "Whiteaker." He stuck his hand out for a shake. "Nice to see you."

"You too, Mayfield."

Palmer sat stone-faced, his eyes on the scratched table top.

Alistair withdrew the documents and the money from his pocket. He shoved the envelope into the middle of the table.

"Five thousand dollars, Palmer. Sign these papers, the money is yours."

Alistair took no pleasure watching Palmer face the dismantling of his manhood. His pallor took on a green tinge. He looked at Alistair with absolute desolation in his eyes. Then he gazed across the room where Juliana, hand on her hip, flirted with another man. His eyes moist and reddened, Palmer's lip trembled.

*Take it!* Alistair wanted to shout.

Lily's husband, elbows on the table, leaned his face against his clenched fists. His shoulders heaved.

Quite suddenly, unexpectedly, Alistair was ashamed of himself. To have brought a man to this.

Palmer wiped his face, unashamed of the tears on his cheeks. He looked again at Juliana laughing, leaning in to the other man.

"She really won't have me back, will she?"

He meant Lily, not the bar girl. Alistair shook his head.

His hand trembling, Palmer reached for the documents. Alistair withdrew a pen from his pocket and passed it over. Without reading a word, Palmer found the lines requiring his signature and signed.

Alistair gathered up the papers. "You're doing the right thing for Lily and Maddie, Palmer. This is a good place for them."

"And you'll take my wife."

"If she'll have me."

Palmer laughed. "You bought her, didn't you?"

"I bought her freedom. She decides what to do next."

When Alistair left, Palmer still had not touched the money. Juliana had watched from the corner of her eye, Alistair was sure. She no doubt knew what was in that envelope.

She brushed shoulders with Alistair as she sauntered back to Palmer's table.

From the River Queen saloon, Alistair road upriver, crossed over at Baton Rouge, and put himself up at the Willow Hotel. All the way, the documents in his pocket scorched his skin.

He told himself he had done only what was necessary. Lily deserved to be free of an abusive relationship she could no longer tolerate. Maddie's well-being was at risk, and so then was Lily's. And he had no reason to expect Frederick Palmer to do the right thing and leave them in peace.

But in those moments when Palmer yielded and signed the divorce papers, he saw what it cost the man. Alistair had destroyed him just as surely as if he'd put a bullet in his gut. How was the man to go on after succumbing to such a shameful transaction?

The shame stuck to Alistair as well. Because he had money, he had acted the despot. And if he had not wanted Lily, and Maddie, for himself, would he have laid a fortune in front of Palmer for the sake of a woman's peace of mind?

His notion of himself as a just man, one who tried to be kind, who tried to be thoughtful was tarnished. He had the means to buy what he wanted. That didn't make him just.

Had Palmer gone yet? Would he say goodbye to his wife and child before he left? Would he have re-masked himself with that sneering, cocky manner he wore to disguise how weak he felt?

Alistair was aware Lily might feel more than relief at obtaining the divorce. She might have residual affection for the man. She might even feel sorry for him if she got a look at the despair Alistair had seen in Palmer when he signed the papers.

She might, by the time he saw her again, realize just how high-handed Alistair had acted. If she believed the worst – that Alistair assumed he had bought her -- she could not feel easy with that. The woman had taken control of her own life when she left Philadelphia. He couldn't imagine she'd welcome feeling he now controlled her.

In short, Alistair felt none of the satisfaction he had expected to feel when he handed Judge Beauchamp the signed documents.

"Sit down, Alistair. Let me look these over."

While Beauchamp read the documents one by one, occasionally making a note on a pad, Alistair concentrated on the testimonials and certificates decorating the judge's chambers. 'Distasteful,' his friend had called the bribe. Yes, it was. Distasteful and perhaps dishonorable. But what else was he to do when otherwise Palmer might have reclaimed Lily and Maddie?

He was too selfish to let that happen. That's what it came down to. He had interfered in a marriage, come between a man and his wife and child. There wouldn't be a clergyman in Louisiana who would excuse that. And yet, he would do it again.

Beauchamp stacked the documents and straightened the edges.

"Everything in order?" Alistair asked.

Beauchamp nodded. "A statement from Mrs. Palmer herself alleging abuse would have strengthened the file, but that issue is for my own satisfaction. I do not lightly deviate from procedure without believing there is ponderous need, but I take the husband's agreeing to the divorce as an indicator of his character. As for the legalities. Palmer's allegation of her abandonment as cause for divorce will stand."

Alistair let the breath out of his lungs. "Thank you, sir."

Beauchamp waved his thanks away. "I need a drink. Join me."
Alistair did not hear that as a request. Likely he was in for one of
his colonel's famous lectures. Well, that seemed fair.

The judge poured them both two fingers of whiskey and sat
back in his leather chair. "*Á ta santé.*"

"*Et à la tienne,*" Alistair said, raising his glass.

"My son-in-law gave me this. What do you think?"

"Very smooth. Better than Peppers, I think."

"Well, if that's your standard," Beauchamp said and laughed.

"I'm very fond of Peppers," Alistair said with a smile.

The judge took another sip and put his glass down. "My wife
was newly widowed when I met her."

"I didn't know that."

"I'd known her husband for years. Knew him to be a gambler,
a drinker, and a womanizer."

"Was he."

"I had it from my sister, a credible witness, that his wife was
quite miserable with him. Don't know that he abused her as your
Mrs. Palmer was abused, but he led her a dreary life, no doubt of
it."

"Yes, sir."

"I see that busy brain working, Alistair Whiteaker. What is the
old man's point, eh?"

Alistair smiled. "I figured you'd get to it in time."

"Patience, they say, is its own reward. Now, Evie was in
widow's black when I met her, so I couldn't court her till her year
was up. But I was smitten, I kept coming round. Luckily, she had a
brother whom I could happen to call on when I knew she'd be
home playing hostess. What are you grinning about?"

"The picture of the terrifying Colonel Beauchamp being
smitten. If only the lads could have seen that!"

"They thought I was terrifying, did they?" Beauchamp turned
that over in his mind and smiled. "Very gratifying."

"I can imagine. Always envied the way you could make a cocky
captain quiver in his boots."

"Yes. A useful skill on occasion. But you had your own
methods as I recall. A look from you was worth a hundred words
from another officer."

"You ever miss it, Colonel? The sense of purpose, the
camaraderie, the men?"

"No. Thank God that's over. You?"

"Not the fighting, of course. But the sense of purpose was heady, I found. But peace time has its own satisfactions."

The judge drew in a breath, ready to tackle the issue. "Alistair, the point I'm trying to make. About Evie. As bad as her husband was, the woman grieved."

Alistair tilted his head, interested.

"She'd invested herself in that marriage. Had stood by the cad for eleven years. Had shared the man's bed, saw to his meals, raised his children."

"I see."

"I hope you do. Give your Mrs. Palmer time to grieve, if not for the loss of the man himself, then for the loss of all her hopes and dreams when she married him."

Alistair looked into his glass. "You think she'll forgive me, for the bribe?"

"You set her free, didn't you? Just don't rush your fences. She likely has to work through it – maybe accept that you're not some perfect knight after all. Maybe decide it's okay if your armor is a bit tarnished."

Alistair stood and stretched his arm across the big desk. "Thank you, Colonel."

Beauchamp shook his hand and held on to it a moment. "You are welcome, Major Whiteaker."

The next afternoon, Alistair collected a copy of the documents the clerk had registered in the state archives. He mounted his horse, took the ferry across the river, and rode homeward.

# Chapter Twenty-Eight

Lily sat on the edge of the bed. Frederick's hairbrush and shaving mug were on the dresser. His valise was on the floor. A black tie hung from the back of the chair.

Maddie had become a happy six year old again since they'd come to live with Uncle Garvey. She slept straight through the night, no bad dreams. She played and laughed all day. But since Frederick had turned up, she had become quiet again.

Lily walked to the dresser and fingered her husband's hair brush. She hadn't seen him since Alistair offered him all that money. A terrible lump rose in her throat. They'd been a family once. But no more. In the last years, she had learned to feel it was normal to live in fear, to feel guilty when he was angry and abusive. Living here, she remembered what normal really was.

She gripped the brush. Dear God, if he should try to take Maddie from her. If only he would take the money and be gone.

But she had to face it: His things were here. He hadn't come to say goodbye. Frederick had not taken Alistair's offer. How could he? Alistair had put him in an unthinkable position. Five thousand dollars to leave his wife and child? A monstrous amount of money, but how could he accept? Even if he didn't want her, he had his pride, and who could live with the shame of such a deal?

She was overwhelmed that Alistair would make such an outrageous offer. He'd been splendid, sitting at the kitchen table, calm and absolutely certain he would prevail. Beautiful and generous and kind. And formidable.

She was in love with Alistair Whiteaker, she didn't deny it. But. For days she'd felt resentment simmering beneath the love.

How dare he? With those few words, he had put a man to shame. And did he think he'd bought her with the same money he offered Frederick? Did he think she was so weak a person she could not survive on her own much less solve her own problems?

She drew a deep breath. If Frederick wouldn't leave her and Maddie, then the solution was simple. She and Maddie would leave him.

She would borrow the money from Uncle Garvey, and he would be the only living soul who knew where she was going. It'd have to be someplace big so she and Maddie could disappear. Maybe New York City. People could lose themselves in a place that big and never be found.

~~~

Lily told Uncle Garvey she was leaving. Dear man, he didn't want her and Maddie to go, but he hugged her and told her she had to do what she thought was best for Maddie. He had enough money in the safe built into the floor under his bed to give her a good start.

"I'll pay you back as soon as I can, Uncle Garvey."

He kissed her forehead. "What nonsense. I'm your uncle."

Uncle Garvey went down to the barn to hitch the wagon. He'd take her to Donaldsonville to catch the late afternoon steam boat. Lily wanted to leave today – it would tear her in two to tell Alistair goodbye. It was better if she just left.

Maddie was playing out back with Dawn. She'd pack first, then call Maddie in to get her face washed.

When Frederick's form filled the doorway, she startled and stepped back. A part of her mind was clear enough to appreciate the symmetry of his coming in while she was packing to run away. The rest of her mind was aboil with fear and frustration and anger.

"My God, Lily. I'm not a monster."

She narrowed her eyes, taking him in. He looked like a man who had not slept in days. Like a man who needed a good meal and a kind word.

"I wasn't expecting you, that's all."

He saw the two valises open on the bed and winced. "You were running away again."

Unbelievably, she saw tears well up in his eyes. Where was the blustery mocking Frederick? Where was the man whose every answer to frustration was an angry blow? At least she didn't smell whiskey on him.

"I won't let you have Maddie," she said.

He nodded, his eyes on the floor. "Where were you running to this time?"

"You're the last person I'll tell."

Frederick walked slowly into the room and sat in the straight-backed chair.

"You don't have to go, Lily. I'm going."

Lily's fingers turned cold as she stood there, staring at him.

His elbows on his knees, he dropped his head. "I took the money, Lily." He covered his face and a sob erupted from deep in his chest. "I didn't know what else to do."

Lily gulped down tears of her own. She could hate him when he acted the bully, sneering and mocking. But to see him reduced to this.

"I'm sorry," he said. "I'm so sorry. I wanted to start over with you and Maddie, but . . ."

But he'd found her kissing Alistair.

"You must despise me, taking the money." He drew in a shuddering breath. "I despise myself."

She sat on the bed between the two valises. "It'll be for the best," she said, her voice hoarse.

"I never meant . . . Lily, I don't know why I . . . "

She could see him now that she wasn't angry or frightened. Sad, of course. And perhaps, eventually, forgiving, but what she realized was how small he was inside. He'd lost his position, his very good salary, and he'd turned into a self-pitying man who beat his wife.

When she married him, she'd thought him the smartest, the strongest, the most wonderful man, but when times got hard, he proved himself a weak man. Perhaps if she'd understood that sooner. But it was over. Truly over, and she was glad.

"When are you leaving?"

He wiped his face with his handkerchief and put it back in his pocket. "Today." He glanced at the dresser. "I'll get my things. You'll let me say goodbye to Maddie?"

"Of course I will. Frederick." She hesitated. "Don't tell her you'll never see her again. Just tell her you'll be gone a long time. Someday, when she's grown, maybe . . . "

"Whatever you want." He stood up and took an envelope from his inside pocket. With a crooked smile, he handed it to her. "Believe me when I say I am aware of the irony of offering you any of my ill-gotten gains, but I want you to have this."

Lily opened the envelope. "Five hundred dollars, Frederick?"

"So you won't be beholden, Lily. To anyone."

She couldn't help it. Tears spilled over her cheeks. "Frederick. I don't need it."

"Take it for Maddie then. Please."

Laughing while she cried, she said, "This will buy a lot of shoes and bonnets, Frederick. Thank you."

"Lily. Will you let me hold you? Just for a minute."

"Oh, Frederick." She stepped into his arms and wrapped hers around his waist.

When they could both be calm again, Frederick stepped back. "I've got to go." He looked down at her and she saw the misery in his eyes. "Lily. There's someone waiting for me in town. I expect you'll hear that."

The terrible weight in Lily's chest eased. She was not sending a selfless man away. He might believe he wanted what was best for her and Maddie, but he was a man who, in the end, looked after himself.

"But I want you to know, Lily. Whatever my faults, I was faithful to you all those years. I swear it."

"All right, Frederick. All right."

Both of them were composed when they went downstairs to call Maddie. There was a package wrapped in blue ribbon on the kitchen table. "For Maddie?"

"Yes. One last present."

Maddie came in, Dawn behind her. "Dawn, sweetheart, will you take a jar of water out to your mama? It's thirsty work hoeing that garden. And Dawn, darling, Maddie needs time with her father this morning."

"Yes, ma'am," she said.

Maddie opened the present. It was a beautiful yellow-haired doll whose eyes opened and closed. She touched the blue eyes carefully, and ran her finger along one long golden curl.

"She's very beautiful. Thank you, Daddy."

"You're very welcome, darling. What will you call her?"

"This is Rebecca. Rebecca Palmer."

Lily saw Frederick blink hard and swallow. She was glad it hurt him. It would make it easier over the years. Whenever Maddie wanted to talk about her father, Lily could say how much he hated to leave her.

Frederick hugged his daughter and kissed her and called her his good girl. "I won't see you for a while, but I will send you letters and postcards so you'll always know where I am. And when you're a little older, you can write me back."

Maddie was very pleased at the idea of writing letters. One more tight hug, and Frederick let her go.

Maddie tucked Rebecca under her arm, called out a quick good-bye, and ran out to find Dawn

"Thank you, Frederick. That was a good farewell. I'll make sure Maddie remembers it."

"You won't mind if I write to her, will you?"

"I hope you will. And I'll help her write you back. I promise."

He stared at her, his dark brown eyes glistening. "I guess this is it, then."

God, this was awful. Much as she'd wanted it, she'd had no idea how painful it would be to end her marriage.

She could only nod, her fingers pressed to her lips.

"All right. I'll just go." He stepped in close and gave her a quick kiss. He could barely speak and his voice came out in a hoarse whisper. "I do love you, you know."

He turned on his heel and climbed into the carriage he'd rented at the livery. She watched him drive away, and she was glad he didn't turn back for one last look.

It was done.

She walked back behind the barn and leaned against the rough boards as she cried out all the regrets and sorrows of the last years. By the time she walked back to the house, she knew her eyes were swollen, but Maddie and Dawn wouldn't notice. They were busy drinking tea and introducing Rebecca Palmer to Dawn's Miss Pitty Pat.

# Chapter Twenty-Nine

The first day back, Alistair arranged for his wagons and horses and mules to be available on election day. No one on his place would miss it for lack of transportation. He checked in with his steward. The surveillance he kept on the school house – they'd run off a couple of kids intent on smearing eggs on the windows, but they were just mischief-makers. His mother had sent a request for a dozen laying hens to be sent to her cousin's estate on the Cane River. And on it went. There simply had not been time for him to ride to the Bickells to see Lily. He was relieved, actually. He wanted somebody else, Frederick himself, he hoped, to tell her she could have her divorce. Give her a chance to get used to the idea before he presented himself. Truth was, he feared she'd turn from him, and it ate into his gut like acid.

The next morning, he spent an hour with his steward and most of the rest of the day working on his account books. The railway and steam ship investments, the costs of growing cane and paying laborers, of maintaining the buildings on the place . . . running his own financial empire was complicated, yet he kept his hand in every endeavor.

Which meant that it had been five days since he'd shoved the documents across the table for Palmer to sign. If Lily had learned of it, she'd be wondering what was keeping him, for good or bad. So he bathed, shaved, and dressed as if he were going to one of his mother's at-homes in New Orleans.

Everyone, black and white, was at the dining table when he arrived. Garvey pushed his chair back. "Alistair," he said, sticking his hand out for a shake. Thomas, too, stood to shake his hand. "Sir."

Rachel pulled out a chair for him over his protestations that he would wait in the sitting room. "No, sir. You come on and eat. I got fried chicken tonight and you know you don't want to miss that."

Fanny got silverware and a napkin for him from the sideboard and smiled at him. Maddie announced, "Major Whiteaker, you have to meet Rebecca. Say 'how do you do, Major Whiteaker,'" she told her doll, and then pretended her lips did not move at all as Rebecca greeted him.

"Very well, Miss Rebecca. And Miss Maddie, how do you do?"

Maddie's smile made the whole sorry week worthwhile. "Very fine, thank you."

So everyone was glad to see him but Lily. He glanced at her as Rachel filled his plate with enough food for three men. Lily feigned great interest in buttering a biscuit.

"How are you, Mrs. Palmer?" he said formally.

She glanced at him. "Well, thank you."

The frost in her voice told him she knew her husband had taken the money. She knew she would have her divorce. And it hadn't made her happy.

Garvey took up the conversation. "We were talking about the election before you came in, Alistair. That does not surprise you, I'm sure. Fanny thinks the women should have the vote, too."

"Do you indeed, Fanny?"

Lily wore the calico dress with the tiny yellow flowers and it looked looser than it had the last time he'd seen her in it, and she had shadows under her eyes. Grieving, as Beauchamp had suggested?

"Yes, sir," Fanny avowed. "Women have the same brains God gave men. We have the same right to be heard as men. Give us the vote, and you'll see less corruption, less – "

"Fanny, you can't just assert there would be less corruption," Thomas argued. "You have no evidence . . ."

Alistair did not follow the debate. He watched Lily very carefully not look at him. She nibbled the biscuit, she rearranged the peas and okra on her plate, and she dabbed at her mouth with her napkin, never once raising her eyes from the table.

He managed to eat enough to satisfy Rachel and waited an interminable time for dinner to be over. He had to talk to Lily alone.

"What do you think, Major?" Fanny appealed to him. "Can women think as well as men?"

"Now Fanny, you're putting the man on the spot," Garvey said.

Alistair smiled. "It's all right, Garvey. I did not spend all those years at my mother's knee without learning the answer to that one. Miss Brown: some women can think every bit as well as some men."

"Oh! That's treacherous!" Fanny exclaimed. "You might as well . . ."

Alistair couldn't hold his attention on the argument and let the conversation flow on without him. Lily sat across and down one place from where he sat.

"Lily," he said softly.

Her head came up suddenly, as if he'd shouted her name. She fastened her gaze on his, but he could only say again, "Lily."

Maddie tugged at his sleeve. "Major Whiteaker, did you know that Rebecca speaks three languages?"

From the corner of his eye, he saw Lily's head was down again.

"Three languages indeed? Let me guess, Portuguese, Slovakian, and Chinese?"

Maddie's response was typical little-girl delight. She giggled, "No, silly. English, French, and Cajun."

When Rachel brought out the lane cake, Lily murmured something and excused herself, her shoes tapping rapidly across the floor. Alistair didn't even say excuse me but strode out of the room after her.

She pushed through the front door and was across the yard when Alistair leapt off the porch after her. "Lily!"

She started running.

He caught up to her and whirled her around by the arm. "Lily!"

She tugged free and marched away from him.

He matched her stride. "Lily, can't you even talk to me?"

She looked like she was about to run again. He took hold of her arm. "Stop. Please, Lily."

She turned her back to him and covered her face with her hands.

"You're sorry about the divorce."

"No!" She turned to him, her face scrunched up and crying. "I mean yes. No, I'm not sorry. But it's all wrong now. How can we -- this is awful. You shouldn't have -- I wanted him to take it, but we shouldn't have -- "

Then it was as he'd feared. She'd decided she couldn't stomach what an offer like that had done to her husband. She couldn't stomach Alistair for offering it.

"I'm sorry."

She wiped at her nose. "Do you know he gave me five hundred dollars of your money?" She laughed, the tears still spilling out. "He caught me just like the last time – isn't that funny?" She tried to laugh again. "I was packing, so Maddie and I could run again, only this time he wasn't angry. He looked . . . Alistair, he looked like he'd been kicked in the stomach."

"But you don't have to leave now." Surely to God she wouldn't leave now.

"Oh, Alistair. It's no good. How can I – "

"Because you think -- you think I believe that I bought you."

"Didn't you?"

He shook his head over and over. "No, Lily. I never meant that."

"You had to have thought that," she said angrily.

"No. All I bought was your freedom so that if you did . . ." He had a hard time taking the next breath. "If you did choose me, you'd . . . you could marry me." He felt like weeping himself.

She stared at him a long time, her eyes red and swollen. He raised a hand to touch her but she shook her head and gazed at the ground.

He felt his breath hitch. He imagined himself dropping to his knees and begging, but it wouldn't help. She had turned against him.

He reached into his pocket for the document and handed it to her. "Maddie is legally yours. You're free, Lily. Free of both of us."

Alistair hardly knew how he got from Lily to his horse, how he managed to ride home. His only awareness was of the black hole in his chest.

# Chapter Thirty

Alistair stood with Fanny Brown when she rang the brass bell calling the children to school. She had lost weight, but the light was back in her eyes. She was going to be all right.

The older children told him good morning, the younger ones went tearing past him full of high spirits on this first day of the new school year.

"How do you handle a room bursting with all that energy?" Alistair asked her. "I don't believe I'd have the courage."

Fanny laughed. "See this?" she said and pointed to her face. In an instant, her smile turned into a hard stare. "Haven't met the child yet can stand up to The Look."

Alistair gave an exaggerated shudder. "A mighty weapon indeed." He put his hand on her shoulder. "I'll leave you to it then. Let me know if you need anything."

He mounted his horse and rode through the plantation. The cane was puny this year, all up and down the river. Just had not been enough rain. Some planters were likely going to go under. They didn't have the capital to withstand a poor harvest on top of having to adjust to paying wages and trying to recover from the damages the war inflicted. His plantation certainly would not show a profit again this year.

He looked up at the sky. Another blistering hot day with not a cloud to tease a little hope that it would rain. He could hold out for a while yet, but eventually, he'd have to do some hard figuring. Which cost more, financially and spiritually, to let the place continue to bleed money, or to lay off all these laborers and let the fields lie fallow?

From an easy amble, his mare suddenly screamed. Alistair heard the crack of a rifle at the same moment he saw his horse's mane blossom red. He clamped his knees tight to keep from falling off when she reared, and pulled her in a tight circle to keep her from bolting.

He bent over her neck, blood wetting his cheek, and rode her for the cover of the windbreak. For all he knew he was riding right into the shooter's line of sight, but he thought the sound had come from the west. Once in safety among the trees, he slid off and tended to his mare.

The blood was flowing, but not pumping. The wound was just on the crest of her neck, in the soft flesh the mane grew from. "It'll be fine, Maisie. It's just a flesh wound," he said, stroking her neck, cooing softly. "Hurts though, doesn't it. You must wonder what the heck happened out there." Maisie was a two year old and so had not lived through the war, had not been trained to charge into a battle with artillery roaring and guns blasting. "Poor Maisie," he crooned. "A bad way to start the day isn't it, sweetheart."

The horse gave one last mighty shudder and settled down. Alistair tied the reins to a tree branch and crept to the edge of the thicket, his pistol cocked. Mostly, he saw green, the cane thick in the fields if not as tall as it ought to be. Nothing to hear but the rustle of all those stalks swaying in the breeze. Not even the birds stirred.

Whoever had shot at him was long gone. Probably. The man was certainly no marksman. Alistair quickly calculated who he'd made an enemy of. Every Yankee in the Union, to start with. But that was over. Frederick Palmer, certainly, though Ed Young said he'd seen the man board the steam ship with Juliana.

Meanwhile, Alistair felt trapped in this little copse of sweet gum. A braver, bolder man might mount his horse and go about his business. Alistair chose to wait a while. He'd like to be steadier in his mind before he stuck his nose out and made a nice target of himself again.

Pistol in hand, he reassured Maisie he wouldn't be long and threaded his way through the trees, all his soldier's instincts on full alert. He circled the ten acres of this particular field, sometimes darting from one copse to the other. His steward had the workers in the western fields this week, and there was not another soul out here.

On his way back to Maisie, he spotted where the rifleman had stood among the trees. There were boot tracks, high-heeled like the Texans wore. And there was the bullet casing. Alistair turned it over in his hand. Careless assassin who leaves evidence like that. Of course, it was very little evidence. Lots of men wore Texas boots. Jacques Valmar, for instance. And lots of men had rifles.

Not a lot of men, however, wanted to kill Alistair.

Could it be Valmar? The man was deranged if he had reappeared where he'd already created so much havoc. Maybe committed other crimes Alistair didn't know about. The man was going to get himself killed.

Alistair thought about who and how that might be done. The most satisfying way, to Alistair's thinking, would be to beat the man to death with his bare fists, then to toss his body into the swamp for the alligators to enjoy. Some people just needed killing.

But it was clear Valmar was not part of the continuing disruptions to the campaign. Cross burnings, harassment, intimidation – all that had persisted in Valmar's absence. For people who spouted a lot of rhetoric about their rights, the White Camellia had little respect for anyone else's.

Back at the house, Alistair turned Maisie over to the head stableman, a man who'd been on the place since Alistair's childhood. "I'll take good care of her, I will," Horace said.

Alistair washed the blood off his hands and arms at the pump and went inside to find Peter Kresky waiting in his parlor.

"Pete. I'm sorry to have kept you waiting. I see you've been taken care of," he said, motioning to the coffee cups and a platter of seed cakes.

"Very well taken care of, Whiteaker," Kresky said, rising to shake his hand.

They settled into their chairs and Alistair poured himself a cup of coffee, luke-warm now.

"I've been reading the paper while I waited for you. The price of sugar has fallen another point this week. It's those farmers in Europe distilling sugar from beets. Who ever heard the like, eh?"

"I hear it tastes about the same as cane sugar."

"Does it? I can't imagine. Do you suppose it's as white as cane?"

"I haven't considered. Interesting question."

"My nephew's back east, in Raleigh. I'll have him buy a pound and see what it's like. The ladies would probably be tickled with pink sugar if that's what it is."

Alistair smiled. "I expect you're right."

They commiserated with one another about the poor cane season this year, about the competition from Europe and Cuba. About trying to make a profit when they had to pay wages, "outrageous" wages, according to Kresky.

"They want the wages, then they want me to supply them with pigs and mules for their personal use, then they want me to pay to feed their pigs and mules. They got no sense of fairness, no sense of how an economy works."

"It's an adjustment, for everybody."

"The damned Republicans in Washington would rather see all us planters ruined than stand up to the Negroes. We're going to have to take care of ourselves down here."

Ah, Alistair thought. Here it comes.

"Some of us plan to do just that. We were hoping you'd join us, Alistair.

"In busting up rallies, you mean? Intimidating people not to vote, or to vote Democratic when it's against their own self-interest?"

"That's what it's going to take, my friend, to get this state back on its feet."

"I presume you're talking about the White Camellia."

"Yes, I am, by God. We need you. You're an important man hereabouts. People listen to you. You need to be speaking out, against the Freedmen's Bureau, to start with. Their policies do nothing but stir up false hope among the Negroes. Keep them expecting more than they can ever have. The black man cannot have the vote. He cannot run this state. He simply is not equipped to understand the complexities of government – hell, he doesn't even understand dollars and cents, much less does he possess the intellect required for higher levels of thinking."

Alistair crossed his legs comfortably. He had heard all these arguments before. "I don't agree, Pete. The Negro is ignorant, I grant you. But that is not the same thing as having no capacity to think."

"Yes, yes, I'm aware of your little experiment with the school. All well and good if some of them learn to read and write. It'll help them to read their wage contracts and so forth. I have no objection to that. But that's a long way from being able to think like a white man. They aren't bred to it, and that's a fact."

There really was no point in debating this with Kresky. Alistair would not change the man's mind. And he had other things to do with his time.

"Let me make myself clear, Pete. I want this – " He waved his hand vaguely, as if to include all of the South. "All of this, wages, freedom, education for the Negroes, I want all of this to work. Slavery had its time. It's over. We need to move on, see what it takes to live together, peaceably and maybe more important to your way of thinking, profitably."

Pete sat back in his chair as if he were affronted. "It won't work, Alistair. It can't work."

"You mean you won't let it work," Alistair retorted. He stood up, finished with this discussion.

Pete rose to his feet, too. "Look, you can't stop the white man from setting things right. It's got to be done. We want you with us, but if you persist in these fanciful notions of equality, you will regret it."

Alistair heaved a sigh. "Pete, how many years have we known each other? It saddens me to hear you threaten me."

Pete gave him a belligerent glare. "You choose to take it as a threat. I merely prophesy. We are not thugs, Alistair. I leave the door open. A man needs friends when times are unsettled. You think about it, you'll see it's in your best interest."

Alistair had said all he wanted to. "Let me show you out, Pete."

The look on Kresky's face indicated he felt the insult. "I can see myself out, thank you."

Alistair wondered if he'd soon have a burning cross on his front lawn.

~~~

Alistair had a new appreciation for how much courage Thomas Bickell possessed as he watched him continue with the campaign. In spite of having his rallies disrupted, of being harassed and maligned, of being thwarted at every opportunity, he persevered.

He wondered if there were something else he could be doing to help. He'd talk to Chamard. He was more closely involved with Thomas, being neighbors with Garvey.

After picking at the chicken and dumplings his cook set before him for noon dinner, wondering what she could be thinking cooking something this hot and this heavy when the heat was so bad all the chickens hid underneath their coop with limp feathers, he wondered what Rachel served today – something light, he bet, like cucumbers and tomatoes with some of that vinegar dressing she made.

He closed his eyes at the image of Lily sitting at the table, Maddie at her side, talking, eating, maybe laughing. He didn't think Lily would feel like laughing. She was too hurt. Hard to sort out what hurt her the most – Palmer giving her up, being dishonorable enough to take the money? Or was it because he, Alistair, had dishonored both Lily and Palmer by offering the money in the first place. And then finding Palmer in a weak moment and pressing him to sign those papers.

He was not proud of himself. But what else could he do? For Lily's sake, he couldn't let Palmer take Maddie away from her. And for his own sake, he couldn't let him force Lily to stay with him. She deserved better. Better than Palmer, and better than himself.

He shoved his plate away and went for his hat.

In the stable he checked on Maisie. Horace had cleaned her wound and slathered it with ointment. She was enjoying a bag of oats, munching in the shade of her stall, a nice breeze coming through the barn. He gave her a neck a pat and saddled up Raven, his young stallion. An indulgence, a horse like this, too temperamental and finely made to be much use pulling a wagon or a plow, but he'd bought him on a whim last winter after he'd deposited his dividends from his railroad interests. His best friend, Marcel Chamard, had been with him and had wickedly urged him on. Alistair didn't have a lot of whims, and yielding to this one had been a great pleasure.

He rode Raven past the fields where his laborers worked and noticed two of the mules wore old straw hats somebody had poked ear holes in. A day like this, he could see the need for it, but Raven – he would not inflict such an indignity on a horse like Raven. He would die of shame, Raven would. But he took it easy on the ride to Cherleu, the sweat rolling down the hollow in his back.

Chamard offered him cool barley water and a cigar. The river breeze freshened the air on the front gallery, and Alistair took his hat off, wiping his forehead with his shirt sleeve.

"How are things with the campaign?" he asked.

Chamard drew on his cigar. "Fairly quiet. You heard somebody took a shot at Thomas a while back. He took it as a warning, not a serious attempt. Just the one shot. He's easy enough to kill, he figures, if that's what they intended."

"Me, too, as a matter of fact." Alistair told him about this morning's rifle bullet grazing Maisie's nape. "Found boot prints, high-heeled, and a bullet casing."

Chamard thought about that, Valmar on his mind, Alistair had no doubt. "Not proof though."

"Nope. Not proof."

Alistair poured himself another glass of barley water. "Got home from that little adventure to find Pete Kresky in my parlor."

"Let me guess. He extended an invitation to become a Knight of the White Camellia."

"He been to see you, too?"

"Sure."

Alistair grinned at him. "I bet you told him what a worthy endeavor he was engaged in and that you would seriously consider joining."

Chamard gave him a sly smile. "Exactly."

"Some would accuse you of insincerity, Mr. Chamard."

He arched his brows. "Me? Never."

Valentine stepped onto the gallery. "He could have told the man he was getting too old for such foolishness, but Mr. Chamard, he don't know he's getting old."

"I'm not. You're the one getting old around here."

And there they went, the two of them, bickering like kids. They enjoyed it.

"Major." Valentine interrupted the banter. "Can I bring you a bowl of pineapple? Got blueberries mixed in with it, it's good."

"You offering any to your lord and master, or just Alistair here?"

"Oh, you want some? Maybe I bring you a bowl, too."

Chamard grinned as he puffed on his cigar. "Perfect example of what my daddy would have called 'uppity.'"

"And some still would," Alistair said quietly.

Chamard sobered and flicked ash off his smoke. "Yeah. They would."

Alistair swallowed. "And the neighborhood? Everybody around here all right?"

"Musette's gone to town. I took her to stay with Nicolette for a while. None of her friends are in town this time of year, but Marcel will squire her around, and Finn and Nicolette are fine company."

Alistair didn't speak of Musette's sad attraction to Thomas. Better they all pretended she was merely his mentor.

"When is she coming back?"

Chamard gave him an enquiring glance. "Week or so, why?"

Alistair couldn't just show up at Garvey's place, not anymore, but he needed to see Lily. He'd like to hear Maddie giggle, too, and have her tell him how her doll Rebecca learned to speak so many languages.

"You haven't had a party in a while. I thought maybe Nicolette might come back with her, sing for us. I have a mean fiddler on my place."

"I see. And if I were to have a party, I'd invite you. I'd invite the Johnstons, oh, and maybe Garvey and Mrs. Palmer."

Alistair nodded gravely. "Sounds like a good idea, Bertrand. I look forward to it."

Chamard snorted.

Valentine appeared with a tray. "We having a party, are we? Good. We can order up some ice and when it comes, I aim to sit on it."

# Chapter Thirty-One

Thomas and his friends campaigned relentlessly. They hardly used the donated money -- everybody wanted to feed them, to shelter them, even if that meant sleeping in somebody's barn or on the floor of an old slave cabin.

In spite of the Army presence, every day they dealt with petty harassment, disruptions, heckling. Thrown tomatoes. One time, the opposition hired a band to play nearby so that no one could hear him. "Must mean we got old Percy Randolph worried," Reynard said.

Thomas was tired, and it was so damned hot. Sweat trickled over sweat, and the bright sun made his head pound. He wanted a bath. He wanted to sleep in his own bed. He wanted to see Fanny.

His fine brown suit was rumpled and dirty. The starch in his last clean shirt had given up yesterday and now his linen itched.

One more day and he could rest. Win or lose, he meant to sleep, eat Mama's cooking, and sleep some more.

But he had to get through today. The crowds had been growing the closer they came to the election. They knew who he was, they knew what he had to say, and they knew what they had to do. If he could just get them to the polls tomorrow.

Cabel was getting good at this. His introductions were getting longer, more impassioned, and more successful at focusing the crowd's attention on the platform. Reynard had managed to get him on an actual stage for today's speech, not just the back of a wagon, and somebody had invested in yards of bunting to drape the stage. Coming up in the world, Thomas thought with a smile.

"And so it is my privilege to introduce the man who will represent you at the Louisiana State Constitutional Convention. Thomas Bickell!"

Thomas summoned the courage to face the increasing fear he felt every time he made himself an easy target. Some days his post office box was stuffed with threats, some of them specific and terrible. One memorable letter had been wordless, merely a sketch in black and red ink, the depiction brutal and explicit. Being shot wasn't the worst fate by any means.

He quickly scanned the crowd as he waited for the cheers and applause to die down. Twice in the last weeks, he thought he'd seen Valmar on the periphery, a rifle in his arms, Thomas in his sights. Each time, he'd disappeared, simply poofed into thin air. He had conjured the man up out of his own dread.

Thomas woke in the night drenched in sweat, terrified. He reminded himself it was hot. They were all sweaty. And he was exhausted. But he could do this. He wouldn't yield to the terror.

With hands raised and a grin on his face, Thomas bounded onto the stage to whistles and applause. He began to speak. In moments, his mind was taken up with the message he had been giving for weeks now, but it was not stale, not to him. The passion took hold of him, the crowd quieted, every man turned to him, listening.

Reynard had hired more guards as the contributions had increased, and in a corner of his mind, Thomas noted them patrolling the edge of the crowd, on horseback and on foot. The inevitable hecklers were soon tapped on the shoulder and quietly escorted from the scene. There were soldiers present, too -- the white men who early on might have fired their guns into the air or charged into the crowd were forced to sit back and glower instead.

"I know what you're up against," Thomas told the crowd, his voice hoarse after so many days of speaking. "I know some of you have been told, 'If you leave the field to go vote, don't come back. You won't have a job.' Some of you have been told if you try to vote, you'll be beaten, your knee caps broken, maybe even your wife and children threatened. Hard choices."

The people were listening quietly. They knew what they faced. They needed courage to take what rightfully belonged to them – freedom, dignity, and power over their own lives.

"You heard what they did on Curtis Field's plantation. Maybe some of you were there. The boss said, 'You work on Sunday, or you don't work at all. You work for half what you were promised, or you don't work at all.' And what did our people do? They stood up for themselves, they stood up for justice. And they did that together! They do not work on Sundays on Curtis Field's plantation. They do not work for less than they contracted for.

"It's a risk, every day's a risk. And it's going to continue this way until we take our own power. The way to do that is to stick together, to vote. Tomorrow, take that risk – go to the polls –

because unless we vote, all of us, then next year, and the next and the next, the boss still going to be telling you Do This, Or Else!"

The crowd hurrahed. Thomas quieted them with a raised hand.

"I see some of you wearing Union Army caps. I see -- " he pointed to a man wearing a faded Army jacket, one empty sleeve pinned up – "some of you who fought bravely to defeat the Confederacy, and paid dearly for that privilege." He looked over the somber faces. "We honor our soldiers. We honor what they did, for all of us, when we carry the fight on, not with rifles and artillery, but with our votes. That is the most powerful weapon in this country – "

More applause. Thomas's voice was all but gone. He raised his arm, his hand fisted. "Tomorrow's the day! I'll see you at the polls!"

He waved, accepting the applause, and clattered off the stage where Reynard waited for him. He grabbed Thomas's arm and pulled him through the crowd. Thomas smiled, gripped the outstretched hands, smiled, and smiled. Reynard got him inside the black-owned shop on the corner and closed the door on all the well-wishers.

"Drink this," Cabel said and thrust a mug of water sweetened with molasses into his hand.

His hands trembled as he lifted the mug to his mouth. He had nearly faltered during the speech – he'd seen, no, he'd imagined, a gunman taking aim at him from the edge of the crowd, and then another and another. He was losing his nerve, and he didn't know what to do but to keep going. That's all he could do, what he had to do. Keep going.

"One more event, Thomas. Just one more." Cabel rubbed his shoulders. "You can do one more meeting."

"These men have invested in you," Reynard said. "They got money, they got influence. You gone need them right on. So you got to get hold of yourself."

He nodded. "I know it. Just give me a minute."

A tall man came from the back room. "He not been sleeping?"

"Valentine." Thomas was absurdly glad to see him.

"Yeah, it's me. I figured I needed to hear one more speech or I might forget to vote tomorrow."

Thomas laughed.

"Drink up. I got you a bath ready and Peep brought you some clean linen."

"Daddy's here?" He strode through the curtains into the back room. All Thomas wanted was to lean his head on his daddy's shoulder for a few minutes. To just close his eyes and lean on Daddy. Instead, he greeted his father with a smile and held his hand out for a shake.

"Son, I don't want to shake your hand." Peep pulled him in for a hug, his arms tight around him, squeezing. "I am so proud of you, Thomas. So proud."

Thomas nodded, swallowing hard. "I'm glad you're here, Daddy."

"Give me the suit and the shoes," Valentine said. "I'll see what I can do with them while you get bathed. You ain't as sweet smelling as you could be."

Thomas stripped out of his clothes, his eye on the steaming hip bath. Hot as the air was, he hoped the bathwater was even hotter, hot enough to loosen every kink in his back.

"Andrew, go fetch some bread, some cold meat, anything." That was Reynard giving orders. The last weeks, as Thomas had needed all his energy to campaign, Reynard had evolved from guard to manager. Without him and Cabel, he couldn't have kept going.

Thomas startled at the sound of glass breaking. "What was that?"

"Stay here," Cabel said. Thomas started to head for the front. "Stay here, Thomas," Cabel barked.

"You half naked anyway," Valentine said. "Get in the tub. Cabel can handle whatever's going on out there."

Thomas eased into the water and sighed.

"Just set there and let the water work on you." Peep handed him another mug. "Drink that while you setting."

Cabel returned. "Just a brick through the window, couple of white boys. Andrew and some others chased them off."

"Do we have enough to pay for the window?"

"I'll take care of it," Reynard said.

Bathed, fed, dressed in clean clothes, Thomas was invigorated. He met again with the group of black men who'd been born free and had accumulated influence in the community. He thanked them for their past contributions and gratefully accepted their pledge of continuing support.

The meeting over, Thomas was still energized. Even though his voice was hoarse, he would have been willing to mount the stage again and start rallying people, but the campaign was essentially over. Tomorrow, Election Day.

They had supper with friends and supporters at Raymond Fick's house, bedded down there, and were up early to watch the polls when they opened at seven.

For all the U. S. Army's presence, there were white men engaged in petty acts of sabotage. First snag was that the appointed polling place was closed. Nobody there but a handful of field hands wondering where they were supposed to vote. Thomas was not surprised. That's why he had a team in place for the day, to direct people to the poll and to ensure there was no overt intimidation, no white men ostentatiously writing down the names of black men who dared to vote, no white men with arms crossed, pistols on their hips, glaring at black men.

Thomas and his team split up, chasing down the election officials, threatening formal complaints, until they finally opened the poll, six blocks away from the advertised location. All day long, either Agent Witherspoon or Major Bodell himself, his expression thunderous at the misdirection, stood across the street from the poll, arms crossed, watching, ready to intervene if there should be trouble.

Right alongside the lieutenant observing the proceedings inside the polling place, Reynard had an official position. He watched every man's ballot go into the jar. When the jar got full, he watched the poll official empty it into the appropriate box. He watched the box. And tonight, when they opened the box to count the ballots. Reynard would watch that too. Between him and the U.S. Army, there would be no shenanigans.

Percy Randolph, the white candidate, stood across the street greeting men, slapping them on the back, laughing with them. The campaign wasn't over, Thomas realized.

He chose a spot further down the block and did the same, greeting, encouraging, and thanking the men who'd gone to considerable trouble, even risk, to be here today.

At seven p.m., all across the state, the polls closed. Reynard and Cabel stayed with the ballot box. Everyone else in Thomas's entourage retired to Raymond Fick's house again. No one went to bed that night. Mrs. Fick fed them at eight o'clock, again at midnight, and again at five. Some of them sipped whiskey or wine, and all of them watched the hours tick by.

At dawn, Andrew and Fick took their turn observing the ballot boxes and the ballot counters, standing elbow to elbow with the soldiers monitoring the election.

At two o'clock in the afternoon, the Donaldsonville band assembled at the stage hung with red white and blue bunting.

Heavy on the brass and the drums, the band called the townspeople to gather. The Director of Elections held up his hands for everyone's attention. He made the usual bombastic speech, then announced the winner.

"I give you our delegate to the Louisiana State Constitutional Convention – Thomas Bickell!"

Cheering erupted on one side of the crowd. Thomas heard only the blood roaring in his ears. He'd won. They'd done it – they'd elected a black man to help draft a state constitution. People were pounding him on the back, grabbing his hand to shake, laughing and shouting.

Across the street, a sullen silence prevailed. Mr. Randolph climbed onto the stage with heavy steps. His speech conceding the election to Thomas was gracious, even-toned, and gave no notice to the hostile murmurings of his supporters.

Thomas took the stage. They had agreed during the night that if he won, his acceptance speech should give no hint of jubilation at having beat a white man in a free election. Keep it short, express gratitude for the opportunity to serve and indicate his intention to be a fair and responsible representative of all the people in St. James and Ascension Parishes.

Thomas gazed at all the black faces, and the few white faces, among his supporters. His first words were a mere croak. People laughed, and he started again, managing a hoarse but audible voice. "Thank you," he began.

He was truly humbled. These people, brave men every one of them, had taken a chance on him, a young, untried black man.

As planned, Thomas kept it short. He thanked them again, waved, and left the stage.

"Wow," Cabel said. "We did it."

Thomas grabbed Cabel in a fierce hug. "Yes. *We* did it. All of us together."

"You gone stick around to be adored a while, or you want to go home now?"

"I want to be adored at home," Thomas said.

"Then let's get out of here."

Once they'd passed through the happy crowd, eager to congratulate Thomas and even to touch him, Thomas and his friends walked through the silent white men and women assembled on the other side of the street. No one spoke to him, no one touched him. But they stared, their faces grim. George Clampett, whom they knew to be an officer in the White Camellia, spat at the ground in front of Thomas's feet.

Thomas ignored him and kept a pleasant expression on his face. When they were nearly through the gauntlet, a white man standing apart stepped forward. Cabel immediately put himself in front of Thomas, Reynard closing in on his right.

The white man had white hair and very red skin. His blue eyes were red-rimmed and intense. "This isn't over, nigger," he hissed.

Cabel stood his ground, blocking the florid-faced man while Reynard ushered Thomas around him.

"Forget it," Reynard said in his ear.

"It's all right, Reynard. I'm fine."

# Chapter Thirty-Two

Bertrand Chamard, along with Albany Johnston, dined at Whiteaker's house talking over the election results. The sun lacked a hand's span of sinking below the treetops when Chamard said goodnight and started home. He'd come up the river road on the way to dinner, but on a whim, he decided to thread through the cane fields to see how Alistair's crop was coming along and took the back road home.

He was past the Dietrich place when he saw half a dozen ugly buzzards hopping around on the edge of the road ahead of him. As he got closer, the stink had him pulling out his handkerchief and pressing it to his nose. In this heat -- . His horse side-stepped, objecting to the odor.

Chamard reined her in and settled her with his hand on her neck. Naturally, he expected the carrion to be a dead possum or coon. But then he spied boots behind the curtain of buzzards.

"Shoo! Scat!" He slid off his horse and ran at the nasty birds, waving his arms.

It was a man, lying face down. The boots of course made him think of Jacques Valmar. Good leather, high heels. The right size and build. He did not want to turn the body over to verify it was him. Even with the handkerchief over his nose, he had to fight his gag reflex.

He pulled his rifle from the scabbard on his horse and fired it into the air three times, again three times, then again, three times. And waited for somebody to come.

Dietrich's plantation was all but abandoned, and the next one over, the Kaufmann's was too, so the four men who responded to the distress signal came from Alistair's place. They were wary, one of them carrying a shotgun, one with a pitchfork.

When they realized it was just one man standing by his horse, his rifle in its scabbard, they came on.

"You got trouble, mister?" The man who spoke already had his hand up to his nose.

Chamard gestured to the body lying just off the road. "Would one of you please fetch Major Whiteaker? We're going to need a tarp or two to wrap the body in. And a wagon."

"Yes, sir. We see to it."

They left him with the noxious remains, the buzzards impatient to get back to their repast. He stamped his foot at the bolder ones inching closer and they scattered.

Deserved what he got, if it was Valmar, murderer, rapist, and a general all around evil creature. Still, it was grisly having red-headed buzzards pecking at a man's remains.

The tree tops began to hide the sun, the mosquitoes' favorite time of day. Some of the flies and mosquitoes wanted to sip from Chamard's skin after they'd sampled the corpse, and that made Chamard finally give up and vomit into the weeds.

He was very glad to see Alistair and the other men arrive. Alistair, made of sterner stuff than Chamard, approached the body without a handkerchief to blunt the smell. He stood with his hands on his hips and contemplated the boots, the man's build, death, violence. Alistair was a man who contemplated pretty much all the time, Chamard had observed.

"I guess we'll turn him over and see if it's him."

He turned to the men standing nearby. "Moses, let me have that pitchfork, if you please." It was the big one they used for haying. Alistair slid it under the corpse the best he could without tearing the flesh and flipped the body over.

The side of his face that had been pressed to the ground had escaped the buzzards' attention. It was Valmar.

"Christ Almighty," Chamard murmured. The chest was torn open by a shotgun, looked like. The blood had soaked into the ground under the body and there were a multitude of beetles feasting on the red protein in the soil, one of them busily burrowing into the flesh.

"How long you think it's been here?" Alistair asked.

"You've seen a lot more dead bodies than I have. What do you think?"

Alistair wrinkled his nose and grimaced. "I'd hoped never to smell a dead body again."

"You ready for us to wrap this poor soul in the tarp?" Moses asked.

"Go ahead."

"So, how long? Two days, half a day?"

"I come by this way this morning. It wadn't here then," Moses said.

Alistair nodded. "Hardly even swelled up yet. Just a few hours, I'd think."

"So he was killed in broad daylight?"

"Looks like it."

The men used the pitch fork to roll the body into a tarp. When they bent over to pick the whole grisly burden up, Moses dropped his end and jumped back with a yell. "There's another body down there."

"Oh Good Lord," Chamard said.

Long stringy yellow hair, worn clothes. "Shipton, I suppose," Alistair said.

"Yeah, that's him," Moses said. "He comes round here selling crawfish and trout once in a while."

"I go get another tarp," one of the men said. Another strode across the road and tossed up his supper.

By the time they'd heaved both bodies into the back of the wagon, it was dark.

"You taking him into the sheriff tonight, Major Whiteaker?" Moses asked.

"We could leave them in the barn overnight," Chamard said, "but then the barn would stink and the horses would complain."

Alistair shook his head. "I don't want them in my barn. Moses, you and Jim get a couple of lanterns for us."

"You want some of us to ride along with you, Major?"

He looked at Moses. "It won't be pleasant. It'll be late before we get back."

"Me and Jim come along." Moses looked at the other two men. "Charlie, you and Cat go on back. Tell the women where we be." Moses and Jim went after lanterns.

"Cat, send me my horse, will you?" Alistair called.

"Yes, sir."

Chamard was glad it was a bright night. A man his age, he needed all the light he could get. Alistair didn't seem bothered whether he rode near the lanterns or not. Used to be, Chamard could see in the dark, too, but not anymore.

When they finally pulled up at the sheriff's office, Donaldsonville had gone to bed. The sheriff's office was always open though. Chamard stepped in first and spoke to the deputy. "Got two dead bodies in the wagon, Jean Paul. I believe we'll need the sheriff."

Paget showed up in his shirt sleeves and without his tie. "What now?" he said irritably.

"Brought you a present," Chamard said pleasantly.

They took Paget to the wagon and unwrapped the bodies.

"God!" Paget said as the smell hit him. He made himself step closer. "Hold that lantern over here, will you?"

The sheriff looked at the ruined face and the shredded chest. "Well, that one's Valmar all right. You can wrap him back up and take him on to the funeral parlor. Tell them not to do anything till Doc Millingham sees him. Now who's this fellow?"

"Moses here identifies him as Shipton."

"Well. That's downright convenient," the sheriff said.

Chamard grinned at him. "It is rather, isn't it?"

"Come on in, gentlemen. Let's get this written up," Paget said.

"

When everyone had described how the bodies were found, the sheriff said, "Major Whiteaker, you had some dealings with Mr. Valmar in the past. Can you tell me what you did all day today?"

Alistair smiled. "I can. I rode the fields this morning with my steward. We had lunch together, then I spent time alone in my office. After that, I had water brought up for a bath. Got dressed. By then, Mr. Chamard and Mr. Johnston arrived. We visited, had supper, smoked cigars and drank. Mr. Johnston left first. Then Mr. Chamard said goodnight so he'd be home before dark and discovered the body."

"I suppose the servants in the house can verify all that? For instance, that you actually were in your office by yourself?"

"Yes."

The sheriff rubbed his hand through his graying hair. "And I suppose every one of them would swear to whatever you wanted them to."

"Most of them likely would. But they won't have to lie."

"Fine," Paget said. "I reckon we know who killed them anyway. Probably that third guy, Fisher. The Yankee from up North somewhere.'

"A double-cross," Chamard said.

"Seems likely to me."

"Can't disagree," Chamard said.

Alistair gave Paget a shrewd look. "You expect you'll catch up to him?"

Paget snorted. "What do you think? I expect your Fanny Brown is as avenged as she's going to get. The man would be a fool to hang around here. But I promised her I'd look for all of them, and I will. If Fisher shows his face in these parts, I'll hear about it, and I'll get him."

"That's all we can ask," Chamard said. "Good night to you, Sheriff, what's left of it."

Chamard and Alistair stepped out onto the board walk and looked at the stars filling the sky.

"I hate riding in the dark," Chamard said.

"You don't have to see. Your horse will do that for you."

"Well, let's go home."

~ ~ ~

Peep brought the news about Valmar and Shipton during breakfast, having heard it from Valentine who heard it from Chamard. Fanny set her coffee down, pale-faced, and Lily closed her hand over Fanny's for comfort. The young woman had become cheerful again, was interested in the political campaign, was teaching. Word of Valmar of course brought all her fears back. And anger. Lily was certain there was anger as well.

Fanny sat back in her chair and stared at her plate. She seemed disappointed.

"Fanny?" Lily said.

Fanny looked Lily in the eye. "I wanted to kill him myself."

"Who could blame you, Fanny."

Fanny shook her head. "I didn't just want it. I thought about it, where, and when, and how. I had it all but planned, just waiting for him to come back to the area." She put her fingers to her forehead. "Foolishness, I suppose."

Lily patted her hand. "Not foolish, not to think about it anyway. Now, if you'd actually killed the man, then I'd tell you it was foolish."

Fanny looked at Uncle Garvey. "Who do they think did it?"

"Sheriff isn't saying, yet."

"They'll suspect Thomas."

Rachel turned from the stove, her hands on her hips. "Thomas didn't kill nobody."

"They may suspect him, but Valmar had plenty of enemies," Uncle Garvey said.

"When did it happen?" Lily asked.

"Probably mid-day yesterday," Peep told her.

"Thomas was probably with lots of people. He always is, even now the election is over," Fanny said. "He can prove it wasn't him."

"I'm sure of it," Uncle Garvey said. "And you were at the schoolhouse with all those kids. Alistair was with people, too."

Lily let out a breath. Her first thought had been to wonder if Alistair was involved. He was sick of killing, she knew he was. But he was a man who took action when he saw the need. He didn't wait for things to just happen.

"Chamard, I don't know about yet. But he's too well thought of for Paget to bother him without knowing flat-out it was him."

"Do you think it was him?" Lily asked, shocked.

"Nah, I'm just thinking about alibis, that's all."

"Peep, did they find any signs where the body was found?"

"No'm. It would have been mighty convenient if somebody had left something, maybe dropped his pocket watch or spelled his name out in blood, but there wasn't nothing, that's what Moses say."

Fanny pushed her plate of eggs and bacon away. "Excuse me," she said and strode from the room.

Lily looked at Rachel. "I'll go," Rachel said. "You finish your breakfast."

"Only trouble I see is if people think Thomas did it," Uncle Garvey said.

Rachel hadn't left the room yet and turned at the door. "Well, he didn't, and that's that."

"Uncle Garvey, what about the third man who attacked Fanny?"

"Well, she said herself, he didn't do nothing but watch. Likely Sheriff Paget won't look real hard to find him, now."

"And you?" Lily said. "Will you be suspected?"

"Might be. But the sheriff can suspect all he wants. He won't find any evidence to show I did it because I didn't do it. Same for Peep." He turned to the man he'd worked alongside for the last twenty-five years. "Unless you did it," he said, grinning.

"Nah, sir. I didn't get around to it yet."

"Well, I got work to do," Uncle Garvey said. "Worse ways to start the day than hearing vermin like Valmar gone to their just rewards. You coming, Peep?"

"Yeah, I'm ready."

~~~

Lily had too much to do to sit and mope. She worked in the garden before the heat kicked in about nine in the morning. She helped out in the kitchen, shelling peas, baking biscuits, stirring the blackberries to make jam.

If Maddie missed her father, she didn't show it. She was loud and boisterous again, as she had been before Frederick appeared .

Yet Lily still found time to brood. She'd be cutting okra, or mending a hem, or kneading dough, and her hands would fall still. Her chest would ache. Her throat would swell. Then she would shake her head to rid herself of images of Frederick's sagging shoulders shaking as he wept. Of Alistair's eyes, full of grief when he brought her the papers and she was so cold to him.

Her hands would attack her task again and she'd tell herself she was a fool. Why feel sorry for Frederick Palmer? He was gone, and she was glad of it. She was free! She and Maddie had a home now. They were safe. And she owed that to Alistair Whiteaker.

But how could she accept him with the taint of $5,000 between them? It was shameful, what they'd done. She couldn't turn around and marry him as if it weren't.

The nights were too hot to sleep even after she'd worked as hard as she could all day. She lay in her chemise, feeling the heat rise up from the mattress and hover in the still air, the only coolness the tears that tracked over her face. She grieved as if she'd suffered the death of a loved one, and it was much as if she had. She had just begun, the same week that Frederick arrived, to hope that she might have a future. And now she didn't.

She woke in the mornings, ill-rested, her hair sweat-soaked, and plunged into the life of the farm. She had what she'd prayed for – she hadn't murdered her husband, and she needn't ever fear him again. Anything but gratitude was nothing more than self-pity. It would stop.

And she needed to stop thinking about Alistair Whiteaker. Yes, she'd fallen in love with him. Yes, he was wonderful in too many ways to count. But there was to be no happy ever after for them. She needed to shake off this lethargy. She needed a diversion.

And yet, when the invitation came, Lily was not pleased. Mr. Chamard's party would include Alistair, of course. She wanted desperately to see him, and she didn't want to see him. He would take one look at her and know she was weakening, know how much she wanted him.

She lay the little envelope on the mantle in the sitting room and found Rachel on the back porch. There was always work to do if you were with Rachel, and that's what she needed.

The girls played under the chinaberry tree serving tea to their dolls. Lily had shown them how grand ladies crooked their little finger as they held their cups, and clearly Dawn and Maddie had become grand ladies.

Rebecca was in sad condition. Her dress was filthy and the hem was torn. Her pretty blonde curls were tangled and leaf-strewn. Lily knew Dawn would carefully lay her Miss Pitty Pat in a patch of grass when they finished their tea. Rebecca would be left wherever she happened to lay, in the dirt or among the sandspurs.

She'd be glad if Maddie were as responsible and careful as Dawn, but she was glad, too, that Maddie didn't treat the doll her daddy gave her like it was a sacred object. It was just a doll, and she treated it much as she did her other toys.

With a basin in her lap, she picked the last of the season's peaches out of the bushel basket at Rachel's feet and set to peeling. Eventually, she fell still as she often did these days, the visions in her mind more vivid than the bowl of peaches in her lap. She'd see his long-fingered hands in her mind's eye, see the kindness, the vulnerability when he laughed with Maddie.

She touched her lip. No one had ever kissed her like that.

She shook her head. Him and his high-handed interference. His assumptions. His superiority. Throwing money at every problem.

"You mad at the major about the money, ain't you, Miss Lily?"

Lily's head jerked around. Was her heart and mind so easy to read?

"Wouldn't you be angry?"

"When I was a girl, a pretty blond man like Major Whiteaker bought me," Rachel said, her eyes on the peach she was peeling. "Took me from my mama and my sisters. I had a sweetheart, too. He probably old and fat now, maybe got him six or eight kids with that girl Portia that kept sniffing around him."

"I'm sorry, Rachel."

"Anyway, this man, he put me in the back of a wagon with some other slaves he bought and drove, seemed like a thousand miles. The men had irons on their feet. We women just had the bracelets. I never seen my mama nor my sisters to this day."

Rachel looked at Lily. "That's what bought means. Your Major Whiteaker, what he did looks more like rescue, to me. You sit here on this porch, free to do whatever you want. You could go back to Pennsylvania, he wouldn't stop you. Miss Lily, you ain't bought."

Finally, Lily said, "But it was ugly. It broke a man."

"That man was ugly, way I see it. And he broke hisself."

Nothing like an ex-slave to put things into perspective for you. Just like that, Rachel made Lily's reservations and disappointments seem petty. Even silly.

"Dawn," Rachel called. "You and Maddie get washed up and I let you roll out pie dough."

"I think we'll have enough for four or five pies," Lily said.

"Maybe we'll stew some. And while the oven's hot I'm gone put the iron on to heat so you can press that pretty green dress."

Well, then. She was going to a party.

~~~

The scent of rosewater surrounded Maddie and Lily as they sat at the window while their hair dried. It was Maddie's task to comb through the snarls in her doll's hair. Lily's job was to hem Rebecca Palmer's new dress.

"If Major Whiteaker were here, Mama, I'd let him smell my hair."

Lily laughed. "I'm sure you would be much admired."

Maddie set her comb down. "Do you think he forgot me?"

Maddie had not worried that her father might forget her. She had not mentioned him at all.

"I'm sure he has not forgotten you."

It had been twenty-two days since Lily hurled those angry, hurtful words at Alistair. If she'd waited until she'd had a few more days to calm down, to think -- but she had lashed out at him while she was still struggling with the end of her marriage, the shame of divorce, the guilt of having turned Frederick into a man with remorse riding on his back.

Uncle Garvey knocked and poked his head in the door. "You be ready in an hour?"

Maddie jumped off her little stool and raced to him. "Smell my hair, Uncle Garvey."

"Hmm. What is that smell? Apple pie?"

Maddie favored him with her delighted giggle.

Uncle Garvey picked her up and gave her neck a giant sniff. "Roses it is. Red ones, I think."

"I'll be ready," Lily told him.

"Maddie, you come on down stairs with me. Dawn and I are about to cut a pumpkin or two."

Without Maddie to distract her, Lily's nerves took over. She felt like a young girl going to her first dance. Her white shoes were worn out and she fretted that she'd have to wear her sturdy brown ones with her pale green dress. "Nobody will care but you," her mother would tell her, but that had never been much comfort to Lily when she'd had a growth spurt and her dress was too short.

She pinned her hair in a twist on the back of her head. That was as fancy as she knew how to fix hair. She stepped into her freshly pressed dress and tied a green ribbon around her neck. She'd have to do.

She collected Uncle Garvey from the kitchen and together they strolled down the lane toward Cherleu. It was a pretty day, but still hot. Back in Philadelphia, the October air would be crisp and the trees would be turning colors.

"Lily, I know I'm not your father," Uncle Garvey said, "but if your father were alive, I think he'd tell you the same thing. Don't go being hard-headed and stubborn. Alistair's a good man, and he didn't do anything wrong."

"Uncle Garvey, I think we both did something wrong. Tempting a weak man to destroy himself."

Uncle Garvey stopped right in the middle of the lane and looked at her. "You giving yourself a lot of consequence, Miss Lily Palmer, crediting yourself with destroying a man. From where I stand, the man made a choice, nobody put a gun to his head." He took two steps and turned back to her. "Lily, you saw a sad man, a distressed and maybe confused man when he left here. But you know Frederick Palmer better than anyone. How long you think he's going to stay sad and distressed with a pocket full of money and a fancy gal on his arm?"

"But how can he go on carrying all that guilt? The remorse he must feel?"

"I never saw a thing to make me think the man was one to dwell on guilt or remorse. Self-pity, plenty of that. Look, he's on his way to a new life. Don't drag yourself down imagining how you would feel if you'd taken the money. He's not you. And he sure as hell is not Alistair Whiteaker."

They took another ten steps in silence, then Lily stretched up and kissed his cheek. "Thank you, Uncle Garvey."

"You're welcome. Let's get on and kick our heels up a little."

"Is Musette back?"

"Supposed to be. Supposed to bring Chamard's daughter Nicolette with her. You met her and Finn McKee at the picnic."

"I remember."

Lily had not worn her bonnet – Alistair told her he didn't like bonnets – and the sun overhead was punishing. It was a relief to climb the stairs and step onto the cool, shadowy gallery of

Chamard's home. The doors were open, and the alley of poplars funneled the breeze from the river to the house.

Musette met them as they entered the parlor, her hands stretched out to grasp Lily's.

"How was New Orleans?" Lily asked her.

She saw Alistair standing at the punch bowl with Mr. Chamard, his back to the door. Mr. Chamard's eyes flicked toward her and then back to Alistair. Alistair began to turn, but Lily looked away.

Musette squeezed her hands. "New Orleans was hot, humid, and smelly. Come say hello to Finn and Nicolette."

Lily felt Alistair watching her as Musette pulled her across the room. She'd tied her corset too tight. She wanted to gulp air.

"Mrs. Palmer," Finn said with a big smile. "How have you survived your first Louisiana summer?"

Ah, she could talk about the weather, that was easy enough. "The heat is unrelenting, isn't it? But the air is so soft here, and fragrant. I won't complain."

Musette's cousin Nicolette wore a light-weight muslin gown with very short sleeves even though it was mid-afternoon. A very sensible accommodation to her need to keep cool in her advanced pregnancy. The four of them engaged in amiable chat until Lily noticed Musette suddenly go stiff and still. She turned to see what had affected her so. A tall uniformed officer entered the room, removing his hat, and looking around.

Finn strode across the room, his hand outstretched. "Colin!"

They greeted each other warmly and then Finn brought the officer over to the ladies.

"Colin, how are you?" Nicolette said, her hand in his. He bent to kiss her cheek.

"I am amazed, I am. Here it is October, and it's still hot."

"Yes, well, we may get a few cool days later this winter," Finn said with a grin. "Let me introduce you. This is Mrs. Palmer, my father-in-law's neighbor. Lily, this is Colin McKee."

"How do you do, Mrs. Palmer," the officer said.

"Very well, thank you."

"And this is Nicolette's cousin, Musette DeBlieux. Musette, this is *my* cousin, Colin McKee."

Musette looked quite pale, Lily noticed. The officer smiled broadly.

"Miss DeBlieux. I'm pleased to see you again," executing a proper bow.

"You know each other?" Finn said.

"I met Miss DeBlieux in town."

Lily had not expected Musette would ever be uncomfortable in a social situation, she being the consummate belle, but she held herself stiffly, her hands clasped at her waist. It was curious, but Lily could spare no more than a thought for Musette and the handsome lieutenant.

By turning her head slightly, she could see Alistair in the corner of her eye. He sipped from his punch, nodding to Mr. Chamard, but even from across the room, she felt the weight of his attention on her. At the moment, he seemed focused on her hemline.

She knew when Mr. Johnston crossed the room to join his host and Alistair, but Alistair didn't seem to notice him. His attention had moved to the ruffles on her lower skirts. She didn't imagine he was interested in ruffles, but she was thrilled he looked at her at all.

She had been unfair when they last talked. Cruel, even. What if he'd made up his mind to dismiss her from his mind, to cut her from his heart. But having a man stare at the ruffles along your hem didn't suggest indifference.

Musette and Lieutenant McKee's polite conversation was no more than a drone. Lily faced Alistair squarely. His eyes immediately found hers.

Mr. Johnston was speaking to him, but Alistair left him mid-sentence. He crossed to her, paying no mind to the other people in the room.

With a stiff bow, he said, "Mrs. Palmer, how do you do?"

"Very well, Major Whiteaker. And you?"

"Perhaps you would like a glass of sangria."

He took her elbow, still not having acknowledged the other guests, and directed her to the punch bowl.

He didn't speak, nor did she, as he ladled the sangria into a cut crystal tumbler. He handed it to her then took her other elbow and steered her toward the gallery.

At the far end, away from the parlor doors, he backed her up against the carved post and stepped a pace away with his hands behind his back.

He looked very grave, Lily thought. There were lines around his eyes she hadn't noticed before. Maybe he had trouble sleeping like she did.

"How is Maddie doing, with her father – "

"She's happy, I think. She doesn't seem to miss him."

"And you?" His eyes were dark, his mouth unsmiling. "Do you miss him?"

"I think of him, Alistair."

He straightened and looked over her shoulder.

"But that's not the same thing as missing him," she said.

He drew a deep breath. "I see."

Lily turned to lean against the gallery rail, looking toward the river. He joined her there, setting his hands near hers. They could just see the river beyond the levee, the trees obscuring their view.

"You heard about Valmar and Shipton?" he asked her.

She didn't want to talk about dead men. She doubted he did either. But it was difficult to say what she wanted to say.

"I heard."

"And Thomas has won his seat to the convention."

"Yes. That's good news, isn't it?"

"Yes. I'm very pleased."

"Alistair . . . "

His hands tightened around the gallery rail and he kept his face turned toward the river.

"I was harsh with you," she said. "I was unfair."

"You weren't unfair." He straightened his posture and clasped his hands behind his back. "My actions were arrogant, and meddlesome. I'm sorry I pulled you into actions you regret."

She made herself look in him the eye. "No. It wasn't like that. I'm sorry I made you feel that all of it, his leaving so broken and sad, was your fault."

"It was my fault."

She shook her head. "No matter how poor you were, you would not have left your wife and child."

He stared at her, his face unreadable.

"Say something, Alistair."

The line between his eyes deepened and his gaze was hard. "I would never leave you and Maddie."

If he would only relax his stiff posture. It was impossible to touch him like this. Her heart contracted. Maybe he didn't want her to touch him.

"I'm grateful to be released," she said, taking refuge in formality. "Thank you."

As sudden as lightening, Alistair's rigid face broke into an angry snarl. "I don't want gratitude, Lily. I didn't do it for gratitude."

She felt the blood begin to flow again. This is what she wanted – something, anything, as long as it wasn't this stony distance between them. She smiled, aware a smile was incongruous after his heated, angry words, but she couldn't help it.

"What did you do it for, Alistair?"

Abruptly, he pressed into her skirts, grasped either side of her head, and kissed her, not a gentle kiss, not an enquiring kiss – a kiss that claimed her. She wrapped her arms around his waist, drawing him in.

When they were both breathless, he kissed her temples, her eyes, her jaw until she laughed.

"Will you marry me, Lily?" he said into her ear.

"Oh, yes."

# Chapter Thirty-Three

Thomas had slept and eaten and lazed for a week. He felt like a new man. His mother had cleaned his suit and starched his clean linen. His father had given him a haircut and Miss Lily had made him a silk tie.

Upstairs, Fanny was being fussed over as Rachel and Lily got her into her wedding dress. Thomas was at his ease, in no hurry. Fanny would be down in a little while, they would take the wagon to the church, and they would be married.

In seven months they would be parents. Even that daunting prospect did not disturb him today. Today they would celebrate with their friends and family, and after supper, he and Fanny would go home to the tiny apartment at the back of the schoolhouse.

Thomas knew Fanny was nervous about tonight. After what she'd been through, her notions about sex were bound to be confused. But he had indulged in pleasurable pursuits with women in his earlier days. He knew what to do to reassure her, to prove to her she was desirable. Most of all, he knew to be patient.

Dawn climbed onto his lap. "Listen." She put Miss Pitty Pat's mouth up to his ear. "I'm getting married today," Miss Pitty Pat whispered. "You see my pretty dress? Do you want to kiss the bride?"

He wrapped his big hands around Dawn's doll and gave her a loud smacking kiss right on the mouth.

He narrowed his eyes at Maddie's doll. "Any other brides around here?"

Maddie delivered her doll to him with a grin on her face. "Rebecca is getting married today, too."

Thomas repeated the enthusiastic kiss to their great amusement.

"When I get married, I'm going to wear a dress just like Miss Fanny's," Dawn pronounced.

At the sound of rustling skirts at the door, Thomas stood up. "And here she is."

Fanny stepped into the room, looking both shy and radiant. Her dress was sky blue, and she had a white lace veil over her hair.

"Ohhhh," Maddie said. "You look like a princess."

Thomas felt his heart thudding hard and strong. This was his Fanny. His life's love, his partner.

He leaned in and whispered in her ear. "You look beautiful."

"And you look very handsome."

"You wanna get married?"

"Today?"

He grinned. "Seeing as how we're all dressed up anyway."

She put her forefinger to her lip. "Well, I guess I can take time out of my busy day to get married."

He pressed his lips to her forehead. "Then let's do that."

The church was full when Thomas took his place at the altar, Reynard and Cabel standing up with him. The black gospel choir in their white robes began the service with their sweet, clear voices. Rachel and Peep walked up the aisle to the front pew and sat down. Miss Lily followed and sat next to Rachel and Peep.

Fanny had no parents, no brothers and sisters, but Major Whiteaker and some of her friends from the old days sat across the aisle to be her family. Next came Mr. Chamard with Musette DeBlieux on his arm. They slid into the pew behind Peep, Rachel, and Miss Lily.

Mr. Chamard smiled and winked at him. Miss Musette looked everywhere but at him. Still, he was glad she was here. Musette had sent flowers to Fanny, had even stopped in to enquire about her while she was recuperating. They had been friends a long time. Maybe they could be again.

The choir raised their voices and the ceremony began. As Maddie and Dawn paraded down the aisle strewing rose petals, everyone turned to see the bride walk in on Garvey's arm.

Her veil was down, but he could see her smile through the fine lace. He grinned back, oblivious to everything but Fanny.

In half an hour, Thomas said, "I will," Fanny said, "I will," and they were married.

He raised the veil to kiss her tenderly on the mouth. The choir burst into a joyous hymn, and Thomas and Fanny marched out into the sunshine.

In the moment they had alone, Thomas leant down and brushed his lips against hers again. "Thank you, Fanny Bickell."

She shook her head at him, smiling.

Their friends overtook them then, some of them throwing rice, all of them chattering and congratulating them.

Everyone wanted to kiss the bride, and Thomas let them, though he kept Fanny's hand in his. Then Cabel swooped in and gave her a kiss that had the other young men whooping. Thomas clapped a hand on his best friend's shoulder, and squeezed, hard.

Cabel came up grinning, Fanny holding on to her veil and looking a little bit flushed, which Thomas was not pleased to notice, but then she grinned at him, not his friend, and he forgot all about Cabel.

When the long day of celebrations was over, Fanny and Thomas drove Garvey's wagon through the twilight to the rooms behind the school house, and they were home.

~ ~ ~

During the afternoon of Thomas and Fanny's celebrations, Alistair came to her with Maddie's hand in his.

"We wondered, Mrs. Palmer, if you would like to drive? We'll be back before they cut the cake."

"Can we, Mama? Major Whiteaker says they have a baby horse in his barn."

"Oh, then we must go."

With Maddie between them, they drove out of the yard and took the river road to Alistair's home. All these months, and Lily had never seen it. He turned the wagon into the front alleyway shaded on both sides by ancient oaks. "Oh," Maddie cried. "It's like a princess's house, Mama."

Gingerbread work trimmed the front galleries, upper and lower. There were three dormers with intricately carved work around the windows. Below the central dormer was a large hexagonal window. And the whole place was gleaming white.

Musette had said the new Whiteaker house was less grand than the one the Yankees had burned down, but it was quite grand enough with the sun shining on all that new paint.

Maddie held her arms out to be helped from the carriage and shrieked when Alistair gave her a twirl before setting her down.

"Would you like a twirl, Mrs. Palmer?" he asked with all the gallantry of a Southern gentleman.

"Perhaps another time," she laughed.

The front door opened and an ancient black man stood there. "This them, is it?" he said.

Lily had expected more formality from the butler in a home like this. He certainly looked formal in his starched white shirt, black coat and tie.

Alistair was smiling. "Lily, this is William. He's been on this place since the world was new. William, Mrs. Palmer and Miss Maddie Palmer."

The old man's grin showed white teeth from one side of his face to the other. "Ya'll come on in. Likely Mr. Alistair gone show you the house."

"William, do you suppose we still have lemons in the cook house?"

"I'll have a look see. I bring you something wet anyway."

"Come in," Alistair said, his hand on Lily's back.

The central hallway stretched the depth of the house with mirrors and brocade chairs lining the walls. The arching doorway revealed a lovely parlor with a grand piano, soft green carpets, and emerald green wall coverings.

"This is the front room of a double parlor. When we have guests, we open the pocket doors and make one large room."

The sofa was upholstered in pale blue, green, and gold silk. The chairs picked up the colors in striped damask. He opened the pocket doors to reveal furnishings very much in harmony with those in the first room.

Holding Maddie's hand, he took them across the hall to a dining room dominated by a mahogany table large enough to seat eight. "When we need to, we can add leaves enough to accommodate twenty."

Lily looked without comment. The life lived in this house was foreign to her.

The room behind the dining room was Alistair's study. Deep maroon walls, heavy brown leather chairs, and a desk that had to be the least elegant piece in the house. It was huge, made of walnut, and battered, scratched, pitted, and dented. A working desk, piled high with account books, newspapers, pens and pencils.

"One more room on this floor." He took them into a room full of light, windows on two walls. The paintwork was brilliant white and soft yellow. There were three upholstered chairs in gold and cream, a settee in gold, and a lovely carpet in greens and yellows. "This is Mother's sitting room, and yours." He lifted the lid of a polished round cabinet next to one of the chairs. "Sewing, embroidery. Should you like your own cabinet?"

"I have a basket," Lily said, a little overwhelmed. She wondered whether Mrs. Whiteaker would live here, too, or would she prefer life in town during the winter. She worried at a fold in her skirt. What if they didn't get on? What if Alistair's mother was disgusted he had married a divorced woman? Mrs. Whiteaker would be ashamed to be seen with her in town, Lily could safely assume that.

"Alistair. Your mother. She's knows I'm divorced?"

His amusement did not reassure her.

"Do you mean would she rather I marry the seventeen year old second cousin she's been pushing on me?" He laughed and cupped her elbow in his palm. "Don't worry about Mother. She has a good heart. And you bring something to this marriage that she craves."

"I do?"

He nodded his head at Maddie who was fingering an elegant porcelain lady in a grand riot of frozen skirts. "My mother wants a grandchild more than anything else in this world." While Maddie's back was turned, he bent his head and kissed her. "She'll love you, Lily, you and Maddie both.

"Let me take you upstairs. These are the only rooms on this floor, except the pantry. You can see that later."

He opened the first door at the top of the stairs and stepped inside. "What do you think, Maddie? Does this look like a little girl's room?"

Maddie let go of Lily's hand and looked around with wide eyes. The walls were blue. The bed's canopy was the same shade, the counterpane white with embroidered blue flowers. On the floor was a round rug perhaps eight feet across with pink and blue flowers.

"Oh Good Lord," Maddie said under her breath.

"Maddie Louise Palmer!" Lily said. "Wherever did you hear such a thing? You may not take the Lord's name in vain. Good gracious, child."

"I'm sorry, Mama," Maddie said, but she clearly wasn't. She was admiring the blue silk slipper chair in the corner.

Lily looked at Alistair, embarrassed at Maddie's rude outburst. He had his arms crossed, looking thoroughly pleased even if his step-daughter-to-be was a horror.

Next to the slipper chair was a miniature replica in the same blue silk. "Oh oh oh. This is Rebecca's chair!"

"I believe you're right," Alistair said.

William entered. "I left you and Mrs. Palmer a tray of lemonade in the front parlor. This child, though, she come on with me now. After you drink your lemonade, Miss Maddie, I take you out to see the foal."

"Oh, thank you," she breathed. She went to William as if she'd known him all her life.

"You even remembered a chair for her doll? Alistair Whiteaker, I believe you are going to be putty in Maddie's little hands."

He grinned at her. "I don't doubt it."

Alistair's hand on her back, he led her across the hall. "This is my room. Our room."

Lily stepped in, her hands clasped together. The walls were washed in a pale gold. The bed was enormous, its canopy and counterpane burgundy and gold.

She swallowed and turned to him. "We're really going to do this?"

Alistair took her hands. "Get married? Yes. We are."

He pulled her close and just held her.

"We're going to be happy in this room, Lily."

She couldn't even talk. This beautiful home. This beautiful, kind man.

He pulled back and drew a small velvet box from his pocket and opened it.

"Oh Good Lord," she said, laughing.

"Do you like it?"

The ring was an opal surrounded by brilliant diamonds. The sun seemed caught in the opal, the light sparkling and dancing through every stone.

"Oh, Alistair."

"It was my grandmother's ring. Left to me for my bride."

"Will you put it on for me?"

Lily's fingers trembled as he slipped the ring on her left hand.

"Will you marry me, Lily?"

She laughed. "I already said I will."

"I want to hear you say it again."

"Then yes, Alistair Whiteaker. I will marry you. And love you all my days."

Alistair shoved the door shut with his foot. He took a step toward her. Lily laughed and backed up a step. He advanced again and she retreated. "Alistair, we can't. Maddie is --."

"In the barn."

He cradled her face in his hands.

"Yes, but -- ."

He brushed his lips over hers and Lily forgot what she was going to say.

# Afterword

The Civil War over, the emancipated slaves were filled with hope. President Lincoln intended to rebuild the South and to advance the Confederate states' reconciliation with the rest of the nation. Legislation coming out of Washington after Lincoln's death enacted laws to deliver protections and rights to the newest American citizens.

Never was there a headier time for black people. Men and women decided where they would live, whom they would work for, and what work they would perform. For a few years, Reconstruction brought dignity and protection of civil rights. For a few years, the black population of America approached equality.

There were many men like the fictional Thomas Bickell throughout the South. They gained power through the ballot box and helped write the new state constitutions, which included the right of black men to vote. They became policemen, sheriffs, and judges. They won office as governors and mayors. They were sent to the Congress of the United States. Black schools sprung up all over the South and black families sacrificed to be sure their children learned to read.

The U.S. Army and the Freedmen's Bureau remained a presence in Southern states for a number of years after the war. Their duties included protection of the ex-slaves from the violence and oppressive manipulations of those whites who refused to accept the world had changed. The Freedmen's Bureau adjudicated disputes between labor and employers, reunited slaves sold off from their families, monitored elections and judicial proceedings, and generally endeavored to keep freedmen from being re-enslaved.

And then.

I've never read a more dispiriting account in history. Many expected Lincoln's Vice President Andrew Johnson to carry on with rebuilding the South at the same time ensuring the rights of former slaves. Instead, accommodating the pressure from Democrats in Congress and yielding to arguments from powerful

Southern planters, Johnson and his administration set about restoring the lands and rights of the defeated Confederate plantation owners who had once enslaved close to four million people.

By 1877, Reconstruction was over. If the goal of the Radical Republicans to ensure equality to the ex-slaves had been realized, there would have been no need for the Civil Rights Movement of the 1960s. Instead, the Ku Klux Klan ascended, Jim Crow laws proliferated, and the black population struggled on.

Among the forces aligned against the blacks, The Knights of the White Camellia rose up in Louisiana intent on returning to the old ways, using threats of violence, economic pressure, intimidation, misinformation, and many "dirty tricks." This group was short-lived, but others across the South carried on the campaign to deprive blacks of basic civil rights.

In this maelstrom of injustice and anger, people like Alistair Whiteaker and Musette DeBlieux had their real-life counterparts in the South. We remember their roles, also, in the greater struggle of black Americans to be truly free.

# FAMILIES OF THE PLANTATION SERIES

**The most important characters' names are in bold.**
*Recurring characters' names are italicized.*

## BOOK ONE: *ALWAYS & FOREVER*
*1830s Louisiana, along the Mississippi River*

*On Toulouse Plantation, The Tassins, a Creole family:*

Grandmother Emmeline Tassin, shrewd mistress of the family business.
Emile Tassin, her son, dreamy, loving, irresponsible.
Celine Tassin, Emile's wife, frustrated, embittered, neglected.
Bibi, a house slave and Emile's beloved, calm, big-hearted, nurturing.
***Josephine (Josie)***, Emile and Celeste's daughter, naïve but ultimately practical
**Cleo**, Emile and Bibi's much-loved daughter, a quadroon, born a slave but blessed with beauty and talent.
*Thibault*, Emile and Bibi's son, born simple.
**Remy**, a field slave, Cleo's lover, sweet-natured, sings like an angel, ambitious and wise.
Mr. Gale, the overseer, a competent and honorable man.
Mr. LeBrec, the second overseer, Cleo's worst nightmare.
Elbow John, a slave.
Louella, a cook.
Grammy Tulia, Bibi's mother.
*Gabriel*, Cleo's child with Bertrand Chamard.

*On Magnolia Plantation across the river, The Johnstons, an American family:*

Mr. and Mrs. Johnston.
Albany Johnston, their son, a good man, though unimaginative.
Abigail Johnston, their daughter.

*On Cherleu Plantation, next to Toulouse:*

**Bertrand Chamard**, a distant Creole cousin to Josie Tassin: dashing, handsome, suave, debonair, charming, desirable, seductive – every woman's dream; important character in Books II, III and IV.
*Valentine*, slave, Bertrand's valet.

*From the bayou:*

**Phanor DeBlieux**, a Cajun: funny, kind, handsome, talented, intelligent, and ambitious.
Lalie, Phanor's sister.
Louis, Lalie's husband.
Nicholas, Lalie's child.
Papa.

# BOOK TWO: *EVER MY LOVE*
*1859 Louisiana, along the Mississippi River*

*On Toulouse Plantation, The DeBlieux family:*

> *Josie Tassin DeBlieux.*
> **Simone**, Josie and Phanor DeBlieux's eldest daughter, in love with her half-cousin, Gabriel, she is intense, loyal, steadfast, passionate, and very stubborn.
> *Musette*, the middle daughter.
> Ariane, the youngest daughter.

*In New Orleans and On Chateau Chanson, the farm next to Toulouse Plantation:*

> *Cleo*, half-sister of Josie Tassin DeBlieux, a free quadroon and a renowned songstress: co-heroine in Book I; mother of Nicolette and Gabe Chamard.
> *Pierre*, a free black man, a musician who marries Cleo in mid-life.
> **Gabriel (Gabe) Chamard**, an octoroon, Cleo's son with Bertrand Chamard: brilliant, passionate, sophisticated (studied medicine in Paris), capable of fisticuffs and surgery.
> *Nicolette Chamard*, an octoroon, a popular songstress, Cleo's daughter with Bertrand Chamard and the heroine of Book III.

*On Cherleu Plantation, next to Toulouse Plantation:*

> *Bertrand Chamard.*
> **Marcel Chamard**, son of Bertrand with his first wife, Abigail Johnston, deceased: suave man-about-town; privileged; important character in Book III.
> **Yves Chamard**, son of Bertrand with his second wife; debonair, secretive, principled, courageous, and seductive.
> *Valentine*, slave, Bertrand's valet.

*On Magnolia Plantation, across the river from Toulouse Plantation:*

*Albany Johnston.*

**Adam Johnston**, his son; insecure, passionate, jealous, drunk too often; important character in Book III.

**Marianne Johnston**, Adam's sister: open-minded, thoughtful, skilled in rose breeding and in creating medicinals; also head-strong, idealistic, and passionate.

Mr. McNaught, the overseer.

John Man and Peter, brothers, slaves.

Joseph, a slave.

Luke, a slave.

**Pearl,** a slave: her heart's desire – to love and be-loved by husband and child.

**Alistair Whiteaker**, a plantation owner, friend to Marcel; important character in Book III; Hero of Book IV.

# BOOK THREE: *EVERMORE*
*1862 – 1866 Louisiana during the Civil War*

**Nicolette Chamard**, heroine, first introduced in Book II; octoroon daughter of Cleo and Bertrand Chamard; talented performer, beautiful, courageous, determined, and principled.

*Cleo,* quadroon, renowned entertainer; co-heroine in Book I, important in Books II and III.

*Pierre*, Cleo's husband.

*Bertrand Chamard*, Creole planter, important in Book I, also prominent in Book II and IV; father of Marcel and Nicolette with his lover Cleo, a former slave.

**Marcel Chamard**, Bertrand's legitimate son, half-brother to Nicolette, Confederate officer; conflicted by his love for two women and by his role as a Confederate soldier of conscience; also in Book II.

**Lucinda**, Marcel's beloved quadroon, a free woman, beautiful, loving.

*Valentine*, a slave, Bertrand's valet.

Val, a slave, Valentine's son.

**Deborah Ann Presswood**, Marcel's white fiancé; spoiled Southern Belle whose heart's desire is to love and be loved by Marcel Chamard.

Mr. Presswood, her father.

**Adam Johnston**, Confederate officer; haunted by his misdeed in Book II.

**Alistair Whiteaker**, Confederate officer, friend of Marcel's and Nicolette's; torn between his heart and his duty; becomes the hero in Book IV.

Dix Weber, Confederate officer, friend of Marcel's and Alistair's.

**Captain Finnian McKee**, Union soldier from Boston; of abolitionist sympathies, bewitched by the exotic city of New Orleans and besotted with Nicolette.

Major Hurshel Farrow, McKee's friend.

General Benjamin Butler, in charge of Union occupation of New Orleans, a historical figure of notoriety for his role in the war.

# BOOK FOUR: *ELYSIUM*
*1867 Louisiana, along the Mississippi River*

*On Toulouse Plantation:*

**Musette DeBlieux,** daughter of *Josie Tassin DeBlieux* who
was the heroine of Book I. Musette is Idealistic, romantic,
and passionate.
*Uncle Thibault,* Musette's mother's half-brother, introduced
in Book I.

*On Cherleu Plantation:*

*Bertrand Chamard,* major character in Book I, also important
in Books II and III.
*Valentine, his valet.*

*On Elysium, the farm behind Toulouse Plantation:*

Uncle Garvey Bickell.
**Thomas Bickell**, former slave, running for public office;
brilliant, charismatic man with a great future.
Peep, Rachel, and Dawn Bickell, former slaves, Thomas's
family.
**Lily Palmer**, Garvey's niece from Philadelphia; haunted by
past sins, she yearns for a life of peace and quiet, but new
love brings her disquiet, pain, and hope.
Maddie Palmer, Lily's daughter.
**Frederick Palmer**, Lily's husband: a disappointed man.

*Other players:*

Cabel, ex-slave, friend of Thomas's.
Reynard, ex-slave, friend of Thomas's.

**Fanny Brown**, former slave, teacher, beloved of Thomas
Bickell.

*Alistair Whiteaker*, plantation owner, former Confederate
officer; a principled man of ideals, valor, and hope.
Prominent in Book III.

Jacques Valmar, criminal.

Nicolette and Finnian McKee, briefly, Bertrand Chamard's daughter and son-in-law..Heroine and Hero of Book III.

# ABOUT THE AUTHOR

Gretchen Craig's lush, sweeping tales deliver edgy, compelling characters who test the boundaries of integrity, strength, and love. Told with sensitivity, the novels realistically portray the raw suffering of people in times of great upheaval. Having lived in diverse climates and terrains, Gretchen infuses her novels with a strong sense of place. The best-selling *PLANTATION SERIES* brings to the reader the smell of Louisiana's bayous and of New Orleans' gumbo, but most of all, these novels show the full scope of human suffering and triumph. Visit Gretchen's Amazon Author Page at

**www.amazon.com/author/gretchencraig**

Made in the USA
Middletown, DE
04 February 2018